FLAMES OF PASSION

"I would have you love me, Brynna," Temple whispered huskily.

He'd lowered himself to the edge of her bed. She felt his weight and the heat of him against her thigh.

"I love no man," she replied. "I never shall."

Her answer shocked him in its simplicity and honesty. He felt anger surge through him, and he reached for her, pulling her up from her pillows to crush her against his chest.

Her mouth opened on a startled denial, but his own lips settled on hers. Stunned, she offered no resistance, then her senses returned and she pushed against his shoulders.

Thoroughly, he kissed her, demanding a response, his arms like bands molding her to him. A languorous warmth swept through her, melting her resistance so she ceased her struggle and slowly her arms crept around him. Dimly she perceived she was about to encourage him to claim all he wished from her and in the taking to end this tumultuous hunger he'd awakened. She was like a fire unleashed . . .

Louisiana Heat

Jennifer Stevens

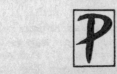

PINNACLE BOOKS
WINDSOR PUBLISHING CORP.

PINNACLE BOOKS

are published by

Windsor Publishing Corp.
475 Park Avenue South
New York, NY 10016

First printing: March, 1992

Printed in the United States of America

Prologue

The silence of the night was broken only by the sound of moth wings rubbing together in a final, agonized frenzy of death against the hot lamp globe and the relentless rhythmic swish of a leather whip as it fell against bare flesh. The brown-skinned girl kneeling on the hard wood floor bit her lip to keep from crying out. Sweat beaded her forehead at her effort not to flinch. She'd learned it was better not to show pain, and she would deny him as much pleasure as she could.

Beyond the lace-curtained window, the plantation lay troubled and still beneath the black, moonless night. In the slave cabins, the servants turned carefully upon their pallets and sought forgetfulness in slumber.

The man raised his whip again. His shirt was sweat-soaked, his eyes glittered with lust and madness. He could feel a tightening in his chest and groin, and now he was caught up in a frenzy of his own, not unlike that hapless moth.

If the girl had glanced at his face she would have known this part of her ordeal would soon be over. But neither

5

participant looked at the other, each was caught up in his own strange need, one to dominate, one to defy.

The lash fell again, and the girl moaned in pain and bowed her head in defeat.

"Daughter of Satan," the man gasped, and flung the whip aside. He towered over her, his chest heaving, the light in his eyes shifting. The girl shivered delicately and remained huddled on the floor, dreading what came next.

"He's finished. I'm going to Cyra!"

"No, Brynna!" Hope Stanton cried out. "Don't go near his room, I beg you." A paroxysm of coughing cut off her words and left her gasping for breath.

"Mama!" Brynna hurried to the sick bed. With shaky hands she mixed a milky concoction from a bottle left by the doctor and held the glass to her mother's lips. Between coughs, Hope tried to swallow. At last the spasm passed and she lay back against her pillows, her strength spent. From some deep protective well of motherhood, she gripped her daughter's hand.

"Promise me," she whispered. "Promise you'll go to Jessica's. I've written to her."

"I've just come back from school, Mama. I won't leave you again."

"You must, you must get away from your father. Wes is—" A cough seized her, shutting off her breath. She fought against it. "He's evil," she finally gasped. "He'll hurt you as he did me."

The girl's brow ridged in shock. "Papa hurt you?" she asked in disbelief.

Between wheezing coughs, Hope whispered the terrible secrets that must be revealed if she were to protect her

6

daughter. "You must take Cyra and get away. You must go to La—"

The wasted frame shook with a seizure. Frantically Brynna tried to help her mother, then, recognizing her inadequacies, ran down the hall to her father's room.

"Papa!" she cried, pounding against the door panel. No one answered. "I need Cyra. Mama's sick." She tore at the knob, but the door was locked. All was silent beyond that portal. The hall seemed thick with something evil and horrible. What went on beyond that door besides the whippings? What other horrible things had her father done that she'd been shielded from. Dread rose in her throat like bile and she threw herself against the panel, pounding on the wood until it seemed it must surely give beneath her small, soft fists.

Suddenly the door opened. Brynna sprang back, her eyes wide and frightened. Cyra stood in the yawning darkness.

"Cyra?" Brynna whispered. "Are you all right?"

Without answering, Cyra turned down the hall. Brynna couldn't resist a glance back at her father's room, but the interior remained in such deep shadow she could see nothing before the door swung shut. Quickly she followed Cyra and saw how her dress clung to her back and lines of blood stained the cloth.

Hope lay pale as death against the pillows. Not even an eyelash twitched as they approached.

"Miz Hope . . ." Cyra spoke at last, leaning close to the woman, but there was no answer. Cyra placed her ear to Hope's chest and felt her pulse. "She's dead!" she said, turning great dark eyes to Brynna.

"No!" Brynna looked at the gentle woman who'd nurtured and protected her through the years. The memory of all that Hope had told her echoed in her head.

"What are we going to do now?" Cyra whispered. Without Hope's presence, what would stop Wes Stanton's cruel acts now?

Brynna raised her tear-stained face. "We're going to see that Mama is properly buried and then we're going to Langtry."

"You'll not leave this house," Wes Stanton said from the doorway. He entered his dead wife's room and spared not a glance for the wasted form who'd once been the lovely, gentle bride who had brought to him the plantation he'd coveted so much. The years since that promise-filled wedding day had been spent in heaping contempt and ridicule on his wife's head. He had no thought of grief to spare for her now. His wrath-filled eyes were pinned on his daughter. "Do you hear me, Brynna? I won't allow you to leave."

"You won't stop me," the girl answered. Though her voice shook, her eyes were hard with determination. "If you try to keep Cyra or me here, I will tell what you did to Mama and what you do to your slaves."

Wes's face grew ugly as he glowered at his daughter, but she didn't cringe as she once might have. She stood her ground, her gaze unwavering.

"Bah! Go then. I'm glad to be done with the lot of you," he shouted, and stalked from the room. Brynna's knees gave way, and she leaned against the side of her mother's bed.

Three days later, when the morning sun had just rimmed the distant hills, Brynna and Cyra crept down the stairs of Beaumont Hall. Often, Brynna glanced over her shoulders, expecting her father to appear at any moment and order them to stay. But the door of his room remained closed. They made it to the front drive; where the carriage waited for them. Their trunks had already been loaded.

"Quick, Cyra," Brynna cried, climbing into the conveyance. *They were going to make it*, she thought exultantly. The slave girl held back, her dark eyes looking distressed.

"I have to go back," she said. "I left my little rag doll behind."

"Leave it," Brynna cried. "We'll get you another."

"Not like this. Miss Hope made this for me, when I first come up to the big house, remember?"

Brynna was touched. Cyra had never seemed to care about the rag doll, preferring instead to play with Brynna's porcelain dolls.

"Go then and hurry!" she urged. "Hurry, Cyra!"

The black girl ran inside. Brynna sat in the carriage twisting her handkerchief in agitation. The minutes stretched by.

"We gots to go, Miss Brynna," Zachary said softly, "if'n we wants to git to Memphis in time to catch that riverboat."

"She'll be here soon," Brynna said, and prayed Cyra wasn't being detained by her father. She'd almost decided she must go inside and find Cyra when the slave girl appeared in the doorway, the rag doll clutched to her breast. Her face bore an oddly triumphant light.

"What took you so long?" Brynna demanded as Cyra climbed into the carriage. "I was afraid Papa had caught you."

"He ain't never goin' to do that to me again," Cyra answered. "I just wanted to say a final goodbye to Beaumont Hall."

The carriage had reached the end of the drive and turned west on the road to Memphis. Brynna looked back

9

for a final glimpse of her home. The sun had risen above the edge of trees, its early light reflecting against the window panes of Beaumont Hall so the house looked as if it were on fire. She would never come back here again, she thought bleakly. The carriage drew around a bend and Beaumont Hall was blocked from her view. She looked straight ahead to a new future and what it might bring.

At Beaumont Hall, the panes reflecting the orange-red sunrise shattered from the intense heat. Smoke billowed through the great hall. Hungry flames licked at the beams and walls. In Wes Stanton's room, the draperies and canopy caught fire, but the man on the bed made no effort to escape. With wide-open, sightless eyes, he gazed upward until the blazing canopy broke free and drifted downward covering him with the cleansing power of fire.

Chapter One

Langtry!

It beckoned, a safe haven for her battered soul. She'd never seen the great plantation, yet she knew it from her dreams.

Langtry!

Where she might rest and rest!

"St. John's Landing!" A deckhand cried the warning.

The cumbersome sternwheeler nudged against the river dock, and darkies leaped to tie off the anchor lines. Amid laughter and chatter, passengers gathered up their belongings and surged down the gangplank to be greeted by cries of welcome from families and friends. Standing on the upper deck, Brynna blotted her brow and chin. She wasn't prepared for the hot Louisiana climate. Spring in Tennessee was often damp and cool, but here the air was already sultry. Her travel dress of gray faille was suffocatingly warm, its heavy folds seeming to weigh her down. Stays jabbed against one breast and restricted her breathing. Her silk parasol was nearly useless against the merciless sunlight. Even the trim buildings of the small river town seemed subdued in its bright glare.

Pushing away thoughts of her discomfort, Brynna watched the happy scene below, feeling lonely and apprehensive. She'd sent a short message to Jessica Sinclair informing her of their arrival, but there'd been no time for an answer. Now she stood wondering what her reception at Langtry would be.

A commotion on shore drew Brynna from her unhappy thoughts, and she glanced at the knot of people gathered around a wagon. A man on horseback jerked at the reins so sharply, the animal whinnied in pain and pranced sideways. A whip was clutched in his meaty fist. Cursing, he guided the horse closer to the wagon bed where three slaves huddled, heads bowed, shoulders hunched in defense against the whip which he drew down in a sharp, wrenching motion. It snapped against the back of the black man, but unlike the others, he didn't cower. He sprang to his feet and quick as a water moccasin striking, grabbed the whip, twisting it around his wrist for leverage. Silently he stood defying the rotund white man.

"Slave traders!" Cyra snorted, coming to stand by Brynna.

Brynna glanced at her maid. Despite their roles as mistress and slave, Cyra had always been outspoken. Since undertaking this journey, she'd fallen into a strange, bitter mood. Little wonder, Brynna thought guiltily, and turned back to the events on shore. Even here in Louisiana, there was cruelty. The scene was too painful to witness yet she couldn't tear her gaze away.

The slave trader's face had gone red with rage and he yanked on his whip handle, but the muscular black man was young and strong. Sweat glistened on his brow as he pulled against the whip. He gazed directly into his white master's face. Fear mixed with anger as the white trader saw the hostility mirrored in the black eyes.

12

"Let go, nigger," he ordered, "or I'll shoot you." One of the women seated in the wagon began to weep quietly, hopelessly.

The black man continued to hold the whip long enough to communicate his lack of fear, then released it abruptly, so the fat man was nearly unseated from his horse. When he regained his balance, he raised his whip again and brought it down across the black man's face and shoulders. Still the black man did not cower. Not by the flicker of an eyelash did he show pain as the trader continued to ply his whip.

Heartsick, Brynna gasped with disgust at the slaver's unwarranted cruelty. Her breath became erratic, and she trembled so, she feared she might fall to her knees. Beside her, Cyra hissed with hatred, her lips drawn back from her teeth in a primitive gesture of rage. Even the onlookers who'd meant to stay and buy slaves turned their backs and walked away.

"If you whip him to death, you won't be able to sell him," a voice called, and gratefully the onlookers turned toward the new arrival.

From her vantage point Brynna could see him clearly, and she drew in her breath, whether from admiration or some foreboding fear she couldn't tell, for the man awakened both emotions in her. Though he was seated on a handsome black Arabian horse, Brynna could tell he was a tall, powerfully built man. His shoulders were broad beneath the finely cut waistcoat, tapering into slim waist and hips. Strong, muscular thighs encased in buff-colored breeches gripped the sides of the spirited black, controlling it effortlessly. The man had taken off a top hat, and his dark hair gleamed blue-black in the sunlight. His face was strong and tanned, his features straight and handsome. It was obvious from his bearing and the quality of

13

his clothes that he was a planter from one of the wealthy plantations they'd passed upriver.

People nearest him in the dirt road bobbed their heads in respectful greeting. The trader had ceased beating his slaves and turned to the man. His thick lips drew back in a cunning grin and he raised his whip again.

"We don't take kindly to mistreatment of slaves here in Louisiana, Shepherd," the man called impatiently. His was a voice of authority. He was used to giving orders and having them obeyed.

"Well, now, sir, Ah don't see as how it's any of your business what Ah do with these slaves unless you're thinkin' on buyin' one."

The planter's lips tightened at such insolence, and Brynna thought he might ride away. But he sat studying the slaves. Brynna noted they were pitifully thin. Through their ragged clothing she could have counted their ribs if she were so minded. Even the towering black man seemed thin for his build. The planter nudged his horse forward through the crowd. "I'll have no slave that's been maimed by your heavy hand," he warned.

"Ah assure you, sir, no such thing has occurred here. Thomas there is an uppity, stubborn nigger who caused his last owner some grief, but Ah've whipped the stubbornness right out of him."

"So I see," the buyer answered wryly. He eyed the slump-shouldered women on the wagon bed. One of them was a mere girl and the belly of the other was rounded with child. "What do you want for the lot?" he asked. The trader smirked.

Brynna could no longer hear the men's voices as they drew closer to dicker, but the memory of the man's deep, rich voice seemed to hang in the air. The deal was struck almost immediately. The trader withdrew with a sullen expression and Brynna guessed he'd not done well in the exchange. The dark-haired man urged his new slaves up the bank to another wagon parked near the wharf.

"We know what he's going to do with his new property." Cyra's voice was heavy with loathing. Brynna looked at her questioningly. "He'll work the man to death in his sugarcane fields and bed the women until he grows tired of them."

"Perhaps not," Brynna said, unable to control the feelings of guilt that plagued her at Cyra's words. "Not all men are like my father."

"How do you know that?" Cyra asked sharply, and Brynna turned away, unable to answer. She had no way of knowing, of course, but she drew comfort from the fact that the slaves had been given food and water. They wolfed down the bread as if it were the first they'd eaten in a while. Even Thomas, the defiant giant, had succumbed to the need for vittles.

"You see. He is kind, after all." Brynna turned to Cyra, somehow pleased by this small reassurance. Cyra paid her no attention, however, for her gaze was riveted on the black man as well. Her pretty brown face was lit by the sunshine, so for a moment she looked like the old Cyra.

"I like that man's manner," she said softly. "I like the way he stood up to that white trader." Her tone hardened and her dark eyes flashed. "I thought he meant to kill him."

"You sound as if you wanted him to," Brynna said, feeling disquieted by Cyra's manner.

"I did," Cyra answered quietly.

Shock washed over Brynna. "Hush," she whispered. "If anyone heard you talk like that . . ." She glanced along the empty deck. Most of the passengers had gone ashore. "Besides, if he'd even tried to kill the trader, he would

15

have been killed himself. And to what avail? He did the wise thing and he was lucky that planter intervened."

"Oh, yes, the benevolent master!" the slave woman sneered.

"Please, Cyra. When we reach Langtry, try to keep such comments to yourself. It's all right that you say them in front of me, but others might not understand."

"You mean you want me to act like one of those slaves, cowering and bobbing my head and saying, 'Yes, ma'am, and no, ma'am'?"

"Just be careful with what you say. Don't cause trouble for us. I don't know what I'd do if we had to return to Papa."

"We ain't ever going back to that man," Cyra said fiercely.

Startled, Brynna stared at her. "What do you mean?"

"Nothing," Cyra mumbled, and turned away.

Brynna made her way down the gangplank. The wharf was teeming with people, ladies in gaily colored gowns, beribboned straw bonnets, and ruffled parasols; men in bright waistcoats and tall hats; and deckhands who moved about languidly, exchanging barrels and crates of goods for bales of cotton and barrels of sorghum to be shipped by steamboat down to New Orleans.

"Excuse me, Captain," Brynna said, approaching the bewhiskered, gray-haired man overseeing it all. "Is there a place I might rent a carriage and driver to take us to Langtry Plantation?"

"Langtry, you say?" the captain asked, squinting one eye as if it might help him hear better. "Mr. Sinclair was just here a minute ago." He looked around the wharf and shook his head. Obviously, the estimable Mr. Sinclair had vanished. Brynna's spirits sank in disappointment. She was weary of the days of traveling and wanted only to be

16

settled somewhere. Here on the wharf there was little breeze. Smells of unwashed bodies, smoke from the belching stack, and the rank odor of river and bayou pressed in on her, so she fought against a rising nausea.

Taking a gold coin from his pocket, the captain tossed it to a young darkie seated on a nearby cotton bale.

"Here, Sammy. Run find Mr. Sinclair. Tell him a lady's waiting for him at the steamboat."

"Yas, suh," the boy said, smiling broadly, and lit off down the dusty street, his brown legs pumping energetically.

"He can't have gone far," the captain said, then, seeing Brynna's pale face, he rushed forward to grip her elbow. "Rest on this bale, miss," he said, guiding her to one. Brynna wanted to resist but she felt weak and her knees trembled. Sunspots danced before her eyes. Gratefully she sank down.

"Here, girl!" the captain snapped, holding out a clean white handkerchief to Cyra. "Run to that fountain in the square and dampen this."

At his imperious tone, Cyra glared back at him.

"Go on, git. Take care of your mistress," the captain ordered, and gave her a shove. Cyra's mouth twisted in a sullen grimace, and she shot an ominous glance at Brynna. Brynna remained silent, knowing she must smooth over Cyra's ruffled feelings later. Before the captain she must hold her peace. Seeing Brynna would not intervene on her behalf, Cyra snatched the handkerchief from him and sauntered away at an indolent pace.

"You got an insolent nigger there," the captain observed, his red face pulled into a frown of annoyance.

"Cyra's good, really. She's been with me for years," Brynna said faintly, and laid aside her bonnet.

"Humph!" The captain's faded blue eyes studied her.

17

"This heat takes some gettin' used to," he explained and, taking one of her hands, he patted it briskly as if that might help her recover. Like most men he felt helpless and ineffectual when confronted with a woman's infirmities.

At last Cyra returned with the dampened handkerchief. Brynna placed it on her brow and leaned against a bale, reveling in the moist coolness, however minute. She closed her eyes, and the noises and smells of the wharf seemed to recede. Dimly she perceived the rattle of horses' hooves, but couldn't seem to rouse herself.

She sensed a presence beside her, magnetic and compelling. A hand, larger and rougher than Cyra's, was laid against her temple. The scent of tobacco and fresh wind and grass came to her.

"How long has she been like this?" a strong, rich voice demanded. She heard someone answer, but couldn't make out the words. She was drifting in a world of fire and brimstone.

"Bring my canteen," the voice commanded, and she sensed movement around her, but there were no people in the world she inhabited, only a dark shadow that floated on the edge. The shadow grew larger. The fiery orange mists swirled and thinned until she could see the face of her father. He reached for her.

"No!" she whimpered and shrank back, but his hands were on her shoulders lifting her. In one hand he held something, surely a whip. Her arms flailed outward. "No, Papa!" she cried. Her arms struck against something solid. Strong hands gripped her arms, pinning them. "No, Papa, please," she pleaded.

"Drink!" a voice commanded, and something was held to her mouth. She felt water, silvery cool against her lips, and she opened her mouth and swallowed the sweet, clear liquid. It soothed her parched throat. She tried to open

18

her eyes, but her lids were heavy and her tongue too thick to speak. Cool clothes were applied to her temples and the back of her neck. She shivered delicately. Fingers unfastened her bodice and worked at the laces of her corset.

"Damn fool female vanity!" the voice cursed. Then she was being lifted and carried by strong arms. She cried out and reached for something solid in this terrifying, shifting world. Her hands fell against something hard and solid and her fists instinctively clasped shut. Something held her strong and sure, so she felt safe again. Her head lolled backward and she gave in to the dull weariness that claimed her.

Temple Sinclair motioned to the driver, and as the carriage lurched forward, settled back impatiently against the cushions. He'd had no intentions of riding in the carriage. Chandra, the black Arabian, was more to his liking, but the girl who rested against him now had clasped his shirt so desperately, he hadn't the heart to disengage her. What on earth had made her cry out like that? What images had caused that look of sheer terror that had claimed her when she looked into his face. She'd recoiled as if she thought he meant her harm. Temple looked down at the slender girl. He barely felt her weight against his shoulder, so slight was she, but he could see the curl of gold-tipped lashes against pale cheeks and catch a whiff of her sweet-scented breath. Even in sleep, her brow was furrowed as if she suffered a great anxiety.

He had little doubt of who she was. Jessica had been fuming for days, ever since the messages from Beaumont had arrived. So this was Jessica's little niece. Not quite the sassy child Temple had expected. Beneath the heavy gray faille and myriad layers of petticoats and camisoles with

19

which women liked to burden themselves were soft womanly mounds. His fingers had brushed against her firm breasts when he'd loosened her clothing. She lay against him like a crushed petal and he found himself studying her sweet, curving mouth. Her skin was flawless ivory except for the faint smattering of freckles across her nose. Chestnut curls hung limply around her ears, their bright beauty dimmed by the dust of travel. Even in such a state of dishevelment, she was a beauty. He wondered about the color of her eyes. They'd been unfocused, dark and haunted when he looked into them.

Their new guest offered some mystery that Jessica would soon ferret out, he had no doubt. He grinned, a dimple flashing in one tanned cheek, one eyebrow rising slightly as he thought of his stepmother. No one could resist Jessica, not even rebellious teenage boys or fainting damsels. With unfailing gentleness and kindness she'd worn down his resistance to a new mother. Her gentle, capable hand had been felt all over the plantation. She'd restored tranquility to their muddled life. He was certain she'd do the same to this frail, broken flower.

Brynna woke in a soft bed. Feeling the whisper of cool, starched sheets against her legs, she imagined herself back in her old room at Beaumont Hall. She opened her eyes and looked around, then uttered a cry of dismay at finding herself in a strange place. Memory returned and she sighed with relief. She wasn't back at Beaumont Hall, so anything would be better. She sat up and looked around. At the first sign of movement, a small brown-skinned girl with wide, round eyes got to her feet and sped out the door. Brynna watched her go and glanced around feeling strange and disoriented. The last thing she remembered

20

was the heat of the wharf and waiting for someone. How did she get here? Where was Cyra?

Pushing back her hair, she noted the light dimity counterpane and canopy of the four-poster bed, the rich, mahogany dressing table and water stand, the airy curtains at the wide windows, shuttered now against the heat, and the chaise longue covered in pink-and-cream striped silk. Delicate pink roses trailed in wild abandonment over the wallpaper, and a muted handwoven rug covered the wide planked pine floor. It was a lovely room, Brynna realized, and her every comfort had been seen to.

Feeling rested save for the pressure building in the lower region of her body, Brynna rose and looked for a necessary chair which effectively hid the chamber pot. She'd no sooner finished than there was a tap on the door. At her command, two servant girls entered, carrying pails of water which they poured into the porcelain tub. Obviously the young slave girl's task had been to inform someone when she awakened.

One of the servants left and the other stayed behind to assist Brynna with her bath. "Ah'm May," the girl said, "Miss Jessica says she'll be waiting for yo' in the parlor when yo're ready."

"Thank you, May." Brynna was touched by her aunt's consideration. She'd longed for a proper bath ever since leaving Beaumont. She slid into the scented water and leaned back in pure contentment. Whatever lay ahead for her, she would face it gladly, but for now she wanted only to savor the soothing bath. She lolled until the water grew tepid, then washed her long hair, holding her head down for the servant to pour cool rinse water over her hair. At last she stepped out and wrapped herself in a linen towel.

"Have you seen Cyra?" she asked May, suddenly

21

alarmed that she might have been left behind on the wharf.

"Yes, ma'am. Cyra's here." A frown dimmed May's smile for a moment, then it returned. "Miss Jessica says for me to help yo' dress dis time."

Something about the girl drew Brynna's attention. She was younger than Brynna, but her slim figure was already ripely curved. Her pert young breasts pushed against the dark calico bodice. She held her head proudly, and her teeth flashed white and sound in frequent smiles. There seemed to be none of the hesitation and unease in this girl that the Beaumont slaves had evidenced. Brynna scowled and turned away, thinking May would have little chance if she'd had the misfortune of living at Beaumont. All too quickly she would have caught the attention of Wes Stanton. Brynna pushed her memories away. They were ugly and best forgotten. She concentrated on dressing herself to meet the Sinclairs.

Her trunks had already been brought to her room and unpacked. Her gowns and petticoats filled the mahogany armoire and high chest of drawers with its pediments and carved rosettes. From the placement of her belongings, Brynna guessed this was meant to be her room during her stay here. Once again she felt grateful for her aunt's hospitality. Some of her anxiety began to fade.

She chose one of the summer gowns she'd packed and directed May in the curling of her hair. The damp ringlets curled easily around the nimble brown fingers. At last, satisfied with her appearance, Brynna rose and prepared to go downstairs to greet her aunt. May led the way.

Stepping outside her room, Brynna paused, gaping at the opulent hall and furnishings. She should have been prepared by the elegance of her own room. Other doors opened onto the hall, and Brynna guessed some belonged to her aunt and her stepson, but what of the others? Surely they weren't all guest rooms. Did Langtry entertain so often then?

May led the way toward one end of the wide hall, where doors opened onto a gallery and a wide, curving staircase led down to the two-story hall. A shimmering glass chandelier hung from the second-floor domed ceiling. Brynna could only stare as she followed May down the carpeted steps. Beaumont Hall had been a prosperous plantation and the mansion house reflected that wealth. She was used to magnificent homes, but none she'd ever seen compared with this.

She was so busy gaping at the lacy plaster frieze work, she didn't notice the dark-haired man standing at the bottom of the stairs until she was level with him. With a start of recognition, she saw that he was the man who'd bought the slaves from the trader that morning. He was as handsome and compelling up close as he'd seemed from a distance. Blue-black strands of hair fell across his wide brow, white teeth flashed in his tanned face as he smiled. His eyes, of a brown so dark as to appear almost black, gazed down at her. His magnetism was so overpowering she stepped backward and in so doing, caught her heel on the narrow step.

"Careful," he said, and his strong, tanned hand gripped her arm. She could feel its heat against her bare skin. Alarm swept through her and was mirrored on her face. Temple saw it and loosened his grasp.

"How are you feeling?" he asked gently. His gaze flickered over her face and gown, taking in every detail from the delicate lace at the rounded neckline to the sprightly, still-damp curls. Her eyes were hazel, warm honey flecked gold, with shadows of green lending a mysterious depth. He stared, then seeing her growing discomfort, stepped back, giving her room to pass or stay as she wished. He was perfectly aware that his tall frame sometimes overpowered others. He used it often in business to his advantage, but never with shrinking, anxious young women with glowing golden eyes and pale, frightened faces.

"You suffered from heat prostration," he went on when she'd made no answer. "You'll have to take a slower pace until you've adjusted to our climate."

"You brought me here?" she stuttered.

"I'm not surprised you don't remember." He smiled, and the stern lines of his face relaxed.

She felt the charm of the man and resisted. "I'm sorry to have been such a bother," she replied stiffly, refusing to look at him.

His smile faded briefly and his straight brows knitted in puzzlement. She was like a butterfly, sunshiny and beautiful one moment, skimming away the next.

"You were no bother. The biggest bother would have been dealing with Jessie if I'd missed you."

"There you are," a high, sweet voice exclaimed, and an older woman entered the hall from one of the wide arches. "Cyra and I had just about given up on you." Her gentle smile included the dark girl who followed her and stood silently watching their reunion. Jessica Sinclair was not a prepossessing woman at first glance. She wore a simple day dress of blue-and-white silk. Her gray hair was brushed smooth from a center part and wrapped into a chignon. The simple style became her delicate features. Her gray eyes were luminous and warm with welcome.

"My dear child. I've been waiting for you patiently, and my great lout of a son has kept you to himself." Temple grinned at his stepmother, then leaned down to kiss her on the cheek. Jessica's smile was warm and loving

24

as she gazed up at the tall man. Watching the two, Brynna sensed a great deal of affection between them. Then she turned her attention to Jessica and found she could not speak. Jessica looked so much like Mama, with her gentle voice and sweet smile, that tears stung Brynna's eyes and she bit her lips to keep from crying. She'd had the vapors once today in front of Temple Sinclair. She had no wish to do so again.

But Jessica seemed to guess her feelings. She folded Jessica into her arms and hugged her. "My dear child," she crooned, rocking back and forth slightly. Her hand fluttered across Brynna's back, patting and soothing. "What sorrow you've endured. First your mother and then your father."

"My father?" Brynna asked, drawing back fearfully. "Is he here?" Had he come for them after all? Would he drag her back to Beaumont Hall against her will, making her endure the torment he'd caused her mother? Had Cyra told Jessica about her father's cruelty? Would the Sinclairs protect them from her father's tyranny? She glanced at Cyra, but the slave woman's expression was guarded. Shame tinged Brynna's cheeks with color. Watching her golden eyes glow and her cheeks color, Temple thought he'd never seen such a beautiful creature.

"You haven't heard then," Jessica sighed. "I feared this might be the case, and I suppose it's best you hear from me rather than a stranger. Come, dear. Let's go into the parlor and have some tea. I'm afraid I have some bad news for you. Are you coming, Temple?"

"Yes, of course," he answered, and Brynna cast him a quick glance wishing he wouldn't join them. She feared what Jessica was about to say. Was Jessica about to send them packing? She didn't want Temple Sinclair to witness her shame.

He guessed her reluctance to have him present and wondered at it. With Jessica on one side of her and Temple on the other, she had little choice but to join them in the parlor. Cyra followed, obviously as reluctant as Brynna felt.

A delicately carved cherrywood tea table sat before an ornate box sofa. Matching chairs had been pulled close. Though the room and its furnishings were elegant, they'd been arranged hither and yon in a manner better suited to the inhabitants. The richly appointed room seemed homier than it might have otherwise.

Temple settled into one of the armchairs, his long legs sprawling across the carpet, his booted feet crossed negligently. He'd affected a pose of ease, but Brynna sensed a tension in him.

"Come, child, and have some tea," Jessica said, handing Brynna an English china cup. The tea smelled of peaches. Gratefully, she sipped, bracing herself for what must surely follow. A great dread was building, so her hand shook. Jessica saw it and her generous heart was touched. Temple saw it and wondered again at the deep, sad secrets this lovely girl seemed to carry.

"Did Hope suffer much?" Jessica asked softly, her faded blue eyes wide and moist with unshed tears.

"No, ma'am," Brynna answered, and drew a deep breath, wanting to say more, yet bound by her fear of something as yet undisclosed and unnamed. Something that lurked ugly and shameful on the edge of a world that had nothing to do with the bright Louisiana sunshine or the fragrant peach tea. She was painfully aware of the handsome man sprawled in nonchalant disregard, his black boottips shiny like hard, cold marble, his aristocratic features unable to hide a touch of impatience. She guessed he'd rather be in his study with a bottle of whiskey than here in the parlor with the ladies. Yet, his manners were impeccable. He accepted the cup of tea Jessica handed him and turned an easy smile upon Brynna.

"How did she die, Brynna?" Jessica persisted, her eyes giving away some gnawing anxiety.

"She—she died in her sleep," Jessica said, grateful that her hesitancy might be attributed to grief and a reluctance to talk of her mother's death. "She'd been doing poorly for some time."

"I understand, dear." Jessica took her hand. "I had to ask. I've worried so about her welfare these past few years since her—accident." Jessica paused. "You're a strong young woman to see your mother buried and then travel here to me as you have, without an escort. I'm surprised your father—"

"I had Cyra," Brynna said quickly, then fell silent. Women were not allowed to travel without male escorts, but she hadn't dared ask her father to provide one. She'd been too fearful he would find an excuse to stop her coming. She twisted her hands in her lap, debating on telling her aunt the truth of her leavetaking, but Temple Sinclair sat watching with eyes that seemed to see right through to her every thought.

"Papa was just too busy to come with me," she said lamely.

"Of course, we don't blame him," Jessica said. "It just seems a pity he didn't. If he had he might be h—" Once again Jessica interrupted herself and cast a quick glance at Temple. He leaned forward in his chair and fixed his smoky gaze on Jessica.

"I fear we may be making this worse for Miss Stanton," he said, observing the pulse beating wildly in the hollow of her throat. "Perhaps we'd better just tell her."

27

"Tell me what?" Brynna whispered, her golden gaze wide and searching on his face.

"Brynna, dear. It's your father," Jessica said gently. "You poor child! There was a fire at Beaumont Hall the morning you left. Your father wasn't able to escape."

"A fire?" Brynna repeated numbly. Her gaze flew to Cyra, who stood in the archway as if ready to flee. Brynna got to her feet and took a faltering step toward the black girl, then paused as images of Beaumont Hall came to her, images of stately columns majestic in the morning light and windows ablaze with the colors of the sunrise. Only it hadn't been a sunrise. Beaumont Hall had been burning then! And her father!

She'd pondered over his failure to come down and see them off, if not out of fatherly love, then to reestablish his control over her, to claim his ownership. She'd been so fearful he'd insist Cyra stay behind, but he hadn't shown his face. Her eyes grew wide as realization dawned. She stared fixedly at Cyra, whose pretty features had twisted with hatred. Her black eyes were hard and brilliant, like polished stones. Only the beads of sweat gathering on her rounded brow gave away her anxiety. With awful clarity Brynna recalled the events of that day. Their hasty leave-taking and Cyra running back inside because she'd forgotten a rag doll Hope had made for her. Brynna had been touched, touched because it was so unlike the practical Cyra. She stared at Cyra and felt the blood roar to her head. A cry of denial began deep within, forcing itself upward. Cyra returned her gaze as if fascinated by the conflicting emotions that played across Brynna's face, but she made no move to help her mistress.

Behind them Aunt Jessica continued to talk in her sympathetic voice, unaware of the tension between the two girls. But Temple saw and wondered at its cause.

Brynna stood with her back to him and he saw her slender body shake like the swamp grass in a hurricane. Even as he leaped to his feet, a cry emerged from her throat, silencing Aunt Jessica's words. Before Temple could reach her, she'd slumped to the floor. Temple knelt beside her, feeling for her thin, reedy pulse and gripping the small heart-shaped chin to turn her face toward him. There was no color on the cheeks or pale, smooth lips. He could see the spidery blue trace of her veins in the delicate eyelids.

"Let's get her to her room," Jessica said, bending over the unconscious girl. Her brows drew together in concern. "I'm afraid I didn't handle that well for her. She's had too much grief for one so young."

Whatever Brynna had felt over her father's death, it hadn't been grief alone, Temple thought, scooping her up in his arms and settling her against his shoulder in a position that was becoming familiar. Whatever secrets those golden eyes hid, she hadn't been prepared for this final bit of news. But then, who could be? She must have been close to Wes Stanton, he thought, remembering how she'd cried out in her delirium before. Now she lay silent in his arms. His nostrils flared, taking in the flowery scent of her skin and hair.

The mystery deepens, he thought, and turned toward the stairs. Jessica followed him, pausing only to speak to Cyra who stood in the hall gazing up at them with narrowed eyes, her face closed and set.

"Cyra, come up. Brynna will need you," Jessica commanded gently and after a moment's hesitation the black girl climbed the stairs.

Chapter Two

"Yo' gwine tell on me?" Cyra asked the next afternoon as she stood at the foot of the big, canopied bed. Her eyes were more defiant than fearful.

"Why are you talking like that?" Brynna asked, stalling for time. Her head ached abominably and she felt weak and quivery as if she might begin to weep at any moment. She didn't want to discuss this with Cyra now, not ever. She didn't want to acknowledge that any of it had happened. She wanted only to pretend that she'd always lived here at Langtry where the sun flowed into the room and across the carpet like warm butter and the light, pristine-white canopy fluttered lazily in the breeze from the open window. Here in this room she felt secure and protected, and she was suddenly aware she'd never felt that way before at Beaumont Hall. A tension had tainted the air, driving peace before it and leaving behind an insidious unease that infected everyone, slaves and master alike. But here she'd found peace in the curl of a flower petal on her wallpaper and the lemon-yellow light streaming across the room. The air had grown heavy and hot although it was not yet midday. Brynna felt dampness forming on her nape beneath the heavy weight of unbrushed chestnut curls.

"Wat wrong wif the way Ah talk?" Cyra demanded, one slim brown hand anchored on a jutting hip. She'd tied a rag around her head like the other house slaves here at Langtry.

"You never talked like that before we came here," Brynna answered tiredly.

"Ah talk like the other slaves now," Cyra answered. "Dat w'at yo' want me to be. Dat w'at Ah am."

"Oh, Cyra, don't be difficult," Brynna sighed, and turned away, hiding her face in a pillow.

"Ah'm sorry, Miss Brynna," Cyra answered, her tone not nearly as meek as her words implied. "Yo' goin' tell Missus Jessie 'bout yore daddy and me and dat fire?"

Brynna sprang upright in bed. "No," she said sharply. "What have you told her?"

"What is it yo' don't want me t' tell, Miss Brynna?" Cyra asked, her expression guileless.

"I—I don't want you to make up lies about Papa." Brynna couldn't look into Cyra's eyes.

"I don't need to make up lies," Cyra said quietly. "Do you want to know what your daddy did to me behind that locked door?"

Brynna clamped her hands over her ears. Cyra laughed, a sharp, cutting sound. "Ah didn't think so. Miss Jessica ain't gonna want to know, eithah, so ah won't say nuthin'."

"I'm sorry, Cyra." Brynna's shoulder's slumped in relief.

"Ain't nuthin' t' be sorry 'bout, Miss Brynna. Ah'm jest a slave. Who'd listen to me anyway?"

"Please, Cyra. Stop this game you're playing."

"We all playin' a game, Miss Brynna. Ah know mah

place now. Ah aim to keep it," Cyra answered, and turned to the door, where she paused and looked back at Brynna with glittering eyes. "Ah'm goin' down to get yore breakfast on a tray, then Ah'll bring yore bathwatah. Is they an'thang else yo' want before Ah go?"

"No, no!" Brynna sighed resignedly and lay back on the bed. Resentment at Cyra's attitude tightened her lips and flared her nostrils. Then she remembered the night her mother died and all the other nights that must have gone before and her resentment gave way to guilt and depression.

A knock at the door interrupted her black mood. At her bid to enter, Aunt Jessica's white head bobbed around the door. She wore a light flowered dress of pink cotton. Its bodice was trimmed with pink ruching and tiny buttons. She looked untouched by the heat and humidity.

"I just came to see how you're feeling today," she inquired.

"Much better," Brynna said, sitting up and unable to hide a grimace at the pain that shot through her temples. "I'm afraid I haven't adjusted yet to the heat."

"It takes a while, child." Jessica hurried to the edge of the bed and took one of Brynna's hands, rubbing the smooth skin absently. "You needn't worry about anything now, Brynna. You're safe here at Langtry. We want you to know you can make this your home for as long as you like."

A weight lifted from Brynna's shoulders. "Thank you, Aunt Jessica. You're very kind."

"Kindness has nothing to do with it. I've looked forward to your visit ever since Hope first wrote you were returning from school and might want to come for a visit." She cast Brynna a quick glance. "As for Beaumont Hall . . ." She paused and took a breath. "I'm sure your father is buried there in the family plot beside your mother. God rest their souls. It's time now we think about the living. By law you inherit Beaumont Hall and all the buildings and slaves and property, but it would be difficult for a young woman of your age to live there and manage a plantation by yourself." She paused, giving Brynna a chance to voice her feelings on this, but at her niece's continued silence, she hurried on. "Temple has made inquiries and the house was damaged beyond repair. There's a buyer interested in the property and he's willing to pay a fair price."

"The property belonged to the Beaumont family, Aunt Jessica. I know my father took over the running of the plantation when he married Mama. But Beaumont Hall belongs to you."

Jessica Sinclair shook her head. "Langtry is my home now, child. I'll never go back."

Brynna heard the contentment in her voice and longed for a place where she could belong, too. Jessica seemed to understand her thoughts without their having been spoken, for she leaned forward and gripped Brynna's hand.

"You don't have to go back, either, if you don't want to," she said fiercely, moved by the defeated look on the young face. "Temple will tend to everything if you want to sell."

"Would he?" Brynna asked gratefully, her eyes flashing with the first hope Jessica had seen there since her arrival.

"Certainly. He offered. He'll leave within a day or two if you wish." She got to her feet and shook out her skirts briskly, then laid a soft, wrinkled hand along Brynna's cheek. "You're going to stay here with us and be my daughter." Her smile lit her face with such radiance, Brynna hadn't the heart to demur even if she'd been so inclined. "Rest, child. Be at peace." The words were like

33

a benediction. Brynna sank against the pillows and watched the door close behind Jessica's bustling figure. She'd found a safe haven, she thought, looking around. Langtry! It would be her home now for as long as she wished. She felt a measure of peace. Thanks to Aunt Jessica's gentle ministrations, the ugly shadows were receding. Perhaps one day they would go away completely.

Almost immediately, she fell into the first peaceful sleep she'd known in weeks, waking only to partake spartanly of the supper tray Cyra had left for her. Afterward she retired once more to her bed and lay listening to the twilight sounds of the plantation. Voices, soft and slurred, called to one another in the Louisiana patois she'd noticed earlier and that Cyra had already adopted. From somewhere crickets whirred their restless, high-pitched melody and the sound of voices blending in deep, rich harmony drifted from the slave quarters. Listen as hard as she could, Brynna couldn't make out the sound of a whip's lash or the helpless cry of someone in pain.

Her eyes closed and she slept again only to wake in the morning feeling restless and imbued with new energy and purpose. Her headache was gone and the lemon light beckoned from beyond her window. She rose and quickly donned a riding outfit with a wide skirt and matching jacket. At home she'd always ridden whatever horse the stablehand brought her, usually some winded farm horse or broken spirited castoff of her father's. Still she'd come to love the feel of the wind on her face and the excitement of an animal beneath her as they raced across the Tennessee hills.

She ran down the stairs, skirted the kitchen and dining room, and let herself out a side entrance. From the side gallery she could no longer make out the stables hidden

34

behind a stand of trees, but she knew they were there, so she set out across the jeweled green lawn. Her quick pace slowed as she was caught by the beauty of the grounds. She'd been faint upon her arrival and seen nothing. From her window she'd been able to study only a small portion of the lawn. She was unprepared for the sweeping vistas of lawn, skies, and moss-draped trees. Gaining a clearly marked lane, she entered the copse of trees where the newly unfurled leaves made a panoply over her head.

Emerging on the other side, she found the stables, freshly painted with a white, railed fence around the pastures beyond. Hesitantly she approached, aware now that she hadn't asked permission of either her aunt or Temple about using their stables. Remembering the black Arabian Temple had ridden, she guessed he took great care with his horseflesh.

Thomas, the black man Temple had bought the day of her arrival, came out of the stable.

"Good morning," she called, noting he looked considerably better than the first time she'd seen him. His face looked fuller, as if he'd been eating regularly, and although a shirt covered his back, she surmised from the easy way he moved that had healed as well. He nodded in response to her greeting but made no answer. Although his demeanor was deceptively meek, she caught the same cold defiance in his eyes as the day he faced the white trader's whip.

"I've come to find a riding horse," she said, trying not to be intimidated by his sullen air. "Do you have a horse no one else rides, something Mr. Sinclair wouldn't mind my using?"

Thomas made no answer, so she thought him dumb, until she saw the direction of his dark gaze. Temple Sinclair had come along the path behind her. Brynna felt herself color slightly and forced her chin higher.

"Good morning, Cousin Brynna," he said, coming to stand beside her. He was taller even than Thomas and she felt dwarfed between the two.

"I was just asking Thomas about a pony I might ride," she said, forcing a smile to her lips but unable to meet the compelling black eyes. "I suppose I should have asked you first."

"This is your home now, Brynna," Temple answered. "You don't need to ask permission for anything here." He turned toward the stables and spoke over his shoulder. "However, if you're asking my opinion, I'll gladly give it."

"I'm asking," she replied, following along behind as he led the way along the stalls until he stopped before one in which a whiskey-colored horse stood munching contentedly on his morning grain. "This is Jarib. His name means He Will Contend. It's an apt name. He'll give you a challenge, if that's what you want."

"Oh, he's beautiful," Brynna cried running her hand along his soft nose. Jarib's brown eyes rolled in their sockets as he looked her over and he made small whickering sounds in his throat.

"He seems to like you," Temple observed.

"Do you think I could ride him?" Brynna asked with shining eyes.

"Only if you allow me the honor of riding with you."

Bothered by the handsome Creole, Brynna hesitated, then captured by the spirited horse, smiled brightly.

"Saddle him up," Temple ordered and moved to one of the other stalls where he began saddling the magnificent black he'd ridden the day Brynna arrived.

"Perhaps you'd like to see some of Langtry," he called as he tightened the cinch.

"You needn't if you're busy," Brynna replied quickly.

Temple frowned at her rejection, yet chose to pretend he hadn't read it correctly.

"I'm never too busy to show off Langtry," he replied, walking toward the front of the stalls leading his mount. A dazzling smile lit his lean face. Brynna glanced away. "You haven't had a chance to see much since arriving," Temple went on, chatting easily as if he hadn't noticed her reticence.

"I've been a bit of a nuisance," Brynna said apologetically.

"Not at all." He stood before her now, Jarib's reins in his hands. His critical gaze moved over her face and downward, lingering only a moment at the fullness of her breasts before coming back to meet her gaze. "You've color in your cheeks. It becomes you."

Her slender hands flew to her flushed cheeks, then she forced herself to a poise she did not feel in his presence. "Thank you. I'm feeling better."

"Good. Come on, I'll give you a hand up." Temple held out his broad palm and, after a moment's hesitation, she placed her small booted foot in it. Gently she was lifted onto the side saddle. Hooking her knee around the horn, Brynna carefully arranged her skirts so only the shiny tip of one black boot showed.

Jarib wickered nervously and pranced forward. Brynna tightened her grip on the reins and talked to the spirited horse in a calm tone. Quickly she brought his skittishness under control.

Temple watched her skillful handling of one of his prized steeds and nodded in approval. "You'll be all right," he said, and swung onto his own mount.

He led the way out along winding bayous and natural levees, past fields of sugarcane resembling a patch of green, flowing sea. Slaves had already begun work, their brown arms flashing rhythmically, the blades of their hoes glinting in the early sunlight. The smell of fertile black dirt hung heavy in the warming air. A white man sat astride a horse at the end of the field, his slouch hat pulled low, his thickening body slumped in the saddle. Now and then he flicked a whip against a post in idle boredom.

"Hewitt," Temple called. The man started and looked around, hastily coiling the whip and tying it to his saddle.

"Mornin', Mister Sinclair," the man said in a singsong accent that might have been beautiful if not for the accompanying whine in his voice.

"Brynna, this is Kyle Hewitt, our overseer." Temple made the introductions tersely.

"How do you do?" Brynna replied politely.

"Ma'am." Hewitt lifted his hat respectfully, but Brynna sensed a kind of insolence in his manner.

"Are you having any problems this morning, Hewitt?" Temple asked, pointedly staring at the whip the overseer had brandished earlier.

"Naw. I thought I saw a cottonmouth, but it's gone now. Ever'thing's fine," Hewitt answered quickly. His eyes shifted restlessly from one thing to another so they never quite met anyone's gaze.

"When the hoe gang finishes here, take them down to the east field."

"Yes, sir," Hewitt answered sharply, his shoulders back, his sharp, darting eyes alert. But when they'd ridden on by, Brynna glanced back and saw that he was once again slumped in his saddle, idly flicking the whip. She sensed a change in Temple as if he were irritated over something.

"You needn't go on with me," she said quickly, although she'd been enjoying their ride. "I can find my way back to the house."

"You haven't even begun to see Langtry," Temple said, smiling at her. His good humor had returned.

"How long has your family owned this land?" she called, urging her horse to catch up with his.

"My great-grandfather claimed most of what you see here," Temple said, slowing down so they rode abreast. "He had less than fifty slaves and he worked side by side with them, draining the land an acre at a time. It wasn't easy, since there were cottonmouths and water moccasins. The slaves were afraid. They wouldn't work unless he worked with them."

"It must have been an enormous undertaking," Brynna said, looking around at the wide, flat fields. "How large is Langtry?"

"We have over seven thousand acres," he answered, and smiled when she stared at him in disbelief. "My grandfather increased the holdings, as did my father."

"You must need a goodly number of hands," Brynna said, thinking of Beaumont Hall's three hundred and fifty acres.

"Sugarcane leeches the soil, wears it out so we have to let some acreage lie fallow. And some of that is still under water," he added cheerfully. "I've left some of it for a bird preserve. I'll take you there someday if you want."

"I'd like that." She clicked her tongue and gave Jarib his head. The horse cantered ahead.

Temple was pleased at her easy manner with him now. She'd become absorbed in the plantation and lowered her guard. Carefully, he nurtured their newfound common ground. He showed her the sugar mill, where in the summer, sorghum was extracted from the sugarcane into

39

great barrels. The mill stood silent now, the great rollers stilled.

Temple explained the workings of the plantation with more details than he might have otherwise if not for her bright eyes and intelligent questions. He thought of Alicia de Jarreau, Cort's sister and a neighbor. He couldn't imagine a similar conversation with her. In fact, Alicia didn't ride horseback, claiming it jolted her delicate constitution far too much. Conversation with her was usually restricted to silly flirtations and silly gossip.

He found himself delighted with his present company and took great pains to point out the wonders of the Louisiana backlands. He showed her the horseshoe lakes formed by the flooding river a hundred years before, the river bluffs, the flat, sloping plains sweeping away to the west, the stand of hickory, pine, cottonwood, and hackberry, and the tupelo which was often mistaken for the knobby-kneed cypress. He showed her the bayous which were used by the Cajuns and Indians in their flat-bottomed boats and explained that some of these same waterways would be closed by the thick lavender growth of water hyacinths come summer. He took her to the piny woods where the best wildflowers, ground orchids, phlox, mints, asters, St. Johnswort, wild peas, and stargrass could be found later and pointed out the early irises growing along a marsh and the sleek dark head of a muskrat in the still waters.

The sun was warm on Brynna's head, and she'd long since discarded her riding jacket as had Temple his. He wore a fine white lawn shirt opened into a deep vee which revealed the tanned skin and mat of hair beneath. Quickly, she looked away, strangely bothered by this virile man.

Birdsongs filled the air, the trills of marsh wrens and

40

tree swallows and many more she didn't recognize. Temple named the black skimmer, the royal tern snipes, as well as ducks and upland plovers. Aloud he wished for his gun and laughed at her soft reprimand.

They came upon the sound of a hundred tiny bells and Temple told her they came from tree frogs. He was surprised she made no moue of distaste at the homely perpetrators, but sat as if entranced, her golden eyes glowing.

At last, when the sun had climbed high in the azure blue sky, he led the way back, taking her full circle so they arrived at the bank of the great Mississippi. Following the river road he brought her back to the oak-lined drive leading to Langtry. The path was a quarter mile long, and the gnarled old oaks formed a leafy canopy over their heads. Brynna was silent as she rode beneath the trees. They must be a hundred years old, she guessed, and they gave a sense of permanency to the land, as if they meant to stand a hundred years more. She thought nothing could impress her as much as the oaks until they reached the end of the drive and she caught her first glimpse of the great plantation house with its sloping roof, graceful columns, and wide-galleried wings. The sweeping lawn had given way to formal gardens where trimmed boxwood hedges contained rose beds and yellow jasmine and clumps of pink azaleas and heavy-budded rhododendruns were etched by crushed shell walks. Giant blue and copper-hued iris vied with larkspur and violets. Flowering redbuds, hawthorn, and magnolia trees provided fragrant pools of shade where white stone benches invited one to rest and contemplate the garden's tranquil beauty. In the center of it all, marbled cherubims guarded a tinkling fountain.

"I used to dream about Langtry, but I never realized how grand it actually is," Brynna said, awed by the size

41

and scope of the mansion before her. Although Temple had never cared to impress anyone with the Sinclair wealth, having taken it for granted most of his life, he was nonetheless pleased by her reaction.

"My great-grandfather built the first main house when he'd finished clearing the land," Temple took pleasure in explaining. "When it was finished he went down to New Orleans and married one of the *filles à la cassettes* sent from France as brides. The girls were called that because they brought everything they owned in little caskets. My great-grandfather was quite a bit older than his bride. He'd spent all his youth building his plantation."

"How romantic," Brynna said softly. He glanced at her face and found her expression wistful and dreamy. He smiled, amused to see she was as normal as most young women her age when it came to a pretty story.

"I'll have to leave you now," he said with some reluctance. "I'm on my way to Tennessee to tend to your business matters."

"I've caused you a great deal of trouble," she said, and he could see her pulling the shell about herself again.

"No trouble, Cousin Brynna. Is there anything you'd like me to see to while I'm there?"

"No, but thank you for asking," Brynna said without looking at him. He sensed she wanted only to forget Beaumont Hall. Why would someone hate their home so intensely, they wished never to return? he wondered. Perhaps he'd find some answers to his questions while he was there.

"How long will you be gone?" she asked.

"About two weeks. Will you miss me?"

She was startled by his question and glanced at him sharply. His eyes flashed teasingly. He watched her reaction. He'd asked, wanting to draw a smile from her, to ease that somber air that claimed her ever since he mentioned Beaumont Hall. But watching the swiftly changing emotions revealed in her expression, he realized that he wanted her to miss him. He wanted her to think of him at odd moments as he knew he would her.

"I'm sure Aunt Jessica will miss you something terrible," she replied honestly.

"Ahh, Jessica," he said, hiding his disappointment, for in truth he didn't understand his own feelings. "That's almost enough." They'd reached the gate posts now and he brought Chandra to a halt. Jarib followed suit.

"I bid you farewell, then, until my return," he said softly, and his rich voice held a tinge of regret. She must have imagined it, she thought. *She* was the one who regretted his going. For one brief hour she'd forgotten the past. He'd made her laugh. For a while she'd felt strong again, untouched by ugly secrets.

A tremor passed over her and she raised her large eyes to meet his. "Goodbye, Mr. Sinclair," she said softly.

His smoldering dark gaze captured hers. "You must call me Temple," he said with a slight quirk at the corner of his mouth. "After all, we are cousins, *n'est-ce pas?*"

"All right, Temple," she answered.

The sunlight caught in her hair. Her eyes were in shadow, her gold tipped lashes hiding the green-gold eyes. He would remember her just like this, a pretty girl sitting easily on the back of a spirited, whiskey-colored Thoroughbred.

"Goodbye, Cousin Brynna," he said and wheeled his horse. Without looking back, he set Chandra at a swift gallop that soon carried him around a bend in the road. She could hear the staccato of Chandra's hooves long after they'd disappeared from view. She wished she'd bid Temple a friendlier farewell. After all, he was making this trip on her behalf. Thoughtfully, she turned Jarib back to the stables. The cicadas whirred in the thick, hot grass and the peace of Langtry seeped into Brynna's very soul. She knew now why Mama had urged her to come to Langtry. She'd known Brynna would be safe here. Brynna thought of Temple Sinclair and wondered if Mama had known how charming and magnetic he was. Suddenly, she didn't feel safe at all. She seemed to stand on the edge of a great precipice and the ground around her was beginning to crumble.

Chapter Three

"Would you like to accompany me tomorrow?" Jessica asked that evening at supper. "It would give you a chance to see a part of Langtry that Temple hasn't shown you. You can learn a little bit about the way we do things here in Louisiana."

"Perhaps I could help you with some of the chores. I don't want to be treated like a guest."

"You wouldn't be," Jessica answered. "But I've often thought I could use an extra pair of hands and a quick young mind."

A warmth stole over Brynna. She wasn't sure if her aunt was only trying to make her feel wanted or if she really needed help. Either way, Brynna faced the prospect of the morrow with renewed anticipation.

After supper, she wandered through the rooms of Langtry, starting with the great parlor with its sculptured Carrera marble fireplace and ornate bronze chandelier. Handwoven flowered carpets covered high-polished floors of cedar and wide-planked pine. Elegant sofas, delicately carved walnut chairs, and mahogany étagères graced the spacious rooms. Marble-topped tables held silver lamps. A large Palladian window dominated one wall, its graceful arch reflected in gold-leaf mirrors. The rest of the windows were really French doors of bevelled glass which opened on to the gallery.

Sheffield silver doorknobs opened mahogany doors leading to a paneled library where a handsome chess table held gold and silver pieces and tall bookshelves ringed the room. Brynna touched the deep wing-backed chairs and for some reason thought of Temple resting here before the fire, his long legs sprawling, his dark hair falling across his forehead in careless disarray while he concentrated on a book.

A lacy arch with ornate plaster frieze led to a large uncarpeted ballroom with silk-covered Hepplewhite chairs placed along the sides and gold-framed portraits of the first Langtry Sinclair and his casket bride gracing the walls.

"There are fifty-one rooms altogether," Jessica told her as they settled over needlework in the small parlor. The painted glass lampshade lent a cozy glow to the room. The doors on to the gallery had been left open to a cool river breeze. Cheesecloth frames kept out the insects. "Too many rooms for one house in my estimation, especially when there are no children." She sighed. "I expect Temple will do something about that one day." She glanced at Brynna, whose cheeks had turned pink.

Brynna buried her head in her work and continued her stitchery. She felt strangely disquieted at the thought of Temple's children. She could scarcely imagine him as a doting father. He was far too handsome. The memory of her own father, stern and disapproving, caused her to pull down the corners of her mouth.

"Try not to be sad," Jessica said softly, misinterpreting

46

her melancholia. Brynna forced a smile, touched by the other woman's kindness.

The next morning she rose at the break of dawn. Cyra made no move to rise and perform her duties for her mistress. Brynna made no comment. She no longer expected Cyra's help. An uneasy pact had settled between them. Hastily donning a simple morning gown, Brynna hurried downstairs. Though mistress of one of the largest and most prosperous plantations in the region, Jessica was already astir and fully engaged with her responsibilities. She was used to rising before her slaves and retiring long after the bells had signaled the end of their work hours. Now she stood instructing the house servants in their tasks for the day. When she'd finished she turned to the overseer Brynna had met the day before. Kyle Hewitt nodded a greeting, touched his hat brim in the briefest show of respect.

"Mornin', Miz Jessica," he said, and his gaze slid to Brynna. His pale eyes raked over her face and figure too thoroughly for her liking. "Miss Brynna."

"What did you want, Mr. Hewitt?" Jessica asked crisply.

"Ah'm puttin' the slaves down along the backland for a few days, yes, have them clearing mo' of thet swamp," he answered in the lilting patois of the Louisiana country people.

"Didn't Temple tell you he wanted the hoe gangs in the cane fields? This weather may not hold," Jessica responded.

"It ain't goin' t' rain, no," Hewitt said. "Ah guarantee it. We can have that bottomland cleared so's we can begin the drainin'—"

47

"Mr. Hewitt," Jessica interrupted him. "First we have to take care of what acreage we have planted. You'd best follow the instructions Temple left for you." She turned away with an air of finality and Hewitt's face suffused with red. Brynna saw his lips tighten into a grim line as he stalked out. Obviously, he didn't like taking orders from a woman.

Jessica seemed unperturbed. "Coming, Brynna?" she called in her gentle voice, and Brynna wondered how she'd been able to rout the blustering Mr. Hewitt so easily. Taking out a key, Jessica led the way along the covered walkway to the kitchen, which was built separate from the big house in case of fires. From there they moved on to the storehouses beyond. A line of servants carrying wooden trays and flat baskets followed.

The storehouse was a sturdy, one-room building with long rows of hams and shoulders hanging from the beams. Tubs of pickled pork and corned beef were stored beneath. The sides were lined with shelves on which rested nine-pound loaves of sugar purchased from the commission merchants in New Orleans, jars of preserves and boxes of dried fruit, beans, and rice. Below the shelves stood barrels of flour and olive oil and cases of wine and brandy.

Jessica portioned out the daily rations of oil, soap, animal fat for candles, leather, needles, cloth, and myriad other supplies. Beside the storehouse, a springhouse had been built half underground to keep its interior cool. A small creek ran through it. Perishables such as cream, butter, eggs, and cheese could be kept there for days. As each servant received the supplies needed, they went off to begin their day's tasks. The fat cook carried her spices and seasonings back to the kitchen where she hung great black kettles over cranes and filled them with spicy filé gumbo thickened with okra. The seamstresses, laundresses, and shoemakers all hurried off to their workplaces. Another day had begun at Langtry.

Tirelessly, Jessica moved about the plantation seeing to the needs of the Langtry slaves. She alone was responsible for their food, clothing, shelter, and medical care. With growing respect, Brynna accompanied her, taking part where she could, standing aside to observe where she must, and ever learning the ways of Langtry as she had never done at Beaumont Hall.

Wes Stanton had ruled his home with single-minded stinginess. Brynna began to suspect her mother's lack of involvement in the running of Beaumont Hall had more to do with her father's jealous guarding of power. He had acquired Beaumont Hall upon his marriage to Hope. After that, it was never her home, but his.

Like most prosperous plantations of its time, Langtry was self-sufficient, growing all the food needed by slave and master alike. Coarse homespun cloth of cotton, linsey, and wool were produced on the plantation's spinning wheels and looms. Plantation seamstresses cut and sewed the cloth into sturdy trousers and shirts and simple gowns.

"By rights the overseerer's wife should see to the sewing and weaving," Jessica explained. "But Ruth Hewitt ran off years ago and her daughter, Betty, has taken over only those duties she took a fancy to and ignored the rest."

"Is she the girl I saw on the porch of the overseer's house?" Brynna asked. She'd noticed the blond girl who was about her age.

"I expect it was," Jessica answered, inspecting a seam.

"I waved, but she didn't wave back."

"Humpf! Sounds like Betty," said Jessica, nodding her approval to the large black seamstress known to one and all as Aunt Clemmie. The woman beamed with pride.

"If she'd had any manners she'd have presented herself up at the big house to meet you."

"That's all right. I'll meet her soon enough."

"She'd have been up there first thing if you'd been wearing pants. Insolent white trash!"

They moved on to another shed where an old man with white wooly hair hunched over a shoe bench, tapping his hammer against a heel. Bits of leather lay on the floor around him.

"Mahnin', Miz Jessica." The old man paused and grinned up at them with his toothless gums.

"Good morning, Zeph," Jessica greeted him. "This is my niece, Miss Brynna, who's come to live at Langtry."

"Mahnin', Miss Brynna," Zeph said.

And so it went all day long. Brynna marveled at the pride everyone seemed to take in their jobs.

A vast number of buildings made up the plantation. The slave quarters were a good quarter of a mile from the big house, and in between lay the blacksmith, wash house, carpentry, weaver's shed, smoke house, salt house, and church—which doubled as a hospital—and the stables and barns.

Behind the main house was a walled garden where vegetables, fruits, and herbs were grown for plantation use. Men, too old to do the punishing labor in the cane fields, were put to work in the walled acre, applying manure to the black raspberry vines, weeding the strawberries, or turning neat rows of the black loamy soil in preparation for planting. Young boys carried pails of water for the tender new shoots while women bent low, baskets at their sides as they harvested early fruits, vegetables, and herbs.

Everyone worked willingly in the garden, for although each slave grew fresh vegetables in his own patch in front of his cabin, he knew when supplies ran out it would be Miss Jessica who gave them extra food rations. Six women were kept busy preserving pickles, catsup, fruits, and vegetables in jars and crocks and barrels.

"In the fall, tasks will be even more demanding," Jessica explained. "Our hogs are killed then and we spend every minute rendering lard from the fat, chopping and seasoning meat for sausage, and curing bacon flanks in brine. Nothing gets wasted, not even the bristles. We make brushes from those. The slaves like the intestines. They call them chitlins."

"I'll help if I'm still here," Brynna said eagerly.

Jessica smiled. "I hope you are, Brynna. But child, you won't be so quick to offer your help when we get to salting the meat. It fair takes the skin right off your hands."

"I won't mind," Brynna insisted. It seemed to her that even the lowliest job on Langtry was a privilege to do.

"You can help when we kill the geese," Jessica went on. "That's not nearly as bad, although I hate the plucking of all that down. We need it for pillows and mattresses. Everyone helps with that, even Betty, although she makes such a fuss and dawdles so, it's almost better without her help."

"Must you labor so?" Brynna asked. "You're the mistress of Langtry."

"That only means I must work harder, *chérie*," Jessica answered. "Langtry has always been famous for its hospitality." Her busy hands fell idle, her eyes took on a faraway look. "My, you should have seen the parties and balls we had when Mr. Sinclair was alive. He loved entertaining, and people loved coming here. They traveled from miles away and sometimes they stayed for weeks."

Brynna remained silent, listening to Jessica's wistful reminiscing. She could never remember Wes Stanton being so generous with his guests. There had been few gatherings at Beaumont Hall.

"Temple's just like his father," Jessica went on. "He likes people and they just naturally turn to him for advice and friendship, but neither of us has felt like entertaining since Etienne died." She shook herself as if from a trance and smiled at Brynna. "Now that you're here, we'll have to plan a party, something small at first, until a suitable period of time for mourning has passed."

"You're too kind to me, Aunt Jessica," Brynna answered. After her father's stinginess, she could never get used to such generosity.

Jessica inspected everything daily, her quick eye assessing the product of her slave's labor, giving praise when it was due and reprimand if needed. Few were needed, for her people were eager to display their handiwork.

By day's end, Brynna was always tired, but Jessica was still going, settling at a table in the small parlor, a lighted lamp nearby while she worked on her plantation books.

"I never realized how much a woman is required to do," Brynna marveled.

Jessica laughed. "We hardly fit the northerner's notion of indolent southerners, do we?" she said, entering a figure in her books. "The shame is that we don't prepare our young women for their future roles." She raised her head and peered over her glasses at Brynna. "I expect you'll be getting married one day. Has any young planter's son been courting you?"

Brynna's golden eyes glowed with laughter and her chestnut curls danced as she shook her head. "There were some brothers of my school friends, but when I went back to Beaumont Hall, they never called more than once." Her laughter died. "I think they were afraid of Papa." She halted abruptly, her words hanging in the air between them. "Not that Papa did anything to scare them away," she amended, gripping her hands together tightly.

"Do you think Temple a handsome man?" Jessica asked, changing the subject, or so Brynna thought. Jessica was perfectly aware she had not.

"He's quite the most handsome man I've ever seen," Brynna said, then turned away abruptly, fearful she'd revealed too much. But Jessica had caught a glimpse of her flushed cheeks. *Ah,* she thought, *my task may be easier than I'd anticipated.*

"I expect he'll marry one day soon. He'll need a mistress for Langtry." She glanced around. "He'll need someone who'll love Langtry as much as he does, someone who'll take care of her and her people."

"Who wouldn't love it," Brynna said wistfully. "It's the most beautiful place I've ever seen. Mama used to read your letters to me and we'd try to imagine what Langtry was like." She paused. "I wish Mama could have seen it. She would have loved it here."

"Well . . ." Jessica said, dabbing at her eyes. "Langtry's a grave responsibility."

"A labor of love," Brynna murmured and, looking somewhat dejected, she settled before the fire and opened a book. Jessica turned back to her ledgers, an elated smile lighting her gentle features.

In the busy days that followed Brynna learned the names of the slaves.

She was awed by Roman, the gentle black giant who served as a blacksmith. Like the round-eyed boy who tended his bellows, she held her breath as, corded muscles flexing, broad back gleaming with sweat, he raised his hammer and brought it clanging down against the redhot iron that would soon shod a horse or plow the black soil. She often visited Caesar, the aging carpenter from whose

53

planing tool fell fragrant oak curls as he fashioned rough-hewn tables for the slave cabins and an occasional fine cabinet for the big house. She poked her nose into the wash house where the laundress, Gloriana, mindless of the hot steam rising from her washtubs and ironing tables, raised her rich voice in hymns of praise. Brynna tried talking in gombo, the singsong French patois, to the three giggling pregnant women who'd been assigned jobs at the spinning wheels during the last months of their confinement. She even walked down to the overseer's house to introduce herself to Betty Hewitt, who languished in a porch swing fanning herself, her bodice unfastened so low, ostensibly from the heat, that a generous portion of white breasts was revealed.

"So yore the cousin from up North," she said with indifference. "The only good Ah can think about the North is that it must be cooler up theah!"

"Yes, it is," Brynna said, and tried her best to carry on a conversation with the other girl. No invitation to sit or offer of a drink was made. Betty managed only an occasional monosyllabic answer now and then. Her foot never faltered in its pushing the swing back and forth. Finally Brynna turned and left, certain Betty would swing for a full five minutes before she realized Brynna was gone.

Her favorite of all the help at Langtry was Lala, who stirred the savory kettles and whacked her slow-stepping assistants with a wooden spoon. Without missing a beat she regaled all who would listen with the latest gossip from other plantations, though how she knew since she'd never once been off Langtry land was more than Brynna could understand. Lala always had something lively to say.

"If yore troubled wif ghosts, jus' burn sawdust and sprinkle the ashes in te corners of yore house," she advised

54

Brynna out of the blue one day. "Dat keep 'em away. Horseshoes work good, too."

"Is that why all the slaves have horseshoes above their doors?" Brynna asked. During a rare idle moment she'd perched on a stool to revel in the rich, savory smells of the kitchen and listen to Lala's folksy talk.

"Dat right," Lala said, brandishing her spoon in the air to emphasize her point. "An' Ah guarantee yo' it work." She turned toward the iron stove and whirled around as if she'd forgotten something. "Don' never walk near a cemetery lessen yo' holdin' the hand of a youngin', an' if'n yo' see a ghost, turn 'round three times real quick and spit on him." Lala sent a fat wad of spittle into the fire as demonstration. It sizzled on the hot bricks.

Brynna slid off the stool. "Thank you for telling me that, Lala," she said gravely. Lala had shared her knowledge out of a growing acceptance of the girl from the North. Not for anything would Brynna hurt Lala's feelings by laughing. Lala's lively conversations had made her feel less lonely since Cyra's withdrawal. "I'll remember what you say and use it should the occasions ever arise."

"Something else, young missy." Lala again shook her spoon. Droplets of rich gumbo flew out from it. "If yo' ever afraid of a dead person, put a bottle of white chicken feathers on his grave. If'n his gris-gris is not too strong, he won't haunt yo' no mo' ".

Brynna thought of her father lying in the family plot in Tennessee. "I'm not afraid of dead people," she said quietly. "They can't do me or anyone I love harm anymore." Lala was looking at her strangely, so Brynna smiled. "What is gris-gris, Lala? Is it part of the voodoo?"

Lala's face lost its shiny smile and her dark eyes dipped downward. "Ah don' know nothing' 'bout no voodoo," she mumbled, then seemed to pull herself together.

"Now, go on. Git out o' mah kitchen. Ah gots supper to make." She waved Brynna to the door and there was nothing to do but leave.

Puzzled, Brynna went in search of Jessica and found her down on her knees in the walled kitchen garden supervising the planting of cabbage plants and snap beans.

"You look troubled about something," Jessica said, seeing Brynna's crestfallen expression.

"I'm confused, Aunt Jessica. Just now Lala told me she knew nothing about voodoo and yet she talked about gris-gris."

"How do you know about gris-gris?" Jessica asked, getting to her feet and taking Brynna's arm to lead her out of earshot of the slaves.

"Cyra told me," Brynna replied. "She's been talking to someone about voodoo. I didn't take any of it very seriously until just now when I saw the expression on Lala's face."

"The slaves are frightened of voodoo," Jessica said. "They don't like to talk about it. Cyra should be very careful herself."

Brynna couldn't suppress a shiver of alarm. "Are you saying it's real?"

"I'm saying the slaves think it's real and that's the danger. Some people think it's harmless, but I've seen some evil things done in the name of voodoo. Keep Cyra away from it."

"I'll try," Brynna said, remembering Cyra's rapt expression as she talked of the power of another world.

Jessica studied her niece's face and took a deep breath. "I don't mean to pry, Brynna, but I've noticed the relationship between you and Cyra is especially close."

"We grew up together. She went away to school with

56

me. We've always been together. She's more like a sister than a slave."

"So I thought," Jessica said, her expression troubled. "For that reason, I've hesitated to say anything to you."

"Please, say whatever you want, Aunt Jessica," Brynna cried, taking her hand between her own. Her young face was filled with such eagerness to please that Jessica felt a wave of happiness. Once she and Hope had been inseparable. The pain of the years apart and Hope's death was eased by the presence of this beautiful, lively girl. She'd seen the kindness and fair-mindedness that was so much a part of Brynna's nature, as it had been Hope's. Yet she sensed the confusion in Brynna's normally sunny spirit. Cyra seemed to be a part of that confusion.

Jessica's lips thinned as she thought of the servant girl. Though she'd rather do anything than hurt Brynna, she was compelled to speak for the sake of her own slaves.

"You must take Cyra in hand, Brynna," she said gently. "She's insolent to my house servants, sullen and lazy. I've seen how she treats you and wonder that you tolerate it. It isn't good for the other servants to see such behavior go unpunished."

"I didn't realize there was a problem. I'll speak to Cyra immediately," Brynna said contritely.

Jessica studied the troubled young face and guessed it was a task her niece dreaded. Jessica wanted to say more about Cyra, but decided against it. Perhaps a reprimand from Brynna would be enough. If not, she'd wait for Temple to return before taking other steps.

Brynna's enjoyment of the day was gone. She had been here two weeks now, and in that time Cyra had grown more hostile and sullen. Aunt Jessica had a right to complain about her behavior and its effect on the other slaves. Outnumbered, often isolated with her slaves, a plantation mistress had to keep a firm hand. Brynna knew she'd let things go too far with Cyra, but she'd been riddled with guilt and Cyra had known that and used it. She must take a firmer hand with Cyra.

But when she approached Cyra that night, the girl quickly turned sullen and defiant. "Ah ain't doin' nothin' wrong," she said, her lower lip jutting mutinously.

"You don't do your share," Brynna said. "When there's work to be done you just disappear. Aunt Clemmie said her son saw you down by the stables this afternoon."

"Yo' got people spyin' on me?" Cyra demanded.

"No, but the other slaves see you come and go as you wish and they wonder why you're given such freedoms."

Cyra rounded on her. "Ah got da right t' freedom." Her dark eyes were wide and unblinking, her mouth pursed in self-righteous anger.

"Is that what's wrong with you lately, Cyra? Do you want your freedom? I'll give it to you and gladly."

"If ah'm free, Ah got no place to go," Cyra said, relenting a little. "Ah got t' stay here on dis plantation, but Ah ain't ever goin' t' let a white man touch me agin."

Brynna's eyes lowered as shame washed over her; then she pushed it away and looked at the slave girl who'd always been so much more than that in her life. "That won't happen to you here," she vowed softly. "Things are different at Langtry."

Cyra made a scoffing noise.

"They treat their slaves kindly here," Brynna insisted. "No one is beaten or starved or abused. You could be happy here, Cyra, if you'd just try."

"That fusty old white woman's got yo' eatin' out a' her hand, but Ah know what she's all about. She makes her slaves work for her, and her son takes his pleasure with the women."

"That's not true," Brynna flared.

Cyra stopped talking and looked at Brynna, a contemptuous smile playing around her lips. "Yo' done gone and fallen in love wif dat man," she accused, "and yo' don't even know him."

"I don't love him," Brynna denied. "We've spoken only a few times, but he appears kind and considerate of all who turn to him for help."

"People thought yo' papa was kind, but we both know he wasn't."

"Cyra, you have to stop remembering what happened in the past. You have to begin to believe in people again."

"Like yo' believe in Mr. Sinclair?" Cyra sneered. "Next time yo' in the slave quarters look at the light-skinned babies and ask yo'self how they got there."

"Get out," Brynna commanded.

Cyra looked at her, startled.

"Get out of my room. I want to rest."

Shrugging, Cyra sauntered toward the door, where she paused and looked back. "Yo' want me to draw yo' bath?"

"No," Brynna said in defeat.

Cyra's laughter was mocking as she closed the door behind her.

Brynna woke the next day with a headache and longed to lie abed, but Cyra's ugly accusations seemed to hang in the air over her head, so she rose and dressed quickly. Cyra's cot was empty, the smooth covers evidence she hadn't slept in her own bed last night. Obviously she'd found someone here at Langtry. Brynna was happy for Cyra. Maybe she'd learn to be content here after all.

Wearily, she made her way downstairs, eager to find something to take her mind off Cyra. She threw herself into her chores. Jessica looked at her dark-rimmed eyes and said nothing, but her dislike of Cyra grew.

By afternoon, Brynna's headache had receded somewhat. Working beside Aunt Jessica, seeing the satisfied faces and healthy bodies of the Langtry slaves, reassured her. Cyra's accusations were false. They had to be. Not all men were like her father. And if she had evidence of Jessica's kindness to those who toiled under her, she felt certain she'd seen evidence of the same from Temple.

She was in the garden picking strawberries with Aunt Jessica when they caught sight of a buggy driving up the oak-lined drive.

"Oh, fiddle, that looks like the de Jarreau carriage," Jessica said, shading her eyes for a better look. "Can't be Clay. He always rides his horse and jumps every fence in sight. Must be Alicia come to see why Temple hasn't been to call on her. I swear I've never seen a woman so set on winning a man as that one. She and Betty Hewitt are a pair." Jessica's nose wrinkled in distaste. "If she had her way, she'd be leading Temple down the aisle this very minute."

There was really no reason for such information to bother her, Brynna told herself, getting to her feet. Absently she brushed at her soiled skirts.

"I was hoping to hold off a few more weeks to give you some period of mourning. Then I planned on having a dinner party or a picnic to introduce you to folks. Do you think you're up to meeting anyone now?"

Brynna spread her dusty skirts. "I'm not very presentable," she said lightly.

"Go up the back stairs and freshen yourself up a bit. Alicia is closer to your age. You might enjoy talking to her."

"All right," Brynna agreed, trying to hide her reluctance. What was this Alicia de Jarreau like? she wondered as she made her way to the back of the house. A very determined woman from what Aunt Jessica said. Brynna wondered how Temple felt about her. She slipped into the back hall and hurried to the stairs. The sound of laughter made her pause. She turned to face a beautiful young woman with the dark eyes and creamy skin of a true Creole. Alicia de Jarreau was dressed in a pale silk gown, its low-cut bodice trimmed with dainty lace and ribbons. The full ruffled skirt was held wide by petticoats, so she seemed to float as she moved across the hall toward Brynna. The black eyes glittered mockingly as her gaze raked over Brynna's disheveled attire.

"You're dressed too poorly to be a Sinclair and you're too light-skinned to be a slave," she said, her tone deliberately condescending. "You must be Jessica's poor little niece from up North, *n'est-ce-pas?*"

"I am from Tennessee and I am Jessica's niece, but how did you know?" Brynna asked stiffly.

Alicia de Jarreau laughed gaily. "Everyone knows everything about everyone around here. What we don't learn for ourselves, our slaves find out for us." Alicia twirled the furled parasol in her slender white hand. "For instance, I know poor Jessica is desperately seeking a wife for Temple, a docile, dull girl who won't challenge her position as mistress of Langtry as she knows I would do."

"I don't think Jessica's like that," Brynna said mildly. "She's really quite nice."

"You needn't defend her. I know what she thinks about me, and the feelings are mutual. After Temple and I are married, and that will be soon now, I'll see that she's shipped off to some relative somewhere. She's lorded it here at Langtry long enough."

61

"Perhaps Temple will keep her here. He seems very affectionate toward her."

Alicia's dark eyes flashed. "Once Temple and I are married, he'll do what I want," she said confidently. "As for you, don't get too comfortable here." Her gaze swept over Brynna's smudged face and plain gown. A smug grin curved her red lips. "Surely Jessica doesn't think you'd be competition." Her laugh was shrill. It echoed in the narrow hall, long after she'd disappeared through the arch to the parlor.

Brynna continued up the stairs to her room, where she quickly washed her face and hands and tried to brush some order into her tangled curls. Suddenly, she threw down the brush and stared at herself in the mirror. Good manners dictated she change gowns and go down to tea with Jessica and her guest, but she was still seething with anger over the things Alicia had said. She wandered to the French doors that led to the wide upper gallery. The sun glinted on the river invitingly. With a last disparaging glance at her tumbling locks, she pushed away any twinge of guilt and hurried down the back stairs and out a side entrance. She lightly ran across the emerald lawn, skirted a white *pigeonnier* with its high ornate peak and copper weather vane and came at last to the river where she watched the brown water roll by sluggishly. A servant called from the stables, and in the distance a bell pealed. Brynna walked along the riverbank, leaving the rolling, tended lawn behind and wandering beneath tall oaks, their spreading branches trailing silver-green wisps of Spanish moss.

The air beneath the trees was cool and refreshing after the hot sun. Brynna walked farther than she'd intended, drawn along the path by patches of wildflowers, which she picked. When her arms were full of phlox, asters, wild peas, and stargrass, she sat on the riverbank and twined them into garlands the way she and Cyra had done when they were children. Smiling at this rare happy remembrance, she placed a crown of flowers on her head and spying an abandoned barque beneath the overhanging branches, placed the rest on the bottom of the boat and climbed in.

Taking up the oar, she pushed the moss-scaled boat away from shore and felt the sluggish stream carry it along. Sighing in pure contentment, she lay back against the bow and dipped one hand in the muddy water. A childhood song came to mind and she sang it in a clear, high-pitched voice. The boat rounded the bend and ran close to shore beneath a willow tree. Brynna stared at the leafy parasol. For this moment in time, all ugliness was left behind. She felt only the beauty of the river and was warmed by the sunlight sparkling on the water.

Temple Sinclair paused to let Chandra drink from the muddy river. He was nearly home. The big house lay just around the next bend, yet he'd paused, captured by the tranquility of the sun on the water. His business in Tennessee had taken far longer than he'd anticipated, but he'd made a good bargain for his little cousin. The effort had been worth the thought of her golden eyes lighting with pleasure when he told her.

He frowned remembering the whispered rumors that someone had set fire to Beaumont Hall, deliberately killing its owner. The answers to the mystery of Brynna Stanton hadn't been found. He'd returned more mystified than ever. He looked forward to seeing her again, to reaffirm her beauty and allure. He'd thought of little else but her soft mouth and those haunted green-gold eyes.

A sound bright his head up. He stood listening. A clear bell-like voice was singing a sad, romantic folk song. A

63

slave had no doubt slipped away from her job to do a little fishing. He could hardly blame the miscreant. The river was inviting today.

Temple waited, his brows drawn into a stern line, arms crossed over his chest, ready to reprimand. A boat rounded the bend, carried on the current, and at first he thought it empty till it floated closer. Then he saw the flower-bedecked girl inside.

She hadn't noticed him yet. She lay against the bow, one slender white arm trailing in the water, her skirts spread wide, wilting flowers caught in its folds, a garland of flowers around her unbound hair. Her eyes were closed, her chestnut curls twined around her shoulders. She looked like an enchanted heroine from a Walter Scott novel or, at the very least, a water sprite. The boat drifted past and struck a log.

"Oh," she cried, and sat up and looked around. When she caught a glimpse of Temple standing on shore, she snatched the garland from her hair.

"You're back," she cried.

"I've just returned," he answered, and waded into the shallow water to retrieve the boat and bring it to shore. She clung to the sides, trying not to stare. She'd forgotten how handsome he was, how tall, how broad his shoulders, how black his hair, how handsome!

His teeth flashed, the water flew from his churning legs in iridescent droplets and fell back to the placid brown river.

"I didn't realize you'd turned into a water sprite during my absence," he said, pulling the boat up onshore. He leaned over the bow and regarded her.

"Have you been to the house yet?" Brynna asked, not knowing how to answer his teasing. She heartily wished she'd been more patient while brushing her hair. It lay in a tangle on her shoulders. Her bare feet peeked from beneath her muddied hem. He thought he'd never seen anything so beautiful as this girl.

"Alicia de Jarreau has come to call," she stammered when he continued to stare.

"I'm afraid I don't know her," he teased, his black eyes staring into her eyes with a boldness that set her heart to pounding. He saw the blush on her cheeks. Her small pink tongue crept to nervously wet her full bottom lip. Nothing had ever looked more inviting. He bent his head closer, intent on claiming a kiss.

"Alicia de Jarreau, your betrothed," she said frantically. Her gaze was fixed on the firm mouth just inches from hers. Temple drew back.

"What?" he yelped, glaring at her.

"The woman you're . . . going to marry," Brynna stuttered, completely intimidated by his scowling brows and jutting jaw.

"Never mind," he snapped, taking hold of her hand and helping her out of the boat. He led her straight to Chandra. "Climb up," he ordered, cupping his hands for her to step into. He was touched by the daintiness of the bare foot she hesitantly presented him. Then, with one lithe movement, she was in the saddle, and his hand lingered on her slim ankle. Nervously, she moved her foot. Temple mounted behind her, his strong arms wrapping around her to take up the reins.

"Which way shall we go?" he asked playfully. "Back to Langtry or to yon enchanted land?"

"Back to Langtry," she answered. "It's enchanted land enough for me." In that moment he guessed how much she'd come to love his home and he felt an overbearing urge to gather her into his arms. But he remembered the Tennessee hills with the mist lying low on the blue-green grass and he wondered that she'd displayed no such passion for it. Was she mesmerized by the size and wealth of Langtry? Disappointment dampened his high spirits. Was his little cousin a mere opportunist like Alicia de Jarreau? Clicking his tongue at Chandra, he turned them toward the big house.

Brynna could feel his hard body at her back and tried to sit straighter. Chandra cantered down the canopied drive and arrived at the main entrance just as Alicia was about to climb into her carriage.

"Temple, you're back," Jessica called, waving gaily. Her mouth fell open when she caught sight of Brynna seated in front of him, then a wide smile spread over her face.

Brynna dared not look at Alicia, and when she finally did, she found the Creole's dark eyes filled with malice. Alicia forced a bright smile and stepped forward to greet Temple.

"What have you brought back, Temple darling?" she called sweetly. "Looks like you have a barefoot little pickaninny."

"Actually, it's a water sprite. I found her in the river. I understand they're very elusive." His voice was husky in Brynna's ears. She dared not turn her head to look at him, his mouth was that close. She kept her gaze straight ahead and was rewarded with a chuckle. Her cheeks flamed. "I understand they bring good luck to the one who captures them."

"Please," she said, pushing against his wrists. Immediately he released her and swung down, reaching up to catch her around the waist and pull her down beside him. In one hand she still gripped the garland of flowers, and now he took it and placed it on her head. "No one ever warned me how enchanting a water sprite can be," he said. His gaze held her captive as his arms had never done.

Alicia's laughter pealed, brittle and sharp. "You've turned poetic," she teased lightly, but her eyes were dark and flat with anger. "Don't tell me you've become enamored of this barefoot child? My dear, do run along and clean yourself up. You want to do your aunt credit after she's been kind enough to take you in."

Snatching the garland from her head, Brynna fled past Aunt Jessica, up the steps, and into the cool, dark interior of Langtry. As she mounted the stairs, she noted the peace and calm of the great house seemed to have vanished, and in the dark shadows dwelled the hint of excitement and danger. She knew what had caused the transformation. Temple Sinclair was home and she suspected that neither Langtry nor she would be at peace again.

Chapter Four

"Did your father have any enemies?" Temple asked at supper that night.

"I beg your pardon?" Brynna answered frantically. Everything about her had gone still—her slender hand holding the plate of Lala's piping-hot corn bread, the pink ruffle of lace across her bodice which normally rose and fell with each breath she took, the bright, newly washed chestnut curls nestled by each ear. Even her heart had stopped beating. She felt a choking need for breath, but was unable to draw it. She was painfully aware of Cyra at the sideboard standing stiff and still as if caught in one of the games they'd played as children.

"I wondered if your father had any enemies of whom you were aware," Temple repeated, his dark eyes focused on her across the wide mahogany table.

It's all right, Brynna tried to tell herself. She attempted to lower the plate of bread to the table, but his next words caught her in a web of terror.

"The local authorities think the fire might have been deliberate." The plate clattered from her nerveless fingers. Her terrified gaze flew to meet Cyra's. The black

68

girl's eyes rolled briefly with fear, then her brow pulled down in a scowl. Brynna forced her gaze back to the table and the broken plate. Lala's corn bread lay among the ruins, sending up inviting whiffs of steam. Brynna thought she would never be able to eat corn bread again without remembering this moment.

"I—I'm sorry," she stammered.

"Temple, you shouldn't have brought this up now," Jessica reprimanded him. "You should have prepared her first."

"I'm sorry, Jess," Temple said, his eyes dark and deep with unfathomable shadows. "My apologies to you as well, Brynna. I should have told you of this more tactfully, but there seems to be no proper way to tell someone of murder."

"Murder?" The blood drained from Brynna's face. Her fingers, icy and nerveless, fluttered across the pink ruffle and down to her lap where she clenched them tightly in an effort to gain control of herself. From the corner of her eye she saw the flutter of skirts as Cyra glided out of the dining room. Through the window Brynna could see her servant's bobbing head as she ran to the kitchen.

"Murder," Brynna repeated through dry lips.

"They think he was dead before the fire destroyed the house."

"No more, Temple," Jessica cried.

"Murder," Brynna whispered, and slid sideways in her chair. Only the curving polished wood arm kept her from the floor. She drooped like some wilted flower, then, by sheer will power, pushed herself upright. She'd had enough of swooning. But Temple was already at her side, his large brown hand settling on her slender arm.

"Are you all right?" he murmured anxiously. She

raised her golden eyes to his, and for one unbidden moment, he saw the terror there.

"Yes, I'm quite all right," she answered, turning away from him. "You've just caught me unawares. My—my father was beloved by all who knew him. No one would want to kill him." She was unaware of Jessica's gaping mouth. She strove only to gain control of her wobbly knees. A hand fluttered to her brow and down to her trembling bosom. "If you'll excuse me, I should like to retire," she said wanly.

"Of course, *chérie*," Jessica said, quickly recovering herself. "You've had one shock after another. Cyra!" Jessica looked around for the slave girl. "Now where can she be? She was just here."

"It's all right," Brynna said quickly. "I have no need of her. I'm quite well."

"But child, you look so peaked," Jessica insisted, catching hold of her hand, "and your hands are icy. Are you coming down with something? Perhaps I should bring you a toddy?"

"Please, don't worry about me," Brynna pleaded, breaking away from them. Her golden gaze flickered from Jessica's kind face to Temple's dark, thoughtful gaze. "I wet my feet at the river today and—and I've overtired myself. A good night's rest will set me right. Good night."

"If you say so, chérie," Jessica answered reluctantly.

Silently they watched her leave, the wide silken skirts of her gown making a whispery sound on the marble floors and trailing behind as she mounted the stairs like clusters of gay pink party ribbons. But her shoulders beneath the soft fabric slumped with despair. They watched her go and looked at each other in consternation. Silently, they regained their seats. The essence of the girl remained in the room, flowerlike and fragile.

"How extraordinary," Jessica exclaimed.

"Was she telling the truth about her father?" Temple asked.

Thoughtfully, Jessica shook her head. "No. Wes Stanton may have been many things, but he was never 'beloved by all who knew him.' "

"You don't suppose that she murdered her own father?" Temple asked the question that plagued him the most.

"No!" Jessica said quickly, loudly, then softer. "No."

Temple sat thinking of all that had transpired. He'd barely spoken of her father and the suspicions surrounding his death. Was that enough to upset a lady of even the frailest sensibilities? He remembered the laughing girl in the boat. For a time she'd forgotten whatever it was that haunted her. For a time she'd been happy.

"Tell me about Wes Stanton," he said finally to his stepmother. "Everything you know."

"It isn't so much what I know for certain," Jessica said hesitantly. "Hope never wrote of anything wrong. Rather it was a question of what she didn't say. All I know are mainly half guesses and suppositions and none of them confirmed."

Temple reached across and took Jessica's hand. A tiny smile curved the corners of his mouth. He would have expected such a statement from Jessica. Her sense of fairness colored every thought, every utterance. "I'd trust your frailest suspicion over a proven fact any day," he said. Quietly, he listened while Jessica told him of all the fears and concerns she'd carried through the years, fears that had grown from each painful, stilted letter Hope had sent. And when she was done, she sighed and leaned back in her chair.

"Can you blame her for looking so scared sometimes?

71

I just want to throw my arms around her and hold her and tell her to cry, but she wouldn't want that. Despite her vapors, she is a strong young woman."

"I'm beginning to suspect that," he replied, and got to his feet. "Perhaps it is time we retire as well."

"Of course, you must be tired from your journey," Jessica replied. But later, after she'd seen to the snuffing of lamps and to the locking of the larder and sheds and made her way toward the stairs, she was startled to see Temple moving along the lower gallery, absently smoking a cheroot. He'd thrown aside his jacket and wore only a loose shirt of white cotton. It contrasted well with his dark hair, and Jessica was reminded again of how handsome her stepson was. As she stood regarding him, he whirled abruptly as if beside himself with anger. One large brown hand raked back his dark locks impatiently. He was truly disturbed about something, Jessica thought, and wondered what slave had misbehaved to such a degree as to bring Temple to this unrest. But he'd had no time to discuss plantation business with Kyle Hewitt and she had mentioned no problems. What then? Jessica drew in her breath in sudden understanding. This anguish was over Brynna. She was certain of it. She'd seen things between them, a glance, a shy smile, and this afternoon when they'd returned from the river, there had been a tension between them. Alicia had sensed it, too. Jessica smiled and turned to the stairs, congratulating herself on the fact that her plan would take less effort than she'd thought.

Brynna was reluctant to go downstairs the next morning, but knew that as certain as the sun had risen and spilled its yellow light through her windows, Jessica would be up the stairs to check on her and fuss over her if she thought something was wrong. Donning a simple day gown of sprigged cotton dimity, Brynna dressed her hair high off her neck against the heat and, with resolve firmly in hand to avoid Temple Sinclair and his probing questions and unsettling dark gaze at all costs, she went downstairs. Her resolve lasted only until the bottom of the great curving staircase, for as her foot touched the bottom step, the door of the large, paneled study opened and Temple stepped out. He looked startled when he first saw her, then he smiled, his white teeth flashing against his tanned skin, his dark eyes brightening, his gaze sweeping over her with such obvious pleasure that color rose to her smooth pale cheeks and her breath caught in her throat.

"Good morning, Cousin Brynna," he said. "I trust you're feeling better."

"Much better, thank you," she replied, trying her best to affect an air of poise and serenity, no mean task as he continued to study her. He was dressed in dark trousers shoved into the tops of soft leather boots and a loose shirt of white cotton, not unlike that worn by the field hands. Obviously he'd planned a day of riding over his fields. She remembered the morning he'd taken her on a tour of the plantation and the way he'd spoken so proudly of it. She wished now she could ride with him and listen to him tell of Langtry's history and the future plans he'd made for her. But that was not to be. She'd come down expecting to help Jessica and remain as inconspicuous to Temple as she could.

"If you'll excuse me," she said demurely, her eyes sedately cast down. "Jessica's expecting me."

"If you could spare a moment, Cousin Brynna," he said, holding his study door ajar. "I'm sure Aunt Jessica won't mind the delay. I need to speak to you about Beaumont Hall."

"Not now. I . . ." Brynna paused, realizing how strange her denial must seem to him. "Perhaps later. I don't want to keep Jessica wa— Yes, all right, for just a minute." She was imminently aware of the heat of his body as she brushed past him into the study. She'd already discovered the book-lined room and decided it was her favorite place in the whole house, but now it carried the indelible stamp of its returned master. A bottle and glass sat out on a sideboard and an ashtray bore evidence of several cheroots smoked since his return. His travel boots lay in one corner and a dark cloth jacket lay at the ready across a chair back.

Temple crossed to a huge mahogany desk, near the French doors. Sunlight spilled across its cluttered top. "Sit down," he invited, picking up a sheaf of papers.

"I'd rather not take that much time," Brynna said stiffly. Temple glanced at her quickly, then handed over the papers.

"This is the offer made for Beaumont Hall and all its surrounding acres. If you agree to it, and I think you should, then I'll need your signature."

"So much money!" Brynna gasped, reading over the papers. "I never realized—"

"I could have negotiated more if there hadn't been extensive damage to the main house, but I believe I've gotten the best possible price for it. You'll be quite a wealthy young lady," Temple said, frowning slightly. She'd uttered no word of remorse that her home was about to be sold. Was money so important to her then? "Are you sure you want to sell?"

She cast him only a slight glance, seized the pen he proffered, and with a steady head, signed away Beaumont Hall. Only when her signature lay in rounded schoolgirl curlicues upon the document did she show any emotion.

Her chest rose and fell with quick breathing and she stood staring at the paper as if transfixed.

"It's not too late to tear up the deed if you wish to keep your home," he said, misreading her agitation.

"Beaumont Hall is not my home," she said distractedly, then raised her chin and clenched her fists. "The devil take it!" Before he could respond, she'd whirled and rushed from the room. He could hear her running footsteps in the marble hall and a distant door swing shut. Temple stood in the silence, remembering the pain in the golden eyes before she'd uttered those final words. Troubled, he folded the papers and placed them in a mail pouch. He'd see they went off immediately. He had a sudden longing to be done with all this business so he need never mention it to his little cousin again.

"Why, child, are you still ailing?" Jessica asked when Brynna came upon her in the storeroom. The servants turned from the filling of their baskets to stare at her with dark, liquid eyes. Brynna was aware her cheeks were flushed and tears filled her eyes.

"I— No, I'm fine, Aunt Jessica," she said, forcing a smile. "I'm looking for Cyra. Has anyone seen her?"

Several of the smiling faces turned away from her and Brynna was all too aware of the dislike some of servants felt toward the slave girl from Tennessee.

"Lala? Have any of you seen Cyra?" Jessica asked.

"No'm, Ah ain't," Lala said. "Thet girl slip around here something awful, especially when they's work to be done."

"That's enough, Lala," Jessica said.

"Thet's the truth, Miz Jessie," Lala continued, and Brynna sensed the sassy old cook spoke the thoughts the others were afraid to express. But why should the others be afraid of Cyra?

75

"I'm sorry Cyra doesn't do her share," Brynna said. "I'll speak to her today." She glanced at Jessica. "Thank you for your patience with us both."

"Huh, ain't nobody kin fault yo', Miz Brynna," Lala went on. "Next to Miz Jessie, yo' 'bout the smartest, hard-workin'est lady in Lou's'annie." The other servants nodded, their bright smiles turned to her once more. Brynna flushed with pleasure that they held her in almost as high a regard as they did their beloved Miz Jessie.

Jessica smiled and continued with her task of doling out flour and salt. "Let's get back to work," she admonished gently. "The sun will be high before we get half finished. Brynna, I wonder if you would gather up some candles for Lala for the kitchen and get some of that calico out of the shed for Clemmie."

Brynna hurried to do her aunt's bidding and fell naturally into the routine they'd established over the past weeks. There was a rhythm to the plantation that soothed her soul and gave her a sense of involvement she'd never had at Beaumont Hall. It had been easy to sign the papers for its sale. Beaumont Hall hadn't felt like home, ever. Only Mama, with her loving smiles and gentle touches, had made it bearable. Brynna had never known things could be different elsewhere. She'd never felt she belonged to the earth and buildings and people, the way she felt here at Langtry.

And yet, Langtry wasn't her home! She was only a guest here. Startled she paused at her task and stood staring at the neat whitewashed buildings and the green blur of new cane in the fields beyond. The thought of one day having to leave burned like an ache in her heart.

"Is something wrong, *chérie?*" asked Jessica, seeing her stricken expression.

"I was just thinking that I should make some plans for

76

my future . . ." Brynna began hesitantly. "I can't impose upon your hospitality much longer."

"Brynna!" Jessica cried with such despair that Brynna glanced up at her. "Are you unhappy here? Have we done anything to hurt you? Was it Temple last night with all the questions of your father? *Chérie*, you aren't thinking of leaving."

"I don't want to . . ." Brynna began, and found herself enfolded in lavender-scented hugs.

"Then you shan't," Jessica said, pressing a kiss upon her brow. "You will stay here as long as you want. Promise there'll be no more talk of leaving."

"I promise," Brynna said, returning her kinswoman's hug.

But later, when she was alone, she thought about Alicia de Jaurreau and the threat she'd made. Once she'd married Temple, she'd see to it that not only Brynna but Jessica as well were sent away. Would Temple allow that to happen? Brynna wondered briefly. She'd heard Hope say once that men did strange things for women they loved.

Brynna had no chance to talk to Cyra that day, for the slave girl stayed out of sight. Nor did she return that night, so with morning Brynna took matters into her own hands and walked down to the slave cabins. May had reported Cyra was staying at Aunt Clemmie's cabin, which was next to the unmarried men's house where the new field hand, Thomas, was staying. Some of the other slaves had seen the two of them slipping off together through the bushes. Brynna had no objection to Cyra's attraction for the black man, but she must attend to her chores and follow some of the rules.

Most of the slave cabins were empty, their occupants working out in the fields and sheds of Langtry. An occasional chicken pecked in the dust along the path, setting up a plaintive squawk as Brynna passed. As she approached Aunt Clemmie's cabin, Brynna heard a scurry of sound within and the plop of a body falling to the ground. Quickly, she hurried to the side of the cabin in time to see Cyra hurrying toward a line of bushes.

"Cyra! If you run away from me, I swear I'll have you whipped." Brynna spoke more sharply than she'd intended, but she was too angry to allow the slave girl to continue her games. Her threat had some effect on Cyra, for she halted as if frozen in midflight. Slowly she turned to face Brynna, her eyes so wide, the whites showed all around the dark pupils.

"W'at you' wan', Miz Brynna?" she asked with exaggerated humbleness.

"Oh, Cyra," Brynna cried with some exasperation. "Stop this act and come here."

"I'z comin', Miz Brynna," Cyra cried, rolling her eyes and bobbing her head to Brynna, but her expression was impudent and mischievous as it used to be when she was pulling a prank on someone. Brynna didn't know whether to scold her or laugh at her antics. It had always been thus between them. And that was the problem. No matter what Cyra did, Brynna had always forgiven her. But Cyra's behavior had become more outrageous with each year, and since they'd come to Louisiana, it had grown intolerable.

"Why haven't you been up to the big house?" Brynna demanded, drawing her eyebrows down to signify her earnestness.

"I heard Master Temple asking you about your father's enemies," Cyra answered without the slave patois she'd affected. "I thought sure you'd tell him about me."

"I never would," Brynna cried in hot denial. "Why would I?"

Cyra sauntered closer, thrusting her face forward, her eyes nearly black with anger. " 'Cause I hated him the most of anybody," she spat out.

Brynna backed up a step. "I know, Cyra," she said softly. "But I wouldn't tell anyone."

Cyra skipped away and stood pleating her skirt between her fingers. Her face took on a sly expression as she regarded Brynna from beneath lowered lashes. "Why do they think someone murdered your daddy?"

"I—I'm not sure. I didn't ask," Brynna said, and suddenly she couldn't look at Cyra anymore. "May said you and Thomas have been together."

The mutinous expression left Cyra's face and she smiled softly, looking more like the old Cyra. "I'm his woman now," she said almost defiantly.

"Oh, Cyra. Don't you know I'm happy for you?" Brynna said quickly.

Cyra looked disbelieving. "Why'd you come down here then?" she sneered.

"Not to take you away from Thomas," Brynna exclaimed. She stepped forward and touched Cyra's arm. "We're family, Cyra. I want only the best for you."

"What you consider the best," Cyra answered sullenly.

"Maybe I know better what's good for you," Brynna snapped, growing exasperated once more. "You can't just stay down here in the slave cabins, doing nothing all day and meeting Thomas at night. Everyone has to earn his keep. That means you as well."

"Everyone has to work to make Master Temple Sinclair a rich man," Cyra sneered.

"Oh, Cyra, we've had this conversation before," Brynna sighed. "He's a fair man. He treats his people well, better than Papa did. Can't you try to cooperate a little bit? Everyone's complaining about you."

"That don't make me no never mind," Cyra snapped. "I'll do what I please and they can just talk. That May is just jealous anyway, 'cause she was making cow eyes at Thomas and he paid her no attention."

"That's not the problem," Brynna answered. "You aren't doing your share. From now on you'll come up to the big house every night after dark. You'll rise early with the rest of us and keep our rooms clean. You'll empty the slops and dust and scrub and help Lala in the kitchen and weed the garden. In short, you'll do whatever May and the other girls are doing. And if you don't do as you're told, I—I'll send you to the fields to be a field hand."

Cyra stood with her mouth gaping open. Brynna had never spoken to her thusly before, nor had she ever given her specific chores. For a long moment the two girls stared at each other, knowing a time had passed between them, a time of friendship, and a new time had come, one of mistress and slave. Brynna's heart pumped heavily with regret, Cyra's nostrils flared with pride and denial.

"Yas, ma'am," she said finally and stalked down the path toward the big house. Brynna stood where she was on the dirt path, in the middle of the slave quarters with the hot sun beating on her back, and shivered. Heartsick, she followed Cyra. Even Langtry in all its beauty and prosperity couldn't soothe her pain of loss.

When she crossed the backyard she saw Cyra seated on a stool outside the dairy, her calico skirts pulled high, a churn between her bare knees, her brown arms pumping rhythmically to bring the butter up. Perhaps it would be all right, Brynna thought. Perhaps when Cyra got over being angry and got to know the people of Langtry, maybe she'd feel happier. Brynna crossed to the larder where Jessie was seeing to the storage of early peas. As she bent to help, Jessica caught a glimpse of her pain-filled expression and knew Cyra was behind it.

In the days that followed, Cyra seemed a model servant, doing her chores without sassing back. But at night she stayed with Thomas until the moon was riding high, creeping in only after Brynna had retired for the night.

Temple never again brought up her father or the suspicions surrounding his death, so Brynna began to relax her guard. With some satisfaction Temple noted the changes in her. The haunted look was disappearing from those great eyes and she no longer avoided him, even managing to scrape up a smile when she passed him in the halls. Their evening meals grew more interesting as she offered her opinions more freely. As always he was struck by her quick intelligence.

The nervous, frightened girl who had first come to them was replaced by a happier one whose laughter pealed on the hot afternoon air as sparkling and heady as the finest wines stored in Langtry's cellars. Temple found his workday disturbed by her presence, the sound of her soft voice directing a slave, the rustle of skirts outside his study, the glimpse of her blue riding habit in the distance. He'd never thought overly much about women. Having been taught by Jessica at an early age about thoughtfulness toward the fairer gender, he'd simply applied the same principle to all women with ravishing results. He'd enjoyed the favors pressed upon him by virtuous ladies and those not so virtuous and given little thought to them once they were out of his bed.

Now a mere slip of a girl from Tennessee with chestnut curls and golden eyes haunted his waking hours. He began returning to the plantation for lunch, instead of carrying a packet into the fields as he'd been wont to do

81

before, and he never missed supper to ride into New Orleans as he'd used to. Jessica Sinclair saw the interest in her stepson's eyes and was pleased.

Someone else watched Temple's growing interest in his little cousin and pouted while considering how such knowledge could be used to best advantage. Betty Hewitt noted Temple's coming and going at noontime and put herself in his path one day. She'd donned her best cotton calico and deliberately left the top buttons undone so the curve of her full breasts was revealed. Her blond hair had been brushed high on her head, accenting her slender throat. The last time Cort de Jarreau had been to visit the Sinclairs, he'd crept up on her porch where she'd been shelling peas and planted a kiss on her bare neck. When she'd coyly protested, he'd proceeded to make up an ode to the beauty of her nape. The peas had sat forgotten all afternoon while Betty had taken him inside and shown him her other delights. He'd been properly appreciative, as would Temple, Betty felt sure, if she were to be bold and make the first move.

So she waited on her porch, and when she saw Temple riding in from the fields, she sauntered out to meet him, a parasol unfurled as if she walked the boardwalks of New Orleans itself.

"Hello, Betty," Temple called when they came abreast on the path. "Are you off to call on someone?" He'd pulled the black Arabian off the path so she might pass.

Betty sauntered by, then paused, blocking his return to the path, while she gazed up at him from beneath her eyelashes.

"Good afternoon, Mister Temple," she called languidly. "Ah'm on my way back. Ah've been down to the slave cabins to direct Aunt Clemmie in her sewing. You have to keep an eye on these niggahs ever' moment or

82

they just get lazy." She twirled her parasol coquettishly and missed the tightening of Temple's lips at her assessment of Aunt Clemmie and her workers.

"Mah, mah. It's a hot day. Ah'm fair on to faintin' from this heat." She fluffed her skirts around her as if seeking relief from their stifling folds. In truth, she'd left off several petticoats, so the thin skirts fell limply around her hips, hugging her curves as she'd wished. A circle of sweat had formed between her breasts, and she reached inside her bodice to sluice it away, all the while her hungry gaze took in Temple's muscular form and the way his cotton shirt clung to his sweat-dampened skin. A wide-brimmed hat shadowed his face and made his dark gaze more mysterious and compelling. Betty shivered delicately.

"Ah swear, Ah don't know how ya'll big men can take stayin' out in this sun for hours on end. You must be thirsty, Temple. If you come up on my porch and set a spell, I'll bring you a glass of lemonade. I've had a pitcher settin' in the creekbed all mornin', so it must be good and cold."

"Thank you, Miss Betty," Temple said, touching his hat brim. "I'm afraid Miz Jessie and Miss Brynna are waiting dinner for me."

Betty pouted prettily. "Ah was so hopin' you could take some time with me, Temple," she said, deliberately dropping the more formal title of address. "Ah have to talk to someone about a terrible decision Ah need to make."

"Shouldn't you discuss whatever it is with your father?" Temple asked, darting a glance toward the big house. How had he gotten himself into this predicament? he wondered mildly.

"Ah'm afraid Ah cain't an' Ah don't have anyone else."

"Perhaps Miz Jessica would be of greater help than I," Temple hedged.

83

"Ah don't think so," Betty answered. "Miz Jessica being such a lady an' all. This is of a nature that might shock her, if you understand mah meanin'. Oh, Ah don't know what Ah'm goin' t' do." Betty wailed and wiped at her tearless eyes with a lacy handkerchief. The parasol dipped low over her face as if to shield her during her embarrassing show of emotion.

Temple glanced at the big house again and nodded. "All right," he sighed, alighting from his horse. "I have a few minutes."

"Oh, thank you, Temple," Betty cried triumphantly. The parasol twirled gaily. She fell into step beside him, chattering brightly. Every now and then she feigned an uneven step on the path and brushed against Temple's bare arm. Her body beneath the thin cotton was lush and warm. Temple felt a stab of desire. He'd spent so much time the past few weeks thinking of Brynna, he'd had no desire to go to town and visit any one of the pleasure palaces at which he was well known and always welcomed. Now his celibacy made him susceptible to Betty's full-blown charms.

They reached the overseer's house and mounted the steps. Betty contrived to trip and fell heavily against Temple, her full unbound breasts pressed tightly to his chest. His arms went out to steady her and automatically slid about her waist. She was uncorseted and he could feel silken flesh beneath the cotton. Her face was close to his and she gazed into his eyes, fluttering her lashes over calculating blue eyes. Her mouth was only inches from his, her lips full and inviting. He caught the whiff of yeasty perspiration and musky female.

"Temple, darlin,' " she murmured, and moved her head so their lips were touching now. Her small tongue darted greedily over his bottom lip and delved inside.

Temple felt his own heat rising, as was the bulge in his loins. His grip on the girl tightened and he hauled her close, his large hands kneading her back and sides and finally working their way around to the full, heavy breasts.

"Let's go inside, darlin', so no one can see us," Betty whispered and, taking his hand, led him inside the overseer's house.

Standing in the shade of one of the live oaks, Brynna watched for Temple. She'd grown used to his arrival for dinner, had even begun to anticipate it so that she came here to this cool spot near the springhouse, where the creek bubbled over stones and the deep shade created a cool oasis in the midday heat. She glimpsed his horse as he came into view far down the path and watched as he drew near. She saw Betty Hewitt saunter out to meet him and wondered what the two of them talked about. Temple dismounted and strolled along with the girl, and Brynna felt some emotion lick at her. She didn't recognize it as jealousy. When Temple turned toward the overseer's house, Brynna felt her chest tighten, and when the two of them stood on the steps in a torrid embrace, she fled her lookout and made her way to the summer dining room where Lala had laid out thick wedges of homemade bread and ham slices, wedges of chilled melon, and buttermilk still cold from the springhouse.

"Temple's a little late today," Jessica said, bustling into the room. Like Brynna, she'd taken the time to smooth back her hair and rinse her face and hands in tepid, scented water.

"I'm afraid he may not join us today," Brynna answered, fanning her skirts to seat herself at the table.

"Why do you say that, *chérie*. Did he send a message?"

"No, I—just thought he must be preoccupied with something important." Her words sounded hollow to her own ears. Jessica studied her averted face and wondered what had happened. Brynna said nothing. She was bitterly disappointed at what she'd seen. Jessica had warned her once about Betty Hewitt. But Temple . . . She'd hoped for something better from him. Now it appeared men were men no matter what. Temple was not unlike her father after all.

"Shall we begin without him?" she asked, passing the plate of melon slices. Little was said as they filled their plates. Though ravenous an hour before, Brynna could eat nothing, so she sat balling bits of bread with her fingers. Her eyebrows were drawn together in a scowl as if she were fighting off tears.

Why, she's hurt about something and trying not to show it, thought Jessica.

"Hello. Am I late?" Temple called from the gallery. Brynna whirled as he stepped through the door. "Sorry. I got tied up with some plantation business," he continued as he seated himself at the table.

"That's all right, dear, you've made it now," Jessica said brightly, and glanced at Brynna expecting to see the scowl replaced by a smile. But Brynna's expression had grown even more stormy and she glared at her plate as if the very flower pattern offended her.

Temple glanced at her, anticipating her bright smile. He saw the gleaming, trembling curls, the porcelainlike skin with its smattering of freckles across her small nose, the soft, pouty mouth, the ivory column of her throat. Even from here he caught the clean flower fragrance of her and he thought of Betty Hewitt, sullen and angry at his hasty retreat. Once he'd entered the darkened, cluttered house, his desire had died and he thought only of Brynna with her laughing eyes and ready smile and quick wit. There was no guile with her. He'd been woman hungry, but not for the charms of Betty Hewitt. Standing in the doorway of the overseer's house, he had known with startling clarity that the woman he desired most in all the world was the one waiting for him at Langtry. At least he'd allowed himself to think she waited. Now he wasn't so certain. Did she feel the same about him?

"Brynna?" he said softly. She raised her head and glared at him with disdain.

"If you'll excuse me, Aunt Jessica. I've wasted enough time. I must return to my chores."

"But, Brynna, you've scarcely eaten," Jessica called. Brynna had already left the room, her head held high, her lips pressed together in prim disapproval.

Puzzled, Temple watched her go. Obviously he had his answer. She did not return his desire. Young ladies of breeding didn't indulge themselves in lustful daydreams as he had done. Sighing, he rose and returned to the mill.

Chapter Five

"Let's give a ball!" Jessica said one evening. Her gray eyes sparkled with girlish excitement. Brynna and Temple looked at her across the dinner table and neither could repress a smile at her exuberance.

"Brynna, *chérie*, I know it's still early after the loss of your parents, but some time has passed and I don't think it would appear too unseemly of us. You need to meet some young people." She turned her expectant gaze to Temple. "What do you think, dear? This house hasn't seen gaiety and dancing for a long while. Don't you think it's time?"

Temple covered her small, wrinkled hand with his own. "If you think it's time, Jessie, then it's time," he answered. "What do you think, Brynna?"

She wanted to resist his smile, his expansive good humor. She wanted to maintain the quiet aloofness between them, but her heart beat fast at the thought of a ball and her cheeks were tinged with color. "A ball!" she half breathed, half questioned. Temple laughed and ruffled a curl on her cheek. His touch was warm and strong against her skin. Brynna drew away, but she couldn't help smiling into his eyes.

"When shall we have it?" she asked.

"When, Jessica?" Temple asked.

"A fortnight from now," she answered without hesitation, then paused. "Oh, Lord! Will that be enough time?"

"It will be. I'll help prepare for it," Brynna said eagerly.

"We'd best get out the invitations. Will you help me write them after supper?"

"Yes, of course I will," Brynna answered. Temple was caught by the change in her. She'd come alive again, the way she could when she forgot some problem that bedeviled her. Her golden eyes sparkled, her curls danced around her head saucy and lively, even her slender body seemed to tremble with excitement.

"I'll check the wine cellar and order champagne from New Orleans," Temple offered. They all paused for breath, then laughed at their giddiness.

"I think," Temple said when their laughter had died away, "a ball is long overdue."

Brynna exchanged a quick glance with Jessica, then her gaze collided with Temple's. Pinpoints of light twinkled in his brown eyes, then his smile faded and he grew almost somber as he stared at her. Brynna felt as if she were being whirled about the room by the force of his gaze.

"You must save the first dance for me, Brynna," he said, and she grew breathless.

"If you wish," she half whispered. Jessica seemed to have faded away. Only Temple and Brynna existed. Then the spell was broken by Temple himself. He pushed back the heavy chair and strode out of the room. Brynna blinked and gazed at his departing stiff back.

"Did I offend him?" she asked aloud.

Jessica's chuckle brought her back to the reality of the room. "Bless me, child. I think you've scared him."

"Scared him?" Brynna repeated in puzzlement.

"Never you mind," Jessie said. "Come help me with those invitations and then we have lists to make, menus to decide, oh, any number of things." She bustled toward her morning room then whirled to face Brynna. "Tell me, *chérie,* do you need a new ball gown?"

"I—why I don't know. I've never been to a ball," Brynna laughed.

Jessica nodded. "Then you need a new gown and so do I. Tomorrow morning we'll go into New Orleans to the couturiere."

True to her word, the next morning Jessica had the carriage brought round. Brynna hurried to don her best dress and bonnet. In her reticule, Jessica bore the hand-written invitations that would be delivered post haste to every neighboring plantation along the river.

"Temple has offered to ride with us into New Orleans," Jessica said, pulling on a pair of gray cotton gloves. Brynna followed her down the wide portico to the waiting carriage. Ben, their driver, was there to pull down the step and help them in.

Temple was already waiting on a mounted horse. He looked splendid in a silk vest and dark-blue cloth tailcoat. His stock was dazzling white as was his smile. Like Brynna and Jessica, he appeared to be in excellent spirits over their plans. "Good morning, ladies," he said, doffing his hat. He settled it back on his gleaming dark head and sat back to study Brynna. Her gown was beige, as were the ribbons and silk flowers pinned to her bodice. A wide-brimmed hat cast her delicate face in shadows and deepened the color of her eyes. Brynna colored under his gaze and lowered her lashes against cheeks gone hot with rushing blood.

"None of that Creole charm this morning, Temple," Jessica decreed, settling on one of the cushions and spreading her skirts so they wouldn't wrinkle. "We've much to do, so we must have our wits about us."

Temple's laughter rang out on the morning air and they started out amid the cheerful call of marsh birds, the horses pulling the handsome carriage at a brisk pace through dappled patches of sunlight. Brynna's hands were clammy with excitement.

"We should have made this trip much sooner," Jessica said, seeing the high color in her niece's cheeks. "I didn't think how boring we country folks must seem to a young woman."

Brynna tore her gaze from the countryside. "I was never bored, Jessica," she said earnestly. "I love Langtry. I would be happy never to leave it."

Temple laughed. "Wait until you've seen New Orleans. She's *magnifique!*"

"I think you'll find it a fascinating city," Jessica echoed.

They were right! New Orleans was like no other city, with her cobblestone streets, colorful shops, and the apartments above with their lacy wrought-iron balconies. The narrow streets were filled with people coming and going, some on foot and some in carriages as elegant as their own. Ladies in ruffled gowns and bonnets walked from shop to shop with a retinue of slaves trailing behind to carry their packages.

Gentlemen in tall hats, carrying gold-tipped canes and smoking cheroots gathered in groups to discuss their investments, crops, and the price of sugar. Fancy octoroon women with gay parasols sauntered down the street followed close behind by small black boys in satin livery.

Negresses hurried along the street, baskets of their mistresses laundry balanced on their heads. On the street corners, freed black men played instruments, while small black boys with pieces of tin embedded in the soles of their shoes tapdanced for the coins the amused planters threw them. The streets were all movement and sound, color and excitement. Brynna could have stayed all afternoon watching and listening.

But Jessica directed Ben to a sedate shop on Royal Street. The words "Madame René, Couturiere" were printed in gold letters across the glass window. "Come, Brynna," Jessica ordered, alighting from the carriage with Ben's help.

"Brynna!" Temple called as she prepared to follow. He leaned from his saddle so their eyes were level. His assessing gaze swept over her. One lean brown hand gripped her chin, turning her head gently from side to side while he studied her. "No insipid pastels for you, little cousin," he said lightly. "You should choose white. It will accent your golden color as nothing else will."

Brynna drew back sharply, nettled at his presumption that she would choose a color to please him. "I abhor white," she snapped. "Nothing would induce me to wear it."

"Nothing?" he teased.

"Nothing!" she retorted, and, turning her back on him, she snapped her dainty little parasol in dismissal and grandly stepped from the carriage. Temple's good-natured guffaw followed her into the little shop.

"Madame, mademoiselle," the shop owner, Madame René, exclaimed. *"Bienvenue!* Welcome to my shop."

The little French woman with the tight pompadour ushered them to seats and clapped her hands. Immediately, a servant girl brought a silver tray with a silver pot of tea and delicate china cups. A plate of small ornate cakes were passed to them. Solicitously Madame René hovered nearby until they were finished, then clapped her hands for the tray to be cleared.

"Ah, you have come to order a beautiful dress, *oui?*"

"Oui, madame," Jessica said, rising to walk about the tiny reception room. "We each desire a beautiful gown, the best you can make. We are giving a ball."

"A ball? *C'est magnifique!*" The little couturiere clapped her hands. "Come to my workroom. We will decide what it is to be." She led them through a door and into a room quite different from the elegantly appointed reception room. Here long tables ran the length of the shop and a bevy of mulatto girls bent over the tables, scissors flashing in their hands as they cut into long, shimmery lengths of cloth, while others sat stitching. Creole women stood in various stages of dishabille while Madame René's assistants measured them.

"Madeleine, do not cut so near the edge, *si'l vous plaît.* Leave room for a good seam or it will ravel, *n'est-ce pas.*" Madame René called instructions to her girls and turned a kindly smile to her customers.

"Careful, you clumsy fool," a voice cried, followed by a stinging slap against a brown cheek. "You've poked me with your needle."

"I'm sorry, ma'am," the girl said, her dark eyes widening to hide her pain. She was quite young, Brynna saw and felt sorry for her. Her pity turned to anger when she regarded the dark-haired girl perched on the stand swaying this way and that to regard herself in the mirror. Alicia de Jarreau was being fitted in a beautiful gown of palepink silk ornately trimmed with ribbons and ruffles. Two large bows nearly obscured the ruffled panel of the flounced skirt.

"Michelle," Madame René called. "Go help Madeleine with the cutting."

Alicia whirled and glared at the Frenchwoman. "Your help is not very adept, Madame René," she said haughtily. "She has pricked me twice this morning. I am not in the habit of being waited upon by your servants."

"Excusez-moi, mademoiselle," Madame replied. "She is new and learning. I had not meant for her to fit you today. I will do that myself."

"That's better," Alicia replied, somewhat mollified. Everyone knew Madame René herself waited upon only her very special customers. It was something of a prestige factor to have the couturiere's sole attention.

"I will be with you shortly," Madame continued smoothly, "as soon as I have waited upon these ladies."

"What?" Alicia cried indignantly.

"Oh, do attend to Mademoiselle de Jarreau's needs," Jessica said. "My niece and I shall content ourselves studying your beautiful fabrics."

For the first time Alicia glanced at Madame René's guests and her outrage turned to simpering graciousness.

"Why, thank you so much, Jessica. I am somewhat pressed for time. Is—is Temple with you today?"

Jessica feigned looking about for him, then shook her head. "As you can see, Alicia, he is not."

The Creole girl's face flamed with color and dislike. She was never sure if Jessica was poking fun at her or not.

"That's a lovely ball gown," Jessica went on, "and you've had it made at such an appropriate time. Brynna, Temple and I are giving a ball in two weeks time. No doubt, my man is even now delivering your invitation."

"Why, Jessica, you and Temple never give balls," Alicia said in consternation.

"Nonetheless, Temple has chosen to do so now. You'd

best watch out, Alicia. You'll have competition with all the eligible men. Temple intends to show off his beautiful cousin."

"I'd wager he's trying to marry her off," Alicia simpered. "He probably grows tired of so many dependent kin on his doorstep."

Jessica's eyes snapped with anger. Brynna seized a swath of material and draped it across her shoulders.

"What do you think, Aunt Jessica?" she called gaily.

"It's lovely, dear," Jessica said, barely paying notice to the lustrous silk.

"Not the right color for you at all, *chérie*," Alicia called, once again preening. In the mirror, her dark gaze, smug and triumphant, flashed to meet Brynna's.

Brynna pretended to study the material, while she strove to cool her irritation. Sweeping it away, she sighed. "I suppose you're right," she said lightly. "Temple said he prefers me in white." She fingered a length of ivory peau d'ange, then glanced over her shoulder at the dark-haired girl. "He dislikes pastels so much." Her gaze swept over Alicia's new gown. "Pity!"

"Come, ladies," Madame René said quickly, not wanting a fight to develop in her establishment. Secretly she was happy to see the lofty Mademoiselle de Jarreau brought down a peg or two. As she passed the ivory peau d'ange, she scooped it up, for her quick eye had seen it was indeed the right color for the beautiful golden-eyed girl. The pale, creamy silk brought out the fiery color of her hair and the flawless skin.

"Good for you, Brynna," Jessica whispered under her breath, and no more was said about the presumptuous Mademoiselle de Jarreau.

The rest of their visit with Madame René was spent under her expert eye in devising ball gowns to outshine all others. By the time they retired to their carriage, Brynna was exhausted and far too excited to want to return to Langtry.

"What was it you said only this morning?" Jessica teased. "At any rate we are not returning to Langtry today. Temple has a surprise planned for you."

"A surprise? What is it, Aunt Jessica? Tell me," Brynna pleaded, but Jessica shook her head.

"It wouldn't be a surprise" was all she'd say. The carriage wound through a narrow back street and halted before a stone wall with a small door placed in the center of it.

"What is this?" Brynna asked wanly. She was far too tired to call on any of Jessica's friends.

"Never fear, my child," Jessica reassured her. "This is home when we are in New Orleans. Come, we will rest for a while until Temple returns." Ben had hurried ahead to ring a bell. A door opened in the wall and a servant bowed Jessica and Brynna in. They were in a tiny, paved courtyard with a burbling fountain in the center and graceful magnolia trees providing deep pools of shade.

"How lovely," Brynna exclaimed, and would have settled on one of the stone benches placed at inviting intervals, but Jessica hastened her toward an outside stairway that led to an upper balcony and second floor.

"This will be your room, *chérie*," she said, indicating a door opening off the balcony. May stood within, and upon hearing their arrival, came to greet Brynna.

"But how did you come to be here?" Brynna demanded, laughing.

"After we left, May and Euphemie packed our bags for an overnight stay and followed us in another carriage," Jessica explained, obviously pleased by Brynna's surprise.

"Where's Cyra?" Brynna asked eagerly, looking beyond May's shoulder.

May cast Jessica a quick glance. "We couldn't find Cyra, Miss Brynna," she said in her soft, quiet voice. "The minute yo' lef' the house, she go down to the fields lookin' fo' Thomas. She say you' dun' mind."

"It doesn't matter, May," Brynna said brightly. "I'm glad you're here."

"Yas, ma'am," May answered quietly, but Brynna could tell from her shy smile that she, too, was enjoying this unexpected holiday. "Ah packed yore nightgown and that pretty green gown. Ah hope Ah done right."

"You did just fine, May," Brynna answered, looking around the airy room. A single bed sat against one wall, a fine netting, meant to keep out the insects while one slept, was pulled out of the way. A washstand with a china bowl and filled water pitcher occupied one corner, a bathtub and rack of fresh linen towels another. Slatted shutters had been closed over the windows onto the street casting cool shadows over a chaise longue. Brynna had thought herself too excited to sleep, but couldn't repress a yawn as May helped her remove her dress and loosen her corsets. Grateful, Brynna splashed cool, scented water over her face and wrists, then sank onto the chaise. The streets below were silent in the afternoon heat. The city of New Orleans rested so it might rise with the cool evening breeze and bedeck itself for the nightly festivities.

The shadows were long, the waning sunlight fell in tattered ribbons through the slatted shutters. Brynna rose refreshed, and pulling on a loose robe May had included in her packing, she opened the French doors and stepped out onto the scrolled ironwork balcony that hung over the sidewalks. Chairs and a small table had been placed at intervals. Taking up a station at one of them, Brynna leaned over the railing to study the people below. The streets were coming alive again. The little shops that closed in the afternoon were reopening, their lanterns blazing to light the wares in their windows. Carriages moved up and down the street, carrying gentlemen to rendezvous with beautiful ladies. Women of the street in gaudy-colored gowns and painted faces called to the passersby with ribald invitation.

As she watched, Temple Sinclair strolled down the street, his long legs moving briskly.

"Temple!" She leaned far over the balcony to catch his attention and wave to him. He looked up and waved. Men on the opposite walk hooted and called to her as well. Suddenly, Brynna was aware of how she must look wearing only a thin robe and with her hair tangling over her shoulders and down her back. Pulling her robe about her throat, she drew back and fled back inside to pick up the brush and tackle her unruly locks. A knock sounded at her door, then it was thrust open and Temple stepped inside. Brynna whirled and gasped when she saw him.

"Excusez-moi," he said, his dark eyes taking in her disheveled hair and the thin robe. "When I saw you on the balcony, I thought you were dressed to receive company."

"I—no, I rushed out after my nap. I didn't realize how I must look. I hope I haven't embarrassed you." Anxiously she gripped the brush.

"Au contraire, cousine," he teased. "I thought never to have seen such a beautiful sight." Brynna stood, flushed, her eyes downcast. "Take your time in dressing," he said kindly. "Then we will have supper together."

"Must we leave this place?" Brynna asked. "I should love to sit on the balcony and watch the people in the street."

"You are a woman of simple pleasure, mademoiselle,"

98

he answered lightly, but his eyes smoldered with unchecked fires. Brynna felt them kindling a flame inside her.

"You forget, I am a simple country girl from Tennessee," she replied, striving for a light tone and failing abysmally.

"Nothing about you is simple, *chérie*," he replied, and the common endearment Aunt Jessica often used herself, became intimate and caressing on his lips. "If you'll excuse me now, I'll say hello to Jessica, then retire to my room to freshen up and await your pleasure." He was gone, striding down the inner balcony with the long-legged steps he'd used in the streets. She sensed he harbored some inner restlessness, as if the very character of the city itself had seeped into his soul. Thoughtfully, Brynna called May to help her with her toilette.

One of the doors opened from the inner balcony into a large salon, simply yet tastefully furnished, as were all things belonging to the Sinclairs. The French doors had been thrown open onto the street balcony and tiny lanterns had been lit. Temple Sinclair stood near the marble fireplace, his back turned to the room until he heard her enter.

"Cousine," he said in greeting, then paused as if struck dumb while he took in her appearance. Brynna was glad she and May had taken so many pains with her coiffure and toilette. She wore an off-the-shoulder evening gown of green silk taffeta. The color changed from dull to bright with every movement she made. The simple full skirt was unflounced, the bodice unadorned except for a slight fichu of lace. She knew she looked her best. Her shoulders rose pale and creamy above the vibrant color. Her chestnut curls had been piled high on her head and fell in a cascade down her back. The shimmery taffeta whispered

as she moved across the room, drawn like a moth to the lights beyond. Temple watched her move, noting her upright carriage, her slender shoulders and proud lines. He'd never seen a female as beautiful as this one.

Brynna noted the table on the balcony set with china and candles. A cart nearby held dishes of food being warmed over braziers of coals. In wonderment she turned back to Temple.

"Your every wish, *ma belle jeune femme,* is my command."

Brynna covered the noise of her pounding heart with light laughter. "Then I shall have to think of something more to wish," she said. "Perhaps a star from the heavens."

"It's yours, mademoiselle."

"Or a fine horse."

"You've only to ask, it is yours."

"I would like the sun to rise at night and the moon by day."

"Done." His eyes sparkled at their play and she was struck by the thought that such as he could throw aside his veneer of sophistication and become a simple youth again.

"I want the Mississippi to flow backward."

"It will do so gladly."

"And I want—" His grip on her shoulders halted her flow of words. She felt his hard body at her back. His breath was hot against her cheek as he bent to whisper in her ear.

"You have not asked yet for my heart, *cousine,*" he said huskily.

"I—I am not yet sure I desire it," she answered, and couldn't still the tremor that shook her.

"What is it you do desire above all else?" he whispered, his hands kneading her bare shoulders.

Brynna swallowed and drew a trembling breath. "I think—"

"Don't think. Say it! What is it you desire above all else? Tell me quick."

"Langtry! I desire Langtry," she blurted. Her heart hammered in her chest. His kneading hands had fallen still and now he slowly withdrew them.

"You are very honest, little *cousine,*" he said wryly.

Brynna turned to stare at him. "Did you not ask me to be?" she inquired, perplexed at his sudden coldness.

Anger struggled with humor in his expression and finally the latter won. "You must always be truthful with me, *ma petite* Brynna," he said lightly. "It is your most endearing quality." He whirled at the sound of someone entering. "Ah, Jessica, you are ravishing as always."

"You're a mite handsome yourself, sir," Jessica answered with rare coquetry and turned to Brynna. "My dear, you are beautiful in that color. You should wear it often." She spied the table on the balcony. "We're eating in," she cried. "What a lovely idea. I'm still rather tired from our afternoon."

"I've ordered shrimp and lobster from Delmonico's, and gumbo and French pastries and wine. Brynna wanted to watch the people in the streets while we sup."

"But we could have done that from the restaurants. The doors are thrown open . . ." Jessica began, then nodded in understanding. "Ah, you are being selfish, Temple. You're keeping her to yourself as long as possible. But the secret of your beautiful cousin will be out of the bag the moment we step into the theater."

"The theater?" Brynna repeated.

"Hasn't Temple told you yet?" Jessica said, leading the way to the balcony and inspecting the dishes beneath the silver-domed covers. Servants waited to serve them.

"Temple has told me very little," Brynna said, casting a quick, happy glance at her devious host.

"We've tickets to the opera tonight," he said offhandedly. "I hope you enjoy the opera."

"I don't know. I've never been," Brynna answered, her eyes wide with excitement.

"It seems this girl has done very little, Jessica. Never been to a ball or an opera. We've been neglecting her education."

"I was away at school," she said defensively, "and Papa didn't allow frivolity. He was a very religious man."

"Well, tonight we shall engage in all manner of frivolities, beginning with this rather excellent wine I've discovered." His long, tanned fingers worked at the cork and he filled their glasses with the sparkling liquid. When all glasses were filled, he raised his in a toast. "Here's to furthering knowledge and frivolity," he said.

"Hear, hear!" Jessica cried, and clinked his glass gaily.

"Hear, hear," Brynna echoed, and drank. The bubbles tickled her nose and she laughed.

"Your turn for a toast," Temple prompted, looking at her. In the candlelight, his eyes looked deep and mysterious.

Brynna thought for a moment, then raised her glass. "Here's to New Orleans, a painted lady," she cried.

"Well done, *cousine*," Temple called admiringly. "A painted lady."

They all drank and toasted and drank until Brynna felt quite giddy, as effervescent as the bubbling wine.

"I think it's time we leave for the opera house," Temple said finally, and Brynna was surprised to see that amidst all the laughter and talk, they had supped quite well. She'd taken little time to note the activity in the street.

102

She'd been too mesmerized by her handsome cousin. She rose too quickly from her seat and staggered slightly.

"Careful," he said, and offered her a bracing arm. They donned their wraps and made their way down the stairs, through the courtyard and to the carriage waiting in the street. A cool breeze had sprung up and fanned Brynna's flushed cheeks. With nightfall, the city had taken on a different character; the lights were gaudier, the music and chatter gayer, more abandoned.

The opera hall was magnificent, with frescoed, domed ceilings and glass chandeliers, velvet-draped boxes, and a broad stage. Although the heat of summer had driven many rich planters and their families out of the city, the reputation of the diva had drawn them back. Cheerfully they strolled through the reception hall, lanquidly exchanging bits of gossip behind frilly silk fans. The men, longing for a final cheroot before curtain call, contented themselves by attending their wives' whims and engaging in small talk.

Temple led Brynna and Jessica in, one female on each arm. People hurried to greet them. Obviously, Jessica and Temple were well regarded by the other planters. Jessica introduced Brynna at every turn until she soon lost track of what name belonged to what face.

"Your niece is quite lovely," Myra Harcourt commented to Jessica after having maneuvered her daughter Coletta next to Temple.

"Thank you, Myra," Jessica answered.

"In spite of her odd-colored eyes."

"They are rather fascinating, *n'est-ce pas?*" Jessica replied serenely. "Did I tell you we're giving a ball. No doubt your invitation has already been delivered."

"Très bien! Of course we will come. Coletta will be

delighted. Have you noticed Temple hasn't been able to take his eyes off her?"

"Oh, *regardez!* There's Aimée de Laussat," Jessica cried, "and her handsome son."

"Oh la la," Myra declared, her attention diverted. "She shouldn't wear that dress since she put on so many pounds, and the color is positively bilious with her complexion."

"Temple, *mon ami.*" A tall, dark-haired man pushed through the crush of people, escorting Alicia de Jarreau on his arm. "You've brought the most beautiful woman in New Orleans. Surely you're going to introduce us."

"Surely not, you devil," Temple declared lightheartedly. "You've broken nearly every feminine heart in New Orleans. I shall warn Brynna of you *immédiatement!*"

"Mon Dieu, does our friendship mean nothing?"

Colletta Harcourt stood forgotten. Pouting, she turned back to her mother, who cast a spurious glance at the group of young people. Temple relented and made the introductions. Courtney de Jarreau took hold of Brynna's hand, bowing deeply before pressing a heated kiss upon it.

"You have captured my heart, mademoiselle," he declared, his dark eyes dancing wickedly. His flirtation was done in such good humor that Brynna found herself liking him immediately. Like his sister, he was dark and handsome, not as tall as Temple, and thinner. His dark eyes held a promise of mischief and his teeth flashed often in a smile. He was witty, slightly rapscallion, and slightly cutting in his remarks about the theater and its patrons, even the diva who would regale them this evening. He made Brynna laugh despite herself.

She wondered briefly if the wine had something to do with her giddiness or the dark lights of Temple's eyes as he cast frequent glances in her direction although he chatted with Alicia. Brynna knew Temple found her alluring. Alicia seemed to guess it as well, for now and then her forced gaiety slipped and revealed a frown. Still smarting from their afternoon encounter, the Creole girl had barely acknowledged Brynna's presence.

"What a quaint little dress," she said in an aside and made no effort to speak to Brynna the rest of the evening.

"We have no guests joining us this evening, why don't you sit in our box," Temple invited, and the suggestion was quickly acted upon. As the gong sounded indicating they should take their seats, Cort de Janneau took hold of Brynna's elbow.

"Do allow me to escort you to your seat," he said, proffering his arm in an age-old symbol of chivalry.

"I shall be delighted, Monsieur de Jarreau," Brynna said, batting her eyes at him from behind her fan. She laughed lightheartedly. Why couldn't she practice such coquetry with Temple? she wondered briefly, and resolved to do so at the earliest opportunity. Over her shoulder she was aware of Temple's hot gaze on her bare shoulders.

"De Jarreau," a loud voice called as they mounted the stairs. Everyone turned to see a scuffle near the door. Two young men in dress coats restrained an intense young man whose dark eyes glared at Cort de Jarreau. The two men, apparently friends, spoke earnestly, and finally all three went off toward the bar where last-minute drinks were being served.

"Goodness, what was that all about?" Aunt Jessica exclaimed. "Wasn't that Pierre d'Abbadie?"

"Come, Jessica, let's proceed to our box," Temple said, stepping forward to take both her elbow and Brynna's. Thoughtfully Cort escorted Alicia.

"I don't understand why he should be angry with me,"

105

he declared. "I've never spoken ill of him or his sister."

"I suspect it is not what you may have said as what you've done," Temple snapped.

"That's preposterous," Alicia snapped. "Everyone knows Francine d'Abbadie has little morals. Besides, she's married now to that dreadful old man." Alicia shivered delicately. "Serves her right, I might say."

"Let us not speak of this again this evening," Jessica said. "We have come to enjoy the opera, not to gossip about some poor girl and her misguided brother."

"I quite agree, Aunt Jess," Cort said, bending to kiss her on the cheek with easy familiarity. Despite her prim expression, Jessica glanced at him with warmth. He'd been Temple's friend for many years. She'd known him as a boy, understood that he'd grown up doted on by an indulgent mother. He'd known no restrictions save those she herself had placed on him when he was a guest at Langtry. He was a charming, well-meaning boy, who'd been given too much of everything in his youth except discipline.

"Have a care, Cort," she sighed. "You are too easy with other people's honor."

"I swear to you, Aunt Jessica, I was not the first to— eh—sample Francine d'Abbadie's charms."

"Do you dare to tell her brother that?" Jessica asked wisely. "I think not. You have boxed yourself into a corner. Pray you will have no further trouble extricating yourself. Now, come, the opera is about to begin."

Suitably chastised, Cort slunk into a chair next to Temple. They had placed the ladies at the front of the box, and now that the drama between them had ended, Brynna was able to attend to the excitement of the theater.

Crystal chandeliers hung from ornately decorated domes and rich wine-red velvet curtains hung along the walls and balconies. There was little time to study the theater, for the lights were extinguished and the curtain opened to a magical wonderland that held Brynna enthralled. Her spirit soared with every rising note of the music, and when at last the curtain closed, she rose as if in a trance and followed the others toward the stairs.

Cort seemed to have recovered from Jessica's earlier reprimand. Now he chatted wittily, commenting on the opera, the talent of the noted soprano, the costumes, and most especially the looks of the girl in the third row of the chorus. In between these observations, he flirted blatantly and outrageously with Brynna until her laughter trailed back to those on the stairs above, and Temple found himself glowering at his best friend's back. All around them, operagoers were talking brightly, their smiles quick and relaxed, for they'd enjoyed the performance.

Brynna and Cort were halfway down the stairs when a shot rang out. Brynna paused. Beside her, Cort gasped and grabbed his shoulder. The crowd fell silent and still as if frozen in time. At the bottom of the stairs Pierre d'Abbadie stood with smoking pistol. Suddenly his friends were there, grabbing the hand that held the pistol.

"Let me go," he shouted in outrage, wrestling with them. "Let me kill that son of a whore, yes, and that painted harlot at his side. They laugh together for what they've done to my sister."

He broke away and raised the pistol again. A woman screamed. Without thinking, Brynna stepped forward the remaining steps until she was level with Pierre d'Abbadie.

"Please, sir. You are wrong to blame Mister de Jarreau. He meant no harm to your sister. Besides, she is married now and all is well."

Pierre d'Abbadie thrust his face toward hers. His eyes were bloodshot, his lips foamed with spittel. He had lost all reason, Brynna realized. "You are not fit to speak my sister's name, you harlot," he rasped out. His mad gaze rose to meet Courteney de Jarreau. "I demand satisfaction," he bellowed.

"I shall be all too willing, but as you see, I am incapacitated," Cort replied.

"Coward!" D'Abbadie cried, his glare taking in Brynna once more. "Coward and whore! You make a good pair."

At his words, Temple pushed forward down the stairs. "Stop it, d'Abbadie. You insult my cousin who is but an innocent girl. Do not draw her into your *petitesse*."

"I make no apologies here. She is in the company of a whoreson. She is tainted by his reputation. Courteney de Jarreau leaves no woman innocent."

"Apologize at once, I say," Temple roared, "or I shall have to call you out."

"She is, as I say, as low as any prostitute who would lay with the likes of Courteney de Jarreau."

Temple's hand flashed, delivering a stinging slap across d'Abbadie's cheek. "My seconds will call on you, sir," he said flatly.

D'Abbadie drew himself up stiffly. "I shall look forward to it, sir," he answered, and followed by his two friends, stalked out of the theater.

Everyone looked stunned. People on the stairs skirted them with sidelong glances and hurried to gather in groups and exclaimed in hushed voices over what had happened. Jessica Sinclair descended the stairs and gripped Temple's arm. Her expression was anxious.

"What is it?" Brynna whispered. "What is happening?"

"You little fool. Temple is about to fight a duel over you," Alicia answered.

"A duel? Is it very dangerous?"

"D'Abbadie has the choice of weapons. There's little doubt he will use the pistol. His reputation is undisputed."

Temple glanced at Brynna's stricken face. "Perhaps for the first time it is," he said lightly. "See how his latest victim still stands."

"At your service, mademoiselle." Cort sketched a quick bow then staggered slightly.

"Oh no," Brynna cried, flinging herself against Temple's arm. "You can't put yourself in danger like this over me. I wasn't insulted, truly I wasn't. He only said those things out of pain for his sister. I'm sure when he's over his anger, he'll apologize. Please don't duel with him. Please."

Temple gazed into her tearful eyes. Never had he seen a more compelling sight, he thought, than the concern on her face. He longed to kiss her. He gripped her hand instead. "You don't understand, *ma petite*. If I don't defend your honor, then people will believe the lies he has uttered are true."

"I don't care," Brynna cried, desperately gripping his arm. "What if you are killed."

"Don't fear, mademoiselle," Cort said, taking her hand. "Temple has fought duels before, and let me assure you he is no mean shot with the pistols. Shall we go?" He pulled her beside him, but Temple was there, placing himself between the two of them.

"You have caused enough mischief for one evening," he snapped. "I bid you good evening. Mademoiselle de Jarreau." He bowed to Alicia.

"Wait, Temple. Have you no need of my services as your second?" Cort insisted.

"I think not this time," Temple answered. "If you were to call on d'Abbadie, even as my second, he might shoot you on sight. You'd best see to your shoulder and then retire to White Hall for a week or two." Without waiting for a reply, Temple led Brynna and Jessica toward the waiting carriage.

"As you wish, *mon ami*," Cort called after them. "I shall call upon you at Langtry, mademoiselle. *Au revoir*." His farewell lingered in the air.

"He behaved very badly," Jessica said finally.

"Cort will never change, you know that," Temple said.

"Still, to cause this tragedy and go off and leave you to handle it seems somehow . . . cowardly," Brynna replied stiffly. Temple glanced at her sharply. Her back was ramrod straight, her lips pressed together in stoic disapproval.

"I thought you liked him," he said gently.

For a moment the firmness of her chin wavered. "I—I did," she said finally. "But he has behaved irresponsibly. I think he doesn't take any of this business of honor very seriously."

"He doesn't," Temple agreed. "Perhaps that is why I've loved him like a brother all these years. He is all the things I sometimes would like to be—frivolous, unthinking, unfettered by responsibilities."

"I wouldn't want you any other way than you are," Jessica said, placing a hand on his sleeve. "Are we all too much of a burden to you?"

Temple squeezed her hand and nodded. "No, I could never be like Cort. I love you and Langtry too much." His great dark eyes turned to Brynna, and somehow she knew she was included in that love. She was suffused with a sense of warmth and belonging.

"Besides," Temple went on. "I have yet to see Cort obey anyone's edicts, least of all mine. I expect tomorrow, he'll be at the dueling field."

"Other people can go to watch the duel?" Brynna asked.

110

Temple laughed, guessing her intent. "It's not a pretty sight, *ma cousine*," he replied. "You'd best stay with Jessica and I shall come back for you when it is finished."

"But I don't want to go, just to watch," Brynna protested. "You may need m— someone."

"That is why I will have my seconds. Now we have returned home. I will leave you ladies here. There is business I must attend before the morning." He got out of the carriage and escorted them inside the walled courtyard. Jessica hurried ahead up the stairs.

"Brynna," Temple called softly, and she paused. The moon cast blue shadows over the still courtyard and lined the edge of the fountain and the bubbling water with streaks of gold.

Brynna felt her chest tighten as she looked up at Temple. "What is it you wish?" she asked softly.

He stepped forward and took hold of her shoulders, his dark eyes studying her closely. She thought he might kiss her, and her heart hammered wildly. Her hand rested against his chest and she could feel the echo of his own erratic heartbeat.

"You are very beautiful," he murmured, his grip on her tightening. Brynna raised her face to him. Her dark lashes lay against her pale cheeks. She felt the nearness of him as he leaned closer, then he touched his lips against her brow and was gone into the magical light of the moon. Beyond the wall, Brynna heard the night sounds of the city. They no longer enchanted. They made her feel frightened and alone.

Chapter Six

Dare she go? Temple had said no, but she couldn't stay behind while he— No, it was unthinkable. She was responsible. If only she hadn't stepped forward to protect Cort de Jarreau and brought d'Abbadie's insults down on her head. She should have realized Cort was perfectly capable of taking care of himself.

Back and forth she paced in her room, listening for the sound of the carriage signifying Temple was home, but he didn't return through the night. Toward morning she resolved to find her way to the place Jessica called the dueling oaks. She'd changed from her opera dress into a simple sprigged cotton. She left her hair uncoiffed, so it hung down her back. At the first hint of light in the east, she threw her opera cape over her shoulders and made her way along the balcony and down the stairs. No one stirred. The servants had not yet risen to heat bathwater and make café au lait for the master and mistress. They slumbered innocently.

From the stairs, Brynna could see a sliver of light at Jessica's window and knew her aunt hadn't rested, either. Such a revelation only convinced Brynna more than ever

112

that Temple was in danger. Only she could do something about it. She would arrive at the dueling oaks, wherever it was, and plead with Monsieur d'Abbadie to retract his words and apologize to Temple. After all, his argument was with Courteney de Jarreau.

She crept across the courtyard and out the gate into the dark street. She had only to find a carriage for hire. She'd noticed several the day before, but there were none in evidence now. Peering down the street with its shuttered windows and dark shadows, she bit her lips to still her chattering teeth. Temple was the one in danger, she reminded herself.

Cautiously, she made her way along the back street. Surely on Royal there would be carriages about. Just as she was about to give up hope, she heard the clop of horses' hooves against the cobblestones. They drew near without any sign of slowing. Desperately, she ran into the middle of the street, her arms flung wide.

"Stop, please stop," she cried as a lone horseman came into view.

"Mon Dieu, Brynna," Courteney de Janneau called, drawing his steed to a halt. The restless animal pranced around nervously. "What are you doing here in the streets at such an early hour? Don't you know how dangerous it is for a lady to be abroad without a chaperone?"

"Oh, Cort. I can't think of that now. I must find a carriage and get to the dueling oaks before Temple is killed."

"Where is Temple now?" the handsome Creole asked.

"I don't know. He didn't come home last night."

"I came to offer my services this morning. I had no idea he would not be here." Cort sat on his horse, considering what to do. "Quickly, Brynna," he said at last, preparing

113

to dismount. "I will escort you back to your aunt, then I'll ride to the dueling oaks."

"Take me with you," Brynna cried, throwing herself against his booted leg so he couldn't dismount. "Please. There's so little time. Jessica said they will meet at dawn. Please, Cort."

"Temple will have my head."

"You must do this for me. You've involved me in this affair," Brynna argued, and knew she was being unfair, but with every passing moment her anxiety grew. Cort saw the passionate entreaty in her eyes and impulsively held out his hand.

"Come," he cried, and swung her up behind him on the horse. "Hold on tightly." He spurred the stallion, and it broke into a fast gallop. Brynna threw her arms around Cort's slender waist and held on for dear life. Wind whipped against her cheeks. The bright-green opera cape flared behind her like bright wings; her hair blew in chestnut streamers.

Cort was an expert horseman, reckless and daredevil. Ignoring the danger to his prized horseflesh on the slippery stones, he raced the animal through the streets and out along the river road. The sun was rimming the horizon, casting a red-gold haze over the park.

At last, in the distance Brynna could see a clump of trees, with one gnarled oak standing taller than the rest. Several carriages were drawn up and men stood facing a clearing. Two figures paced away from each other, their pistols pointed rigidly upward. Fearful of startling the duelers, Cort slowed his horse, yet pushed it in a fast canter toward the clearing.

Brynna could make out Temple's tall figure and hear the arbitrator counting. The duelers waited for the final count. As if in slow motion, she could see d'Abbadie begin to turn, his pistol brought level and cocked.

"Temple!" She screamed the warning. Her cry mingled with the terrifying blast of the pistol. A patch of red grew on Temple's shoulder. Cort jerked his horse to a halt. The watching men turned to stare at the commotion. Brynna paid them no attention, for her eyes were riveted on Temple. He stood ramrod straight, making no sign he'd been wounded. D'Abbadie's eyes widened in awareness of his predicament. He'd fired his shot, now he stood defenseless before Temple Sinclair. Temple cooly raised his weapon, sighted along its barrel, and fired. Pierre d'Abbadie fell to the ground.

"No," Brynna whispered, hiding her face. She'd never seen a man killed. She'd never dreamed Temple could shoot a man in cold blood. She couldn't bear to look at him. The seconds and a doctor rushed forward to examine the fallen man. Temple stood with the gun dangling from his hand, his gaze fixed for the first time on Cort and Brynna. They could read the rage in his eyes.

"Sir, a most generous shot," the doctor called. "Monsieur d'Abbadie lives."

"He didn't kill him," Brynna gasped.

Cort shrugged negligently. "Not Temple!" he declared proudly. "He's eminently fair to everyone, even a fool like d'Abbadie."

"Seems to me d'Abbadie was not the only fool in this affair," Brynna answered, her anger at the thoughtless Creole returning now that the danger was past.

"Forgive me, *chérie*. I vow to change my ways and cause you to think well of me. Perhaps as well as you think of Temple." With that *bon mot*, he turned his attention back to the scene before them. Brynna's cheeks flamed, but she made no answering retort. Courteney de Jarreau

115

had misinterpreted her concern for her cousin. She would have to set him straight, but not now.

Temple stalked to the injured man. The doctor rose to tend his wound, but he brushed him away. His eyes were black as he studied his opponent. "Enough blood has been shed over this, d'Abbadie," he said. "Let us have done with it." He turned away and relinquished the pistol to a second.

"I think it would be wise if we quit this place, *chérie*," Cort said, studying the degree of anger displayed by his friend. "Unless you've a mind to risk Temple's wrath for the comfort of his carriage."

"I'm quite able to return with you," she answered, suddenly aware she might have displeased both Temple and her aunt. "But please, do hurry. Perhaps if I reach Aunt Jessica before he does . . ."

"A wise choice, indeed," Cort laughed, seeming well pleased about something. He wheeled the horse and spurred once more to a gallop. Brynna clung to his waist while the wind whipped her hair to a wild tangle and did its best to cool her hot cheeks. Temple glanced up in time to see them streaking away, Brynna perched precariously like some colorful, exotic bird behind Cort on the galloping stallion. Cursing beneath his breath, he leaped into his carriage and set off at a swift pace toward the city.

By the time Temple reached the townhouse, Brynna had freshened herself. May had brushed her wayward curls into a demure, rolled crown around her head and the story had been told in part to Jessica, who had gently chided her, then thoroughly questioned her on Temple's condition. When Temple strolled into the salon, Brynna was occupied in stitching a sampler while a cup of thick, dark chocolate cooled before her.

"Good morning, Cousin Temple," she greeted him almost shyly.

"Don't you good morning me," he raged, shaking his finger at her. "I should spank you for what you did this morning."

"Temple, do sit down and calm yourself," Jessica admonished gently. "I see you've been wounded. I must tend to it immediately."

"It's merely a scratch," he shrugged dismissively and continued to glare at Brynna.

"Nevertheless, it must be seen to." Jessica ordered her medicine kit to be brought, and when it arrived, she insisted upon Temple removing his coat. He fumed. She fussed, but she was heartily grateful to see the tall, lanky figure of her stepson.

"Now, as to Brynna . . ." she said as she worked over him. "Although it's true she shouldn't have gone to the dueling grounds, she did so out of the purest of motives."

"Did she tell you how she went?" he sputtered.

Jessica turned a rebuking eye on Brynna, who had the grace to blush and lower her eyes. "Perhaps she's not had the time to tell me everything," Jessica allowed.

"She arrived on the back of Cort's horse, her arms wrapped around his waist as if they were Gypsies, her hair all uncurled."

"I'm sorry if I've displeased you," Brynna said. "I was most anxious to arrive there in case I should be able to do something to stop the duel."

"You should have had more faith in my ability to handle this, Brynna. Cort should never have brought you there today. God alone knows what people thought when they saw you galloping about on the back of his horse."

"Are you so tempered by what others think?" Brynna asked quietly, somehow disappointed if he were to answer yes. He sensed the mood of her question and stopped his angry pacing.

"Not for myself, but for you, little *cousine*," he answered.

"Temple is right, my dear," Jessica said. "People so love a good gossip. Cort should have known better."

"*I* should have known better," Brynna said. "In my concern for you, Cousin Temple, I put common sense aside. I shan't do so again. Now if you'll excuse me, I'll prepare for the trip home."

Her words were said without rancor, if a little crisply, so Temple stood with his mouth hanging open, wondering if she'd just won their argument.

"Was it so bad?" Jessica asked when Brynna was gone. His arm had been bandaged.

Temple glanced at her. "In truth, I feared for her life more than her reputation on that half-wild stallion of Cort's. When they galloped away over the field she looked . . ." He paused, his hands spread before him as he thought back to that scene. "She looked magnificent," he said finally. "Like some ancient warrior princess riding with her master into battle."

"I see," Jessica said. And indeed she did.

In the days that followed, the plantation was a beehive of activity. Menus were planned and replanned. Hams were chosen and put aside for the event. The making of pralines, a wonderful buttery candy filled with pecan halves, began. Rum cakes were made ahead, wrapped in rum-soaked rags and stored, their heady aroma permeating the pantry for days. As they neared the big day, chickens were slaughtered and kept in the spring house until the morning of the ball when large cast-iron pans would be filled with heated oil and the coated pieces fried.

Fresh shrimp were purchased from the Cajun fishermen who plied the bayous. Wines were selected. Jars of sparkling fruit punches were concocted and put to chill in the spring house. The shelves there were already filled with pecan pies and coconut cakes.

Even the gardeners nursed choice plants and cast an eye at the heavens for good weather to hold. Tender spring peas were brought from the garden and the first of the tomatoes.

In their zeal to make Langtry even more beautiful, the rooms were nearly torn apart. Servants scrubbed and waxed the wide plank floors in every room. The marble entrance was cleaned with extra care, and for the rest of the time before the ball, people checked their soles before gingerly crossing it. Windows were washed until they sparkled, silver-plated doorknobs polished until they gleamed. Even the chandeliers were lowered and each tinkling piece of glass washed and rinsed in vinegar water.

Everyone worked hard and willingly, for even the servants were excited about the coming festivities. All save Cyra who grumbled and grew sullen. Brynna ignored her. Nothing could dampen her anticipation of her first ball.

Temple's wound was healing nicely. The duel had become a brief memory of her visit to New Orleans.

Madame René and her assistant brought their new gowns and stayed overnight to finish fitting them properly. When Brynna pulled hers over her head, she was startled at the low-cut bodice and the sophistication of the gown. She'd never owned one like it. Temple had been right. Her skin gleamed with a delicate warmth she'd never known she possessed. Her hair was loose and spilled across her shoulders. She wished Temple were here to see her now. Meeting Brynna's gaze in the mirror, Madame René picked up one of the gleaming strands.

"Ah, mademoiselle, if only you could wear your hair like this for the ball, you would steal away every man's heart."

Brynna blushed, fearful of having her daydream found out and swept the long strands into her hands. Giving them a twist, she wound them around her head. Madame René regarded her silently then nodded.

"*Oui*, this is much more suitable for the ball, and still the men will turn to look at you so often their wives will hate you."

"Oh, no. I wouldn't want that." Brynna turned a shocked face to the little Frenchwoman.

Madame Rene laughed gaily. "Ah, mademoiselle, so serious. You are very young and beautiful. You must enjoy this time. I have seen the way Monsieur Sinclair looks at you. I have heard he fought a duel for you. Your future is made."

Brynna looked after the departing couturiere, puzzling over what she'd meant. Then she glanced at the image in the mirror and couldn't help preening a little. The skirt had been adorned with insets of lace. The silken ruffles rustled around her ankles prettily. The ivory color had been broken by streamers of ribbon at the waist and around the flounces. The bodice had been lowered to show her gleaming shoulders and tiny knots of ribbons tied in clusters around the gathered edge. The curve of exposed bosom seemed almost indecent, and she wondered if she should call Madame René back and ask her to raise the bodice. Then, thinking of Temple's eyes when he looked at her, she chose to leave it just as it was.

Temple had been strangely aloof ever since their trip to New Orleans. At first she'd thought he was simply angry with her and it would soon be over. When it was not, she spoke to Jessica, who assured her that Temple never held a grudge. What then could it be? She was too busy with preparations to dwell on it overly long. Perhaps he was as preoccupied as Jessica and she were.

"Were you pleased with Madame René's work?" Temple asked that night at supper. He'd tucked the volatile little Frenchwoman into a carriage for her trip back to New Orleans that afternoon and now felt free to ask this question.

"Her work is exquisite," Jessica said. "Her reputation is well earned, wouldn't you say, Brynna?"

"Oh, yes," Brynna replied. "My gown is the most beautiful thing I've ever owned."

"Then it may befit the pretty mademoiselle who wears it," Temple said gallantly. Brynna blushed beneath his gaze and sought some other topic of conversation.

"Are the de Jarreaus coming?" With her eyes lowered to her plate, she didn't see his frown.

"Of course," he replied. "Cort wouldn't miss the chance to dance with every pretty girl who puts in an appearance."

Brynna laughed. "He is something of a ladies' man, isn't he?"

Temple studied her face. "Doesn't this bother you?"

Startled, she met his gaze. "Why would it?" she asked simply, and saw a smile grow somewhere in the dark, mysterious depths of his eyes and spread to his face.

"No reason, *cousine*," he said, falling back on his pet name for her. For the rest of the meal and the days that followed, he was in the best of spirits.

The hot Louisiana sun spread moist heat thick as molasses over the black soil and lush vegetation. Cicadas filled the air with their shrill singing. Jessica was up early supervising last-minute details. Despite her aunt's admonishments to stay abed and rest, Brynna hurried downstairs to do her part. She was too excited to sleep. Guests would begin arriving anytime from noon on. Those coming from the farthest distance would arrive in time for the ladies to rest in one of the guest rooms. Then they would dress for the ball and arrive downstairs refreshed and unwrinkled.

The doors of the ballroom had been thrown open. Everything gleamed from its recent scrubbing, from the curlicues of the ceiling cornices to the waxed floor. Gilt-edged chairs sat in a row along the walls for those who needed to rest between dances or simply to watch. At one end of the great room, a small stage had been erected, and it was here that an orchestra hired from New Orleans would provide the music.

The flower gardens had been carefully culled of their choicest blossoms and those farthest from the house had been literally stripped of their bright foliage, all for the huge bouquets that graced every room. The table and the sideboard were set with fine English china and gleaming silver and crystal. At the right moment, Lala's servants would carry out the dishes of food she'd spent two weeks preparing.

Even the slaves hadn't been forgotten. The field hands had been given a holiday from their labors. Down at the slave quarters, a hog had been slaughtered and was put to barbeque on an outdoor spit. The women who weren't helping with the ball were in their cabins busy preparing dishes of rice and beans. Temple had ordered a barrel of tafia brought out. Made right there on the plantation of cane juice, the rum had been set aside especially for the slaves' holiday drink. One barrel would allow each man, woman, and child one cupful of the raw brew. They sang as they prepared for their own festivities, anticipating the taste of rum, the dancing, and the food.

When the hot sun had reached its apex, Jessica shooed Brynna inside to bathe and rest. She retired for a nap as well, something unusual for Jessica, but she knew the dancing would last far into the night and she must remain gracious throughout it all. Sometime in the somnolent afternoon heat, Brynna was awakened by the arrival of the first carriages. She didn't even bother to rise. She knew Jessica would go down to greet her guests briefly and show them to a room, where they, too, would soon be slumbering.

But now she found herself unable to sleep, and summoning May, she ordered her bath and lazed in the delicious tepid water until her fingers were wrinkled as a prune. Wearing only the lightest of cotton wrappers, she sat on the upper gallery while May fluffed her hair dry with a towel. Bored, Cyra came to join them, although she made no offer of help with her mistress's toilette.

"How's your crop this year?" A man's voice sounded below them.

"Barring hurricanes, droughts, or floods, we should bear a good crop this year," Temple answered. The two men were seated on the gallery below. The fragrant odor of tobacco wafted upward.

"Begnaud tells us you've tried some new methods of planting. You didn't windrow this year."

"Thas' Mistah Harcourt," May whispered in her ear. "His wife and daughter mus' be restin'."

"I think I met him in New Orleans," Brynna whispered back.

"No, I didn't windrow, and with this hot spell, I'm glad I didn't," Temple was answering. "But I did try planting my rows farther apart."

"Farther apart?" Harcourt exclaimed. "Why, man, it'll take yuh twice the fields to produce a good crop."

"It's true I don't plant as much per arpent as I once did, but the plants are superior." Brynna was surprised she could follow the men's conversation. Once she hadn't known arpent was the Creoles' measurement for three-quarters of an acre.

"Even more importantly, I'll be able to use a plow to weed my plants."

"Suh, don't tell me you're about to use the plow in your fields after planting. Why, your Nigrahs will cut down more plants than they leave."

"I don't believe so," Temple answered. "The biggest expense on the planter is his labor force. The plow should do that and free us from some of this dependency on slaves."

"Ah see," Harcourt said stiffly. "You seem to have taken up some of the ideas of the northern abolitionists."

"Not entirely," Temple answered mildly. "Slavery is an abomination in which we've all been forced to become involved, regardless of our personal sensibilities on the subject. The truth is, we planters need the black laborer. They've done much to further the development of this region, but the toll has been hard on him and on the planter. If we can try new technology to end this inequality, it behooves us to try."

"Yore papa never talked like that, suh. I knew Etienne Sinclair from the time he was a young man working to build his plantation to the day he died, and he was a staunch supporter of slavery."

"He was a staunch supporter in the development of sugarcane in this region, Mr. Harcourt, and so am I. But if you knew my father, you knew he was the first to try new ideas. Ten years ago we all planted our cane two and a half feet apart. The last year of his life, he began to experiment with wider rows and with keeping back the best seeds and cuttings instead of the worst. That's one of the reasons our crops are improving. Other planters are beginning to try some of these things and they're working for them as well."

"Hrumph. I believe in mah daddy's way of doing things," Harcourt insisted.

"But you aren't competing in your father's world," Temple snapped impatiently, and Brynna could imagine him, his expression alight with enthusiasm and commitment to his crops. Willingly he shared his expertise with any who asked. Why wouldn't men like Harcourt listen to the young men with their younger ideas.

"Even your father bowed to the need for rotation to rebuild the soil," Temple reminded his guest. Brynna could tell he'd forced himself to a more genial tone and knew the effort it must cost him.

"Umm, well, yes," Harcourt answered reluctantly. His crops had been declining over the years. "Perhaps I will try holding back some of my better cuttings this year."

"That's wise of you," Temple rejoined. "Could I offer you a mint julep, sir?"

"You could indeed, suh," Harcourt answered. "Have you had any troubles with yo'r Nigras lately?"

"None," Temple said. "The Langtry slaves are not mistreated, so I have few problems with them."

"Jacques Fortier had some trouble on his place down near Houmas. Some of the barns were burned. No one was killed, except the ringleader. They hung him."

Their voices faded as they walked to Temple's study.

Brynna glanced at Cyra, and was startled to see her maid's face was twisted with bitterness.

"Why, Cyra, are you all right? Are you feeling ill?"

125

Cyra shook herself as if coming from a trance. "Ah guess Ah am feelin' porely," she answered. "Ah believe Ah'll go down and ask Lala for one of her potions."

"Oh, she'll be busy, Cyra. Let me ask Jessica for something." But Cyra hadn't waited for her consent. Without looking back, she hurried along the gallery and down the back stairs. Silently, May and Brynna watched her go.

"How strange," Brynna said worriedly. "She's not even going in the direction of the kitchen."

"Maybe she go down t' the slave quarters and ask Aunt Clemmie. She'll fix her up good as new in no time. Aunt Clemmie has a gift."

"Perhaps that's it," Brynna said doubtfully, thinking of when Cyra had fallen ill. She'd been so engrossed in the men's conversation she hadn't noticed her friend.

"If she doesn't come back in time, will you help me with my hair and gown," she asked May.

The young woman nodded happily. "Ah was thinkin' of a new way to do yore hair, Miss Brynna," she said shyly. "Would you let me try it."

"Of course," Brynna cried. "You always make me look special."

"Thet's 'cause yo' is, Miss Brynna," May answered.

While May worked on her hair, Brynna tried to recapture her festive mood, but Cyra stayed in her mind. She hoped Aunt Clemmie helped her. She had little doubt Cyra would see Thomas while she was down there.

The moment of truth was at hand. Brynna stood before the mirror, suddenly wishing she had ordered the neckline raised. Too much of her firm, curving breasts were revealed. What would Temple think? Frantically she draped a scarf across her bodice.

126

"Yo' don' need that, Miss Brynna," May chided. "All the ladies be wearin' gowns like that, some lower. Some act like they want t' show ever'thang they have to offer. Yo' look beautiful and yo' still look lak' a lady."

"Do you think so?" Brynna asked, breathless. "Perhaps I should ask Jessica's advice. It's not too late to change."

"Miz Jessica already gone down to check on things," May answered.

"I'll go down and ask her," Brynna cried, suffused with doubts. "Wait for me, in case I need to change." She hurried to the door and whirled. "Take out the green silk taffeta that I wore to the opera," she ordered, and was gone. She'd gained the top of the stairs when she saw Temple in the hall below. She tried to draw back, but it was too late. He'd already seen her.

"Brynna," he called, coming to the bottom of the stairs. She had no recourse but to go down. Taking a deep, trembling breath, she descended, her eyes downcast, her hair ringing her head like a chestnut crown. She had no idea how beautiful and innocent she looked. Temple watched her descend, and with each step that drew her closer, the muscles in his chest grew tighter so he could barely breathe by the time she stood on the step above him. Slowly she raised her head and their eyes met. Her face grew pale. Her pink, soft lips trembled and her shoulders barely moved as if she, too, were unable to draw a breath.

"You are the most beautiful woman in the world," he whispered. "You take my breath away."

"And you mine," she answered honestly. He was resplendent in a dark coat, gold-shot vest, and white shirt and stock. His dark trousers hugged his slim hips and long legs. He was elegant and handsome and his smile was warm and for her alone. Brynna guessed later it would not be so. No wonder the odious Mrs. Harcourt had pushed her awkward daughter Colletta at him. What mother wouldn't want such a handsome man for a son-in-law. Then she thought of Alicia. Apparently Mrs. Harcourt didn't know he had already made his choice.

Temple saw the light go out of her eyes and grasped her hand. "What's wrong?" he demanded, meaning to pledge his very life to bring back her smile. Brynna shied away from his touch. She couldn't tell him the truth.

"I see the de Jarreaus have not arrived yet." She uttered the first thought that popped into her head. Temple drew back, his lips tightening.

"Not yet. They will be here soon," he reassured her. Glancing at the floor, he chose his words carefully. *"Cousine,* I hope when Cort arrives you will be as circumspect with him as you are with me."

Her chin jerked up at his words. "Of course I will be, Cousin Temple," she answered with mock courtesy. "Surely, you do not expect less of me or of your friend?"

"Mais non," he said. "I meant simply that Cort has grown so used to flirting with every young woman in such a careless manner, her reputation is sometimes damaged from it."

"I promise to do nothing to shame you or Jessica," Brynna said stiffly, her cheeks coloring at his reprimand.

Temple saw he'd offended her. "I know you would not," he said quickly, but the damage was done. Holding her head proudly high, she passed him and reclimbed the steps to her room, where despite May's protestations, she changed from the ivory dress with its daring décolletage to the demure green silk taffeta she'd worn to the ball. She was certain Temple would not have seen fit to speak of her behavior if not for the revealing cut of her gown. She did not make her way downstairs again until she heard the sound of arriving carriages. Temple's eyes widened in disbelief when she descended and took her place next to him in the receiving line.

"What happened to your beautiful new gown?" Jessica whispered when there was a lull.

"A seam let go," Brynna whispered back. "You look beautiful, Jessica."

"So do you, my dear." She sighed. "When you're young, you have no need of a new gown to make you beautiful. The gods have blessed you, my dear. Temple can hardly keep his eyes off you."

"He's watching my behavior," Brynna muttered beneath her breath and turned an illuminating smile on their next guests, the Jarreaus.

Monsieur de Jarreau was a tall, handsome man like his son, but years had robbed the dark eyes of their devil-may-care lights. He greeted Jessica and Temple formally and welcomed Brynna to Louisiana. She found him charming and distinguished, and wondered how such a somber man could have produced a son like Cort.

Alicia's lips tightened in vexation when she saw Brynna standing next to Temple, then her gaze slid over the younger girl's dress and she smiled brittlely.

"How charming you look," she said. "Haven't I seen that gown before?"

"Yes, I wear it often," Brynna replied with false serenity. "It's my favorite gown."

"You should never wear any other color," Cort said, stepping forward to take her hand and kiss each cheek. Temple stood at the front of the line, forgotten and ungreeted. Scowling he cleared his throat.

"Bon soir, mon ami," Cort cried, turning at last to him. "You look like a thundercloud tonight. You haven't forgotten this is a ball."

129

"Don't pay attention to him," Alicia said, clinging overly long to Temple's hand and raising her face for a kiss. Jealousy surged through Brynna as she watched Temple bend to place a kiss on her cheek. Alicia's full lips pouted prettily, then she smiled. "I'll save a dance for you, *mon cher*," she said huskily, and finally trailed away into the ballroom. Cort went off to find a knot of young bachelors who stood sharing drinks and brutal assessments of the richly gowned and beribboned planters' daughters. All agreed, few could hold a candle to Temple's newly arrived cousin.

Brynna had begun to think the receiving line would never end. She'd never known there were so many neighbors and friends of the Sinclairs. They came in a steady line and Jessica introduced Brynna to each and every one. Her fingers were crushed, the back of her hand bearing the imprint of dozens of kisses, her ears growing red from the compliments, sincerely and insincerely given. Most of the mothers saw Brynna as a very real competition; that is, until they'd entered the ballroom and spoken to Alicia, who took great care to reveal to one and all the events at the opera and the duel the next morning.

By the time Brynna entered the ballroom, the buzz of gossip had been repeated and embroidered upon many times so it bore little resemblance to even Alicia's petty version. The orchestra had been playing quietly, but now that Temple had appeared in the doorway, it swung into a spritely melody that set feet to tapping. Temple turned to Jessica and held out his hand.

"I'm fairly faint from standing so long," Jessica cried, pressing a handkerchief to her bosom. "Do take Brynna out for the first dance."

Temple smiled down at his stepmother, his eyes twinkling dangerously. "You were never a good matchmaker,

130

Jessica," he said. She flushed, surprised he'd found her out. Yet he seemed to harbor no anger for her attempts. He turned willingly to Brynna.

"May I have the honor?" he asked.

Brynna sketched a curtsy and was about to take his arm when a slender masculine hand grasped her waist. "I've been waiting to dance with the most beautiful girl here," Cort said, and before either of them could protest, he whisked her away.

No sooner had the dance ended than one of the other young men came to claim her hand. It wasn't until much later that Temple was able to claim his dance.

"Are you having a good time, little *cousine?*" he asked, looking into her laughing eyes. Her color was high, her eyes sparkling, her pretty mouth curved in a smile.

"I never knew a ball could be so exhilarating," she giggled. "I wish I could go on dancing forever."

"You won't feel like that in a few hours," he predicted, "but never mind. The night is young and you've suitors aplenty."

The dance ended much too quickly and supper was announced. Temple escorted Brynna to the dining room. She knew they drew many speculative glances as they walked from the ballroom.

At first she wasn't aware of the things being whispered about her. But Temple was called away and she walked alone to the gallery to catch her breath. She nodded courteously to those she passed and was surprised that her greeting was not returned. Nor had any of the women approached her throughout the evening. At first she'd thought it was because she was so busy dancing, but now they made their disapproval plain. Although she was a guest of the Sinclairs and been accorded every bit of their vast hospitality, to the others, she was naught but an interloper.

"I heard she was a penniless relative from up North," someone whispered in a voice loud enough for her to hear. Brynna paused. "She's nothing more than a poor relative and them trying to pass her off like she's somebody."

"Did you see the way she stood in that receiving line just like she was a Sinclair herself?"

"That gown is the same one she wore to the opera two weeks ago. I'll bet she doesn't have a cent to her name."

"She'd better mind the way she behaves then, gallivatin' around the countryside on the back of a young man's horse."

And so the buzzing went on, fired first by Alicia and then the mamas of marriageable young women who would brook no competition and especially not from a poor, misbehaved northern cousin. The cut was slight; good manners to their hosts declared it should be so. Jessica and Temple never knew that few, if any, had spoken to Brynna. When the music recommenced, the invitations of the young men to dance dwindled to nothing and Brynna was left sitting on the sidelines, her cheeks flushed with mortification, her chin held high.

"Don't pay them any mind, *chérie,*" a pretty young woman said. Her gown was beautiful and cut daringly low. Her dark hair was coiled around her head most becomingly. Brynna judged her to be of about the same age as herself, but the other girl possessed such poise and charm as to seem older.

"I really don't mind," Brynna answered. "I don't know many of them anyway."

"That is your good fortune." The girl made a moue of

132

dislike. "I'm Francine Beynaud. My brother fought Temple in a duel a few weeks ago."

"You're Francine d'Abbadie?" Brynna exclaimed unthinkingly.

"Ah, I see you've heard of me. The scarlet woman," Francine said lightly. "No, no, make no apologies for the things you may have heard." She giggled and leaned close. "They're probably all true."

Brynna laughed despite herself. Francine wasn't at all shamed by the scandal connected to her name. Pleased by Brynna's reaction, Francine looped her arm through Brynna's and walked along the brick-paved gallery. Brynna liked the young Creole woman. She seemed more like a classmate from school than the notorious Francine d'Abbadie Beynaud.

"Did you love Cort very much?" she asked finally, comfortable that she wouldn't offend her new friend.

"Cort? *C'est magnifique!* But I do not love him."

"Oh." Brynna was disconcerted by her answer.

"Perhaps I love him a little bit," Francine said. "He has been a great friend to me."

"But I thought—" Brynna hesitated.

"That we are lovers? No, *chérie!* Ah, you are confused." Francine leaned her head close to Brynna's. "So was my father." She laughed delightedly.

"Let me tell you my story. I have always loved Guy Beynaud. As a little girl I said I will grow up and marry him one day. He always brought me ribbons and presents." She paused, her dark eyes growing serious. "When I grew to womanhood, he no longer brought me gifts or paid me any attention." Her pretty mouth pouted. "I took matters into my own hands and declared my love for him, but he said he was too old, that I should find a handsome young boy for a husband. Imagine! My father agreed.

133

They would not listen to my arguments. They said I was too young to know my own mind." Her smile turned impish.

"So I looked among the handsome young boys. I searched and I searched." She shrugged. "I could not help it if I found no one who pleased me, nor could I stop the gossip. Alas! I was ruined. No one would have me as a wife, except Monsieur Guy Beynaud."

"Oh, Francine. How brave and wonderfully romantic of you."

Francine laughed gaily. "I have a secret I will tell only you." Her dark eyes shone. "I went to my husband a virgin bride."

Brynna blushed at Francine's frank revelation. They had followed the brick path all the way around the house and come again to the front gallery. Beyond the opened doors, couples whirled in a lilting dance.

"Are you sorry that others think so badly of you?" Brynna asked. "Your brother was nearly killed."

"Pierre is such a hothead, looking for a reason to fight a duel. But I have told him the truth. I won't have him use me as an excuse for his temper. As for the rest, I care not what they think. They are stuffy and far too conventional. I shall never inflict such restrictions upon my daughters as they do on our generation of women."

"You aren't bothered by their snubs?"

Francine scoffed. "Guy Beynaud is a wealthy man with much influence here. They don't dare snub his wife." She giggled. "They all came to my wedding, absolutely certain they were about to see a cowed, penitent bride. Their jaws dropped when they saw my white gown." Brynna couldn't help but laugh. The two girls clasped each other's waists and giggled behind their fans.

"I see you've found some amusement this evening,

chérie," a masculine voice said from the shadows. The girls swung around.

"Guy," Francine cried with obvious delight and affection. "Come meet the only sensible woman at this party, other than Jessica, of course." A tall, distinguished man stepped from the shadows. He was quite handsome, with black hair silvered at the temples. His body was lean and fit. No wonder Francine had set her cap for Guy Beynaud.

"Mademoiselle, welcome to Louisiana," he said when Francine had finished the introductions. Taking her hand, he bowed slightly, then turned to his new bride. "Would you like to dance, *chérie?*" His tone was husky and intimate, making Brynna feel she was intruding simply by being there.

"Mais oui, my love," Francine answered softly, and curtsied a farewell to Brynna. Guy Beynaud led his beautiful wife into the ballroom, and for a while the women seated along the walls had something else to whisper about besides Brynna. She couldn't restrain a smile. Somehow their snubs mattered less now. Furthermore, she'd gained an unexpected new friend. She barely noted the whispers about herself.

Cort noticed, though. He heard the talk and saw the snubs and he came to claim her for a dance. "Don't worry about what they think," he admonished, sorry his wayward behavior had helped bring her to this impasse. "I claim the rest of your dances and they can think what they will."

His kindness brought a smile to Brynna's face. She followed him to the floor and laughed gaily as he whirled her into a fancy dance step. For the rest of the evening Cort hovered over her, bringing her glasses of punch, sitting beside her when she was too tired to dance, strolling beside her along the gallery when the room grew too hot. Since he'd never paid such prolonged attention to a young woman before, his attentiveness drew immediate comment from the dowagers so jealously observing.

"Looks as if your cousin has made a conquest," Alicia said to Temple as they watched the couple glide around the dance floor. "I've never seen Cort so enamored of a woman before."

Temple's lips tightened. "I'm pleased she's having a good time," he answered bleakly, then, unable to bear watching any longer or to hear Brynna's peal of laughter at Cort's repartee, he excused himself and joined the other gentlemen on the gallery for a cheroot. The ball he saw had been an unqualified success. The muffled laughter of their guests, the couples strolling through the moonlit gardens, the frolic of the dance, and hum of conversation all pointed to that. Yet, standing in the moonlight, he thought of the bright flame of a girl moving across the dance floor in another man's arms and he felt unaccountably sad.

Chapter Seven

The ball was over. The guests were gone. Brynna stood on the gallery with Temple and Jessica and watched the last carriage roll down the oak-lined drive. A twinge of disappointment settled over Brynna. Somehow the ball had not been all she'd hoped for. She wasn't certain what she'd expected. Certainly, the fact that the ladies and their daughters had chosen to snub her was disheartening, but her dissatisfaction went deeper than that. She glanced at Temple. He seemed to have had a good time. He'd danced nearly the whole evening with Alicia de Jarreau.

"I swear I never saw people stay so late before," Jessica said. "I suspect they were having such a good time, they didn't want to leave."

Temple put an arm around her shoulders. "You were always a gracious hostess, Jessica," he observed. "People were happy to see Langtry entertaining again. It's been long overdue."

Jessica sighed. "I suppose you're right. But I'm so tired right now, the thought of ever having another ball is beyond me. What about you, Brynna?"

As they'd talked, Brynna had sagged onto a hall settee,

feeling like a wilted flower, certain she looked the same. "One ball is enough," she answered and couldn't repress a yawn.

Temple laughed. "You've exhausted yourself by dancing every round with Cort," he said lightly. Brynna studied him from beneath lowered lashes. He seemed in the best of spirits over the idea that Cort and she had spent so much time together.

His expression sobered. "Come, little one. Let's go to bed," he said, and before she knew what he was about, he bent and scooped her up in his arms.

"I can walk," she protested.

"You don't look as if you can," he answered, and led the way up the stairs. "Coming, Jessica, or would you like to wait and I'll come back for you."

She chuckled. "I think as my last official act as a hostess, I'll manage to get to my bed. Good night, Brynna dear . . . Temple." She hummed a little tune under her breath as she followed them up the stairs. She'd worried tonight, watching each of them act charming and dancing with other people. Except for that one dance, they'd seemed not to know the other was alive, but she'd seen something in their faces just now, something they'd tried to hide from themselves as well as each other.

Effortlessly, Temple carried Brynna up the stairs and to her room as if she were a piece of fragile porcelain. Pressed against his chest, she felt his heart pounding and wondered if it were from the exertion or something else.

"Here we are, m'lady," he said lightly, and placed her on her bed with a flourish. She was reminded of the day he came upon her at the river. He'd been lighthearted then, but beneath the playful air, something had stirred between them. She felt it now.

She lay back against the pillows. Her shimmery green skirts flared over the white linen counterpane in a bold contrast that only highlighted her bright beauty. Temple's eyes darkened and he drew away sharply. Desire coursed through him and he longed to tear away the delicate cloth and expose the warm, tender flesh beneath. Visions of what he could do to this dainty female whose beauty tormented him brought a sheen of sweat to his brow. He would plunder that sweet mouth with kisses, loosening her glorious hair and wrap it around them both, and taste the forbidden ambrosia of her breasts. All evening she'd tantalized him, with glimpses of her adoring face turned toward Cort, of a slender body weaving with Cort's in dance, of laughter like a golden cord drawing him close, mocking his jealousy. He saw the wariness in her eyes and his lips tightened in self-control.

She saw the dark emotions warring in his gaze, emotions she could not name, but her body echoed of its own accord. His eyes glinted with dangerous lights and suddenly she was afraid. She suppressed a shiver. She didn't want him in her room. It was too much of an invasion into her peaceful world. He was too large, too masculine, too alien. Too disturbing. She felt violated, defenseless. His dark gaze moved about the room, noting the flutter of lacy petticoats discarded over a chair, a silk stocking draped over the bedpost. Her scent filled the room, her perfumes and soaps lay on the dressing table, a half-written letter on her desk. Discarded slippers lay on the floor, and the beautiful ivory gown spilled across the chaise.

His gaze stopped on the pale silk and came back to her. "Why didn't you wear your new gown?" he asked huskily.

139

"A seam let go." She blurted out the lie.

"Pity," he said, turning away from her and raking his hands through his dark hair. "You looked very beautiful in it when you came down the stairs."

"I—I didn't like it after all," she said, sitting up quickly. "I think I shan't wear it again."

His head came up and he studied her. He saw the slump of her shoulders, the way her elbows clamped close to her sides. "You should never be afraid of your beauty and femininity," he said. "You are very desirable." He saw the stiffening of her body. She looked vulnerable and afraid, and he guessed his presence added to her discomfort. All passion fled from him. "You must be tired," he said. "I'll leave you."

"I *am* rather fatigued," she answered stiffly.

Temple studied her for a moment more, then moved toward the door. "Good night then," he said softly.

Her eyes, wide and startled, met his briefly. "Good night," she murmured and turned her head away.

Quietly Temple closed the door behind him and stood wondering why she displayed this anxiety in his presence. If not for her obvious enjoyment of Cort's attentions, Temple might have thought her afraid of men altogether. He thought of her ease around Cort and, scowling, stalked off to his room.

Within her room, Brynna waited for his footsteps. Her heart pounded as she thought of him standing outside her door. Would he come back? What would he say, what would he do? What would *she* do? She remembered the look on his face as he'd glared down at her. For a moment she'd thought he meant to kiss her, not the chaste cheek-pecking that was done so casually by all, but something more.

"Thet man want yore body." A voice echoed Brynna's

train of thought. She jerked around and looked at Cyra seated on the edge of the bed.

"Where did you come from?" Brynna demanded.

"Ah was on the balcony waitin' fo' you. Ah come to help yo' undress fo' bed on account of yo' so dainty and helpless yo' can't do it fo' yo'self." Cyra answered sassily and sat on the edge of the bed as she used to do when they both were children and had things to share with each other. Brynna knew she should reprimand her, but she was too happy to have the old Cyra here tonight.

"Ah saw the lust in his eyes," Cyra said, her face looking sly.

"You didn't!" Brynna flared. "Temple isn't like that."

"He's a man, ain't he? All men are like thet."

"Temple doesn't think of me that way." Brynna cried, and jumping off the bed, she began to struggle with the buttons on her gown. Cyra made no move to help.

"Temple's jus' like any other man," Cyra answered languidly. He thinks anythin' in petticoats been put here on earth for his personal pleasurin'."

Brynna whirled at the implication of Cyra's words. "Temple takes good care of his slaves. He doesn't . . ." Her words dwindled away.

"The same way he takes good care of the overseer's daughter," Cyra sneered. When Brynna remained silent, she walked to the window and looked out. "Sometimes, late at night, I hear cries from the barns and the sounds of somebody being whipped."

Brynna clutched her gown to her bodice, her eyes wide with denial. Slowly she shook her head. "It's not true," she said softly. "Temple wouldn't mistreat his people."

Cyra's grin was cynical and disbelieving. Brynna longed to slap her. "Get out," she said instead. "I don't need you anymore tonight. Get out."

141

Insolently, Cyra stood before her a moment longer, then she left the room, her laughter floating back to mock Brynna.

The days following the ball were quiet and contemplative. Brynna tried hard not to think about Cyra's hateful accusations against Temple. She avoided Temple as much as possible. He was puzzled by her behavior, but summer had begun in earnest, and with it came a new set of problems and responsibilities.

The days were long and hot; the air so heavy Brynna could scarcely draw a breath. The soil beneath her feet burned right through the soles of her shoes.

Temple had taken to rising before dawn to roust the work gangs. They were set to plowing the rows of sugarcane almost the moment the first ray of light topped the flat horizon. Temple worked them until the sun was at its highest peak, then he dismissed them for a few hours. Desultorily they made their way back to their cabins, where they dozed in the hot afternoon heat. When the sun rays slanted low in the sky, he sent them into the fields again until darkness forced them to halt. The water wagon was in constant use carrying fresh water to the toiling slaves.

Despite herself, Brynna was drawn in admiration for the way Temple worked alongside his men, staying in the saddle for long hours. She had never known a planter to work such long hours. Yet she knew that if he left the supervision of the work in Kyle Hewitt's hands, the slaves would be driven beyond endurance.

Brynna suspected the man drank. More than once, she'd seen the house slaves pull aside from him or divert their gazes when he was present. She recognized their fear and was troubled by it.

Brynna and Jessica had taken to rising earlier than usual to set the house slaves to their tasks. By the time the sun had heated the yard and outer buildings to an unholy pitch, the slaves were allowed to rest. Brynna and Jessica spent the afternoons in the cool inner rooms of the big house. Sometimes they stitched until the threads clung to their sweating fingers, sometimes they just sat and talked. Jessica told her tales of her childhood with Hope at a time when life had been happier and innocent for Brynna's mother. Brynna had never known her mother any way other than as an invalid. It was hard to picture her running and swimming and tending to her favorite pony. Somehow she felt even sadder for the way her mother's life had turned out.

Temple joined them occasionally for a glass of lemonade. Brynna would grow stiff and uncommunicative and finally make her excuses to retire to her room. She knew Jessica and Temple were puzzled by her behavior, but she couldn't explain.

Many times Temple went straight to his room to sleep a little. Brynna knew he was pushing himself far harder than he should. He'd lost weight, and deep creases marked his lean brown cheeks. Brynna realized she had condemned him without hearing his side. What if Cyra were wrong? Temple's actions were not those of a hard, uncaring master. Then she remembered Betty Hewitt and her anger at Temple increased.

Fearful of seeing further evidence of his indiscretions, she never waited for Temple's return as she had once.

Cort came to call with surprising frequency, and although he sat on the porch visiting, he lingered long after Aunt Jessica had gone to bed so he could talk to Brynna.

Riding in late from the fields, Temple would hear their laughter and see their two heads bobbing close together as they shared some bit of conversation. The first time it had happened, he'd stalked to the front gallery to escort Cort to his horse. Cort had ribbed him so badly about being jealous, he'd stayed away after that. With each visit from Cort, Temple became a little more aloof to Brynna. Finally he stopped joining Jessica and her for their afternoon tea.

One afternoon Brynna was late returning from the slave quarters where she'd delivered one of Jessica's remedies for a toothache. The heat had grown so oppressive, it seemed to push her downward into the very soil. She felt shorter, flattened, as if all life had been squeezed from her. Even the sky was leeched of color by the insidious rays. The trees and grass were diminished by dust, and everything seemed as sullen as she felt.

The dust rose from the path and mingled with her sweat, making her itch. She could smell her own body and longed for the coolness of the big house and the tepid bath she'd ordered brought up to the spare bedroom which had been turned into a permanent bathing room. She was resolved to lolling in it for the rest of the afternoon. She'd dispensed with so many petticoats and undercoats that she wore only a light cotton shift under her dress. Puddles of perspiration had stained the cloth, making it cling to her damp skin.

Wearily Brynna pushed away escaping tendrils of hair, rounded the corner of the spring house, and stopped short. If she were able to give a detached thought to this moment, she might have said, that even when she became an old woman she would never forget the sight before her. Sunlight through live oak trees dappled the ground and sparkled in the flowing creek water. Temple Sinclair crouched on the bank, his head thrown back, his wet hair streaming water down his neck and onto his shoulders. His wide-brimmed hat was clutched in one hand and the other draped casually over one knee. She could see the cords of his throat as he swallowed. His white shirt was stained with sweat and dirt from the fields, his pants and boots caked with grime. He seemed transfixed staring at the green oak leaves overhead. He looked exhausted and at the end of his endurance. She wanted to touch him, to soothe his brow with a cool hand, to make the worry lines turn to laughter, to comfort the large, loose-limbed body that had seemed so indefatigable. In all her time here at Langtry, he'd never seemed touched by the human frailties of others; now she saw a man who gave of himself to his land and people. Her heart went out to him.

She must have made a sound, for he turned and caught sight of her. "Cousin Brynna," he called with something of his old teasing. His tired expression eased somewhat as he smiled at her.

"Temple," she said, pausing beside him. She was conscious of her disheveled, unkempt look. She had no way of knowing the admiration and affection he felt for her labors for the plantation. "You look very tired," she said softly. Her glance was sympathetic. The stiffness that had existed between them since the ball was gone for the moment.

"I am," he acknowledged. "The slaves aren't working as well, either."

"It'd help if there were just some rain now and then," Brynna complained, and leaned forward to cup creek water in her hand and let it dribble over her face and neck. It felt heavenly.

Temple glanced at the pale sky beyond the canopy of trees. "I hope rain is all it does . . ." he began, then paused

145

as his gaze swept back to Brynna. She sat with her head thrown back, much as he had done earlier. Her skin was shiny with water. Her bodice had become soaked as well, and now it clung to her young form, outlining her firm breasts and taut nipples. Temple fought the urge to put his mouth against the tantalizing mounds and suckle. She was an innocent girl with no knowledge of a man's lust. He'd have to lead her gently to those acts of passion. He blinked, surprised at his thoughts. He'd been drawn to her from the beginning, had desired her and abstractly wooed her, jealous of Cort's every attention to her, but it was only now that he had clear intentions of what he wanted. He was going to marry this little cousin of his. He smiled, intensely glad they were not related by blood.

"What do you mean?" Brynna prompted when he didn't continue.

"Umm?" Temple was still preoccupied with his thoughts. He stretched his long, booted legs out on the grass and stared into the creek.

"You said you hoped rain was all it did. What more could happen?" Her golden eyes had darkened with worry.

"There might be some hail, or too much rain so we would have some flooding," he said, not voicing his real concern lest he scare her more.

Silently she sat contemplating his words. "Have you ever had tornadoes down here?" she asked finally.

He should have known he couldn't fool her or cosset her. She was too intelligent. "We call them hurricanes," he answered.

"Are they as bad as tornadoes?"

"I expect they are," he answered, relieved to talk freely about his worries. "When one hits, they destroy a sugar-cane crop, uproot trees, blow over outbuildings. If ever

146

you see the sky turn a lemon yellow, head for the big house."

"I'll remember that," Brynna said. "What about you and the slaves. Aren't you in danger of being caught in the fields?"

"We keep a lookout in this kind of weather, so we can have some warning." Aware of her fear, he forced a smile and took hold of her hand. "Don't worry about it too much," he admonished. "You might worry one right down on us."

"I wouldn't want to do that," she answered pertly. Her lips curved in a smile, but her eyes were still dark and brooding.

Temple did his best to repress a yawn. She got to her feet quickly.

"You should rest," she observed. Her gaze took in the sweaty shirt. "I had the servants bring up bathwater for me earlier. You're welcome to use it. It will cool you so you can rest better."

"I wouldn't dream of it," Temple objected. "You're hot, too." But she'd already leapt to her feet and was moving toward the big house. "Brynna," he called, but she didn't look back.

By the time he climbed the stairs, she was out of sight. May stood at the door of the bathing room, fresh linen towels thrown over her arm.

"Miss Brynna say Ah give these t' you', suh," she said shyly. "Yore bath is ready." When he took the towels, she sidled away. Temple glanced into the bathing room. The tub was filled and waiting. Temple peeled off the sweaty shirt. Despite his protestations, he was grateful for Brynna's generosity. With a sigh he slid into the lukewarm water and thought he'd never felt anything so wonderful in his life.

147

At first he just soaked while he daydreamed of a girl, a woman-child with sweet bare breasts and unbound red-gold tresses plaited with wildflowers. When he felt the heat in his groin, he pushed away the image, briskly soaped himself, and rinsed. The water contained a hint of lemon, reminding him again that this bath had been intended for Brynna. He wondered briefly what her skin would taste like and smell like if she'd bathed in it. Desire coursed through him again so that he cursed and stood up. The water sluiced off sleek muscular shoulders and legs. Black hair lay flat against his chest and groin where his rigid member testified all too readily to his recent train of thoughts. His thick black hair clung tightly to his nape until he ruffled it with a towel, intent on drying it.

Brynna was gone long before he'd brought the towel from his face and begun drying his broad chest and flat middle. She hadn't meant to watch him at his bath. After his protests, she'd been sure he hadn't taken advantage of her offer and decided she might as well make use of it after all. She'd arrived just as he stood up, and the sight of him, tall and sleekly, frankly masculine had opened a floodgate of emotions and responses she'd never experienced before. Mouth gaping, she'd stood and watched, until some reason struck her again and she slipped away to her room, where she sat on the edge of her bed, fists clenched in her lap, and tried to dispel the image of Temple Sinclair nude.

She threw herself across her bed and buried her face in her pillow, the hope of a bath forgotten. Finally, even the image of Temple rising from his bath was pushed aside by other images, memories that haunted her and made the golden bubble of her newfound security frighteningly fragile. At last she slept, and in the freedom of slumber, shed the tears she'd held back.

Temple slept like a baby in cool, lemon-scented comfort and dreamed again of a water sprite who rose from her flower-strewn bark to sprinkle droplets of lemon-scented water upon his brow and tempt him with her ivory-and-gold breasts. He awoke with new resolve regarding Brynna. No longer would he retire from the scene when Cort came to call. He intended to make it very clear to one and all that he had designs on Brynna himself. He would leave no doubt in her mind as well, and if she chose to reject him, why, he'd just keep wooing her until he broke down her resistance. The thought was a tiny, dark cloud over his bright dreams. If she chose Cort over him, what would he do? *One thing at a time,* he told himself. Tonight, he would become Brynna's suitor.

But that night Alicia rode over with Cort, and while Brynna, cool and elegant in a simple white-sprigged frock that made her look like a fresh-faced schoolgirl, laughed at Cort's repartee, Alicia chattered brightly in Temple's ear. He could barely contain his annoyance at this turn of events. What in God's name was Cort saying to her that she found so amusing? He knew for a fact that Cort could be witty, but even he soon tired of Cort's incessant quips. Wasn't she intelligent enough to seek more substance? *Of course she was!* he thought angrily. *Maybe not,* he thought deflatedly. Perhaps she liked his sly humor. She laughed often enough.

Round and round his thoughts went, and all the while he sought to answer Alicia's pretty flirtations with the gallantry they deserved. It was hard to do when once again Brynna's laughter pealed out. Alicia made a moue of anger. She'd seen how often Temple's glances strayed to his little chit of a cousin.

"It's such a beautiful night," she sighed. "Why don't we walk down to the river, Temple?" She leaned close, so her breasts brushed against his arm. "Perhaps we can catch a breeze there?"

"Certainly," he said, rising and gallantly escorting her from the gallery. "I'll get a lantern."

"Oh, don't do that," she pleaded prettily. "Let's just walk and savor the moonlight."

Shrugging, Temple took her elbow and led her down the drive toward the river. It was dark beneath the oaks. Their shiny leaves shut out the moonlight.

"My goodness, I hadn't realized how dark it would be," Alicia said coyly. "I might be frightened if I weren't with such a strong, brave man." She clutched his arm tighter and contrived to move closer, so now their hips brushed as they walked. For once he was grateful for the full petticoats women chose to wear.

"How's your father?" he asked to put Alicia's mind on a safer subject. "Are his fields being affected by this drought?"

"I suppose so," she answered dismissively. "I do get so tired of hearing everyone talk about crops and the weather. Seems to me there are topics much more appealing."

"Is your father worried about the weather?" Temple ignored her batting eyelashes and persisted in his chosen topic.

Alicia sighed pointedly. "He keeps mumbling something about a drought and rain," she answered. Suddenly she whirled and threw herself into Temple's arms. "Oh, Temple, let's not talk about it anymore. It's just too depressing. You may kiss me if you wish," she said archly. Before he could answer, she wrapped her arm around his neck and pulled his mouth down to hers. He'd known she was bold. She'd done this before. At first he'd been amused by her blatant interest in him, then cautious. Now he felt her mouth move beneath his and found himself wondering what Brynna's sweet kiss would be like. For a moment, he returned her kiss as fervently as she could have wished, imagining he was kissing Brynna, then he drew away. He had no desire to encourage Alicia's scheming.

"We'd best go back," he said.

"Oh, Temple, must we?" she whispered, moving her breasts against him in a wanton, suggestive manner not unlike Betty Hewitt's.

"It's growing late," he said, taking her hand and starting back to the house. "I rise early these days, for like your father, I'm concerned about the future of my crops."

"This is just too dreary," Alicia answered, lagging so as to slow his steps. In courtesy he was forced to match his pace to hers. She smiled up at him forgivingly. "I swear I would go to New Orleans, but there's been rumors of Yellow Fever again."

Temple's head jerked up. "I hadn't heard that," he observed. "Is it an outbreak?"

"They don't know yet," Alicia answered casually. "If it's only in the Nigra community, it can hardly be considered an outbreak. God knows it's the only way to weed out some of those hovels. They breed like cattle."

Temple's lips were taut with anger by the time they reached the gallery again. "It's been good of you to call tonight, Cort," he said, going directly to his friend. "But I rise before dawn and so must of necessity retire early."

Brynna was quick to echo his words. She'd seen the two figures merge on the path and guessed Temple had kissed Alicia. The other girl's expression was victorious.

Getting to her feet, Brynna smiled at Cort fondly. "I'm afraid Jessica and I have taken to rising early as well so we can finish with our tasks before the heat is too intense."

151

She held out a hand and smiled at Cort to soften her farewell. "Thank you for coming. You are a most generous friend."

Cort's dark eyes glowed with purpose as he bent low over her hand. "It is not my intention to remain merely a friend," he said so all heard him. He placed his lips against the back of her hand for a prolonged kiss. Brynna flushed with embarrassment. Jessica rose and gathered her needlework. Temple scowled.

Only Alicia seemed to find her brother's declaration amusing. Her laughter was indulgent. "It seems my brother grows more enamored each visit," she said lightly. "Perhaps wedding bells are indeed in order before the year is out."

Brynna snatched her hand back. "Good night, Cort," she said somewhat grouchily and turned abruptly toward the door.

"Good night, Brynna," Cort called cheerfully. He cast a mocking glance at his friend. "Temple, *mon ami*," he said, slapping the taller man on the shoulder. "Come, Alicia. We've been politely dismissed." He led his sister to their carriage.

"Good night, Temple darling," Alicia called back. Standing at the door, Brynna heard her endearment and bit her lip. Her expression was nearly as black as Temple's as she made her way to her room.

Preparing for bed, Brynna was preoccupied, so she made little response to May's cheerful prattle. Finally the little maid fell silent, and when her tasks were complete, bade her mistress good night. Brynna settled into bed guiltily. She hadn't meant to be short-tempered with May. The pretty slave girl had served her well ever since Cyra and she had quarreled. Turning out her light, Brynna tried to sleep, but the memory of Temple's tall

152

form bending over Alicia's in a passionate embrace haunted her.

Why should she care? she thought irritably. He was a womanizer, a cad, a man of the lowliest sort. Everything Cyra had said about him must be true. She thought of Betty Hewitt and the way Temple had met her on the path for their little midday dalliance. What of Cyra's insinuations? He wouldn't take advantage of his women slaves in such a fashion. Not all men were such ogres. It was too ugly to contemplate. She fell into a fitful sleep.

The next morning she rose with a headache. The heat was even more oppressive, the very air sullen. Even Jessica, who never seemed to mind the heat, paused often to wipe her brow and draw a breath. Brynna noticed her eyes were feverish, her face drawn.

"Jessica, you aren't getting a fever, are you?" Brynna cried, remembering Alicia's careless words about an outbreak of yellow fever in New Orleans.

Jessica smiled wanly. "No, child, never fear. I'm just hot like everybody else. My, I hope we have a rain soon. It would cool things down considerably. It might help the crops some, too."

"Is Temple worried?" Brynna asked.

Jessica nodded. "All the planters get worried along about now," she said. "They planted their crops last fall and they've nursed them along for nearly a year. They've invested a lot of time and money in them by now. They can't afford losses."

Brynna paused. "I heard Temple talking to Mr. Harcourt the day of the ball. Mr. Harcourt said Temple was a fool to be experimenting with his crops the way he was."

"Mr. Harcourt is not a far-seeing man the way Temple and his father have been," Jessica snapped. Seeing Brynna's concern, she smiled with affection at this girl

153

who had embraced Langtry so fully. "You shouldn't worry," she said. "Temple knows what he's doing."

"I'm sure he does," Brynna hastened to say. "I just thought that if there's anything I can do, I want to do my part."

"There's always danger of one sort or another," Jessica reminded her. "Our plantations thrive or go under on a whim of the weather. It's part and parcel of the sugar business. All planters are a little bit crazy, I guess. The trick is not to lose your nerve. Now enough of this dismal subject. Let's go down to the spring house and get a glass of cold buttermilk."

Obediently, Brynna followed Jessica, but her thoughts returned time and again to their conversation. What would happen to Langtry if the crops failed? Would it be put on the auction block like so many other failed plantations? Brynna couldn't bear to think of that happening to the lovely, serene land.

Through the morning they struggled to ignore the prickly heat and attend to the needs of the plantation, but by noon Jessica was swaying. Brynna dropped the basket of peas she'd been shelling and rushed to put an arm around her.

"Aunt Jessica, I don't know how we let the time slip away from us. It's already past noon. We have to let the slaves rest. They're fair ready to drop, if we don't."

Jessica peered up at her weakly. "I expect you're right, dear," she mumbled. "I'm feeling a bit tired myself."

"Let's go to our rooms. There's bound to be a breeze from the upper gallery and we can have May bring us some cold soup."

"Yes, all right," Jessica said, and allowed herself to be led up the stairs and to her room. Frantically, Brynna called for May. While the slave girl removed Jessica's outer garments and helped her into bed, Brynna poured cool water into the washbowl and bathed Jessica's cheeks and wrists.

"I do feel cooler," Jessica sighed as Brynna pressed a cold cloth to her brow. "I believe I'll sleep for a little while."

"That's a good idea, darling," Brynna whispered. "I'll be in my room if you need me."

"Nonsense, why would I?" Jessica demanded with something of her old crispness.

Feeling easier about Jessica's condition, but still too restless to sleep, Brynna paced the upper gallery. Should she inform Temple that Jessica was sick? she wondered. Through the distant trees, she could see his horse making its way back along the path. She would run down and talk to him, she resolved, making her way to the back stairs. A movement along the path caught her eye. Betty Hewitt was sashaying out to meet Temple. Her yellow hair was gathered in an untidy knot on top of her head, her blouse was opened low over her breasts, and her skirts were limp, signifying she wore no petticoats beneath. Beneath one arm she carried a jar of lemonade. Straddling the rutted path, she waited with obvious purpose for the man on horseback. Without another glance, Brynna turned back to her bedroom. She'd make no attempt to speak to Temple today. If Aunt Jessica worsened, Brynna would send a message by May.

Refusing to allow one thought of Temple and Betty Hewitt together, Brynna took off her clothes and crawled into bed, pulling the mosquito netting securely around her.

Chapter Eight

By late afternoon Jessica was no better. Temple hadn't returned to the house. Brynna assumed he'd spent his midday respite with the overseer's daughter. Briefly she wondered where Kyle Hewitt had been while Betty entertained male callers in their home. Perhaps he didn't mind as long as the caller was Temple Sinclair, or perhaps he hadn't much choice. Temple was his employer and could terminate him if he wished. Perhaps that was why the overseer was so sullen and uncooperative.

Another thought came to her. Perhaps his dalliance with Betty Hewitt was the reason Temple hadn't let the inept overseer go. All afternoon she went over the affairs of the estate, and anything that appeared wrong was laid at Temple's doorstep. When the evidence of his loutish ways seemed insurmountable, she remembered his tired face when he rode in from the fields, the passion with which he discussed Langtry, and the new techniques he hoped to try. She ended by being more confused than ever.

She must put this business from her mind, she told herself, standing at the dry sink to wash her face and neck and straighten her hair. She'd spent too much time worrying over Temple Sinclair's needs so that even now, the memory of him stepping from the bath, his member rigid and ready, brought color to her cheek. Only by sheer will power did she keep herself from speculating further on his prowess as a lover.

Taking herself firmly in hand, she crossed the hall to Jessica's door and knocked. There was no answer within. Thinking Jessica had likely already gone downstairs, she opened the door and stuck her head in just to be sure. What she saw caused her to swing the door wide and hurry to the bedside. Jessica tossed about on the tangled sheets, her hair and gown sweat-soaked and odorous.

"Jessica!" Brynna whispered, then, running to the door, she shouted for May. Quickly, fresh cool water was brought and Jessica's face and neck bathed. Her lips were already cracked and dry from the fever that claimed her.

"Quick, May. Tear the gown away from her and bathe her arms and legs. We have to get her fever down." The two women worked frantically. When the water had grown too warm, Brynna carried the basin to the top of the stairs and called for Euphemie and Floria. The house slaves sensed their mistress was badly ill. Quietly, they climbed the stairs hauling fresh water, bringing lemonade which Brynna tried to coax Jessica to drink.

"I don't know what to do," Brynna said, wringing her hands. "Floria, go down and tell Lala to send for Temple. Be quick."

"Yas'm," the girl said, and scooted off on her errand. Brynna turned back to the bed where Jessica lay gasping for air. It would be some time before Temple would be found, and in the meantime she must do something for her aunt. May's eyes stared at her trustingly, certain Brynna would know what to do.

"May," Brynna called. "Go down to the sewing shed and get Aunt Clemmie. Tell her Miss Jessica has a fever. Tell her to come quick."

"Yas, ma'am," May said, and scooted out, her brown legs churning in her haste. Frantically, Brynna rewet the cloth for Jessica's brow and wracked her brain for some remedy for fever which her aunt might have mentioned.

"Euphemie, run down to the kitchen and tell Lala to give you some vinegar. Hurry." Euphemie bustled away. She was back in no time.

"Lala say the vinegar's locked away in the storehouse," she reported. "Miz Jessica's got the key." Euphemie's eyes rolled in distress as she considered her mistress's helpless condition.

"Stay with her and keep applying the wet cloths," Brynna ordered, and hurried to the small desk where Jessica kept the plantation keys. Taking up the ring, she hurried downstairs and through the back hall. The air was so heavy she could scarcely breathe. Her anxiety only made it worse. She raced to the back gallery and into the yard and came to an abrupt halt. Though only midafternoon, there was little light. Ominous black clouds set on the horizon in the southeast, the hapless earth shielded at last from the sun's burning rays. But a more deadly menace threatened them all. No leaf quivered in the stillness. On the path, a slave cast a fearful glance at the sky and ran toward the barns.

After a quick glance around, Brynna ran to the storage shed where the vinegar was kept stored in large crocks. A growl of thunder sounded in the distance as she fumbled with the locks. At last it was opened and she hurried inside the pungent, dark interior. She was barely able to make out the shape of barrels and crocks. Snatching up a dipper, she scooped vinegar into a tin bowl, then hurried from the shed, not taking time to lock up. Back in Jessica's room, she dipped the cloth in the clear vinegar and bathed her aunt's face.

"Jessica, you can't die. You just can't," she whispered, remembering the futile struggle to help her mother before her death. "I won't let you die. Do you hear me?" Frantically, she worked, bathing over and again the woman's arms and brow. Jessica roused in her sleep and mumbled a protest.

"Jessica Sinclair, don't you die, do you hear me?" Brynna sobbed. She was unaware of the sweat that formed on her brow or the bodice of her gown. She concentrated solely on the gentle woman who'd been her friend and teacher for the past months. She had no idea of time passing. Aunt Clemmie came waddling up the back stairs, out of breath and awed by the richness of the big house until she saw her beloved Miz Jessica on the bed.

"Lawd, have mercy," she cried. "It's the end of the world. God's comin' t take his angels back with him and then he's goin' t' sow death and destruction on the rest of us."

"Not now, Aunt Clemmie," Brynna cried. "What can we do for her?"

"We can't do nothin', Miss Brynna. The Lawd goin' t' take this here saint as surely as we standin' heah."

"Well, I won't let him have her," Brynna cried, trying to shake the massive old woman's shoulders. "You have to help me. I've bathed her with vinegar water, but I don't know what else to do. We have to try something."

"Ah'll steep her some red pepper tea," Clemmie declared. "Mebbe dat'll help, Ah dun' know. Mebbe some powder of rhubarb, maybe some camomile tea."

"May, run tell Lala to brew some camomile tea."

159

The girl was back in no time with a pot of the brew and an amulet of clay and rooster feathers. Gingerly May held it before her, her nose crinkling in distaste. "Lala say hang this on Miz Jessica's bedpost. It'll help chase away the devils."

Brynna barely glanced up. "We need all the help we can get," she said absently. Carefully she spoon-fed the tea down Jessica's throat and rewet the vinegar rags on her brow. Helplessly, she looked at the feverish woman, uncertain what else to do. A rumble of thunder reminded her of the building storm. Hurrying to the gallery, she looked out at a world that had lost all its color. The trees and fields of sugarcane stood like black silhouettes against a gray sky. A wind had come up now, blowing leaves from the palm trees and rattling the gnarled old branches of the oaks. Brynna's skirts whipped around her as she contemplated the sky. Where was Temple? she wondered frantically. She'd never felt so isolated before, as if she'd been set down on a deserted island with only the scared servants, the feverish woman inside, and the approaching storm. She looked toward the path leading to the fields and saw Floria sprinting for the big house. Cyra was right behind her. Perhaps they'd found Temple and he was on his way home, she thought, and hurried to meet them.

"Ah couldn't find him," Floria half sobbed. "Ah tried, Miss Brynna, but the storm started comin' and Ah got afraid."

"It's all right, Floria." Brynna soothed the shaking girl. "He must be on his way here." She looked around at the circle of frightened faces. "Let's get things closed up before the storm reaches us. May, you and Euphemie make sure all the doors are securely latched. Lala, put out the fires in the kitchen. There's no sense on taking a chance. We'll eat a cold supper. Floria, get Tadeo and

160

Oby to help you bring in the furniture from the gallery. Store it in the downstairs hall. Aunt Clemmie and Cyra, stay with Aunt Jessica in case she needs help."

The door behind them opened and was flung back against the wall by the rising wind. Brynna whirled, certain Temple had returned. Betty Hewitt stood in the doorway, her eyes wide with fright, her hands nervously twisting her skirts.

"My daddy hasn't come back home yet. Ah wondered if he was here with Temple." Brynna noted her easy familiarity with Temple's name.

"No one is here except Aunt Jessica and myself," she stated coolly.

Betty lingered, casting a quick glance over her shoulder at the whining wind. "Ah hate storms," she said vehemently. "They're sometimes so mean, you can't tell which way they're comin' and goin'. You just know you'd bettah get out of the way."

Seeing her nervousness, Brynna relented. "You're welcome to stay with us till it's over," she offered.

"Thank you kindly," Betty said brightly. "Ah believe Ah will stay here and talk to y'all a spell. It gets kind of lonesome down yonder all by myself."

"Yes, I expect it does," Brynna said, not unkindly. Betty Hewitt was a pretty young girl who liked attention. Although she went into New Orleans nearly every weekend, Brynna guessed living out here must be boring for her. Perhaps she should have made more of an effort to be friends with her.

"Come and help us fasten things down," she said, trying to include the other girl.

Betty made a moue of dislike. "I'm not one of the slaves on this plantation," she said haughtily. "I don't work

161

beside them." Disdainfully, she pulled her shawl and her offended pride about herself.

Brynna stared at her in anger, sorry now she'd invited the girl to stay no matter what the weather outside. "Since you feel that way," she said evenly, "you may wait in the parlor."

Regally, Betty turned to the parlor and seated herself on a fine sofa before the fireplace. With a proprietory air she glanced around the elegant room, then, posing herself with affected stiffness, she called sweetly to May.

"Bring me a pot of tea at once."

May glanced at Brynna, and without acknowledging the woman's order, continued with her chores. Betty's face reddened an ugly shade.

"Why that uppity niggah," she cried. "I shall see to it that she's whipped for her bad manners."

All sympathy and resolve to befriend the overseer's daughter had dissolved almost immediately. Brynna whirled on their unwanted intruder.

"We do not whip our people at Langtry, Betty. Surely, you're aware of that yourself."

"Ah gave her an ordah!" Betty sputtered. "It's not good for the slaves to be allowed to disobey."

"You're right, of course," Brynna replied firmly. "However, they are attending to my orders right now. If you desire anything from the kitchen, you'll have to walk down there yourself and get it." Without waiting for an answer, Brynna whirled and left the girl sitting alone in the parlor.

When she'd seen that all was secured below, she climbed the stairs to Jessica's room. "How is she, Aunt Clemmie?" she asked, placing a cool hand against Jessica's brow. Cyra sat huddled in a corner.

162

"She's some quieter," Aunt Clemmie muttered, "but Ah dun' like thet fever."

"She feels a little cooler," Brynna said, and paced worriedly to the window. The black clouds were approaching with a morbidly slow speed. "How long will it take the storm to reach us?" she asked.

Aunt Clemmie left off the humming under her breath. "Sometimes, they takes an eternity," she said. "They's mighty slow gettin' here. Seems like the waitin's the worse thin', until the storm hits an' yo' learn diff'rent."

"I'm worried about Mister Temple." Brynna voiced a fear that had been nagging at her.

"Lawd, don't worry 'bout him, child. He done lived through too many of these heah storms. He knows what to do to protect hisself an' his men. Won't nobody git hurt, not if Mistah Temple kin help it."

Only partially reassured, Brynna took a deep breath and turned away from the window. There was nothing to do now but wait, wait out Jessica's fever, wait for Temple's return, and wait out the storm. Aunt Clemmie was right. The waiting was the worst. Wearily, Brynna sank into a chair by Jessica's bed. The wind had increased outside the window. Its howl was that of some wounded demon come to wreak vengeance on puny mankind. Aunt Clemmie prayed and sang humns. May and the other house servants crept into Jessica's room and took up vigilance around the room. The long hours dragged into evening.

"Is anybody up here?" a voice called, making them all sit up in anticipation, but the cry came again, and everyone sank back in their places. Betty Hewitt came to the door of Jessica's room.

"Where is everybody?" she called.

"Shh. Jessica is very ill," Brynna warned, feeling guilty

again because she'd forgotten all about their infuriating guest.

"What's wrong with her?" Betty asked, coming into the room.

"She has a fever," Brynna answered from between clenched teeth.

"A fever!" yelped Betty, jumping back. Her eyes grew wide and scared again. "Yellow fever?" she asked loudly.

Nervously the black women looked at one another. Secretly they'd been afraid of that very thing. Hearing the white girl say it out loud, somehow made it more menacing.

"I don't believe it's yellow fever," Brynna said quickly, and crossed to the bed to show the other servants how unconcerned she was for her own safety.

"What if it is?" Betty insisted. "We got to do something. We can't just sit here in a bedroom with a dying woman."

"Jessica is not dying," Brynna flared, her eyes dark with fatigue and her own unspoken fears. Her nerves were raw with worry. Deliberately, she lowered her voice. "Jessica is getting better," she said calmly, but her hands smoothed her skirts in an agitated motion that was not missed by Betty or the house slaves. Taking a deep, steadying breath, Brynna pushed back tendrils of hair.

"I think we'd best think about a little supper while we still can," she said. She couldn't eat a bite herself, but she had to get the minds of everyone on something else besides Jessica's mysterious illness and the coming storm. "Aunt Clemmie, feed Jessica some more of that camomile tea. Euphemie, you help her. Dampen the cloth on her forehead." She glanced around the huddle of people who seemed to look to her for guidance. If they only knew how helpless she felt.

164

"May, you and Floria and Cyra come with me. Betty, you come, too. We'll need to get drinking water and food and candles." She paused, thinking. "Let's see, what else will we need?" No one offered suggestions. They depended on her. "Let's go down," she said, and led the way through the hall and down the stairs. The great halls and elegant parlors were eerily silent and barren. A single lamp burned in the parlor where Betty had sat. Brynna made a mental note to put it out on her way back. Now they used it to guide them down the hall to the back entrance.

"Where y'all goin'?" Betty Hewitt asked, hanging back.

"We have to go to the kitchen," Brynna said, looking at the girl in surprise.

"Ah ain't goin' out there again," Betty whined.

The wind screamed outside the door and Betty drew back even further. Brynna could hardly blame her. The sound was disheartening, especially now that darkness had fallen. But they had to go outdoors and along the covered passageway to get to the kitchen and spring house. If they tarried here too long concerning themselves with Betty's fears, the other women might become too frightened to go as well.

"Stay here and hold the door for us," Brynna said, and stepped out on the gallery. She wasn't prepared for the force of the wind. It toppled her back against the wall. Quickly, she struggled aright and turned to the other women.

"Brace yourselves!" she called, and without looking back to see if they followed, she started down the roofed passageway. Once they were away from the house, the wind tore at their clothes and hair. Its claws were fierce and stinging. The thought came that they shouldn't have

165

left the house. The storm was too far along. Yet she'd had to do something to still the fears of the servants.

Head down, Brynna strained against its pull and finally reached the kitchen. She was grateful for the solid strength of its brick walls. A brush of an arm told her May was at her side. Gratefully, she turned to smile at the girl. Behind her Floria huddled against the building. There was no sign of Cyra. Brynna turned back to the kitchen and grasped the door handle. The door flew inward with a burst of sound that brought screams of terror from the dark shadows.

"It's me, Miss Brynna!" she called. A lighted candle sat in the center of the oak table. Brynna moved forward so the light fell on her. May and Floria lent their weight to the closing of the door against the pitiless wind. Lala's assistant, Maisie, came out of the shadows. Behind her stood Benjamin, the young boy often sent to run errands for the household.

"Are you all right?" Brynna asked. Silently they nodded, but their faces reflected their fright.

"Help us gather some food and water and candles," Brynna ordered, "then we can all go back up to the big house."

"Us, too, Miss Brynna?" Maisie asked anxiously.

"Both of you." Brynna nodded. Silently, they all moved around Lala's kitchen gathering the necessary things to make it through the night. A black kettle of gumbo sat on the cold hearth. The thick iron pot had held its heat.

"We'll take this," Brynna said, thinking she would try to spoon a little of the warm stew for Jessica. "Bring some bread." She nodded at the fresh loaves in the warming chamber at the side of the brick fireplace. May and Floria had already gathered water and cups. They placed bowls and spoons in a basket along with the bread and a knife and candles.

"Let's go," Brynna said, taking up the warm kettle of gumbo. They hesitated by the door as if preparing themselves, then stepped out into the buffeting wind. Brynna turned to make sure the door was secure, and in that moment a memory came to her of another door she'd left unlatched. The storage shed! Even as she remembered, the slapping sound of wood against wood came to her.

"Maisie!" Brynna called, holding out the kettle. "Take this to the big house."

"What yo' goin' t' do, Miss Brynna?" Maisie asked.

"I've got to go close the door on the storage shed."

"No, Miss Brynna," May cried. "Yo' be hurt in this wind."

"I have to, May. I left it open this afternoon. The supplies will be spoiled if it rains."

"No-o, Miss Brynna," May screamed after her, but Brynna didn't pause to argue any further. This must be done. Some instinct told her once this was over they would need whatever food the storage shed held. She ran over the grassy lawn, cursing herself for her impatience this afternoon. She'd been so worried about Jessie. In the dark her foot fell on an uneven section of ground. With a cry she sprawled forward, giving her ankle a mighty wrench.

She lay gasping for air; the wind snatched her very breath away. She was sure the ground heaved beneath her, then chided herself for such fancifulness. It was only the motion of the wind. It beat at her head and tossed her long strands of hair over her eyes, so she became disoriented.

Pushing her hair back and holding it with both hands, Brynna raised her head and squinted her eyes trying to make out the direction of the storage shed and the big house. From this angle the buildings appeared distorted and elongated. She longed to simply bury her head in her arm and lie here.

"Miss Brynna," May called from behind her, and wearily she got to her feet. Standing aright, she was forced to bend against the wind as she staggered toward the shed. The door slapped back and forth. Grateful to have reached it at last, she rested a moment, then grabbed the door handle and fought with the wind. At last her numb hands replaced the hatch. Quickly, she dug the keys out of her pocket where they'd lain bumping against her thigh. When the door was securely locked, she sprinted toward the house. So intent was she on reaching its safety, she didn't pay attention to the crack of wood until it was too late. She heard May scream and looked around. A pecan tree wavered against the black sky, then pitched downward toward her.

Brynna screamed and felt the jar of limbs bearing her down. *I'm going to die,* she thought. She hit the ground with a stunning force and felt herself pinned there by sharp, cutting weights. For a moment she lay stunned, then heard May screaming for her. The black girl raced across the yard.

"Miss Brynna!" she screamed, circling the tree.

"I'm here, May," Brynna cried. "Help me!" She caught hold of the grass, pulling up great handsful as she tried to crawl from beneath the frightening weight. Suddenly, she felt a warm hand grasp hers.

"Ah got yo', Miss Brynna. Ah got yo'," May cried triumphantly. "Pull. Pull real hard."

Brynna tugged with all her might against May's outstretched hand. The slave girl had lain flat on the ground to reach Brynna. Brynna worked herself forward inch by inch. The branches clutched at her skirts, trying to pull her back. Above, the winds shrieked in mockery at their puny efforts.

"Come on, Miss Brynna. Yo's comin'," May encouraged her. With one mighty tug she was free. With her skirts half torn from her, she crawled forward and away from the tree.

"Are yo' all right, Miss Brynna? Can you stand?" May asked anxiously, crouching beside her.

"I don't know," Brynna swallowed back her sobs and pushed her tangled hair away from her face. "Help me stand."

Tentatively and with May's help, she got to her feet. Except for the soreness of her wrenched ankle and a million stinging scratches from the gnarled limbs, she seemed whole. She'd been pinned only by the top of the tree. She shuddered to think what would have happened if the tree trunk had landed on her. With May helping her, she limped back to the house. Cyra and Betty stood in the doorway, staring out at them with wide, uncertain eyes. Bitterly, Brynna noted they'd made no effort to come out and help her. Only May had risked her own safety for Brynna's. Cyra had the grace to look shamefaced when she met Brynna's gaze. Once they reached the great hall, Cyra lent her shoulder on one side and together she and May got Brynna back up the stairs.

"Betty," Brynna gasped. "Turn out the lamp in the parlor. If the wind blows it over, it could start a fire." Obediently the white girl ran to do as bid. There were no pretentious airs about her now. She was genuinely frightened. May and Cyra helped Brynna to the chaise longue in Jessica's room.

"Is she any better?" Brynna asked. Aunt Clemmie was trying to coax a little tepid tea down the feverish woman.

169

"Her fever's broke," she said, "but she ain't woke up. Ah's mighty worried over her." The big woman's shoulders shook.

May brought water and towels and knelt to tend Brynna's scratches. Her skirts had protected her somewhat, but some of the wounds were deep and bleeding heavily. May bathed and bandaged them. When she was finished, Brynna went to relieve Aunt Clemmie. May and Floria passed out bowls of gumbo and Lala's bread. The servants ate. Betty Hewitt turned up her nose at such simple fare, but when no one paid her any mind, she gulped it down quickly enough.

Brynna was too preoccupied to eat. She sat beside Jessica's bed, gripping the thin, wrinkled hand. Where was Temple? she wondered for the hundredth time. But at least Aunt Jessica looked a little better. The fever had lessened and she lay against her pillows, looking pale and incredibly fragile. She should have seen Jessica was ailing, Brynna thought dismally. She should have known the heat was too much for her, that she was working too hard, that she'd been too quiet of late. She should have noticed, but she'd been too busy concerning herself with Temple Sinclair and his *affaires d'coeur*. Her self-blame and disgust were complete.

Having eaten, the servants seemed less fearful, although the wind outside the shuttered French doors had increased. They sprawled on the floor around the room and talked quietly. Aunt Clemmie had started singing her hymns again. Her soft, rich voice soothed them all. Now and then some debris was flung against the shutters with a crack not unlike a pistol shot, causing them all to gasp and look around expectantly. With a loud crash one of the shutters was torn free, and now leaves and branches were flung against the windowpanes, threatening to break the

170

glass. With the shutters gone, the storm became more real to those within the room. The wind roared and the first drops of rain were driven beneath the gallery roof and against the doorpanes. Everyone in the room sensed the storm was building to a fury now. Their long wait was over, but would they survive what came next?

A blast of wind blew a tree branch against the railing of the upper gallery. It hung there tapping insidiously. Even Aunt Clemmie stopped singing to stare at it. They were so intent on the raging storm outside, they didn't hear the footsteps on the stairs. Brynna didn't know Temple was there until she heard Betty Hewitt's cry. The overseer's daughter flew across the room and threw herself against Temple. Automatically his arm settled at her waist. Her hands clung to him and she wept copiously. One hand gripped her shoulder, but his gaze had gone around the room until it settled on Brynna.

"Are you all right?" he demanded.

Brynna nodded.

Temple looked around the room once more. "Where's Jessica?" he asked.

"She was taken by a fever at midday. She's been unconscious ever since." Brynna moved aside so he could see Jessica lying in her bed. Impatiently he set Betty aside and strode to the bed.

"Her fever's down now, but she hasn't awakened." She paused, fighting back tears now that Temple was here and she didn't have to put on a brave front anymore. Her hands twisted anxiously. Temple put an arm around her, and she leaned against him for a moment, drawing strength from him; then she straightened, her young back stiff, her shoulders thrown back. For the first time, Temple saw the condition of her tattered clothes and bloodstained petticoats.

171

"You're hurt," he said, his voice filled with dismay.

Brynna shook her head. "Don't worry about me. Jessica's the one. We didn't know what to do. We've bathed her with vinegar water and given her camomile tea and some herbs that only Aunt Clemmie knows about. Then we've just waited. I sent for you, but . . ." She halted her flow of words, knowing she was babbling.

"We were in the far fields, trying to save the crops as best we could," he said, and slumped on the side of the bed. She saw that lines of weariness marked his face and his wet shirt was dirty and torn in places. Her heart went out to him as she thought of him braving the storm for as long as he dared in an effort to save some of his crops.

"Then I had to see the slaves were taken back to safety," he continued. His voice was gravelly with fatigue. "I thought Jessica could take care of things here. She's been through these hurricanes before. I didn't know you were alone." He regarded her gravely.

"Other than Jessica, we made out fine," she hastened to reassure him. As if to make mockery of her brave words, the wind tore the limb loose from the railing and sent it crashing through the window. The remaining shutter ripped away and went careening away into the darkness. Both doors were flung open. The wind blew the curtains straight back, like streamers. The servants screamed.

"Get into the hallway, up against the wall," Temple ordered, jumping to his feet and striding to the window. Closing the French doors, he upended Jessica's chaise longue and wedged it against the fragile portals. The tinkle of glass panes being blown from their casing filled the air.

"Brynna," he shouted, racing back to the bed. "Get into the hallway."

172

"Aunt Jessica," she cried.

"I've got her." Temple swooped Jessica's slight form up in his arms and carried her to the upper hall. Brynna hobbled along behind. Gently he placed his stepmother on the carpet and lowered himself beside her. Brynna knelt to tuck a coverlet around her aunt. Jessica was moaning, but her eyes remained closed.

"Do you think she's in pain?" Brynna whispered tearfully.

"I don't know," he answered, and she knew he felt as helpless as she did. Once again the wind tore at the graceful mansion as if angered that it stood in the face of so much fury. Shutters and a portion of the railing were ripped away. A small window at the end of the hall was blown out, but they were safe where they were. Temple gathered Brynna close, shielding her and Jessica with his own body.

The sound of sobbing rose above the shriek of the wind. The very rafters seemed to shake from the onslaught. Prayers were cried out and lost in the pitch of the wind and the roar of hailstones on the gallery floor.

Then it was gone. The storm's energy was spent. The hail stopped as abruptly as it had begun. Silence hung over them, so loud they could not hear it. Slowly, the servant women ceased their weeping and raised their heads. Brynna looked at Temple.

"Is it over?" she whispered disbelievingly. He nodded and released her. Getting to his feet, he crossed to the broken window and peered out. To the south, sullen clouds still tainted the sky, but in the west a sunset was streaking the horizon. "Brynna, come quickly and look," he called. He was grinning boyishly. Brynna crossed to the window and looked at the glistening pebbles of ice that

173

covered the gallery and lawn. In the waning sunlight, they reflected with a brilliance of diamonds.

"It's looks like a fairy tale," she whispered.

"Diamonds for mademoiselle," he said, and reached up to smooth a strand of tangled hair.

"I must look terrible . . ." she began self-consciously.

"You've never looked more beautiful," he answered. His dark gaze captured hers and they stood thus, silhouetted in the broken window by the glow of sunset. "Thank you for all you did during the storm."

"It was nothing!"

"You took care of Jessica and Langtry. You're very courageous." His gaze was warm on her face.

Embarrassed, she turned away. "Hadn't we better see to Jessica?" she asked, the worry with her again now that the storm was past. Temple gathered up Jessica's slight form and carried her back to her room. As he placed her on the bed she opened her eyes and looked around.

"Temple? Brynna? What are you doing in my room? My, I've slept the afternoon away. I've got to get up." She took hold of the covers as if to throw them aside and get out of bed. Temple pushed her back against the pillows.

"You'll do nothing of the sort," he said firmly. "You've been ill, Jessica. You're staying there." Bewildered, she looked from one to the other and at the servants who'd crept from the hall into her room.

"Clemmie?" Jessica said wonderingly. "What're you doing up at the big house? Is someone sick?"

"Yas'm, Miz Jessica," Aunt Clemmie said with tears raining down her brown cheeks. "Yas'm, someone was shorely sick."

"Oh, Jessica," Brynna cried, taking her hand. "We were so afraid you were going to die."

174

"Nonsense!" Jessica said crisply. "Who broke that window and put my chaise up like that?"

Brynna looked at the window and back at Temple. The lights in her eyes danced mischievously. "Temple did it, Aunt Jessica," she said primly, and said no more. Temple's laughter rang out as Jessica scowled at him.

"I can see we have a passel of explaining to do with you, Jessie," he said, and sat down on the bed beside her. Brynna watched the two of them together, saw the love and tenderness between stepmother and stepson, and she felt like giggling and crying at the same time. The long hours had been fraught with too-intense emotions. She felt happy tears burn the back of her lids, and not wanting to come between Temple and Jessica's reunion, she slipped from the bedside.

"Brynna, where are you going?" Temple asked before she could steal out of the room.

"I'm going to my room. I need some privacy," she answered brightly. "I'll come back." She hurried away before he delayed her further. Once she'd reached the sanctity of her room, she gave way to her sobbing laughter. Her hands trembled as she pressed them to her mouth.

"Thank you, God," she whispered, "for making Aunt Jessica better and thank you for keeping Temple safe."

She forgot to pray about Langtry.

Chapter Nine

Brynna woke with a start. She'd been having a dream of walking through the rooms of Langtry with the wind shrieking through broken windows. There had been a sense of dread, as if some great unknown tragedy was yet to come.

But when she opened her eyes the sunshine lay in gay streamers across her bed. The humidity that had plagued them for days was gone. Brynna leapt out of bed and ran to throw open the French doors. Stepping out on the gallery, she looked around at the devastation the storm had wrought. Trees and bushes lay twisted and broken. Debris lay everywhere on the green lawn. A line of field hands had been put to work clearing the lawn of fallen limbs and branches. The great alley of oaks stood like sentinels, their graceful branches untouched by the fierce gale, but the gardens were badly damaged. Slaves moved among the rows pruning and tending the bruised plants. Brynna was surprised Jessica wasn't among them. Jessica! She'd forgotten about the fever.

She flew indoors and dressed quickly, struggling to fasten buttons and snaps and brush her tangled hair into some semblance of order. She'd gone to bed last night without tending to it. When the curls were free of snarls, she caught them back with a ribbon so they fell loosely down her back. Without taking time for more than a splash of water on her face, she hurried to Jessica's room. What if the fever had come back during the night and no one had known she needed doctoring, Brynna thought guiltily.

Her guilt was put to rest when she heard Jessica's tired laughter. It echoed even in the hall, mingling with masculine chuckles. Brynna hesitated, reluctant to intrude on Temple and Jessica.

"So tell me," Jessica demanded in a more serious tone, "how bad are the crops? Are we about to lose Langtry?"

Lose Langtry! Brynna's head spun. The hurricane had ruined all of the crops. Brynna knew what disaster such a storm could bring about. Most plantations were heavily mortgaged, the money going into the next year's crop. Temple had gambled heavier than most on his new techniques and now those crops were gone. But to lose Langtry! They couldn't!

Tears coursed down her cheeks as she stepped into Jessica's bedroom. Jessica's smile died as she caught a glimpse of Brynna's face.

"Why, child, what's the matter with you?" she demanded gently.

Temple looked up, his bright smile dying away as he saw Brynna's distress. She couldn't look at him, couldn't bear to see his brave front.

"I couldn't help overhearing what you said . . ." she began.

"What?" Jessica said, then smiled as she realized what Brynna had heard. "But, child, we—"

"Oh, you don't need to hide the truth from me and

pretend everything is all right," Brynna rushed on. Gently, Temple touched Jessica's arm and warned her to silence. "I know the crops are ruined and you're in danger of losing Langtry. That just can't happen, it can't!"

"What would you suggest we do?" Temple asked somberly.

Eagerly Brynna moved forward and gripped the mahogany bedpost. "I have the money from the sale of Beaumont Hall. I will give it to you and gladly."

"But child, we—" Temple's touch on her arm silenced the old woman. Puzzled, she glanced at him and back at her niece.

"That's very generous of you, little cousin," Temple said, rising and pacing about the room. He'd bathed and changed his clothes since last night. Dark trousers were shoved into well-polished boots. His vest was fine cloth and his stock starchy white. A matching coat lay over the foot of the bed.

"Were you planning to go to New Orleans today?" Brynna asked. "If you are, I'll go with you and transfer my funds to your account."

Slowly, Temple shook his head. "I can't take your money, Brynna," he said, "but I thank you for the generosity of spirit and the love you bear Langtry to make this offer."

"But you must use it. I insist!"

"Impossible," Temple said, and repressed a chuckle.

"Why?" Brynna stood before him, her eyes wide and direct, her chest rising and falling slightly in her excitement. "I should like to think I had a small part in helping Langtry."

"That money is for your dowry, cousin," Temple teased her. "If you give it away, I may be stuck with an old maid on my hands or I might even have to marry you myself."

The words were said in jest, but both of them were caught unawares. For one startled moment they stared into each other's eyes. Then she wheeled away.

"You don't have to do that," she said stiffly. "The offer was made without conditions." The air around her seemed to barely move, she held herself so rigidly. Temple studied her profile. The gold-tipped lashes curled against ivory skin, the soft lips were pressed together firmly without the coyness of a pout. The simple dress she'd donned so hurriedly hugged her sweet curves. A heavy tendril of chestnut hair coiled over one shoulder. He stood beside her, seeing her fiery beauty, and the words were blurted out before he had thought them, rising from some yearning place in his soul.

"It is the only way I will take your money," he said huskily. Jessica's head came up. She'd known before that he was teasing; now she heard the serious intent and drew a breath. *Not like this, Temple,* she wanted to cry. *There's a better way to win her.*

Brynna glanced at him and moved away. "I do not require that of you, cousin," she answered softly. "I give you the money and happily."

"Would you deny me my sense of honor?" Temple demanded. "A few short months ago I rode off to Tennessee to handle your affairs and now you expect me to take your money and give nothing in return."

"I require nothing," she repeated, trembling slightly. "I want to do this for Langtry, for Aunt Jessica and—and for you. You've all been very kind to me, providing me with a home."

"Wouldn't you want to make your home at Langtry

permanently?" he asked, watching her face for the swiftly changing emotions it revealed.

For the first time she met his gaze. "If you marry me, you will be mistress of Langtry," he continued.

"I'd never have to leave!" she said wonderingly.

"Never. You'd be my wife and bear my children, the future heirs of Langtry."

Her dreamy smile faded. She blushed and looked away from him. "I cannot!" she said reluctantly. " 'Twould be unfair of me to take advantage of you at this time. Take the money, I beg of you." She tried to flee, but he was there blocking her way, one strong hand gripping her shoulder so she was forced to look at him.

"We both love Langtry," he said softly. "I want to share it with you. I'll have the money no other way. Will you marry me, Brynna?" She looked away then, her gaze going to the window and the green lands of Langtry beyond. To be a part of this black soil, to know on waking every morning and sleeping every night that she belonged here and would never have to leave was a dream come true. She closed her eyes so she would see the sweeping lawn and trees and fields. She closed her eyes against the temptation, and stood shuddering in his grasp.

"Will you marry me?" he repeated.

"Temple, leave the child alone," Jessica called. "This is not the way . . ."

"Will you marry me, Brynna?" He shook her slightly.

"Yes," she whispered without looking at him. "Yes, I will marry you."

His hands fell away from her. His dark gaze held her. "In three days," he said gently. "Jessica will be well. We'll be married in the parlor."

"I need more time," Brynna protested. "I have no bridal dress."

"Wear the ivory gown," Temple suggested huskily. "You were very beautiful in it."

Brynna raised her trembling hands to clamp them over her lips, and at last she met his gaze. His eyes glinted with dark lights that struck to the very heart of her.

"Don't look so tragic," he said gently. "This is supposed to be a happy occasion."

"I—I am h-happy," she hiccuped, her eyes filling with tears. She lowered her hands and he saw she was smiling broadly behind the tears. His heart soared with a special joy too quickly daunted by her next words.

"I shall never have to leave Langtry." She turned joyously toward Jessica. "Oh, Jessica, I'm so happy," she cried elatedly and sped across the room to throw herself into Jessica's arms.

Temple stood watching her and felt disappointment build. He'd longed for her to come to him like that, but she'd turned to Jessica. Her happiness seemed centered on Langtry rather than him. He would change that.

With her head close to Jessica's, Brynna didn't look up as Temple left the room. Only later when she heard the clatter of hooves against the drive did she go to the gallery and watch his departing figure.

Why had he insisted on marriage? she wondered. She'd offered the money without conditions; still he'd insisted. Perhaps it was a matter of pride for him. Once she married him, her dowry would go to him automatically. Was he so in need of money for Langtry that he would enter a marriage without love? She had no illusions that he might. There had been no word of love spoken between them. This was a marriage born of a different kind of love, a love for Langtry. He'd made this sacrifice for Langtry, while she—she had only gained that which she wanted, never to have to leave this place. She would work dili-

181

gently at Jessica's side, learning all that was needed to run the plantation. Temple would never regret his sacrifice.

She looked over the lands of her domain and unbidden came the memory of other things said in Jessica's room. Temple had said she would be his wife and someday bear the future heirs of Langtry. Someday! She would have to face those duties as well. Pacing along the gallery she thought of Temple and of her father. She had little knowledge of men and what they expected from their wives except what she'd seen between her mother and father. She shivered. Could she bear such humiliation and unhappiness? One day Temple would expect heirs. She paused, staring at the gold-tinged fields; even broken and destroyed as they were, they were beautiful and awakened a sense of pride in her. She belonged to the land now and it belonged to her. Like Temple she must make sacrifices for it and someday she would produce an heir if that were required of her. She would pay whatever price was necessary to be a part of Langtry! With the issues firmly resolved in her mind, she strolled along the gallery with a troubled heart.

Three days later, as Temple had decreed, the wedding took place. Madame René was hastily summoned from New Orleans to add a swath of Valenciennes lace across the bodice of the ivory dress. The fear and destruction caused by the hurricane were forgotten in the excitement of preparing for the wedding. Lala fussed over not having time to prepare traditional fruit cakes for the wedding, but she whipped up a four-layered coconut-pineapple cake and dozens of pies. The furniture was moved back to the parlors and polished until it gleamed. The flower garden had fared badly in the storm; still, enough flowers for a bridal bouquet were found and carefully nurtured. Invitations to only a few close friends were sent out.

"It's best anyway," Jessica said brightly, "since you are still in mourning for your family." She paused and studied Brynna's closed face. "My dear child, are you certain this is what you want? You can still change your mind."

"This is what I want, Aunt Jessica," Brynna answered serenely.

Jessica appealed to Temple. "Why in God's name have you forced her?"

"I love her, Jessica," Temple said patiently. "I want her for my wife. Have you objections to her you haven't told me?"

"No, of course not," Jessica snapped. "It's just that to do it this way—"

"She might not have married me otherwise," he answered sadly. "I was afraid she was growing too fond of Cort."

"You dolt," Jessica said angrily, and stamped out of the room. Startled, Temple looked after her. Jessica had never spoken to him in that manner before.

The morning of the wedding dawned fresh and sunny. May came to help Brynna with her hair. "Yo're goin' t' be the mostest beautiful bride in these parts," May exclaimed when she was dressed. The lace had not detracted from the gown's beautiful lines. It covered Brynna's shoulders and fell softly just below her collarbones. The richness of the fabric was repeated in the glow of her skin and the gleam of chestnut hair piled high on her head. A small cap of matching lace held a short veil which floated like a cloud behind Brynna. Taking up the garden bouquet of roses and baby's breath, Brynna turned toward the door.

"Cyra!" she cried as she caught sight of the figure

standing there. "I was afraid you wouldn't get here in time. It wouldn't have seemed right to get married without you. We talked of this so often when we were girls."

Cyra remained silent, her eyes scathing as she looked at Brynna's fine gown.

"Don't you want to wish me happiness?" Brynna asked softly.

"Yo' won' be happy with him," Cyra predicted, shrugging her shoulders.

"Don't say that," Brynna cried, reaching out to catch her friend's hand. "Cyra. This is my wedding day. Put aside your bitterness and share this day with me."

"I got married, too," the black girl answered.

"Cyra, when?" Brynna's expression was filled with happiness for her.

"Last month, Thomas and me jumped the broom," Cyra said, referring to the simple ceremony the slaves practiced.

"You didn't tell me," Brynna chided. There was so much she wanted to say, but she sensed Cyra's anger was ready to explode at the first wrong word. "I'll have to think of a wedding present for you."

"Maybe a silver candlestick for my fancy table," Cyra scoffed. There was no laughter in her glance.

"Maybe," Brynna said, and drew back, defeated at last by Cyra's bitterness. "I'll speak to Temple about a cabin for you and Thomas."

"They's ready for yo', Miss Brynna," May called from the top of the stairs.

Brynna looked Cyra. "Won't you stay and join the festivities?" she pleaded. "There's food and drinks and dancing."

"No, thank yo', Miss Brynna," Cyra said with exaggerated humbleness, but her anger overtook her and her

184

voice grew hard-edged as she continued. "If I stay up at the big house, I can only watch the white folks dancin' and eatin' and laughin'. If I go back down yonder with my own kind, I can do the dancin', eatin', and maybe then I'll feel like laughin'."

Brynna was silent, her gaze sad as she studied Cyra's defiant face. "I'm sorry things are as they are, but I can't change them. I can only do my best to see the slaves aren't mistreated or made to do without. I promise to work toward that."

"We's lucky to have a mistress like yo'," Cyra said, once again affecting the slave's patois.

Feeling defeated, Brynna turned away from her. This was her wedding day and she had no wish to quarrel. She moved toward the stairs. Below, people were waiting for her, people who would wish her well and laugh with her and give their love and support. Here there were accusations and rage over a system she hadn't started and couldn't end.

"Brynna," Cyra called, and Brynna paused, for Cyra had put aside the false humbleness and spoken to her as they once had a lifetime ago.

"Yes?" Brynna asked, looking over her shoulder at the slim black woman.

Cyra smiled at her. "I brought you a wedding gift." Her gaze held Brynna's as she moved closer.

"You didn't have to . . ." Brynna began, suddenly apprehensive of what Cyra might say or do.

"I wanted to bring you this present today," Cyra whispered hoarsely, shoving her face close to Brynna's. Her dark eyes glittered with triumph.

"What is it?" Brynna asked, anxious to be done with Cyra and descend the stairs to her wedding.

"There's little white babies being born down in the slave quarters!" Cyra said, and smiled serenely.

"I don't know what you mean," Brynna stammered, her heart thudding louder in her chest.

"Babies with black mommas and white poppas," Cyra said with great enjoyment.

"I—I've never seen any," Brynna whispered, backing away from her.

"They're there. Go down and see for yourself. Marie's baby was just born."

"Why are you telling me this?" Brynna demanded. "Temple is not the father."

Cyra made no answer. Her smile was knowing and full of pity.

"He's not that kind of man. He's good to his people."

"He's a white man. They're all alike," Cyra answered softly. "Don't believe me. Go down and see for yourself." She moved away down the hall then, glancing over her shoulder. Her black eyes studied Brynna's stricken face without remorse for the pain she'd caused. She reached the back stairs and was gone, leaving her ugly insinuations like dark clouds over Brynna's wedding day.

"Miss Brynna, they's waitin'," May urged again. Slowly, Brynna made her way to the top of the stairs. The people waiting below turned their faces toward her. Temple's dark eyes met hers. His teeth flashed in a proud smile. Brynna thought of Cyra's accusations. They weren't true. They couldn't be, she thought frantically, and swayed as if she might swoon. A hum of dismay rose from below, but she grabbed hold of the railing and righted herself. She couldn't go through with this. The music began, and after a moment's hesitation, she began the descent down the stairs. At the bottom, Temple smiled, took hold of her arm, and led her into the parlor where the priest waited to make them man and wife.

Temple saw her face as she descended the stairs. It was dull with fear and disgust. Did she hate him so much? he wondered. Had he been wrong when he'd read caring and burgeoning desire in her glance? He couldn't have been. He'd lain awake these past three nights remembering that beautiful face, alive and too revealing, those dark eyes, startled by his words into telling her dearest secrets. She'd looked into his eyes, unprepared, and he'd read the same longings, the same needs he'd felt himself.

He blinked and looked at his bride again as she glided down the stairs. Her expression was closed, her thoughts and feelings her own and never to be shared. She reminded him of that first day she came to Langtry, crying out against some unnamed horror. Her time at Langtry had brought her peace, had given her a reason to laugh again, to risk a part of herself. He would have that woman for his wife and in his bed. He'd show her the depths and fire of his passion and he would coax the same response from her. Her innocence would give way to the fullness of womanhood, and the conquest would be a sweet surrendering for him.

She placed her hand in his and side by side they walked to the parlor. He heard the faint perfumed swish of silken skirts, saw from the corner of his eye the high color on her smooth ivory cheeks, and felt a tremor in her small hand. He pressed her fingers gently to reassure her, then they were standing before the priest and the words were being said. Temple answered firmly, without hesitation. Brynna waited long breath-stopping moments before responding, and when she did, her voice was low and filled with pain.

187

Temple glanced at Jessica and saw his concern mirrored in her eyes. Had he made a mistake after all? Had he pushed her too soon? Was she unaware of his feelings for her? Had she decided she loved Cort after all but was beholden to Temple because of her promise over the wretched dowry?

" 'What God has joined, let no man put asunder'," the priest intoned, making the sign of the cross over them. "By the power of God invested in me, I pronounce you man and wife."

It was done! They were man and wife. Brynna's heart beat so fast, she feared she might faint. Temple turned her to face him and lowered his head. She knew he was about to kiss her, their first kiss, before all his friends. It was just for show, she reminded herself, and steeled herself not to pull away. At the last minute, she turned her head, so his lips caught her just on the corner of her mouth. Her veil hid her temerity from the rest of the room, but she felt Temple's hot breath against her cheek as he sighed. His hands rested lightly against her waist; then he tightened his grip, crushing her against him for one brief moment before he released her. The guests chuckled indulgently.

Seated nearby, Alicia turned her head away when Temple's dark head bent over his bride's in a kiss. How could he have married her? she raged. He couldn't love that simpering ragtag relative of Jessica's. She'd thought he was disinterested in his little cousin. She'd come to Langtry that night to assure herself it was so. Temple hadn't seemed to mind Cort's dancing attention on the plain little cousin.

She had no special graces, no witty small talk, no money or connections. How, then, had she snared Temple? Alicia's speculative gaze flew to the girl's tiny waist. That full skirt could cover much. Color high, Alicia leapt to her feet and pelted the couple with rice as they walked side by side out of the room. All around them, guests called out well wishes. Alicia remained silent, but her eyes narrowed maliciously. She spied Cort and joined him. He was especially handsome today with his dark-burgundy coat and buff trousers and vest. She knew he must have taken extra care with his appearance.

"Smile, brother dear," she said archly. "This is supposed to be a joyous occasion."

He glanced at her sharply, then relaxed his features in an easy smile. "And so it is, sister dear," he replied affably. "Even more so for me, I'd wager."

"And why is that, pray tell?" Alicia bit back.

"Because if Temple had not married her, I would have done so myself and my bachelor days would have ended. Close call, eh?" His smile turned mocking as he glanced at his sister's lovely face. "What of you, dear Alicia? Are you able to put aside your designs upon our estimable bridegroom and be a friend to his beautiful wife?"

Alicia's chin raised proudly. "I do not make it a point to gather women as my friends," she said scathingly. Then her voice turned purring and calculating. "But I shall certainly keep my friendship with Temple intact."

"Alicia, none of your machinations," he warned. "She's young and innocent."

"Perhaps not so innocent after all, my lovestruck brother. She's a mewling, simpering imposter, and I shall take great joy in exposing her for what she truly is."

"Leave her alone, Alicia. I warn you," Cort said flatly. His good-natured smile of a gallant had vanished, and in its place the cold, deadly intent of a man of purpose. His coldness unsettled Alicia.

"Why do you protect her so?" she demanded. "She's

not Creole as we are. She could never be good enough to marry one."

"You showed no such discrimination when you thought I was courting Brynna, *n'est-ce pas?*" Cort's voice was raspy with anger. Between the revealing folds of her full skirts and his coat, he caught hold of her wrist in a bone-bruising grasp. Alicia's eyes widened in pain. "Smile, dear sister," he muttered while his own lips curved in a boyish grin. "Perhaps you made no objections because you thought I would remove your competition for Temple."

"I knew your penchant for the women, *mon cher,*" Alicia whispered back venemously, although she smiled and nodded to other guests who filed out of the parlor after the bride and groom. "You would never have thought to marry this pathetic little creature."

"I loved that 'pathetic little creature', as you so generously put it." Cort's hand turned slightly, twisting her arm sharply. "She's the most beautiful, gentlest woman I've ever known, and I would have asked her to marry me if Temple hadn't asked her first."

"I would never have allowed her to marry into the de Jarreau family." Alicia gritted the words from clenched teeth. "Now let me go. You're hurting me." Cort released her, but his dark head remained close to hers.

"Not as much as I will if you do anything to cause Brynna unhappiness," he warned softly.

Rubbing her wrist, Alicia stared into his dark eyes. "You fool," she said, her lips twisting into an ugly grimace. "You really have fallen in love with her."

"Yes," Cort said simply, and moved away from her, his dark gaze still pinning his sister's in a warning she knew not to ignore. Ever since they were children, she'd been able to control Cort only to a point and no further. When he wore that stubborn, dangerous look she saw in his face now, she knew she'd gone too far. Well, so be it. She would pretend friendship to the scheming little usurper. That would please both Cort and Temple. And somehow, she would see Brynna paid for this day.

"Temple's new wife is very beautiful, isn't she?" Myra Harcourt said, stopping beside Alicia. Her eyes were bright with malice. Her daughter, Colletta, was in tow as usual. Alicia pinned a smile on her face and turned to greet the odious woman.

"She's quite lovely for one so young and in her condition," she said sweetly.

Myra blinked. "Condition?" she repeated avidly. "Has she been ill? I understand Jessica was down with a fever during the storm."

"Brynna is not suffering from a fever," Alicia said as if one privy to well-kept secrets. Taking up her fan, she waved it tranquilly. "I'm afraid her condition will take several months to overcome."

"Months?" Myra repeated, frowning in puzzlement. Then her face cleared in understanding. "I wondered at the haste of this wedding. Why, the shameless, ungrateful little trollop. Such wickedness, and right under Jessica's nose after all her kindness." Myra Harcourt's jowls quivered with indignation. "My dear, how can you bear it?"

"I shall as we all must—pretend a friendship to her in spite of her odious behavior. I'll do it for dear Jessica and Temple." Brynna smiled at Myra bravely. "You know, of course, I have told you this in the strictest of confidences. You must not tell a soul."

"I won't, I swear," Myra cried.

Alicia glanced at Colletta. "My dear child, you should never wear that color," she observed and, head high, walked away. She left behind a mother so bristling with the need to gossip, she did not even berate her daughter for the color of gown which she herself had chosen. She sidled past the crowd in the hall and with Colletta tagging behind, hurried to the garden where she told Madame Kerlerec, who hurried away to tell her best friend.

By the time the newlyweds had joined their guests on the gallery, everyone knew how Brynna had shamelessly contrived to trap Temple into their marriage. Their sympathy lay with the noble young planter. They took great pains to speak to him warmly, and with exquisite finesse, put Brynna in her place. Once again she met the onslaught of their censorship and wondered what she'd done to bring it down on herself.

Temple appeared not to notice what was happening, but Jessica was too wise in the ways of the planters' wives and daughters not to guess. Hadn't she met the same snubs when she first married Etienne Sinclair? At every opportunity, she paused to chat with Brynna, putting an arm around her for a quick hug, or straightening her train with the pride of a mother, showing to one and all that Brynna was now a Sinclair and must be treated accordingly.

"Don't worry, dear," Jessica whispered, thinking the distressful look on the bride's face was the result of their guests' behavior. "They'll come around. They did for me and they will for you."

Brynna tried to smile, but the attempt was sad enough to break Jessica's heart. "I'm not bothered by those people," Brynna said. "I just have to remember that no matter what, I have you and Langtry."

"And Temple," Jessica reminded her softly. Stricken-faced, Brynna turned away. Bride's jitters, Jessica told herself, but she was troubled. Brynna should have been radiant and indeed had appeared so earlier this morning,

192

but now her eyes were shadowed and bruised-looking, the glow was gone from her. She looked like one of the porcelain dolls in the windows of the shops on Royale Street in New Orleans, beautiful but lifeless.

The guests moved indoors to the dining table, where a sumptuous buffet had been set out. Servants moved around the house and gardens with trays of champagne and wine. When all had been served, Sidney de Jarreau raised his glass in a toast to the new couple. Amid laughter and cheers, everyone raised their glasses. Temple placed a possessive arm around Brynna's waist and pulled her close. When all had drunk, he raised his own glass.

"To my beautiful bride," he said. "May she know nothing but happiness and love here at Langtry."

The guests fell silent, but they raised their glass in a toast as Temple had bade them. Puzzled, he looked around the room. An awkwardness had fallen over the gathering.

Cort stepped forward. "Here, here," he cried. "To the most beautiful bride in Louisiana." He drained his glass. "And now, *mon ami*, since you have taken the only girl I ever wanted, I demand the right to kiss the bride."

"By all means," Temple said graciously. Cort moved forward and grasped Brynna's hand. The room was silent as everyone listened to what had occurred. After all, was it not only a few weeks ago that her name, like that of Francine d'Abbadie Beynaud, had been so scandalously linked with Cort de Jarreau. Perhaps the child she carried was not even Temple's. Unsuspectingly, Cort bowed low over her hand, pressing a fervent kiss on the soft, pale skin.

"Madame Sinclair," he said formally and with great seriousness. "I pledge you my friendship as I have given Temple. If you ever have need of help, you have only to ask."

193

"Hear, hear!" Monsieur de Jarreau echoed his son's words with pride. The music had begun playing and Temple reached for her hand.

"This time, I claim the first dance, Madame Sinclair," he said teasingly. His hand settled at her waist, guiding her out onto the floor. Her ivory skirts flared wide as he whirled her about. Even the most callous of onlookers was moved to admit, they did indeed make a handsome couple. Temple's dark handsomeness was a sharp contrast to her vivid beauty. Round and round they danced until the room whirled and Brynna's face grew pale. If not supported by Temple's strong arm, she was sure she would fall to the marble floor. She gripped his arm tightly. Temple felt her trembling touch and was moved by it.

"Tonight, Madame Sinclair," he whispered close to her ear, "I shall show you how well loved you are."

The music swelled and she heard no more, but it had been enough. Tonight! She'd given no thought to their wedding night, assuming theirs had been a business arrangement, assuming they would have time to come to know each other better. But what more did she need to know of him? Cyra had told her enough. Tonight! She could not bear the thought.

Chapter Ten

The plantation was silent. The guests had left, taking their gaity and laughter with them. Jessica, still recovering from her bout of fever, had retired immediately. Now, Brynna and Temple stood alone in the great hall. Euphemie was extinguishing the last lamps, so shadows deepened around them save for the glow cast by the last lamp on the hall table, the lamp that would light their way up the stairs and to their room.

"Come, *ma femme*," Temple said, looking at her tenderly. "It is time for us to retire."

"I—I'm not tired just now," Brynna said hurriedly, and turned her back to him. Her heart was pounding so urgently in her chest, she thought he must surely hear it.

"Neither am I," Temple said huskily. He reached out to touch a curl that lay against her nape, then bent to kiss the soft ivory skin where it had rested. Brynna shivered and took a step away from him. Temple controlled his racing pulse. He must give her time, he reminded himself, teach her to desire him as he so desperately wanted her.

"I . . . we need to talk," she said rather desperately, turning to face him at last. His smoldering gaze consumed her. "We—we did not speak of this." She could not meet his eyes.

"We did not speak of what, *ma petite?*" he asked, reaching for her. His hands were gentle but firm on her waist.

"Of this," Brynna cried, breaking away from him. Temple took a step after her and halted, his brows drawn together in a scowl. She faced him, her fists clenched, her chest rising and falling with each strangled breath.

"You'll have to be more specific, *chérie,*" he said patiently, but she could hear the edge of anger growing in his tone. "What do you wish to say?"

"That I should share your bed was not part of our agreement."

"You agreed to be my wife."

"Nothing more."

"I ask nothing more."

"But not a true wife," Brynna cried, taking a step backward. "I give you my money willingly for Langtry, but I cannot give myself."

"You agreed to be my wife," Temple repeated in a louder voice. "That means in all ways, *chérie.*"

"I meant, only to . . . to bear your name," she blurted wildly. "I do not love you as a husband."

"You'll come to love me," Temple said after a moment's pause. In the face of her rejection, pride prevented him from uttering his own feelings. "You have only to give it a chance." She remained silent. "Surely you did not imagine I meant to enter a marriage in name only. I want children, Brynna, yours and mine, future heirs to Langtry." In his earnestness he moved toward her, but she backed away from him until the wall was at her back, and there she crouched. The look on her face drove him to a fury.

"Dammit, Brynna," he shouted, and in his frustration,

raised a hand to rake through his hair as he was wont to do when vexed. She saw the raised hand and cringed. In that moment he reminded her of Wes Stanton. How many times in the night had she heard the nightmarish sounds between her mother and father, first the shouted blasphemies and the soft pleading, followed by the sound of blows falling against unresisting flesh. Old terrors sprang before her and she screamed.

Anger gave way to concern and Temple moved toward her.

"Don't," she cried, her eyes dark with terror. "Please don't."

"Brynna!" He caught hold of her shoulders, shaking her slightly. "You've no reason to be afraid of me. In God's name, did you think I'd force myself on you?" His dark gaze captured hers.

Reason returned to her. This was Temple. He'd never harmed her, only protected her. "I'm sorry," she sobbed, hiding her face behind her hands. "I'm tired and—and the day has been long."

"I understand," he said soothingly, and lifted her in his arms.

"No!" she cried out softly, her eyes pleading with him again.

"Shhh! I'll not harm you, Brynna," he crooned. "You're my wife. I'll always treat you with honor. We'll wait until another day. Rest against me." His words were reassuring. Her head ached. Wearily, she lay against his shoulder. He smelled of brandy and cigars and all things masculine, things that might have once made her wary but now almost seemed pleasant.

As before, he carried her up the stairs, but instead of turning down the hall to her bedroom, he carried her to his.

"No," she whimpered.

"It's all right," he crooned. "Your things have already been moved in here." He kicked the door to his room and it swung inward. May leapt up. She'd been dozing while waiting to help her mistress undress. Temple nodded curtly and she scurried from the room.

Tears filled Brynna's eyes as she saw May leave. A sense of betrayal swept through her. Temple had lied about his intentions. He was just like Papa.

He placed her gently on the huge bed that dominated the room. Brynna made no more outcry, her heart was frozen, unable to beat or feel pain. Numbly she waited for what was to befall her.

Temple knelt at her feet and gently removed her slippers, then her silk stockings. His fingers brushed against her skin, making her shiver. He towered over her, his weight resting on the one knee anchored on the bed beside her.

"Turn over," he ordered gently. He quickly unfastened the tiny buttons of her gown and just as efficiently unlaced the corset and petticoats beneath. They were whisked away, leaving her in her thin chemise. Temple barely glanced at her, but she saw his lips were clamped tight. Next he turned his attention to her hair, pulling away the veil and the pins that held it in place. Her curls tumbled free and fell over her shoulders. He looked at her then, his glance hot with passion. He lifted a thick chestnut strand feeling its silken texture between his fingers as he raised it to his lips.

"You are so beautiful." His breath was rapid and harsh, his face somber, almost stern, as he gazed at her. He dipped his head slowly and claimed her lips in a kiss, their first real kiss. She had no chance to turn away as she had after their wedding. His arms blocked her on either side, like columns that supported his body, holding it away from her. His lips were firm and warm on hers. A shivery tingle started somewhere deep inside her and moved outward making her tremble slightly, but this time not from fear. Her chin tilted only the tiniest bit, then tucked down into her chest as she sought to withdraw the contact. But Temple had noted that small response and his eyes were bright with elation until he saw her eyes.

"You promised," she whispered.

"Oui, I promised," he sighed, and drew back. He stood staring down at her in all her fiery-gold beauty and now he trembled with the effort he knew it would take to walk away from her. "I shall never break a vow I've made to you, Brynna," he said softly. "Tonight, I pledge you my heart and mind, everything I am as a man. You need never fear me. You will come to love me as much as you do Langtry. Your sons will ride across this land beside me and they will be children born of love and passion between us, not duty. I promise you this from the bottom of my heart."

He was gone then, stalking out into the night, cursing a man named Wes Stanton and all the things Jessica had told him about Brynna's father, cursing himself for not listening to Jessica and taking more time to woo Brynna, cursing the very moon itself, which chose to shine too brightly. He went to his study and downed a glass of bourbon and then a second until the tightness around his groin eased a little. He wasn't sure what to do about the tightness around his heart. It was his wedding night and he'd envisioned a much different ending. Even now the memory of Brynna lying pale and golden against the white sheets sent the blood coursing through his veins. Best not to think about it. Impatiently he set aside the whiskey and, lighting a lantern, he let himself out a side door and made his way through the darkness.

Brynna lay where he'd left her, staring up at the strange canopy above, her thoughts jumbled and confused, her heart beating sluggishly as it had when she was a child and the noises in the next room had diminished and she'd cried herself to sleep. Now she wept and she wasn't sure why. Temple's last words echoed in her head. He wanted her to love him. Did that mean he loved her? Why hadn't he spoken the words? Her rejection hurt him deeply. She'd seen it in his eyes. Yet he'd been kind to her, taking care of her tenderly as if she were a beloved child. But his words and kiss had made it clear he wanted more than a child. He expected her to be his wife in all ways. Could she? She wanted to, oh, but she wanted to.

She drew a breath and turned restlessly on the bed, surprised at the revelation her thoughts brought. Did she love Temple then? She thought back over the weeks and months she'd spent in this house, the times she'd seen him tousled and warm from sleep, sipping his first cup of coffee before going off to the fields, and she'd seen him covered with filth from those same fields, his eyes weary, his shoulders slumped, but always with a ready smile for her. How generously he shared everything with her, his lands, his home, even his friends. Had he not shown her in every way how honorable his intentions for their life? What more could she expect of him?

Cyra's accusations came back to her. They'd never been far from her mind, even when she exchanged her wedding vows with her husband or when he'd gathered her in his arms for their wedding dance. The awful images of Temple and his slave girls had mocked her as she'd smiled at their wedding guests and borne their cuts. She'd longed to hurl her knowledge of his transgressions at

Temple when they argued in the hall below, but she could not speak of it. No woman would, she knew. Even Mama had pretended not to know of such things. Brynna clasped her hands and turned on her side. Tears slid down the side of her face onto the pillow.

Temple was not a monster. Other men visited the slave quarters. Every plantation had its share of mulatto children running about. She was being too sensitive. But could she accept the love of a man who indulged in such indiscretions? No, her heart cried, and tears began anew.

When she had exhausted herself with weeping, she thought again of Temple's generosity, his kindness to his slaves, the way he worked beside them, the way he cared for them and for her. She thought of the warm laughter and his thoughtfulness to Jessica. He had made his vows to her both in the parlor and here in the bedroom and she knew he meant them. As his wife, she would be treated with the same consideration as he showed his stepmother. She would be loved and protected, but who would protect her from him? And did she need such protection? she asked herself. Hadn't she felt herself drawn to the tall, graceful body. Hadn't his dark, smoldering glances awakened a flame within her, so she'd dreamed of his kissing her and more that her innocence could not yet imagine?

Too restless to stay in bed, she rose and crossed to the washstand and splashed water against her tear-reddened eyes and flushed cheeks. Donning a cotton robe, she walked to the open French doors. The moonlight gilding the oak leaves drew her to the gallery. The peacefulness of Langtry seeped into her troubled soul. This was her home now, and the feeling was rich and reassuring. She must put aside her fears and Cyra's gossip and find happiness with her husband. She felt better for her resolve and wondered where Temple was. She would tell him of all her thoughts and plead with him for patience, and in the weeks and months to come she would contrive to please him in all ways.

Tomorrow she would tell him. She turned toward their room, but a glint of light in the distance caught her eye. Puzzled, she walked along the gallery trying to discern what it was, finally making out that it was a man walking with a lantern. But who would be abroad at this hour? Temple!

Her heart twisted with the sure knowledge it was he. In her preoccupation with Cyra's accusations she'd forgotten about Betty Hewitt. Surely Temple would not seek out the overseer's daughter on his wedding night. She had turned him out, Brynna reminded herself, remembering his passion-filled eyes. What should she expect. Fidelity! The word was a cry in her heart. Her hands gripped the railing until the knuckles whitened with the effort not to call out to him. But even as she watched through tear-filled eyes, the figure carrying the lantern moved past the overseer's house and continued on the path toward the slave's quarters. And then she knew that the small glimmer of hope that Cyra's accusations were untrue was gone forever. Silently she turned away from the sight of her husband and made her way back to their room.

She did not see Temple the next morning. He didn't return to their room, doubtlessly too ashamed to face her after so quickly breaking his promises to her, she thought bitterly. She dressed in an everyday gown of pink muslin. The color pleased her today because she knew it was not Temple's favorite. She tied an apron around her waist much as she did every day she worked around the plantation, then went down to join Jessica.

"Good morning, child. You needn't have come down today. Why didn't you laze in bed?"

"Why didn't you?" Brynna replied, glancing at Jessica's pale face. "You're still not recovered from your fever. You should be resting."

"I grow testy when I have nothing to occupy my mind and hands," Jessica said. She studied the girl before her. This was not the glowing face of a new bride. There were smudges beneath her eyes testifying she'd slept little, but her lips bore no evidence of a lover's kiss and, Jessica saw with dismay, Brynna was not meeting her eyes. There was no shy reddening of the cheeks or coy avoidance of eye contact. Something was horribly wrong.

"You and Temple should have had a honeymoon," Jessica said, tentatively probing.

"We couldn't possibly be away from Langtry at this time, Jessica, you know that," Brynna said without glancing up from her breakfast plate. She'd eaten little, pushing the food about with her fork. "Temple needs to be here to salvage as much as he can from the storm and you aren't well enough to handle things by yourself."

"I'm truly sorry, I couldn't."

Brynna's stricken gaze met hers then. The girl leaped from her chair and knelt beside Jessica's. "It's not your fault, darling Jessica. I don't want to go anywhere else. I'm happiest here at Langtry."

"Are you happy, *chérie?*" Jessica asked, taking hold of the soft young hands.

"Mais oui," Brynna said, and smiled wryly at her first attempts at the French that was so easily interspersed in all Creole conversations.

Jessica was not to be deterred. "Are you happy with your marriage to Temple?" she persisted. "We haven't rushed you, have we?"

203

"No, of course not," Brynna answered, but she looked away. Rising, she moved around the table, her skirts rustling briskly. "The day is getting away from us," she said softly. "Lala and the other slaves are no doubt waiting for us."

"No doubt," Jessica said. "Why don't you go ahead without me. I feel the need to sit in the sunlight a moment longer."

"Are you all right?" Brynna fixed the woman with a worried gaze.

"Yes, I'm quite all right," Jessica said. "But you are mistress of Langtry now and I have no need to work so hard. Now go, go." She made shooing motions with her hands.

Brynna hesitated only a moment more, then, picking up the ring of household keys, she turned to the back entrance, where the slaves were gathered waiting for their day's rations and instructions.

Mistress of Langtry! Brynna felt her shoulders lift at the thought. Jessica had prepared her well. She knew what she must do to set the daily events of the plantation in motion. At the back door, she paused, took a deep breath, and walked out onto the gallery. Broad smiles were turned her way.

"Good mahnin', Miz Sinclair," the slaves called cheerfully.

"Nice mahnin', Miz Sinclair."

"Please, continue to call me Miz Brynna," she instructed with a smile. "Nothing has changed." She walked along the covered brick passageway to the storage sheds and she knew *everything* had changed. She was mistress of Langtry. The wonder of it stayed with her all morning, making her forget her unhappiness for a time.

* * *

She didn't see Temple all day, but that evening he returned from the distant fields, riding behind his slaves, conversing with Kyle Hewitt about something. Brynna stood on the upper gallery and watched them approach. When they reached the barns, Temple turned aside. Where was he going? she wondered briefly, and sadly went inside. She'd finished with her chores early and had taken time to bathe and change into a fresh dress. May had brushed her unruly curls into a simple yet regal crown around her head. At the first glimpse of Temple's return she'd set the slaves to filling a bathtub for his convenience and now she checked to see it was ready before going down to the parlor. Seating herself demurely on one of the sofas, she took up her needlework and bent over it with assiduous concentration. She was determined that Temple should see a tranquil wife upon his return.

"Brynna," he called, stamping through the hall. "Brynna, where are you?"

"I'm here," she answered, and stayed seated on the sofa, her skirts carefully spread around her, her slippered foot resting daintily upon a stool. She was determined he should see she was the epitome of respect. She would shame him from his despicable habits by her very piety.

"Brynna!" Temple appeared in the doorway. He was covered with mud and sweat, but his eyes glowed with anticipation. He took in her prim demeanor, and laughter sparkled in his dark eyes. In a few long strides he was beside her, his hand clasping her stitching frame and laying it aside.

"Come with me," he ordered grasping her hand. "I have something to show you."

"But I—"

205

"Hurry!" Temple led her out of the hall and out to the gallery where his horse waited. He lifted her into the saddle and sprang up behind.

"I have no time for a ride," Brynna protested primly. "The servants will be serving supper soon and your . . . your bath is already drawn." She felt his warm, hard body pressed close to her and smelled his earthy sweat. Although it was not an unpleasant odor, it was vaguely troubling, making her too aware of the man.

"That can wait," Temple said enthusiastically. He kicked the sides of his mount, and they cantered down the path past the overseer's house. At the sound of his approaching horse, Betty came out onto the porch. When she saw Brynna cradled in Temple's arms, she disappeared inside again with a flip of her skirts. Temple paid her no mind. He guided the horse down the path she'd watched him follow the night before, but then he turned aside to the stables.

"Here we are," he said, alighting and reaching up to pull her down beside him.

"Why are we here?" she demanded, feeling cross and exasperated. He seemed to show no anger for her rejection the night before. Taking her hand, he headed for the stable door. Brynna had to run to keep up. At last they halted beside a stall.

"Take a look," he said in a low voice filled with wonder.

Brnna peered into the stall. A tiny foal rested in the hay, her red-brown coat gleaming, her eyes big and brown and slightly scared-looking in her small face.

"Oh, she's beautiful," Brynna breathed, stepping inside and falling to her knees in the hay. Her hands smoothed the glossy coat and touched the wet black nose. "She's perfect."

"That she is," Temple said softly, looking at Brynna. "She was born last night. I just happened to walk down here when her dame was in labor. I thought about going back to the house to get you, but you'd had a big day. I knew you were tired."

"Not that tired," Brynna cried, then bit her lips. Too tired to be a wife, but not to see a mare foal, she thought and avoided his eyes for a moment.

"I thought you might like to have her," he said, moving into the stall and kneeling beside her.

"Oh, Temple, do you mean it?" Her face was glowing with happiness. He reached out a hand to chuck her chin.

"You are not a conventional wife, Brynna," he chided gently. "You barely acknowledged the diamonds I gave you for a wedding present, yet you go all starry-eyed over a foal."

"But she's far more beautiful than diamonds," Brynna cried, bending to place her forehead against the tiny ears. They felt like the softest velvet.

"What will you call her?" Temple asked, enjoying the delight his new wife displayed so guilelessly for her wedding gift.

Straightening, she looked at him. "I shall have to think of something," she said softly. "It must be as special and beautiful as she is." She smoothed the foal's coat, her forehead wrinkled in thought. Then her face cleared and she smiled at Temple shyly.

"I shall call her Malka. It means queen. She shall be a queen."

"That will make two here at Langtry," Temple said, and couldn't resist reaching for her. Before she could protest, he placed a kiss on her soft lips and drew back.

"We'd better go back. Supper is ready and Jessica will be waiting for us," she said, getting to her feet. Then a thought came to her. "You were down here last night?" she asked.

"Yes, I told you. I thought about coming back for you."

"I wish you had, Temple," she cried, her eyes shining. Impulsively she threw her arms around him and planted a kiss on his chin. "Thank you for the most wonderful gift of all," she cried, and before he could take advantage of her mood, she whirled away and ran down the path. "I have to tell Aunt Jessica," she called over her shoulder.

Temple tossed the reins of his tired mount to a stable-hand and followed her down the path. His new wife was as changeable as the spring winds, he thought, happy he'd done something that pleased her so much. He could see now that life at Langtry would never be boring. As he traversed the hall past Jessica's room, he heard Brynna's happy chatter and Jessica's answering laughter.

"Mister Temple, yore bath is ready," May called from the bathroom. Gratefully he slid down into the scented water. He was tired. He'd slept only a few hours on a bundle of hay in the stables and had gone directly to the fields from there. Now he felt the tepid water slough away his fatigue along with the dirt and rose to towel himself, his mood buoyant. Was that from the bath or the memory of Brynna's quick kiss on his chin? he wondered idly.

Supper was a gay affair, with Brynna chattering brightly about the foal and her plans for it. Jessica, too, seemed more rested for her release from some of the responsibility. Looking around the table at the two women who meant the most to him, Temple thought this was a better wedding supper than the night before. But when they'd gathered in the parlor, and Brynna sat once more with needlework before her like some great barrier, the conversation held awkward gaps. Fearful her presence was causing the problem, Jessica excused herself, pleading fatigue.

"I'll go up with you, Jessica," Brynna said quickly, laying her hoop aside.

"There's no need to do that, child," Jessica rebuked gently. "Stay and talk with Temple. I'm sure he'll desire your company."

"He won't mind," Brynna said without glancing at him for confirmation. "I'm quite exhausted."

Temple got to his feet. "It seems we're all in need of retiring early," he said. He bent to kiss Jessica's brow, then turned to Brynna. "You go on up, darling," he said, looking into her eyes. "I'll see to things down here and then I'll be up."

"All right," Brynna said calmly, but her pulse leaped in her throat. He was only putting up a good front for Jessica's benefit, she told herself, and followed her aunt up the stairs.

"Good night, dear," Jessica said, pausing before the bedroom door that Brynna was to share with Temple.

"Good night, Aunt Jessica," Brynna answered. There was nothing else for her to do but enter Temple's room. Once there, she paced the floor frantically. Oh, why hadn't she thought to have her things moved back to her own room? She'd forced every thought of Temple and his expectations from her mind, concentrating solely on her tasks around Langtry. She'd stuck her head in the sand, she thought bitterly. At last she tired of pacing and decided that since Temple had not yet come to his room, he intended to sleep elsewhere. Getting out a fresh cotton nightdress, she quickly got ready for bed. The stiff white folds of the gown enshrouded her figure, so its long hem covered even her toes. Then she let out her hair and plaited it loosely into one fat braid down her back. Turn-

209

ing to the wash basin she performed a sketchy toilette, her thoughts on Temple.

She was grateful for his thoughtfulness. It wasn't that she wasn't ready to become his wife. He had been very endearing in giving her the beautiful foal. She'd been incredibly happy to know he'd spent the night in the stables and not . . . She let the thought drift away. She'd condemned him without hearing his side, just as she'd believed Cyra's accusations. The degree of unfairness she'd shown Temple bothered her. If he came to their room this night, she would become his wife, she thought bravely. All women make such sacrifices at one time or another. It was expected of her. Her mother had made them, Aunt Jessica had made them, and she would, too.

As if on cue, the door opened and Temple stepped inside. Color flooded Brynna's cheeks.

"Oh!" she gasped and fell silent, her golden eyes wide and apprehensive. "I thought you meant to sleep elsewhere."

"This is my room, Brynna," he said, as if explaining something to a child. "I'm used to my own bed."

"I see," she said, nervously twisting the starchy cotton of her gown. She looked like a school girl with her hair braided and the high-necked gown. Temple turned away and began to undress.

"If you would like me to go elsewhere, I will," she said, moving toward the door.

"I should like you to come to bed," Temple said, his voice heavy with impatience. "You are my wife." He'd removed the loose cotton shirt he wore. His chest was tanned and muscular, his middle sleek and taut. Now his hands went to the belt at his slim waist. Cheeks flaming, Brynna turned away, her frantic gaze darting here and there. It fell on the round mirror above the washstand,

and she caught a glimpse of a long brown thigh. She shut her eyes, but her mind expanded on that brief glimpse reminding her of Temple rising from his bath that day before the storm. Her pulse thundered in her ears. She felt hot and breathless.

"You can turn around now," Temple said. "I'm under the covers." When she made no move, his voice rose. "Brynna! Come to bed."

She took a deep breath and turned. He lay beneath the covers, but his broad chest was bared. She saw the mat of glossy hair sworling down toward the covers and remembered it covered his belly as well. Gulping, she took a step forward. Temple's dark gaze followed her.

"Come to bed," he repeated in a softer voice.

She had little choice, Brynna realized, unless she expected to change rooms in the middle of the night, and what a fuss that would create with the servants and Aunt Jessica. How could she possibly explain it? Besides, hadn't she only moments before vowed she would become Temple's wife as he wished. With the air of a martyr, she raised her chin and marched to the other side of the bed. Temple took up an enormous amount of space, she saw, and got in carefully so as not to touch him. He lay with his back to her.

When she had settled herself rigidly on her back and was sure her gown covered every inch of her legs and even her feet, she took a deep breath and waited. Surely, this would soon be over. She would think of something else, she told herself naively, the new foal and a list of tomorrow's chores. She counted the folds of the canopy above her head. When Temple made no move, she turned her head. His back was still to her. Of course, he couldn't know of her change of heart, she thought warily.

Clearing her throat, she tucked the covers tightly over her chest. "I'm ready!" she croaked out.

Still no response from the other side of the bed. Taking another deep breath, Brynna tried again. "Temple, I've thought it over and decided you were right. I'm ready to be your wife," she said all in a rush.

Her words were answered by a deep sigh and a soft snore. Brynna sat upright, her outraged gaze studying her husband's back. He was sleeping! While she lay here trying to find the courage to consummate their marriage, he'd gone right off to sleep.

Anger and humiliation swept over her. Had he no idea how hard it had been for her to swallow her pride. Hadn't he cared? She lay back against her pillows. Didn't he want her anymore? Had her refusal last night so disgusted him that he no longer desired her? What of the children he'd wanted? Had he given up all thought of them? She lay puzzled by the ways of men, half relieved for her reprieve, half angered at his rejection.

Finally, she fell asleep and some time during the night she burrowed against the warm, masculine body that occupied most of the bed.

Chapter Eleven

Temple woke with an unfamiliar warmth at his side. He tried to sit up and found himself tangled in silken strands of red-gold hair. Carefully, he turned to face his wife. Her hair covered her eyes.

"Ummmfgh!" she muttered irritably. Grinning, he gently brushed aside the tousled curls and looked at her delicate features. How could he have gone to sleep so quickly with this beauty in his bed? he wondered. Only fatigue of the highest degree had claimed him; otherwise he would have made a concerted effort to claim his husbandly privileges. Had he been dreaming when a small voice declared she was indeed ready to fulfill her wifely duties?

A frown puckered his brow as he gazed at the smattering of brown-gold freckles dusting her lovely nose. He didn't want Brynna in his bed as a matter of duty. He wanted her as filled with passion and desire for him as he was for her. Let other planters content themselves with dutiful wives and dusky-skinned mistresses on the side. This fiery girl would be both to him. He would woo her and seduce her until her senses reeled, and when at last she came to him, he would strip away all false modesty and pretensions genteel society had taught her. He would teach her to understand her needs as a woman and to glory in them without reserve, without shame. The thought of that moment flooded him with such desire, he was forced to role away from her and get out of bed, lest he demand his rights this very moment.

Time! He must give her time. She had crept into bed beside him like a lamb going to a slaughter. She would grow used to his presence, to the scent and heat of his body lying next to her in bed, and when she'd accepted him, nay, when she'd learned to draw comfort and joy from having him next to her, he would teach her to love him. Time! And a miracle, for he wasn't sure he could keep his resolve not to rush her.

Casting frequent glances at his wife sprawled on his bed, he performed a quick ablution. When he was dressed and ready to leave, he paused for a final glimpse of Brynna. It must last him all day.

She'd kicked aside the light coverlet. Her virginal white gown rode high on her hip, displaying a graceful curve of thigh and leg. Her feet were small and dainty, he saw, her toes like delicate flower petals. Her fiery hair fanned out on the pillow behind her leaving her profile in soft relief against the white linen. Her lashes were a dark-gold smudge against her cheek. There was a vulnerability to her that touched him deeply. He would protect her until his last breath, he thought fiercely. Whatever her life at Beaumont Hall with that scoundrel of a father, she would never know unhappiness again. Tucking the mosquito netting around the bed, he left the room, closing the door softly behind him.

Brynna heard the door close and sat bolt upright. Where was she? She relaxed as she looked around and remembered. She'd spent a second night in Temple's room. Then came the memory of her humiliating offer of herself to a man who had cared so little he'd fallen asleep. That scenario would not be repeated, she told herself, stepping out of the bed and reaching for her clothes. She would have her things moved back to her own room this very day. If Temple didn't want her in his bed, she was only too happy to leave it. A clatter of horses' hooves drew her to the French doors. Throwing them open, Brynna stepped out onto the gallery. The boards were cool beneath her bare feet, the air heavy and moist. Beyond the railing, Brynna saw Temple astride his black stallion galloping toward the fields. The sun was just rimming the far trees, its whitehot light burning away the haze.

Restlessly, Brynna strolled along the gallery. Smoke hung over the chimneys of the distant cabins. The slaves were up and around, some already streaming toward the cane fields. The stable boy who'd brought up Temple's horse jogged along the path to the barn, stopping now and then to pick up a stone or to catch a grasshopper along the path. Normally this bustling domesticity calmed her unrest. Not today. She thought of Temple's long, sleek body lying beside her in bed. How strange to have him so near in such intimate contact, yet so aloof. What would have happened if he hadn't fallen asleep, if he'd rolled over and taken advantage of her offer? The thought stained her cheeks. Turning back to her room, she hurried to wash and dress herself.

The restlessness stayed with her throughout the day, so finally Brynna slipped away for a ride on Jarib. With the awful summer heat and Jessica's illness, she'd given up riding. Now she felt the horse moving beneath her and the wind whipping her hair from its demure chignon and exultation sang through her. She gave Jarib his head, neither urging him forward nor holding him back. The Thoroughbred seemed to enjoy the chance to stretch as much as she. At last he slowed and, mindful of the heat, Brynna turned him toward the river, where she allowed him to drink and graze a bit while she lay under a tree and daydreamed idly. Only when her dreams turned to Temple and yet another night in his bed, did Brynna rise and remount.

Following the old river road, she made her way toward Langtry. She heard the clang of machinery and the call of men before she rounded a bend and came upon the sugar mill. Chandra was tied to a post, so she knew Temple was near. He came around the low-roofed, open-sided building and paused. His face lit with pleasure, making her feel warm and tingly. Her hand went to her wind-tossed hair. She wished she'd worn a hat.

"You've come to see the mill," Temple said, coming to help her dismount. His dark gaze took in the simple white cotton bodice and black cloth skirt. Her curls lay vivid and alive across her shoulders. Her ride had put color in her cheeks and a sparkle in her eyes. She had little idea of how she'd changed from the tense, sad-eyed girl who'd come to Langtry months before. Taking hold of her hand, he led her toward the rectangular building.

"We've started processing some of the sugarcane damaged in the storm," Temple called above the racket of the engine. "It's a bit green and the yield won't be as high this year, but we'll realize some profit."

"I'm happy to hear that," Brynna shouted, then put her hands to her ears.

"This is our new steam engine," Temple laughed, and led her forward with pride. "We've begun using a double set of iron rollers, so we extract far more juice than our old method with wooden rollers powered by mules."

"It's quite overpowering," Brynna said, not wishing to show less interest than he had enthusiasm.

Temple laughed. "I know it's terribly noisy, but it's worth the bother. Look here, after the cane has been squeezed between the rollers and its juice extracted, the juice runs down to those vacuum pans where it's boiled."

"I thought you used open kettles," Brynna said, looking at the contraption of drums with hoses running to and from them.

"We used to," Temple explained, "but we couldn't maintain an even heat with an open kettle, and the sugar was inferior. This is something new. We can produce more and better sugar. It uses less fuel, too."

"Is that good?"

"Very good. Some planters have gone to coal, but I balk at that. We've been experimenting with the bagasse."

"What is that?"

"The waste after we put the stalks through the rollers." Temple had led her past the vast rollers and the hissing motor and steaming vents to the tropical outdoors.

"What do you think?" he asked, falling into step beside her as she returned to her horse. The noise of the mill diminished. There was a boyish eagerness about Temple, and Brynna sensed he truly desired her comments.

"I'm impressed," she answered truthfully. "But you continually amaze me with your modern thinking on this. You seem always to be at the forefront of new experiments."

"Once we take out the waste and find the best approach to raising and milling sugarcane, we'll be able to make it a better-paying crop for Louisiana," he answered, slapping at his boot tops with his riding cane. "This part of Louisiana can't bear some of the crops the northern parishes can. We've already found indigo can't grow here. The insects eat it up. Right now, sugar is an unpredictable business at best. Sugarcane wasn't really doing well here in Louisiana until we got our hands on ribbon cane." He smiled deprecatingly. "I'm boring you with all this talk."

"Indeed, you're not," Brynna hastened to say. "I want to know everything about Langtry." She turned toward the river, which flowed strong and pulsing like an artery in the heart of Langtry. She wondered if she could make Temple know how much she loved her new home. "Sometimes I can't believe I truly belong here," she sighed.

"Langtry wouldn't be the same without you. You've conquered us all," Temple replied softly, and wondered if the day would come when he could speak words of love to her without Langtry standing between them.

Brynna cast a sparkling glance over her shoulder, her smile winsome enough to stir his heart. A river breeze fanned the chestnut curl resting over her heart, making it tremble. He longed to reach for it and feel its silken coil in the palm of his hand.

"I have no wish to conquer," Brynna was saying, "only to be a part of Langtry. That's why it gives me such pleasure to use my inheritance . . ." She paused as another thought struck her. "Haven't you need of my signature to transfer my funds into Langtry's account?"

"We haven't needed the money yet," Temple explained, his face averted.

"But what about the crops? Haven't we lost most of them?" Brynna persisted, her golden eyes searching his.

He couldn't lie to her about that. The devastation lay in the fields for all to see. "We lost two-thirds of our crops," he answered gravely. "Better than some planta-

218

tions, worse than others. But I won't need your money until later."

"When the bank loans come due?" Brynna said with quick understanding. "It is there whenever you're ready for it."

"I know," Temple said, placing a hand on her shoulder. "And I thank you for your generosity."

For a moment, she thought he meant to kiss her. She hesitated, wanting him to and afraid he would. "I have to go," she said quickly. "I've left Jessica alone too long and she's still not able to handle all the responsibilities although she tries to."

Temple bent to give her a hand into the saddle and when she was perched high above him, he took hold of her hand. She didn't draw away.

"I'm glad you came down to see me, Brynna," he said with such obvious pleasure, she didn't tell him she'd only been for a ride and stumbled upon the mill. His hand was warm clasping hers and his eyes smoldering with dark, unfathomable lights.

"Will you ride out to see me again during the day?"

"Yes, if you wish," Brynna answered with breathless stiffness. "I must go." She fled then, galloping down the narrow dirt path as if the very demons of hell were after her, when in fact, it was only her feelings she ran from.

Temple watched her ride away, his expression filled with regret. Every day it became harder to maintain the lie with which he'd trapped her into their marriage. His lips thinned now with impatience at his blundering. He should have waited, as Jessica had advised. He should have wooed her and won her over, but he'd seen the look in Cort's eyes and heard the easy laughter between the two of them. Never before had he deliberately thwarted his friend in anything he wanted, but he'd known ever since that day he'd found her by the river with flowers plaited in her hair that he loved her and wanted her for his wife. Now he cursed himself, fearful he might have driven her away by his haste.

"I will win her over," he vowed, standing by the swollen river with the wheeze of the sugar mill in his ear. Without her, Langtry would mean little to him.

Brynna made her way along the river, then turned up the path Temple often used to return home. Her thoughts were full of her handsome husband. She admired him more than any man she knew. He was progressive and daring, unafraid of hard work, dedicated to Langtry's good and the well-being of its people. He treated everyone fairly, even his lowliest slave. She thought of Cyra's accusations and thought they rang with a certain falseness. She should see for herself, Brynna decided, and reined the horse toward the slave quarters.

More than likely, Marie would be in the sewing shed. New mothers were put to work there, so they could be near their babies. Glancing around for any sight of Cyra, she dismounted. She had no wish for Cyra to know she'd come to see Marie. She must hurry, for soon Temple would release the field hands and they would return to their quarters. Gathering up her skirts, she made her way to the sewing shed and had to pause outside the door to still her racing pulse and regain her breath.

When she was calm, she pushed open the door and walked in. Aunt Clemmie sat at a loom, her hands and feet working rhythmically. Marie and Tilly sat in a hard chair against the wall, sewing in their laps, their babies on pallets at their feet. Involuntarily, Brynna's gaze was drawn to Marie's baby. Though only a few days old, she could see by the pale milk-chocolate color of his skin that he was part white. Marie looked up and saw her gazing at her infant.

"Yo' wan' sum'pin', Miss Brynna?" she asked uneasily.

Tilly exchanged a glance with Aunt Clemmie.

"I—I haven't been down to see your baby yet, Marie," Brynna said, crossing to the black girl. "Are you both feeling well?"

"Yas, ma'am." Marie smiled fondly at the sleeping babe. "He never give me no trouble, Miss Brynna, not with the birthin' or nothin'. He a good baby."

Brynna smiled gently. Marie waited expectantly. "He's a beautiful baby."

"Yas, ma'am, he is." Marie's shoulders rose in pride.

"Have you notified his father yet?" Brynna asked softly. Marie jerked her head up and stared at her with soft, doelike eyes.

"No, ma'am," she said finally. "I reckon he knows." Her words sent a spear of pain through Brynna. She turned to go, then paused at the door.

"He's a fine boy, Marie," she said. "What have you named him?"

The black woman's face beamed with satisfaction. "I'se goin' t' name him Templeton," she said proudly.

Brynna closed the door very gently and slumped against it. Marie was going to name her baby Templeton. What further proof did she need?

"Yo' been to see Marie's baby?" a grating voice demanded. Brynna straightened and stared into Cyra's dark, cynical eyes.

"I stopped to talk to Aunt Clemmie," she said with feigned nonchalance. "Where have you been these past few days, Cyra? You can't just come and go as you please."

Cyra returned her gaze with derision. "Yo' tol' me to get out, 'member?" she said softly.

"I didn't mean for good," Brynna answered sharply, although at that moment, she wished never to see Cyra again. "You have to do your share, Cyra, just like all the other . . ." She paused.

"Jes' like the other slaves," Cyra finished the words for her. "Yas'm, Ah do that." Her eyes snapped with rage, her mouth twisted bitterly. The silence between them was sharp and cutting. Brynna realized the friendship they'd once enjoyed was forever gone, destroyed by Wes Stanton and his cruel appetites.

Cyra watched the play of emotions across Brynna's face, following each one effortlessly as if she were thinking and feeling the same. And why not. Hadn't everyone said they were as close as sisters. Cyra's mouth twisted with rage and she held out a small pouch. White chicken feathers stuck out from the sides.

"I can make Marie and her baby disappear, if you want me to," she said, and the slurring accents of the slave quarters were gone. She spoke the words sharply and clearly, as she'd always done back in Tennessee. Perhaps that was what made them seem all the more menacing, because she sounded so much like the old Cyra, giving comfort and offering advice. Brynna's eyes filled with hope that all was not lost between them until she spotted the pouch Cyra held.

Instinctively, Brynna recoiled. "What is that?" she demanded.

Cyra's lips twisted in a malevolent smile. "It's a little gris-gris," she said. "Black magic."

Brynna pressed backward against the door. "Where did you get it?"

Cyra's smile faded. "I got it from the voodoo woman in New Orleans."

"New Orleans?" Brynna whispered. "You were never there."

Cyra laughed and shook the bag in Brynna's face. "Black magic can do anything. Even get rid of your enemies."

"Marie's not my enemy," Brynna said sharply.

"Yo' want t' get rid of yore husband?" Cyra asked brightly, rolling her eyes. Once again she'd affected the language and stance of the field slaves.

"No, never," Brynna shouted, striking at the pouch. It fell to the ground between them. All humor had disappeared from Cyra's face as she stared into Brynna's eyes. Brynna pushed herself away from the shed door and ran down the path. Cyra's laughter, wild and mocking, followed her.

Brynna made her way back numbly to the big house. Her anger at Cyra almost obscured the pain over Marie's baby. Absently she instructed May to move her belongings back to her old room. The little maid looked at her with puzzlement, but hurried away to do her mistress's bidding.

Brynna was strangely silent the rest of the day.

"What's troubling you, child?" Jessica asked gently.

"My goodness, Aunt Jessica," Brynna answered brightly. "What could possibly be wrong?"

Jessica pried no further, but all afternoon she cast troubled glaces at Brynna. Something was bothering the girl, she thought. Probably the same thing that bothered Templeton.

Supper was a quiet affair that night. Several days had passed since the cooling effect of the storm and the heat had crept back as punishing and relentless as before. After a light supper, Jessica and Brynna took their needlework to the upper gallery, hoping to catch a breeze from the river. Temple came to join them and smoke his pipe. Brynna was painfully aware of the pale blur of his white shirt in the dark shadows. His booted feet were sprawled in front of him, his big body slumped at ease in his chair. Yet, even when relaxing, he exuded a restless energy.

She'd come to know him well enough to understand he would sit still for only so long before he would be up and moving, pacing around the gallery or going to his office to work on plantation books. For now, there was a semblance of familiar camaraderie that awakened yearnings in her that they could indeed be a true family. But how could she accept him in her bed when he dallied with his slave women? She grew so agitated, she was forced to put aside her needlework.

"You're quiet tonight, Brynna," Temple said, ever conscious of her moods. Perhaps she was thinking of him, as he had been of her ever since she rode away from the mill.

Brynna fidgeted, wishing she could ask him outright about Marie's baby. "I'm rather tired," she said faintly.

"You work much too hard around here, dear," Jessica said fondly. "You need to take some time off. Even if Temple can't get away from the plantation for a honeymoon, you could take more time for yourself. Pamper yourself a bit. You've certainly earned it."

"I agree," Temple said, leaning across to take her hand. "Why don't you rest a bit and in a few days, perhaps I could take time to go to New Orleans." He pressed her hand warmly.

Before she was forced to answer, the sound of hoofbeats sounded on the crushed-shell drive. Temple rose and walked to the rail. Happy for the diversion, Brynna joined him there. The oaks were dark shadows now, hiding the identity of their unannounced guests until they were nearly upon them.

"Cort!" Temple called down to the rider. "I thought it might be you."

"Good evening, Tem," Cort answered, then tipped his hat to Brynna. "Miz Sinclair."

"My goodness, you don't have to sound so formal. I'm still Brynna," she answered, and was rewarded by a quick flash of a smile.

"Who's that with you, Cort?" Temple asked, referring to the other riders.

"Good evening, Temple." A fleshy man rode forward into the lamplight. "Miz Brynna. I'm sorry my wife and I couldn't be here for your wedding. We were hit worse than some by that storm."

"I'm sorry to hear that, Alcee," Temple said, and Brynna remembered meeting Alcee Fortier and his wife, Madeleine, at the party Jessica had given.

"Won't you come up and have a glass of lemonade with us, Mr. Fortier?" Brynna asked.

"Much obliged, ma'am, but I've got to ride on home tonight. I just stopped by to ask Temple if he's had any trouble with his slaves."

"None that I'm aware of," Temple answered. "Have you?"

Alcee Fortier nodded grimly. "Something's going on," he said. "My Nigras have been getting restless. I even had a couple of them run off. I've never had that before. I treat my people good. They've got no call to take off like that. The other day I came upon a pouch containing some bones and chicken feathers. None of my people admit to knowing about it."

225

"We all deal with the slaves' superstitions and this voodoo they espouse," Temple said.

"That's what some of the other planters said," Fortier revealed. "I've been out talking to them most of the day, but they all say it's gotten worse lately. Some of them have picked up rumors from their slaves that this new outbreak is stemming from Langtry."

Brynna felt her heart slow. Temple looked at her and then at Jessica. "Have either of you noticed any signs of our people practicing voodoo?"

"Only Lala, with all her potions and superstitions," Jessica said. "And you know that's harmless."

"No, I've seen nothing," Brynna said, reminding herself that she had no proof that Cyra was practicing voodoo. A pouch meant nothing.

"I'm sorry, Alcee," Temple called down. "But I will keep an eye out and let you know if I see anything."

"Much obliged. Good night, ma'am," Fortier called, and tipping his hat in a final farewell, spurred his horse down the drive. Cort followed suit, his dark gaze going one last time to Brynna. She didn't notice. She was busy trying to remember every word Cyra had uttered to her that afternoon. She was torn between her need to protect Cyra and her loyalty to Temple and Jessica.

"How very strange that they should think our people have something to do with this," Jessica was saying. She fell silent and Brynna knew she was remembering the rumors about Cyra. The gentle gray eyes studied Brynna until she could bear the scrutiny no longer.

"I believe I'll retire," she said, getting to her feet.

"Of course, dear." Jessica held her cheek to receive Brynna's kiss.

"I'll be in soon," Temple said absently.

In her worry over Cyra, Brynna hadn't spoken to him

about her move back to her own room. He would discover it soon enough, she consoled herself. No doubt he would be happy she was gone. He would have the freedom to come and go to his many paramours as he wished.

Brynna was quiet as May helped her prepare for bed. After she dismissed the girl and just settled herself beneath the covers, there was a knock at her door.

"Come in," she called, thinking it was Jessica. The door swung inward and Temple stood in the opening. He was scowling darkly and his fists were clenched as if it took great effort to control himself. Brynna felt her heart constrict.

"D-did you want something, Temple?" she asked, trembling beneath his fierce gaze.

"Perhaps, madame," he began, biting out the words from between clenched teeth, "there is a reason of which I am not aware for your removal to this room."

"I—I thought we might both rest better in our own rooms," Brynna began. "I have no wish to offend you, Temple. I'm grateful that you've given me your name and Langtry as my home."

"Then, by God, show me how grateful you are by returning to my room and becoming my wife as you should."

Her cheeks flamed with color, wariness gave way to a burgeoning anger. "Do you mean I must pay for the privilege of being mistress of Langtry. I thought I had done that. I have given you my inheritance. I have nothing more to give."

He stalked to the bed and gazed down at her. Her vibrant curls were caught back by a blue ribbon. Her skin glowed with warmth. Her nightdress was virtuous in its long sleeves and high neckline, but the thin material clung to her shoulders and breasts. The dark areolas of her

227

nipples were an inviting shadow. Temple leaned over her, his face scant inches from hers.

"You have given me nothing I value, Brynna," he rasped. "I want you in my bed as my wife. If you won't come willingly, then I will take you there by force."

"You wouldn't dare." Splinters of lights danced in her golden eyes and she glared at him with more impudence than he'd seen her display since her arrival at Langtry. Her fear of him seemed to have lessened somewhat, he thought with satisfaction, at the same time he attempted to subdue her rebellion.

"I would dare," he warned her with such quiet intensity, she knew he would. She glanced away from him and took a deep breath, trying to calm herself and find a way out of this dilemma.

"Would you force yourself upon me, even if I have no love for you?" she asked in a small voice that shook him.

"I would have you love me, Brynna," he whispered huskily. He'd lowered himself to the edge of her bed. She felt his weight and the heat of him against her thigh. Her gaze darted here and there. "Are you unable to love, Brynna?" he asked gently.

She remembered the humiliation of the night before when she'd offered herself only to find he'd fallen asleep. She hugged her pride to herself and nodded miserably.

"Why?" he asked patiently, trying not to show the hurt her anger caused him. "Why can't you love me? Do you love another?" His heart pounded in his chest as he waited for her answer. Had he made such a wretched mistake after all?

"I love no man," Brynna replied. "I never shall."

Her answer shocked him in its simplicity and honesty. Feeling helpless in the face of her implacable attitude, he felt anger surge through him. He reached for her, dragging her up from her pillows to crush her against his chest. Her mouth opened on a startled denial, but his own mouth settled on hers, his tongue delved into the sweetness of her. Stunned, she offered no resistance, then her senses returned and she pushed against his shoulders, her small fists pounding ineffectually. He kissed her thoroughly, his tongue touching hers, demanding a response, his teeth nibbling her lower lip, his arms like bands molding her to him.

A languorous warmth swept upward melting her resistance so she ceased her struggle, and slowly her arms crept around him, her sensitive fingertips felt the smoothness of his skin, the power of the muscles beneath his thin shirt. Very little separated them, and the heat of him seared her breasts. Her tender nipples ached from being pressed against the solid wall of his chest. When he saw she no longer resisted, he slowly lowered her back against the pillows and now she felt the full length of his body pressed against hers. One knee had settled between her legs, a hard thigh pressed against her mound. The muscles of his manhood leaped against her soft belly, causing a fluttery ache to begin and spread outward.

She gasped for air, fitting her mouth against his, seeking the pressure of his lips. Her hands skimmed downward over a hard, muscular back and taut middle to the flare of buttocks. Dimly she perceived she was about to press against him, to urge him closer, to encourage him to claim all he wished from her, and in the taking to end this tumultuous hunger he'd awakened. He was stunned by her response. She was like a fire unleashed, burning free. He noted her awkward innocence and the pulsating needs that even he hadn't dared hope existed.

"Brynna," he whispered hoarsely. His hands reached

for the fullness of her breasts, cupping them, kneading them until she moaned and pulled away from him.

"No," she cried, curling herself into a ball, hiding her face with shame. "Please don't," she wept. Temple lay beside her, hearing her weep, his body aching for release from the passion she'd aroused. Yet he heard her piteous cry and his anger died.

"Don't cry, Brynna," he soothed, stroking her gleaming hair with one big hand. "This is the way it should be between a man and a woman."

"I can't. I told you I can't."

"Why? Tell me so I'll understand and can help you." When she didn't answer but lay shaking her head from side to side while silent tears slid off her cheeks and wet her pillow, he tried again. "I know about your father. I know your mother didn't have a happy marriage. But I'm not like your father. I'll never hurt you, Brynna, I promise. I'll always cherish you and take care of you. I'll make you laugh and forget how to cry. I promise."

"Don't make promises you can't keep," she cried, taking her hands from her face and glaring at him. "You are like my father already. I know you are. I've seen . . ."

"You've seen what?"

"Nothing." How could she speak of this to him. It was a secret too many plantation wives carried in their hearts. "Please go. I'm tired." She lay against the pillows like a crushed flower.

Temple rose and stood looking down at her. He couldn't leave her here like this. If he did, they were doomed. He must break through her barriers.

"Just tell me one thing," he said, his chest rising and falling with each breath. "Do you love Courteney de Jarreau?"

She raised her head and looked at him in puzzlement.

230

"Cort?" she said, as if he'd suggested the most incredible thing. "Of course not."

Temple's scowl vanished, replaced by a wide grin. "Then, my wife," he said, bending to swoop her up in his arms, "I refuse your request to leave you. You are returning to our room and our bed. I will give you time to adjust to me, but I will enjoy the pleasure of seeing my wife slumbering beside me."

"You must be mad," Brynna cried as he walked down the hall with her. "Take me back at once."

"Shh! Do you want to wake Jessica and the rest of the household."

"If I must," Brynna declared. "I shall scream the house down. Then how will you explain?"

"No, *chérie,* how will you explain a wife who doesn't wish to share her new husband's bed?" He'd reached his room again and strolled to the bed. He placed her on the coverlet and straightened, frowning down at her sternly. "Tomorrow, May will return your things to this room and here you will stay. The servants will be informed not to remove your belongings again, and every night I shall go down the hall and claim you if I must, but you will not escape me, Brynna." He bent close to her, his dark eyes smoldering, his fingers caressing strands of her hair, his voice soft and coaxing when he spoke again. "Your kiss tells me something different than your words," he murmured, "so I choose to believe your kiss. You are not a cold woman, Brynna. Soon I will overcome this fear and anger you hold in your heart and I will teach you to love me."

I already do, she thought desperately. *That is why I'm so afraid.* But she didn't say the words. Silently she watched as Temple blew out the lamps. Moonlight streamed through the French doors, casting pools of light on his

231

body as he removed his shirt and boots and then his pants. The memory of that lithe, hard-muscled body pressed against hers brought a stirring in her blood. Flouncing on her side away from him, she pulled the covers over her head. She felt the mattress give as he got into bed. At once he moved toward her, putting an arm around her waist, nestling her against him spoon fashion. She tried to hold herself rigidly away from him. He only laughed.

"Good night, my stubborn little wife," he said softly. For a long time they lay like that, and she could tell by the tension in his body and the bulging warmth against her buttocks that he was not asleep.

He knew about her father! But not everything. No one knew everything. If Temple had known what a monster her father truly was, he would never have married her.

His presence was soothing and she soon found herself yawning. Right before she fell asleep, Temple shifted his arm, so one big hand fell against her breast cupping it gently. When she awoke in that first soft gray light of dawn, she found she'd turned in the night and lay pressed against Temple. One bent knee lay across his. They were touching from shoulder to hip as intimately as if they'd just made love. Dimly, she thought of drawing away, but the feel of his body against hers was too pleasant to deny. So she lay half dozing, half dreaming. She was unaware that in her dreamy state, her hips moved against him rhythmically in an age-old invitation that finally drove him from his bed and out into the fields of Langtry.

Chapter Twelve

True to his word, Temple did take a few days off to accompany Brynna to New Orleans. He would conduct some business matters while he was there as well. Determined not to interfere in any way in what must serve as a honeymoon for Brynna and Temple, Jessica stayed behind.

They left early in order to reach their destination before the heat of midday. Temple rode beside Brynna in the open carriage, and she felt herself swell with pride at the picture she and her handsome husband must make riding into the city. Wanting to do her new husband credit, she chose a favorite gown of sheer white gauze. The modest bodice was lace-and-ribbon-trimmed and the full skirts, held wide by the number of crinolines she'd donned, was ruffled and flounced. A wide-brimmed hat of white straw and lace shaded her eyes from the sun. Temple delighted in looking at her. Other than carefully spreading her skirts and opening the frilly white parasol upon first entering the carriage, she'd made no fuss about herself. Nor had she asked him to fetch her gloves or retrieve her reticule. They lay beside her on the carriage seat, forgotten as she concentrated on the scenery.

Temple chatted lightly about the countryside and the people who inhabited the fabulous plantations on the outskirts of New Orleans. He'd put the worries of Langtry behind him for a few days and concentrated on charming his wife. Brynna was not immune to Temple's dark good looks and flashing smile.

"I'd nearly forgotten how gay and exciting New Orleans is," she exclaimed, turning from side to side so as not to miss the sights and sounds.

"Living at Langtry with Jessica and me must seem rather dull to you at times," Temple said, watching her glowing face.

Brynna tilted her head and met his gaze with directness. "You know that isn't true," she scolded gently. "You only want me to repeat yet again how much I love Langtry and Jessica and y—" Her words tumbled to a halt. "Did you see the little Pierrot on the corner?" she exclaimed with forced excitement, but her blush gave her away.

Dancing lights flared to life in Temple's dark eyes as he looked at his flustered wife. She'd nearly included him in her list of people she loved. Tonight! he vowed. Tonight.

The carriage drew to a stop before the courtyard gate of the Sinclair townhouse. Temple alighted and then helped Brynna.

"Are you tired?" he asked, leading her into the courtyard.

"No," she said quickly. "I'm much too excited to rest now."

"Then wait here where it's cool. I'll see our trunks are taken up and then, my pretty wife, I have a surprise for you."

234

"What is it?" Brynna asked excitedly.

"Patience, *ma petite*," Temple said, and, humming to himself, he disappeared in the lower region of the townhouse. He was back in no time followed by a servant bearing a basket to the carriage. She had no time to wonder what all that meant, for she'd heard a soft whimper of sound from Temple's hat, which he held against his side.

"What is that?" she asked, looking at his pleased expression.

"That is my surprise for you," he replied mysteriously. "Let's see, shall I make you guess first?"

"Don't tease me," Brynna begged prettily. "I can't guess what you've done."

"Are you certain?" Temple asked as his hat shook impatiently and a sharp bark emitted from it.

"A puppy? You have a puppy!" She laughed and clapped her hands in anticipation.

Temple held out his hat, and a small ball of fur with a wet black nose and moist tongue poked his head over the brim. His eyes were hidden by a floppy fringe of hair.

"He's adorable," Brynna cooed, and gathered up the wriggling fur ball. He was so tiny, she could cover him with her two hands if she chose, except that the puppy hadn't stopped moving since she picked him up and his tiny pink tongue had already licked her fingers. "I love him," Brynna said, holding the tiny dog against her cheek. Tears burned the back of her lids as she looked up at Temple. He was moved by her obvious pleasure, but then after the foal, he'd guessed she'd be pleased by this gift as well.

"I'll bet you had a managerie of animals when you were a child." He was sorry he'd spoken the moment he said the words. Her brilliant smile faded and she hugged

235

the puppy against her breasts in an oddly protective gesture.

"I wasn't allowed to have animals of my own," she said softly. "My father said everything on the plantation belonged to him." She stopped speaking abruptly and shrugged as if pushing away the hurt. "I really didn't mind though. I—I will cherish Malka and and . . ." She held the dog at eye level. "I must find you a name," she cried with gay delight. The intense sadness of a moment before was gone, forgotten that quickly, and he knew her ability to hide such hurt had come from long years of practice. He tried to take solace in the thought that she'd actually shared something about herself with him. He was making progress, or was he? Silently, he cursed her father and wished him alive so he might call him out.

"I have another surprise," he said, delighting in the stunned disbelief in her eyes.

"Two surprises at once?" she cried. "This is too much, Temple. You'll spoil me."

"I'm trying my very best to," he replied, taking her elbow. "You'll have to come with me for our next surprise."

"What about the puppy?"

"Bring him along. We'll put our heads together to think of a name for him."

She was pleased! It showed in her bright flashing gaze, in the lilt of her voice. She was pleased, and so he was pleased. He'd already given orders to his driver, and now he settled back against the cushions to watch his wife and her new pet. The puppy seemed as taken with her as she with him. Its furry tail wagged furiously and its happy little yips brought peals of laughter from her. People passing in other carriages turned to look at them, and Temple saw the admiring and indulgent smiles when they looked at the pretty girl and her puppy.

"Where are we going?" Brynna asked when the carriage turned down Esplanade Avenue. Ahead lay the entrance to the city park.

"Are you hungry, Brynna?" Temple countered her question with one of his own. "I noticed you scarcely ate breakfast."

"I was much too excited."

"Then you must be ready for my next surprise." The carriage had entered the park, winding around lagoons until they came to a grassy plot of ground shaded by moss-draped live oaks. Snowy egrets waded the shallow lagoon. Weeping willows bent low, dragging their slender branches in the glassy pool. Temple signaled to the driver to stop.

"This looks familiar," Brynna said, looking around with wide eyes. Her gaze snapped back to meet his. "Surely you don't intend to fight another duel."

Temple's laughter was deep and rich. "The dueling oak is some distance from here," he reassured her. "We are going to have a picnic." Even as he spoke, the driver had taken the basket from the carriage and spread a quilt on the grass.

"A picnic!" Brynna exclaimed, jumping to her feet in excitement. Temple helped her from the carriage and watched as she lifted her skirt with one hand and ran across the grassy clearing. Her delighted gaze came back to him, time and again. Lights sparkled in her beautiful eyes. With the guilelessness of a curious child, she placed her puppy on the blanket and rummaged in the basket.

"I wasn't hungry," she called, waving him to join her, "but now I am. You've brought wine and those favorite little sausages I like so well, and cheese and bread and

237

fruit." She popped a grape into her mouth and impatiently tossed her hat on the corner of the blanket. With a ferocious growl, the puppy trotted to it and attacked a silk flower. Temple and Brynna laughed. "You'll have to name him something in keeping with his nature," Temple warned. "None of these cuddly, babyish names."

"You're right," Brynna replied, seating herself on the edge of the blanket. Taking out two plates, she prepared a generous portion of everything for them both. "I shall have to name him after a famous General. Washington, perhaps."

"Attila the Hun or Ivan the Terrible sounds more appropriate," Temple suggested, rescuing her hat.

"You're a generous, thoughtful man," Brynna said, tearing off bits of bread and sausage to feed the puppy. Her lighthearted manner was gone.

"Here now," Temple admonished her teasingly. "I'm all of that and more, but it's no reason to become melancholy and serious. We're on holiday, *n'est-ce pas?*"

"Mais oui," Brynna replied pertly, and settled down to eat. There was no awkward groping for subjects of conversations between them. Brynna's lively mind took in all subjects. She ate heartily, Temple saw, without false modesty, and when she'd finished, she kicked off her shoes, rolled off her stockings, and rubbed her bare feet in the grass. Sunlight filtered through the trees, dabbling her full skirts with yellow light. Relaxed and contented just to sit here in the sunlight and enjoy the sight of his wife playing with her puppy, Temple's lids grew heavy and before very long he'd dozed.

Brynna let him sleep. Even the puppy had tired himself and lay cuddled in her lap. With nothing to divert her attention, Brynna's gaze moved time and again to her husband. How tired he looked. He was working far too

238

hard, trying to save Langtry, she was certain. She thought again of her inheritance. Temple hadn't taken the money yet, no doubt from a sense of pride. She gazed lovingly at his sprawled form. A man of Temple's nature would hate to take money from his wife. He was accustomed to giving, as his presents indicated. Her hand went to smooth the fur ball asleep on her lap. A frown rippled her brow. Most men gave their wives expensive jewelry. Temple had been forced to give her simple gifts like a foal and a puppy. Not that she was complaining. She much preferred them to gems which she must lock away. Still, his gifts said something about his financial state. What if he desperately needed the money for Langtry this very moment and was too embarrassed to ask? Brynna's stroking of the white fluff halted. This was really too ridiculous. She would transfer the money to Langtry's account on her own and nothing need ever be said about it again. Having made up her mind, she was anxious to be done with it.

"Temple," she said softly. He made no stirring. Carefully, she leaned over him, studying at close quarters the lines and textures of his face, the wide brow, lean cheeks, and firm mouth. She knew how those lips felt against hers, the havoc they wrought. Forgotten were her plans to transfer her money. She sat mesmerized by the sight of her sleeping husband. She longed for him to wake up, so she could hear his voice and see the passion and desire in his eyes. Gently, she blew against his eyelids. He grunted and rolled his head to one side. Mischievous laughter glinted in her eyes as she lowered her head and blew against his ear.

Temple moaned softly and rolled his head back so their lips were wonderfully close. She longed for the courage to press her lips against his. Instead, she pursed them and prepared to blow against his eyes once more.

Suddenly strong hands seized her, pulling her forward against an unyielding chest. A mouth, hot and demanding, claimed hers. Brynna held herself stiffly, then relaxed in her husband's arms. She had brought this on herself, she acknowledged, so she must submit. But simple acquiescense grew to tentative participation, and finally to outright response. She fit her mouth against his with less awkwardness than she had before and, when his tongue stroked against hers, she melted against him. The kiss was long and thorough. Brynna gave no thought to any passersby who might see them. She was too immersed in the ardent passion of her husband's kiss.

At last he drew away. "If we keep this up, we may well break a city ordinance," he said softly. Cheeks flaming, Brynna drew back and fussily smoothed her skirts. The puppy still slept on her lap.

"I was trying to wake you to remind you about your appointment this afternoon."

The teasing playfulness left his expression and he sat up. "Ah, yes, reality intrudes," he said ruefully. "Still it was an idyllic interlude." His glance was sultry. "Perhaps we can repeat the pleasurable experience this evening?"

"I—I shall look forward to dining with you," Brynna said, and rose so quickly, she sent the puppy tumbling head over heels onto the pallet. He shook himself and barked sharply, conveying his indignation. They laughed at his antics, glad for the diversion.

Quickly they packed up the remains of their picnic and walked back to the carriage.

"Thank you for the lovely picnic," Brynna said, "and for the puppy." She paused, struggling with the need to say something further and fear of revealing herself too much. "You really aren't like my father, you know."

They'd reached the carriage now, and Temple had

lowered the step for her to enter. At her words, he paused, his gaze searching. "Thank you for trusting me, Brynna," he said huskily, taking hold of her hand.

"It isn't just that," she said quickly, shying away from too intimate a disclosure of her feelings. "I enjoy your company. You make me feel happy about things, and you're thoughtful and kind." While he sorted out her rush of words, she sprang into the carriage by herself and primly settled her skirts about her. Touched by the things she'd said and the contrasting moods of his wife, Temple seated himself across from her and watched as she played with her puppy. Half child, half woman, she was utterly enchanting. With every moment he spent in her company, he grew more ensnared by her beauty and touching vulnerability. Tonight, he exaulted. Tonight, she would be his in all ways.

Brynna stood on the banquette and watched the carriage roll away with Temple in it. He turned once to wave and she waved back. When he was out of sight, she hurried to her room, where she settled the puppy on her bed and freshened herself. When she felt she looked her best, she sped down the stairs and let herself out of the courtyard without notifying any of the servants of her intentions. She wanted to complete her business at the bank and be back home ahead of Temple.

She hurried down the street in search of a hired carriage and was soon conveyed to the New Orleans Bank and Trust. A uniformed guard bowed her into the establishment and a smiling bank teller escorted her at once to Monsieur Laussat, the bank president. Brynna recognized him as one of the guests at her wedding.

"Mrs. Sinclair!" he said effusively. He held a chair for

her to be seated. "I'm honored by your visit," he continued, seating himself behind the ornately carved wooden desk and assuming an officious air. "How may I help you?"

"I've come about my account, Mr. Laussat . . ." Brynna began, placing the tip of her parasol on the floor beside her and twirling it slightly. Perhaps she should have waited for Temple, she thought nervously, then pushed the idea aside. If she were able to help run a plantation like Langtry, she was certainly capable of tending to her business affairs. Laussat had watched the emotions play over her face with masculine indulgence. She reminded him of his own daughter, who was always overdrawn on her allowance and needing to wheedle more for a new petticoat or trinket.

"No doubt you need to make a withdrawal from your account here," he said indulgently. "That can be arranged." He picked up a pen, dipped it in the inkwell and glanced up. "How much would you like?"

"All of it," Brynna answered.

A splotch of ink marred the spotless blotter. Monsieur Laussat fixed her with a reproving glare over the rim of his glasses. "All of it? My dear child, are you aware of how much money is in your account?"

"Mr. Sinclair has told me," Brynna replied, growing irritated by his condescending air. Her chin raised to a regal angle, her large eyes darkened with a warning he did not read. "Is there a problem, Mr. Laussat? Do you not have that much money on hand?"

"Yes, of course," he said quickly, but he laid down the pen and rubbed his palms together in perplexity. "I just fail to see how you could have need of all your inheritance at once. Unless of course you wish to remove it from our establishment and place it elsewhere."

Brynna took pity on him. Head tilted slightly so the brim of her hat shadowed her eyes, she smiled graciously. "Let me hasten to end your discomfort, Monsieur Laussat," she said. "I have no desire to take my money from your bank. I wish merely to have all of it transferred to the Langtry accounts."

"Transferred to the—" Laussat's troubled expression cleared briefly, then he frowned as he thought of all such a move would entail. "You realize of course that once that money is transferred into the Langtry accounts, you may not draw on it without authorization from Temple Sinclair."

"I'd not given it any thought," Brynna answered honestly, "but it doesn't matter. Please transfer the funds as I've asked you."

"Mais oui, madame," Laussat said, taking up the pen and writing swiftly. "You are wise to put your inheritance in the hands of Temple Sinclair. He will be able to invest it far more prudently than you yourself could."

Again the banker's condescension rankled. "I feel I've just invested my funds prudently, Mister Laussat," she replied.

"Yes, of course. I didn't mean to imply otherwise," he said quickly, but they both knew he had. He laid aside his pen. "It is done!" he exclaimed, smiling down at her. Business concluded, he rose and extended his arm to escort her from his office and to the door of the bank. Heads turned to watch the pretty girl walk by. As they neared the door, Brynna spied the hired carriage and was reminded of yet another problem. Cheeks blushing, she turned to the pompous banker.

"I'm afraid I'm without funds to pay the hired carriage," she said, with some embarrassment.

"I'd be honored to take care of that," Laussat said,

pulling a thick wallet from the inside pockets of his coat.

"Brynna, *chérie*, how wonderful to see you again," a gay voice called. Alicia de Jarreau approached and placed her cool cheek against Brynna's. Startled at this uncharacteristic display of friendship, Brynna could only stare. "What is this?" Alicia asked archly, looking at Laussat's wallet and the money he held in one hand. "Don't tell me you're transacting a withdrawal here on the banquette in front of the bank?"

"It's a personal loan . . ." the banker began, flustered at Alicia's comments.

"Surely, the wife of Temple Sinclair, one of the wealthiest planters in the country, doesn't have to borrow from the town banker. How distressing."

"It's only a small loan," Brynna said stiffly. "I've managed to come away without funds to pay for the hired carriage. Now if you'll excuse me, I must be on my way. Temple will be expecting me."

"Come, my dear." Laussat helped her into the carriage and paid the driver with instructions that he was to deliver his passenger back to the townhouse on Royal Street without delay. Stepping away from the curb, Laussat bowed slightly in farewell.

"Brynna!" Alicia's peremptorial cry caused the driver to stay his whip over the team's backs.

"What do you want, Alicia?" Brynna asked with some reluctance. She wished only to be away from the other girl.

Alicia placed a dainty, glove-clad hand on the carriage door. "I wasn't aware you and Temple were in town. Are you staying at the townhouse?" Brynna nodded. "I'll come have tea with you this afternoon."

"Oh, I'm not sure . . ." Brynna began.

"Well, if you don't want me to come," Alicia sniffed. "I

was only trying to be friends. After all, the Sinclairs and the de Jarreaus have been good friends since our great-grandparents' day. I'd hoped only to extend the effort to you."

"Alicia, wait!" Brynna called. "Of course, I'll look forward to your coming for tea," she lied. "I just wasn't sure what Temple's plans were."

"My goodness, Brynna, he'll be delighted to see me. I'm certain of that. If he's cross with you, I'll speak to him on your behalf. I've always been able to make him do what I wanted." Her smile was mocking and assured as she stepped back from the carriage.

Brynna thought about the beautiful Creole all the way home. Alicia de Jarreau seemed to think she still had some influence with Temple, yet she hadn't been able to get him to marry her, Brynna comforted herself. However, she couldn't overlook the obvious. Her husband was something of a ladies' man and she'd simply have to come to terms with it. She couldn't be jealous of every woman who threw herself at him. Yet, he wasn't the debonair roué Cort was, nor had she ever seen him deliberately behave flirtatiously with another woman. Something else drew the women to Temple Sinclair—the dark Creole looks coupled with a warmth and charm that was as much a part of his nature as the steadfast devotion to his plantation and family. Intuitively, women knew he would never treat them heartlessly.

Her thoughts were full of Temple as she alighted from the carriage and made her way upstairs. The puppy ran to greet her with tiny yelps of pleasure and soft slurps from his pink tongue. Laughing, Brynna sat on the edge of the bed and played with him a while, tumbling him about while he emitted ferocious growls. Tired at last, he curled up beside her and fell asleep. She longed to rest a while herself, but her bath had been brought and she wanted to be fresh and beautiful when Temple returned from his appointment.

Sliding into the tepid water, she leaned against the high back of the tub and thought about the picnic with her husband. His eyes had been filled with dark lights that thrilled her from head to foot. Every part of her tingled just to think of his kiss. She remembered the night at Langtry when she'd almost succumbed to his caresses. There'd been anger and suspicions between them then. The anger was gone now, the suspicions allayed for a time. Idly she wondered what might happen between them this night.

Sighing, she used the washcloth to slosh water over her shoulders and neck. It ran in tepid streams over her heated skin. The rough washcloth brushed against her sensitive nipples and she drew in her breath, remembering how Temple's hand had possessed that breast, how her body had responded with turgid, tumbling demands that threatened to overwhelm her. Tonight, she thought breathlessly. Perhaps tonight she would learn what all these troubling emotions meant.

Rising, she dried herself and, with the help of Darcie, Jessica's New Orleans maid, she slipped into a gown of pale-yellow silk. Though the color was one of her favorites and looked well with her coloring, she wrinkled her nose in distaste. The addition of a white lace-trimmed pelerine beneath the collar and the gigot sleeves made her look like a prim schoolgirl. Brynna stood before her mirror bunching her heavy hair first on top of her head and then into a cascade of curls behind each ear in an effort to see which way made her look more grown-up and sophisticated. She grew more exasperated with each attempt.

"Ah fix yo' hair so yo' look like a lady," Darcie reassured her, but before she could brush the curls into its intricate design, Sully knocked on the door to announce Alicia de Jarreau had come for tea. Hastily, Brynna caught the heavy silken curls back with a matching ribbon and went to the main salon to join her unwanted guest.

"My dear child," Alicia said effusively, kissing the air near Brynna's ear. Drawing away, she looked around the richly appointed room with a proprietary air and settled herself on the sofa before the tea table. The puppy had followed Brynna into the room and now he ran to greet the guest, his tiny white furry tail wagging a welcome. With a grimace of distaste, Alicia shook her skirts to shoo him away.

"You must be frank with me, Brynna dear," she said, taking on the role of the hostess and pouring out tea. Her dark eyes were calculating and avid with curiosity. "Is Temple being perfectly beastly to you about pocket money? You mustn't feel ashamed. After all, as I told you earlier, I do have some influence with him. Of course, this must be dreadfully hard for you, marrying a wealthy planter only to find yourself unable to touch his money. That is why you went to the bank this afternoon, isn't it?"

Brynna seated herself in a lolling chair and took the cup offered by Alicia. The puppy promptly leaped into her lap and settled down. Brynna met the other woman's gaze serenely. "Temple is a thoughtful and generous husband," she said sweetly. "If you knew him as I do, you'd never think him capable of anything less."

Alicia's smile vanished. The teapot clattered sharply against the delicate cup. "Then why did you go begging to Monsieur Laussat?" she persisted. "You must be sensitive to your position as Temple's wife. The Sinclairs are a fine old family here in Louisiana."

"My mother was a Beaumont," Brynna answered

firmly. "They were an equally important family in Tennessee. I come to the Sinclairs with credentials no less admirable."

Alicia studied her with a hard, speculative gaze. She hadn't expected this usurper to show such spirit.

"If your mother's family is so important in Tennessee, why did you come here?" she demanded.

"Because Jessica and Temple invited me," Brynna answered. "And once I came and saw how beautiful this country is, I chose not to leave."

Silently, Alicia stirred her tea, her mind working furiously over the things Brynna had revealed. Brynna knew the other girl was still puzzled over the swiftness of her marriage to Temple. The puppy stirred and growled ferociously.

"Brynna!" A voice filled with impatience and male indignation called out. Temple had returned, and in a foul mood, it seemed. Casting a quick glance at Alicia, Brynna hastily rose and ran to the gallery.

"Did you call me?" she asked worriedly. This was not the same man who had wooed her in the park earlier. His eyebrows were pulled down in a dark scowl. His long legs stalked the length of gallery and brought him back again at the sound of her voice.

"I spoke to Monsieur Laussat," he said without preamble. "He told me you were at the bank today."

"I— Yes," Brynna said faintly. Then she raised her chin and met his gaze with more courage. "I had business to attend to there."

"Yes, and he told me of your business. Why did you do it, Brynna?"

"But that was our agreement," she replied in puzzlement. "You hadn't gotten around to making the transfer of funds. I thought you might—might—." She stuttered to a halt.

Temple's gaze softened as he looked at her troubled face. "You thought my pride might be wounded at having to take money from my wife?"

"Yes, oh, don't say anything more," Brynna gasped, remembering Alicia sat inside the parlor. "We have a—"

"And you thought since our marriage was based on my acquiring your inheritance that you'd see it was done." Temple's gaze was warm on her.

"Please . . ." Brynna interrupted. "Won't you come inside for a cup of tea. We have a visitor."

Temple frowned. "Who would be calling on us here?" He moved toward the doors leading directly into the parlor from the gallery.

"Temple, darling," Alicia cried, rushing forward in a whisper of silken skirts to take hold of his hands and offer her cheek for his kiss. Leaning against him in an intimate pose, she smiled with delight, as if the two of them were lovers meeting again after a long separation and kept from a more intimate embrace only by Brynna's presence.

Brynna bit her lower lip. She'd had quite enough of her unwanted guest and her manipulations.

"Come, sit with me and tell me everything you've been doing. I've missed our long chats." Alicia wound her arm through Temple's and guided him toward the sofa. She drew him down beside her, brushing aside the small puppy who'd since taken possession of the sofa. He went tumbling to the floor and, looking somewhat disgruntled at such treatment, shook himself.

Alicia leaned close to Temple, her dark eyes reflecting adoration, her smile soft and girlish. Brynna clenched her fists in her lap and ignored the puppy's restless bark.

"I ran into Brynna at the bank today," Alicia was

saying prettily. "She arrived in a hired carriage and had to borrow funds from Monsieur Laussat to pay for it. I've just been pointing out how important her position is as your wife and that she must make an effort not to embarrass you in such a manner."

Temple drew back from Alicia's grasping hands and fixed her with an amused gaze. "I believe my wife only adds luster to the Sinclair name," he said softly. One dark eyebrow lifted whimsically. Brynna had seen such a look before when he was irritated with a guest and trying his best to maintain a decorous front. She felt her own anger melting and leaned back in her chair, a serene smile on her lips.

Alicia looked from one to the other of them, her brow puckering. "I'm sure she will grow into it," she commented wryly, and studied her hands for a moment. "How fortunate for you, my dear, that you had a large dowry."

"I'm not sure I understand what you mean," Brynna said.

"I'm afraid I do," Temple answered.

"I simply mean," Alicia began as if carefully seeking her words, "having a large dowry improves one's chances of making an advantageous liaison."

"Don't you mean marriage?" Temple asked brusquely. "Brynna and I are married." Impatiently, he got to his feet. "It was good of you to call on us, Alicia." His tone made it clear the social call was over. Alicia remained seated, her lips fixed in a smile that never reflected in her eyes.

"How long will you be in New Orleans?" she asked, drawing on her gloves with deliberate care.

"We have only a few days before we must return to Langtry. Obviously, we wish to make the most of every

250

minute," he answered pointedly, "since it is our honey-moon."

"Jessica didn't come with you? My, Brynna, you've put her in her place rather quickly, haven't you?" Alicia's unkind insinuations brought color to Brynna's cheeks.

"Jessica still hasn't recovered from her fever bout," she answered, and would have gone on if Alicia hadn't let out an outraged scream.

"Get that horrid little creature away from me," she cried, jumping to her feet and shaking her skirts. The puppy sat back on his haunches, his small black nose wriggling, his tiny mouth opened wide in pleased regard for what he'd done. A spreading pool of moisture gleamed on Alicia's satin slippers and stained the hem of her gown. "You little beast," Alicia cried, and kicked at the puppy. With a yelp he went tumbling backward.

"Oh, don't do that," Brynna cried, running to rescue the tiny white fluff ball. "He didn't mean to soil your slippers."

"Your dog is just as—as *malfaisant* as you," Alicia said, her eyes glinting maliciously.

"Alicia!" Temple's voice was a crack of thunder ending her impetuous words. "You forget, mademoiselle, that you are speaking to my wife. I will not support such insults to her."

Speechless with rage, Alicia glared back at him and then at Brynna. Without another word, she gathered the soiled skirts to the side, well away from her, and flounced out of the room. Wordlessly, Brynna watched her go. Temple followed her to the gallery and returned only after he was sure she'd departed the courtyard below. When he returned to the parlor, he paused and regarded his wife. She stood with the small furry animal clutched to her bosom, her eyes wide and defensive.

251

"Truly, it was an accident," she exclaimed, afraid he would be too angry to allow her to keep the puppy.

"Pity," he said. "I thought it was too well done to be entirely accidental." Temple's eyes glinted with humor. Brynna felt the tension ease from her, then, at the memory of Alicia's outrage, she couldn't repress a chuckle. Temple's laughter joined with hers.

"Have you thought of a name for this fine fellow yet?" he asked, taking the puppy from her and holding it aloft. Nearly dwarfed by Temple's large hands, the puppy yipped and wriggled until Temple brought him closer. "He's not only handsome, but quite astute as well." The puppy put out a tongue and licked Temple's chin.

"I thought I might call him Beauregard," Brynna said, coming to stand beside her husband and stroking the white fur. Immediately, the puppy turned his attention to her, covering her fingers with affectionate little licks.

"The name's bigger than he is," Temple observed, "but I approve." He turned his glance to Brynna. "I approve of everything."

She blushed beneath his praise. "Then you aren't angry with me for transferring my funds over to the Langtry accounts?"

"How could I be angry for an act of trust and commitment such as you've made?" His dark gaze robbed her of breath. "There's no going back now, Brynna. You know that."

"Yes, I know," she answered, and knew they were no longer speaking of dowries or Langtry. She'd made a commitment to their marriage just as he had. Now they would move toward their future together. And tonight, neither doubted their marriage would be consummated.

Chapter Thirteen

Intent on making this night memorable in every way, Temple took her to Antoine's, a popular new restaurant with an enviable wine cellar. Obsequious waiters escorted them to one of the best tables and presented menus with a flourish. Temple ordered pompano en papilote, les huitres frais aux agrumes, poule faisane rotie à la liqueur des Pères Chartreux, and because he knew she was still child like enough to enjoy it, he finished with meringues glacées. But Brynna was too nervous to pay attention to her food. Time and again, as she glanced at her handsome husband, she wondered what the night would hold for her.

At last the table was cleared and only goblets of sparkling wine sat before them. Brynna had lost count of the number of times she'd sipped from her glass only to have it refilled. Her head was giddy and she felt a wonderful urge to giggle and float away over the heads of the other diners. Sometime or another Temple had taken a firm hold of her hand and she was certain that was all that kept her anchored in her chair.

"Have I mentioned you're the most beautiful woman

in the room?" Temple murmured, leaning close. His dark eyes held magnetic lights.

"Several times," she said lightly. "You're liable to turn my head if you continue."

"Shall I stop?"

"No!" Her head was close to his. She smelled his masculine scent. "I've never had my head turned before."

"You've never had a man tell you how beautiful you are?" His voice was low and teasing, his glance bold with promises that made her shiver deliciously.

"Never a man whose opinion mattered to me," she answered.

"And do I matter to you, Brynna?" His husky voice made her feel shaky inside, as if she were caught in an earthquake.

"You are my husband," she hedged.

"A fact for which I shall be forever grateful," he said, and raised her fingertips to his lips, kissing each one as tenderly as if she were a beloved child.

"D-do I matter to you?" she asked softly, scarcely aware she'd uttered the words, so loudly did they sing in her heart.

"More than Langtry itself," he answered so fervently, she pulled away, needing to distance herself from this happiness she felt so she might draw a deep breath and calm her racing pulse.

Temple reached inside a pocket and pulled out a velvet box, placing it before her with a small flourish.

"What is this?" she exclaimed, eyes shining brightly. She loved presents.

"Open it and see for yourself, *ma petite.*" Leaning back, he lit a cheroot and watched with pleasure as she opened the box. It contained a pendant of fine topaz ringed by emerals and tiny diamonds. Her mouth rounded with surprise and admiration.

"Let me fasten it," he said, taking the necklace from the box and placing it around her neck. As his fingers fumbled with the clasp, he noted the smooth white skin of her slender neck.

"It's beautiful," she exclaimed when the pendant was in place, "but you've given me so many things already."

"I couldn't resist when I saw it," Temple said huskily. "It reminded me of your eyes, but now I see the beauty of the stones can never match your magnificent eyes." Once again he took her hand. His dark gaze captured hers. "You take my breath away when you look at me like that. Your eyes are filled with warmth and passion. I want to know more about the passionate woman revealed by your glances. Shall we go?"

"If you wish," Brynna said faintly. She rose and felt the room sway around her. It seemed every eye was on her. Brynna put a hand to her forehead. Temple was there, placing a steadying arm around her waist. Gratefully, Brynna leaned against him as he guided her from the restaurant. Indeed, other diners did pause to watch them, thinking they'd never seen such handsome lovers.

In the carriage, Temple pulled her into the protective curve of his shoulder. Giggling slightly, Brynna leaned her head back.

"I've had too much wine," she said, and giggled again. Temple's chuckle sounded in her ear, warm and intimate. His body heat was comforting and disturbing at the same time; still, she snuggled into it, feeling whole and strong and ready for whatever mysteries the night held.

"Your eyes are filled with moonlight," Temple whispered in her ear and placed his lips against her smooth cheek. The clop clop of the horse's hooves matched the rhythm of her thrumming pulse. "Great golden eyes that see all the way into my soul," he said, trailing tiny kisses across her cheeks and down to her jaw. "They learn my secrets, manly secrets that only you should know. They see my love for you." Soft kisses brushed her eyelids. "My desire." His lips touched the tip of her nose. "My needs, which I can no longer deny." His lips claimed her then. His kiss was gentle, maddeningly controlled.

She wanted more. Her arms snaked around his neck, pulling his head down, deepening the contact of their mouths. Her tongue, soft and hesitant touched his lips, timidly seeking. His arms folded her to him, molding her soft body to his sleek, hard one. She opened her mouth to him, but he remained restrained, making her wait, making her ask for what she wanted. His teeth nipped her soft mouth, then his kiss gentled once more. He cradled her against his chest, stroking her back. She wriggled closer, suddenly hating the petticoats and layers of silk that held them apart. Boldly she sought his mouth, her small white teeth closing over his full lower lip as he had done with her. She heard his moan and felt him shudder against her. Startled, she grew still, assimilating the sudden knowledge that he was as moved by her as she by him. Raised as she was in a household where women had no power and certainly never over a man, she was stunned by this revelation.

His passion awakened, Temple wasn't content to rest quietly. Once again his lips claimed hers, his large hands stroked and caressed with building intensity, first her back and waist and then upward to the soft mounds of her breasts. Brynna's breath drew in sharply. A languor swept over her, so she whimpered softly. The carriage stopped before the walled courtyard. Temple stepped down and reached for her, gathering her in his arms.

Moonlight gilded the fountain and cast a blue-silver light over the bricked walk as he carried her across the courtyard and up the stairs to their room. Once there, he released her legs, letting her body slide downward against his, while his lips claimed hers for kisses that left her breathless. At last he drew away and lit a lamp, turning the wick low so the room was cast in golden shadows. Darcie looked inside to see if she was wanted, but without taking his dark gaze off his wife, Temple waved the servant away.

"I'll need her to get out of my dress," Brynna protested.

"You have me," Temple said. "You have no need of anyone else."

Amid kisses and caressing strokes, he unfastened the buttons that held the silk gown closed. With maddening slowness he undressed her, drawing the yellow silk from her young form, feasting his gaze on his wife's body. Next came the loosening of petticoats, which he insisted upon doing. His hands settled on the rounded curve of her buttocks, kneading her flesh, awakening strange longings until she fairly wanted to tear at the lacings of her corset. Slowly, teasingly, he peeled away the layers of cloth, bone, ribbon, and lace that separated the two of them, and when she stood before him, blushing and shy in her nakedness, he took away the pins that held the shiny coils of hair in place. It cascaded around her shoulders and down her back. He bent to bury his face in the fragrant strands, then pushed them away to taste the sweetness of her flesh.

She remembered his strong, masculine body rising from the steam of his bath and now she longed to see and touch him. What she must turn from seeing before, she now sought with unmaidenly passion. She undressed him as he had her, feeling him tremble as she brushed the

257

ruffled lawn shirt from his shoulders and fumbled with the unfamiliar fastenings of his trousers until at last he pushed her hands aside and flung off his own clothes.

Her cheeks grew hot, her gaze darted away from the sight of lean hips and long, tapering legs. But she'd thought of him often since that day she first saw him at his bath, and curiosity overcame shyness, so at last she gazed at him boldly, noting the sinewy muscles and sloping planes of his body. She'd never thought a man could be beautiful. She realized with a rush now that her husband was. She touched where her gaze led her. Tracing with one finger over the rippling broad shoulders down to the sworl of hair, the hard flat nipples that puckered as hers did when she touched them.

He waited, breathing deeply, while she explored, until her questing hands touched the tumultuous leaping muscle of his manhood. With a groan of helplessness he swept her into his arms and carried her to the bed. His pulse was racing, but he bit his lips to still his needs. She was a virgin. He'd wooed her to this place, he wouldn't risk losing her for one runaway moment of passion. Gently he stroked her slim body, suckling her breasts until she arched beneath him and looked at him with wonder-filled eyes.

"There's more to come, my sweet," he whispered, and stroked lower over the curving planes of hips to the warmth of her woman's mound. He felt her stiffen, then relax as he continued to stroke, and only when she began to stir beneath his hand, did he stroke more intimately, waking her to new delights until she lay gasping and moaning. He kissed her, his tongue delving deep while his hand repeated the rhythmic dance on her body. He felt her shudder and jerk, and he rose and entered her, gently at first until the first shock of his invasion had passed, then deeper. He felt the resistance of her maidenhead, heard her muffled cry as it gave way. He cradled her, rocking her gently until the pain had receded. When he felt her stir again, he plunged against her, free at last to answer his own needs. His hands guided her slim legs to wrap around him. He raised her hips and thrust into her. He gloried in her answering movements and felt a roaring consume him like a summer hurricane sweeping in from the gulf. Dimly he heard her cry out. The sound was filled with surprise and triumph, then stilled as they began the long, sliding ride to a wondrous new place neither had ever known before.

They slept, twined in each other's arms, and woke in the night with the lamp still burning. In its burnished light, she grew shy, her gaze evasive, until he captured her mouth. Then the shy maiden wrapped her arms and legs around him and moved wantonly. Her eyes were shiny with emotion when she met his gaze. Awakened to passion's wonders, she planted tiny kisses over his chin, throat, and chest and downward until, with a groan, he stopped her. She was innocence, unaware of what she did, but his own body reacted with a hunger of its own, and he knew there were some lessons better left till later.

He cuddled her next to him, but she pushed away from him, climbing astraddle him, her pert breasts bared to his searing gaze. He cupped them in his hand, feeling the heat of her nipples against his palms. Her soft buttocks rode against his manhood with each wriggle she made until he'd grown hard and turgid again. Her red-gold hair spilled around her and onto his stomach, tickling his skin. Lifting her at the waist, he settled her on top of him, thrusting upward into her and seeing her eyes open wide in surprise at his entrance.

She arched as if in pain, and he reminded himself he

must be careful yet. She was still too new at this game of love. But she drew a deep breath and adjusted herself. Gently she rocked herself, her expression filled with pleasure, then her golden eyes darkened and glazed with intensity and her movements became larger and swifter. She made little gasping sounds as she moved against him and cried out, arching against him before falling forward like a broken flower. Her hair covered them both, her sweat-sleeked body rose and fell as she drew in short breaths of air. Temple held her until their breathing returned to normal, then he pulled the cover around them, so she wouldn't grow chilled. Her eyes were closed now, her muscles slack with fatigue. Her golden lashes lay against her pale cheeks as she drifted toward sleep. Temple smoothed the hair from her cheek and she stirred, calling out for him.

"Shhh, *bébé*," he whispered softly. "I'm here. I'll always be here."

"I love you, Temple," she sighed, and slept.

He lay awake for a long time, his heart too full to sleep. He'd won that prize which he'd so deeply sought, and its taking was more glorious than anything he'd imagined. She'd been as giving in love as she was in all things. The shadows were behind them.

When he woke in the morning, Brynna was seated in a chair near the windows, demurely dressed in a white sprigged muslin dress, her glorious hair twisted neatly into a loop on top of her head. When she saw he was awake, she rose and lifted a tray from a nearby table.

"Good morning," she said brightly, placing the tray before him. Black coffee and fresh beignets had been arranged for him. "I've brought your breakfast," she said shyly, avoiding his gaze.

"Brynna," he said, catching her hand. "Kiss me." Her

gaze flew everywhere, from the tray to his chin to the door of the room as if someone might be waiting without. "Kiss me," he repeated and, at last, her gaze met his. Obediently, she leaned forward and placed her lips against his. Her breath was sweet, her lips soft. His hand fumbled in the coils of hair, removing the hairpins. She tried to draw away, but he held her prisoner until the last pin was gone and her hair tumbled about them. Then he lowered his head and suckled one breast through the constraining muslin. He heard her draw her breath in and laughed triumphantly.

"Take off your clothes, wife, and come back to bed," he ordered.

"I can't. The servants!"

"The servants be damned," he cried, pulling her forward so he could undo the buttons of her bodice and touch the sweet, cool skin of her breasts with the tip of his tongue.

"I truly can't," she cried, pulling away from him with some reluctance.

"Why not?" he demanded, then struck by her crimson cheeks, he paused and laughed outright.

"Did I use my new bride too harshly?" he asked teasingly. "Then never mind, come sit beside me and share my coffee."

Willingly, Brynna complied. "What shall we do today?" she asked brightly, and he was delighted at her easy manner with him. A barrier had been torn down forever last night and he meant never to have another one between them.

"Would you like to go to a horserace?" he asked, and laughed at her enthusiastic reply. "First, we'll finish breakfast," he chided. She buttered the croissants for him and poured cream in his coffee, and with such charm, he thought, he might never take his eyes from her. Perched on the edge of his bed, she fed him, breaking off tiny bits of roll for him and herself, raising the cup to his lips, wiping his mouth, kissing his chin, and then repeating the process until they forgot time and place, so lost were they in each other.

"I'll be late for the race," Temple exclaimed at last, pushing aside the tray and leaping out of bed.

"Are you racing?" Brynna asked in surprise.

"That's why I had the groom bring Chandra from Langtry," Temple replied. He stepped into the tub and sloshed water over his body. Brynna watched him openly, glorying in the fact she could do so without shame or reservation. He was her husband and, after last night, she had no doubts that she was his wife. He'd branded her as surely as if she'd been his slave. Caught in the novelty of watching her husband dress, she barely left time to change into a more suitable gown and have her hair recoiffed. With a knowing smile, Darcie arranged the strands for a second time that morning. When she was finished, Brynna perched a lace-and-plume-trimmed straw bonnet on her head and tied the bow beneath her chin. Temple's eyes widened in appreciation when he saw her.

"I'll be the envy of every man at the race," he said, escorting her down the stairs. The city streets were filled with people as the carriage rolled by on its way to the city park. Other carriages had fallen into line headed for the same destination. Once inside the park, the driver turned the carriage toward a grassy clearing where a racing oval had been marked out. Carriages filled with planters and their wives ringed the racing grounds.

"Brynna," a voice called, and Brynna waved to Francine Beynaud. Temple directed Ben to pull the carriage next to the Beynaud conveyance.

"Will you be all right here?" he asked, alighting and taking Chandra's reins.

Happily Brynna nodded. "Be careful," she said, leaning over the edge of the carriage to peer at him.

"Give me something of yours for luck," he ordered, pulling her down to kiss her. Brynna drew out a lace-trimmed handkerchief. "I give you this and all my love," she said softly, feeling like Guinevere.

Temple tucked the handkerchief into a pocket. "I shall carry it next to my heart, always," he answered gravely. Then he leaped into his saddle and galloped toward the starting line.

Francine had watched the tender exchange silently, and when Temple was gone, she called again to Brynna. "I didn't know you'd come to New Orleans."

"We took a few days for a h-honeymoon," Brynna replied, then blushed.

"Ah, so that is the way of it," Francine teased, and laughed when Brynna blushed yet again. "Temple Sinclair is a very handsome man, very strong. He once had a reputation with the ladies."

"Yes, so I've guessed," Brynna said, frowning slightly at the memory of Alicia and Betty Hewitt.

Francine laughed gaily. "Do not be jealous, *ma chère*. A man must gain his experience from somewhere. He must have his *babiole*. Now his wild days are behind him. He is pleased with his new young wife. Observe how he looks back to see that you are watching him."

Indeed, Temple had looked back. Brynna waved gaily to him.

"Ah, *petite*, how your face gives you away. You love this

263

husband of yours. How different from the *tragique* face of the bride."

"I've decided not to think about . . . about his life before. I will concentrate only on our lives together."

"Bravo, *ma chère*," Francine exclaimed. "Now you are becoming like the Creoles. We do not bother our heads with that which we cannot change. We enjoy life as it is now." She paused and twirled her parasol. "I see you have another admirer." Gaily she waved to someone.

Brynna glanced around to see Cort de Jarreau staring at her. When he saw he'd been caught, he urged his horse closer, cheerfully greeting Francine before turning to Brynna.

"Cort!" Brynna exclaimed. "I'm so glad to see you."

"Are you?" he asked, his dark eyes studying her lively face. She was more beautiful than he remembered.

"We've missed seeing you. You didn't stay when you called with Monsieur Fortier."

"That is true," Cort said, shaking off his somber mood and adopting the light flirtatious tone she was more familiar with. "Did you miss me, Brynna?"

"Temple and I both miss you," she said carefully, but her eyes flashed with laughter. She liked Cort for all his careless antics. "Tell me, will you be challenged to a duel today or have you behaved yourself."

Cort threw back his head and laughed. She teased more boldly now and he hated to think such a minor change had been brought about from Temple; but her eyes sparkled with assurance and she carried herself like a woman instead of the shy virgin she had been. The lights in his eyes grew somber.

"I have no mind to fight a duel," he said far more seriously than he'd intended, "unless it was with Temple."

The laughter died from her eyes and she blushed. "If you hadn't earned such a reputation as a rake, I might almost believe you," she said with forced lightness. "No doubt you're wearing the favor of half the ladies here."

"No doubt," he said, smiling cheerily. "Would you care to add yours?"

"I've already given mine to Temple," she replied.

"I wonder," Cort mused, "if Temple really knows how fortunate he is."

His look was too piercing to be ignored. Brynna knew he was hurt and she was sorry for the rift between Temple and him since their marriage.

"You will always be my friend, Cort," she said. "I love Temple. I think I've loved him from the first moment I saw him."

"Then I'm happy for you, Brynna," Cort said, and wheeled his horse away. With a debonair flourish he cantered to the starting line. Brynna saw Temple glare at him, but Cort only saluted and called a challenge.

"Ah, *chérie*. You have done something I never thought any woman could. Cort is in love with you," Francine observed.

"He doesn't love me," Brynna replied. "He's only miffed because I'm the only one who resisted his charms."

"I do not think so, *chérie*," Francine said. "You have done very well in the short time you've been here. You have won the hearts of two of the most eligible bachelors here."

"I care about the heart of only one," Brynna answered.

"If that is so, *ma chérie*, then take some advice," Francine said. "You have made an enemy. I suspect it is Alicia de Jarreau. She wins her duels with a *langue chargée*, a sugar-coated tongue. Be on guard, *chérie*. It is one thing for

265

the *bonne compagnie* to gossip about me, but to gossip about you is something else altogether.

"Thank you for the warning, Francine," Brynna said. "But she can't hurt me. I'm Temple's wife now and there's nothing she can do about it."

"Perhaps," Francine replied. "*Regardez*. The race is about to begin."

A shot went off and the men on horseback spurred their mounts forward. The horses galloped around the track throwing clods of dirt and sod from beneath their hooves. The planters and their wives called out encouragement to their favored horses. Chandra was at the head of the pack. Excitement gripped Brynna so she leaped to her feet.

Cort was close behind Temple. The two men galloped side by side, their arms pumping as they vied with each other. The race ended with Chandra a full neck ahead of Cort's horse.

"So you've won again," Cort called out, holding his horse to a canter.

"It was a good race," Temple answered. "You nearly won."

"No, it seems I had little chance after all," Cort said, glancing at Brynna in the carriage.

Temple grew still, knowing they no longer spoke of the horserace. He held out his hand. "Then let us shake and be friends, as we've always done."

Cort sat stiff and unreachable and Temple feared he meant to ride away from him, but the handsome face creased in a smile and Cort took his hand. "Friends as always," he said. But when the clasp was broken, Cort sat staring into Temple's eyes. "If you ever do anything to hurt her, I'll be there and I'll do everything I can to win her away from you."

Temple was shocked at the wave of jealousy that swept

266

through him. "She's my wife, Cort. No other man will ever claim her, not even one I call a friend."

"Then guard her well, friend," Cort said. "You have only to fail once."

Temple's face was hard with anger as he thought of all the men who'd been cuckolded by his dashing, careless friend. "Don't ever give me cause to call you out, Cort," he warned. "I will kill you, if I have to."

"So the lines are drawn, *mon ami*. We know where we stand," Cort cried, and spurred his horse away. Thoughtfully, Temple watched him go, then turned toward his carriage.

"Temple, you won, you won!" Brynna cried, throwing her arms around him so he was nearly unseated. Her enthusiasm restored his good humor. He collected his purse, redonned his jacket, and instructed the groom in Chandra's care. Then he climbed into the carriage beside his exuberant young wife.

"You brought me luck today," he said, taking her reticule and tucking the winnings from the horserace inside. "This is for you to spend as you wish while you're in New Orleans."

"But that is your money. You won it," Brynna said. "Besides, I have little need for money."

"Nonetheless, you shall have some funds in your pocket in case you see some *babiole* you want. I've made arrangements with Monsieur Laussat for you to draw against the Langtry account anytime you choose."

"I wouldn't take money you might need for Langtry," Brynna exclaimed.

Her eyes were wide with disbelief that he expected she would. Taking her small gloved hand in his, Temple sighed. "Brynna, I have something to tell you," he began.

267

"I hope you won't be angry with me. I'm afraid I've misled you."

"You have?" she asked warily, and waited for him to go on. When he didn't, she drew her hand from his. "You don't really love me, is that what you wish to say?" she demanded stiffly.

Temple's laughter rang out until he saw the distress in her eyes; then he put his arm around her and pulled her close, not caring who saw them.

"I shall never stop loving you," he said solemnly. Instantly, her smile was back.

"Then nothing else matters," she said. "I forgive you for anything you might have said or done."

"Even if I tell you I've tricked you into this marriage."

She paused considering for a while. "If that's so, you've only tricked me into something I wanted anyway."

Temple studied her beautiful face. "Never have I felt such love as you arouse in me," he said. She blushed and glanced away, but her eyes were bright with happiness when she looked back at him.

"Perhaps you'd better make your confession," she said lightly.

"Langtry has no need of your inheritance," Temple said. "Even with the damage to this year's crops, we are quite solvent."

"Then why did you insist you would take it only if I married you. You needn't have married me at all."

"I wanted to marry you. I used your dowry as an excuse because I thought . . ." He paused, loathe to bring up his fears concerning Cort, yet determined to put all fears and secrets behind them. "I thought you might be falling in love with Cort."

"Cort! Impossible!" she scoffed. "He's a roué, a flirt. He would never be serious with a woman. He would never care for her and protect her as you do. Besides, I could never have loved him, Temple, not as I love you."

Seated at a sidewalk cafe, Alicia de Jarreau had finished regaling the society matrons of New Orleans with her latest findings about Temple's new bride.

"He married her only for her dowry. He has no love for her. If only the fool had come to me, the woman he truly loved, but his pride stood in his way."

"How fortunate, *chérie*, his pride does not stand in his way now," one of the women observed, indicating the passing carriage. There for all the city to see, Temple Sinclair bent over his young bride in a passionate embrace. Alicia stared after them, then with a snap of her parasol, stepped into her carriage and ordered it away in the opposite direction.

Unaware of the sensation they had caused, Brynna and Temple held hands until they reached the house on Royal Street, then hurried to their room, where they spent the rest of the afternoon. When they emerged for supper, Brynna's mouth bore evidence of Temple's kisses and she was so fatigued she could scarcely eat her supper. Temple pulled her onto his lap and fed her from his own plate, then carried her back to their room, where they remained until morning.

"Welcome back," Jessica Sinclair called as their carriage pulled to a stop before the front entrance. Amid a flurry of petticoats and ribbon-tied boxes, Brynna rushed forward to embrace the older woman.

"Oh, Jessica, I missed you so," she cried, drawing back. "I've brought presents for everyone, that length of cloth

269

you liked so well at Madame René's, ribbons for May, candy for Lala, eyeglasses for Aunt Clemmie, and—and so much more. I hope I haven't spent too much money. Temple said I hadn't, but I wasn't sure."

"You look wonderful," Jessica said, smoothing the soft cheek.

"Oh, Jessica. I've never been so happy," Brynna sighed.

"It shows."

"Did I tell you about the race Temple won or that we went to that new restaurant everyone is talking about?"

Jessica listened to her babble away, her sharp old eyes catching the happy lilt to her voice, the sparkle in her eyes. Temple came to hug Jessica and she saw the same change in him. *Praise be to God,* she thought. *They've worked out their differences.* Brynna's happiness was contagious. The gifts were brought inside and passed out to all the servants until only one remained.

"This one's for Cyra," Brynna said. "Where is she?"

"I'm afraid she's remained down at the slave quarters the entire time you were gone."

"I see," Brynna said, and the old haunting sadness flitted across her face.

"What is it?" Temple asked, but she only shook her head, forcing a smile to her lips again.

"Nothing. I'll give this to her tomorrow."

"Is there a problem with Cyra?" Temple insisted, although he, like the rest of those at Langtry, had come to dislike the slave girl. He wasn't quite sure why, but some instinct told him she should be watched.

Brynna shrugged aside his question. "Cyra's in love with one of the field hands. Thomas, the one you bought the day we arrived."

270

"I remember him. He's a good worker, intelligent and strong."

"Do you think so?" Brynna's face cleared. "I don't imagine Cyra would love him if he were not." She rose and picked up her reticule and bonnet. "I'm going upstairs. I'm rather tired. There's been so much excitement."

"Go ahead, dear," Jessica said. "You needn't come down until dinner is ready. I'll send May for you."

Jessica watched her go. "She seems so happy now. I'm glad things have worked out between you."

"We love each other, Jessica," Temple said, as if still awed by the fact.

"What of this slave, Thomas?" Jessica asked.

Temple got up to pace the floor a bit. "I didn't want to tell Brynna, but I've suspected Thomas is behind some of the trouble we're hearing complaints about. I've ordered Hewitt to keep an eye on him."

"Hewitt," Jessica snorted. "I had some trouble with that one while you were gone. He tried to whip one of the slaves without just reason. The poor man had injured himself and was trying to keep working. Hewitt wanted to whip him for malingering."

"What did you do?"

"I stopped him and had the man taken to the hospital. He's got an infection in his foot and will be out of the fields for a few days."

"I'll speak to Hewitt."

"There's something else," Jessica said. "I've overheard some of the slaves talking, just bits and pieces. Whenever I ask them if there's any trouble, they clam up. I've never had that before. Our people have always been open with us except about one thing."

"Voodoo?"

271

"Voodoo!"

"I'll keep watch, Jessica," Temple said, bending to drop a kiss on her withered cheek. "Now, I think I'll ride out to the fields and see what's happened while I was gone."

"Temple," Jessica called. "It's good to have you and your wife back." He grinned and hurried out. Jessica listened to his booted footsteps on the gallery and crushed-shell path beyond. It *was* good to have Temple and Brynna back. She felt restless without them, restless and somehow threatened. She wasn't familiar with such feelings and now she was glad of a reason to scoff at them. Sighing, she rose and made her way out to the garden. Everything was right with Langtry again. Her beloved family was back.

Chapter Fourteen

Brynna lived in a fairy tale world of happiness. Her days were filled with the satisfying task of running Langtry, her nights with the insatiable demands of the passion she and Temple shared. When she tried to rise in the morning, bleary-eyed and tired from their long night of lovemaking, he would gently push her back against her pillow and urge her to rest. When she awoke later, he would be gone, but on her pillow would be a rose, fresh picked from the garden or a sprig of spirea for her hair. Temple's thoughtfulness touched her deeply, and if she'd ever imagined herself incapable of loving him more, she soon discovered there were new depths and breadths to her feelings for him.

The long summer was drawing to an end in a flourish of picnics and barbeques, so their weekends were kept as busy as their weekdays. Jessica often accompanied them, for her strength had returned and with it the bloom to her cheek. It amused Brynna to see that Sidney de Jarreau often sought out her aunt, hovering over her solicitously, bringing her cups of punch or cold tea and seeing she was seated in the shade. At dances, he escorted her onto the floor so often that tongues were wagging behind opened fans. Jessica seemed unperturbed by the stir her romance with Sidney de Jarreau was causing.

"I'll never remarry," she informed Brynna as they bent over a tub of fresh-picked snapped beans. "Etienne was the only man I've ever loved."

"What was he like?" Brynna asked dreamily, wanting to know all she could about Temple's father.

"He was very handsome, like Temple," Jessica declared, "and fair-minded and honorable." She continued for some length, only too happy to reminisce about the man who'd given her so many years of bliss. "So you see," she ended finally, "as good a man as Sidney de Jarreau is, he could never compare to Etienne. That's why I could never marry him."

"I understand how you feel, Jessica," Brynna said. "I could never marry again, should something happen to Temple." The thought was so devastating that for a moment she had to squeeze her eyes tightly against the pain behind her eyelids. Tears rolled down her cheeks and she wiped them away, embarrassed to be so emotional.

Since returning from New Orleans, Temple had had to work extra hard to make up for his absence. After a long day in the fields, he often returned and spent some time in his office pouring over his accounts.

"I'm sorry, darling," he said, kissing Brynna lingeringly one evening when Jessica had pleaded a headache and retired early. "I hate to leave you alone, but I must have this bookwork done before we start cutting."

"*Bafouillage!* Is that not what the Creoles say?" Brynna murmured between light kisses. "Don't worry about me. I have many things to do." She reached for her needlework and deliberately took a stitch. Temple grinned, obviously relieved.

274

But when he had closed himself in his study, Brynna found herself restless. Bored with her sewing project, she threw the frame to one side. She wished Cyra were here. They would talk as they used to, and she would tell her how happy she was. But Cyra no longer came to the big house. Brynna was reminded she still had Cyra's gift. She would take it to her friend. Though dusk had fallen outside the windows, Brynna felt no fear as she retrieved the gift from her room and made her way down the path to the slave quarters. Greeting the slaves who sat smoking and visiting outside their cabins, Brynna hurried to the last cabin in line, the one Cyra shared with Thomas. No one was about. Disappointed, Brynna considered what to do. Where was Cyra likely to be now?

A low, throbbing noise coming from the woods claimed her attention. Curious, she walked around the cabin to an overgrown path leading into the woods. She could hear the sound better now. It was the slow, pulsing beat of a drum. Casting a quick look around, Brynna started down the path. She was foolish to do this, some rational part of her chided, but this was Langtry land and she was safe here, another part argued.

The path led into the woods a short distance to a small clearing. Fires were lit around the edge of the clearing. A larger one lit the center. Their flickering light cast an eerie glow over the scene.

Brynna hesitated, puzzled by the gathering of slaves. Why were they meeting here instead of up in the slave quarters or the church where they held their normal get-togethers? But as she watched, the reason became all too clear.

The drum had increased in rhythm now. The black bodies began to move, slowly at first, then in an increased frenzy. Suddenly a woman in a loose flowing red robe and white turban appeared before them. At first Brynna didn't recognize Cyra. Her eyes were closed as if in a trance. She began to dance without moving her feet, her body twitching and bobbing, exciting the onlookers to a more fevered pitch.

The drums had become louder, their thrumming like a pulse in Brynna's head. She wanted to turn and run, but she seemed rooted to the spot, her gaze pinned on the brightly lit spectrum in the clearing.

Cyra's dance had become wilder, more abandoned. Her brown hands pulled the encompassing folds of the red robes high, revealing her gleaming brown thighs. A large black man had joined her in the clearing. Thomas! And in his hands he held high a cottonmouth snake. Its flickering tongue looked evil, its body writhed to free itself. The slaves drew away when Thomas danced close, shoving the snake toward them menacingly.

A rooster was brought out and placed on the ground; its feet were bound. Thomas danced around the frightened chicken and released the snake beside it. Immediately, the slaves drew back, forming a ring, their voices crying out with alarm and something more, something evil and untamed. The rooster flapped its wings in a futile attempt to escape the deadly snake.

Brynna could watch no more. Turning, she ran back along the path until she reached the slave quarters. Walking along the dusty street before the cabins, she was aware of every dark gaze pinned on her. When she turned to confront them, they quickly averted their eyes. They knew she'd gone into the woods to see the ceremony and now they wondered what she would do. Why hadn't these people gone as well? She saw the answer in their averted faces. They were afraid, afraid of voodoo, afraid of what terror and retribution it might bring to them.

Thoughtfully, Brynna made her way back to the house. She would have to tell Temple and Jessica. They must know at once. She remembered Fortier and some of the other whispers she'd heard from the other planters about the troubles they were having. Who had brought this evil to Langtry? Why had Cyra allowed herself to be caught up in it?

Cyra! She couldn't tell Temple yet, not until she'd warned Cyra, made her see she was courting disaster, perhaps even death. She hated to keep anything from Temple, but she must try to save Cyra from her own folly. Tomorrow morning she would go to see Cyra and tomorrow night she would tell Temple of what she had found. With a troubled heart, Brynna made her way to her room and was grateful Temple was still downstairs working on his books. She wasn't sure she could have kept herself from blurting out what she had found. She lay awake long into the night, and when Temple finally came to bed and whispered her name, she feigned sleep so she wouldn't have to lie to him.

Brynna woke with an excruciating headache, from lack of sleep she guessed. Tiredly she rose and performed only a sketchy toilette before making her way downstairs.

"Oh, there you are, dear," Jessica called cheerily. "You're just in time to give me a hand. I need someone to supervise the canning of these snap beans. Could you do that, dear? Marie and the girls know what to do, but sometimes they forget the amount of spices and what not."

"Certainly, Aunt Jessica," Brynna answered, grateful for the reprieve. She felt too tired to confront Cyra. Later, she reassured herself. She had all day to go down to the slave quarters.

The day passed quickly. Glass jars of green beans sat in

neat rows attesting to their productivity. Normally Brynna would have been filled with a sense of accomplishment. The knowledge that she had to speak to Cyra had hung over her head all day, and now she could find no more delays. Pausing at the spring house for a dipper of cold water, Brynna girded herself emotionally and walked down the familiar path. The sun was hot on her head and shoulders.

She thought of the things she meant to say to Cyra and felt the anger that had been building ever since she'd seen Cyra at the forbidden voodoo ritual. By the time she reached the slave quarters, she was breathing heavily from her exertions and her determination.

"Cyra!" she called, standing outside the last cabin. No one answered. Brynna went up on the porch and put her head inside. The cabin was sturdily built with a wood plank floor and a brick fireplace at one end. A ladder led to a loft above. A rough table, littered with dishes, and several chairs stood before the fireplace. On the hearth sat a kettle half filled with some unpalatable mass. Although the main room was spacious enough for a cabin, there was little room to walk or sit for the clutter of clothes and belongings. Whatever Cyra did with her days, she did not spend them cleaning her cabin. Brynna withdrew and stood on the porch looking around. Where would Cyra be at this hour of the day?

A hunch carried Brynna around the cabin and to the path that led to the clearing she'd visited last night. Slowly, she made her way through the trees, loath to return, wary of what she might find.

Cyra was in the clearing. She sat near a tree stump, her head wobbling as if she had no control of it. Her eyes rolled in her head. When she spotted Brynna, she attempted to rise and fell back to the ground.

"The mistress of Langtry," she said in slurred tones.

"Cyra!" Brynna cried, running to her. "What's wrong with you? Have you been drinking?"

"No, Mistress Sinclair," Cyra answered, and took a swig from a fruit jar.

"Rum!" Brynna cried. "If you're found out, you'll be whipped."

"Ain't Ah jus' been found out?" Cyra demanded. She'd managed to still the wobbling of her head. Now she put her hand to her temple and moaned. "Wha' yo' down heah for, Brynna. Yo' ain't goin' t' whip me."

"No," Brynna said, and sat down on the stump. "I don't even care if you're drunk, except it's a fool thing to do, and you're going to have a big head when you sober up."

"Then Ah won' sober up," Cyra answered, and took another drink.

"Don't drink anymore, Cyra," Brynna pleaded. "I've come to talk to you."

"Ah'm listenin'," Cyra answered with indifference.

Brynna paused, trying to think of a way to start. Now that she was here with Cyra, she knew none of her previous plans would work.

"Cyra, I came here last night."

"Ah know!"

"You know!"

"The voodoo queen Cyra knows all, sees all."

"Voodoo queen! Cyra, you can't mean that," Brynna said firmly. "You must stop this voodoo nonsense at once. If you don't, you're going to get into trouble."

"Who's going to cause me trouble?" Cyra demanded.

"Monsieur Fortier and Cort de Jarreau rode out to talk to us before we went to New Orleans. They've heard rumors that the voodoo practices that have been bother-

279

ing their slaves came from here. If they find you're doing it, too, you might be sold off. I couldn't bear that Cyra. You must stop."

"No!"

"Why! Why can't you be happy. I'm happy here, Cyra. I love my husband and you have Thomas. For the first time in our whole lives we're free of my father's tyranny."

"Your father?" Cyra scoffed.

"Things are different here, Cyra. I love Temple. He's kind and good. You love Thomas. We have the means of happiness here. We must guard it, protect it. You're going to ruin everything. I can't protect you if you're found out."

"Po' little Brynna," Cyra said. "Don't try to protect me. Ah'll take care of myse'f."

Seeing it was impossible to reason with Cyra, Brynna got to her feet. "I came down to warn you, Cyra, that I'm going to tell Temple what I saw last night."

"Yo' goin' t' tell on me?" Cyra repeated in disbelief. Brynna could see sobriety returning to her with jarring reality. Cyra leaped to her feet and shoved her face close to Brynna's. "Yo' won't. Yo' wouldn't do dat t' me."

"I'm not going to keep it from my husband."

"Why not?" Cyra's eyes were hard and threatening. "Yo' don't have t' tell him nothin'."

"I won't keep secrets from him. He's my husband. We tell each other everything."

She took a few steps backward. Cyra followed her, cat-quiet and wary stillness a part of her stance. "Ever'-thin'?" she asked softly, and grinned. Something about the grin made Brynna's blood run cold.

"Did yo' tell him about Wes Stanton? Did yo' tell him ever'thin' 'bout yo' mama?" Cyra advanced after Brynna. "Does he tell yo' 'bout his trips down t' the cabins?"

"He doesn't go there," Brynna cried, and remembered the nights she'd fallen asleep before Temple came to bed.

"Are yo' sure?" Cyra asked. Her smile was enigmatic and full of knowledge Brynna didn't want to share.

"I'm sure!" she cried.

Cyra's smile broadened. Her eyes were muddy-looking from the rum she'd drunk, and a strange light lurked in the dark irises. "The slave woman, Africa, is goin' t' have a baby," she said softly. "The father is a white man."

"No! You don't know that," Brynna cried. "You're only guessing. You're lying. I don't believe you."

Cyra's eyes gazed deep into Brynna's. "I know," she said softly. "Cause Ah got a second sight. Ah know what things have happened in the past and what's comin' in the future."

"No one knows that," Brynna scoffed.

Cyra only smiled again. "Yo' won't tell him 'bout the voodoo," she intoned. "If yo' tell him 'bout me, Ah'll tell him 'bout all of us. Yo' want me t' do that, Brynna?"

Brynna stared into Cyra's cruel eyes. Slowly she shook her head in denial. "I don't know who you are," she whispered.

Cyra thrust her face just inches from Brynna. "I am the voodoo queen, daughter of the high priestess Laveau," she chanted. "I have the power."

"I'm going to tell Temple what I've seen," Brynna said stiffly, "and if you're caught performing voodoo, you will be punished and I'll not say a word on your behalf." She whirled and stalked back along the path.

"Yes, yo' will," Cyra called after her. "Ah'll cast a spell on yo'. Yo'll do what Ah say."

Despite the alarm it might have caused the other slaves, Brynna ran through the slave quarters and up to the big house. She arrived at the porch, sweating and gasping for air.

"*Chérie*, you act as if you've been chased by demons," Jessica said with some alarm. "Are you all right?"

"I'm fine, Jessica," Brynna gasped. "I—I just wanted to get back and bathe before Temple returns home."

"You'll likely not see him until late tonight, child," Jessica said. "He's starting the slaves to cutting some of the north fields."

"I see," Brynna said, debating on talking to Jessica about Cyra's behavior. She had no desire to worry her aunt needlessly. Troubled, she climbed the stairs to her room. Lolling in a tub of herbal-scented water, she was able to put Cyra and this business of voodooism in its proper perspective. By the time she'd dried and dressed herself and settled on the gallery for a glass of lemonade, she was able to scoff at Cyra's attempts to make herself seem important. Perhaps she wouldn't tell Temple after all. That brought her to Cyra's final prediction, the one that Brynna had been trying to forget all afternoon. Another half-white baby was going to be born on Langtry. Cyra had said it was Temple's. The pain bit deep in Brynna's heart. *He couldn't have,* she told herself. *At least, he won't any more now that we're married.*

She was glad he wasn't coming home early that night. She couldn't bear looking at him after what Cyra had claimed. Too depressed to eat supper, she retired early and had fallen into an exhausted sleep by the time Temple returned from the fields. He stood over the bed, looking at her face in slumber. She slept with the innocence of a child. He longed to wake her and make love to her, but she looked far too tired. Besides, his own body had been pushed beyond all limitations this day. He contented himself with a quick bath and cuddling her against him as he fell instantly into an exhausted sleep.

The mills were working again. She could catch the faint rumble of them if she stood very still and concentrated. Gray-black plumes of smoke marked the distant sky where Temple and Hewitt had the field hands.

"They're burning the stubble from the fields they've cut," Jessica explained. "They'll let the land lie fallow for a few months and plant again. Some won't be replanted for three or four years."

On the long evenings when work was done Brynna wandered disconsolately along the gallery, not allowing herself to feel or think over the accusations Cyra had made against Temple. Brynna thought only of those magical nights in New Orleans with her husband, the way he'd held her and wakened her to a world of need and passion that could not be denied now. She loved him, had loved him almost from the first moment she came to Langtry and he loved her, too. She was sure of it. But a man's way of loving, she began to see, was different from a woman's. Could she accept this darker side of her husband's nature? Could she turn a blind eye to it, pretend it didn't exist, as her mother had tried so hard to pretend with her father? Hope Stanton had been trapped in a loveless marriage, where she had been pressured by the very nature of their society to remain. Was Brynna now trapped in the same way, by sentiments of love and fidelity and southern womanhood? With each empty hour spent pacing the gallery, beneath the dwarfing magnificence of the brick columns, she sought answers to her doubts, and with the answers came pain and disillusionment and finally a terrible cynicism. She was indeed trapped, a prisoner of her love for Temple and Langtry. She felt the silken cords tighten too harshly and some inner core railed against them.

Jessica saw the war going on in Brynna and didn't understand the reason for it. Had Temple done something to wound the girl? Had they fought? Was Brynna's youth a stumbling block between them? They'd seemed so happy, so in love, when they'd returned from New Orleans. Now that the excitement of marriage had worn off was Brynna growing bored with their quiet life and a husband who spent too many hours working his plantation? Surely not. She'd observed Brynna's devotion to Langtry and her level-headedness. She wouldn't have changed. What then caused the dark circles beneath the golden eyes? What caused her shoulders to slump so pathetically when she thought no one observed?

"Are you feeling well, child?" Jessica asked gently as she and Brynna supervised the weaving of new cloth.

"I should ask that of you," Brynna replied evasively. "You've had no return of that fever?"

"None," Jessica replied. "But I'm inquiring about you, *chérie*. You seem distracted. Are you sure all is well with you?"

"I'm just tired, Jessica. There's so much to do at this time of year."

"I expect you miss seeing Temple more often, too," Jessica persisted.

Brynna turned away. "Yes, of course, that, too." Deliberately she busied herself at a loom, checking the coarse hickory cloth which would be used for the slaves' work clothes.

Jessica watched her with a worried expression. She hated to interfere, but that evening, she waited for Temple to return from the fields. As had become her habit recently, Brynna had retired early. She seemed to spend more and more of her time in her room.

"Have you noticed a change in Brynna of late?" she queried as she poured a glass of wine and carried it to Temple. He'd bathed the field dirt from himself and changed into a clean jaconet shirt and dark trousers. His blue-black hair was still damp and gleamed in the lamplight. Sitting as he was, with his shoulders slumped from fatigue and his eyes dark and puzzled, she felt a wave of maternal love. He'd been her son for so many years and she'd been fulfilled by their affection for each other. What hurt him hurt her. Now, she took a rare glass of sherry for herself and settled in a chair near him.

"I've had the feeling she's been avoiding me," he said now, looking at Jessica with hurt-filled eyes. "She claims she's just tired, as we all are, and perhaps that's it."

"Perhaps!" Jessica agreed. "The summer was one of immense change for her. She may just need some time to adjust to everything."

Temple looked at her. "You don't think that or you wouldn't have spoken to me."

"No, I don't think that. I'm concerned about her. She's losing her bloom. There's no laughter anymore, and she used to laugh nearly all the time. The servants have noticed it, too. They love her and miss her cheerful nature."

"Has Alicia been to call?" Temple demanded suddenly.

"Only once," Jessica answered, "and she made her usually attempts to *bafouer*, but Brynna handled her superbly. No, Brynna's melancholia began soon after you returned from New Orleans."

The two sat pondering. Suddenly, Temple snapped his fingers, his eyes shining. "Is possible she is in a delicate condition?" he asked excitedly.

285

Jessica studied his beaming face. "There are rumors that is why you married her so hastily."

The light died in Temple's eyes. "That could not be true," he answered quietly. "It is too soon for a child of mine to bring about this malaise, unless . . ."

Jessica saw the doubts forming in his eyes. "Don't let gossip destroy your trust in her. She is a girl of impeccable reputation."

"Cort has overcome a girl's strict upbringing more than once," Temple cried, leaping to his feet so quickly the chair tipped backward.

"Temple, I beg of you," Jessica said, "do not voice this accusation to your wife."

He seemed not to hear her. His hands were clamped around the delicate wine goblet so intensely, his knuckles were white and she feared the glass might break. With a slosh of red wine, he placed the glass on a nearby table. His dark gaze was fixed on the door and the stairs beyond.

"Temple, please don't speak of this tonight. Wait until you've had time to think about it."

"I'm sure that's good advice, Jessica," he said, "but my wife and I have a promise of no secrets between us. If she carries Cort's baby, I must know."

"You condemn her without cause, I'm sure," Jessica asserted. "She loves you."

"That I would hear from her lips this very night," Temple said, and stamped out.

Watching him go, Jessica berated herself for her meddling. She'd thought only to help, instead she'd caused untold trouble. She prayed Temple would approach his wife with the love she knew he felt, yet she'd seen his flare of pride and anger. He was not a man to be tricked, even by the woman he loved.

Brynna awoke with Temple bending over her. His face

286

was cast in dark shadows from the lamp's dimmed glow, yet she sensed something in his eyes that caused her to come fully alert.

"Temple?" she said softly, pushing herself upright. "Is something wrong?" Her voice sounded small in the tense stillness of the room. He drew back from her, turned his back as if seeking some calmness within himself, then whirled to confront her.

"We have said there will be no secrets between us, no lies, only truth and honesty."

"Yes, Temple," she said faintly, dropping her gaze to the coverlet as she thought of the secrets they both kept.

He saw the dip of her lashes and read evasion in it. "Brynna!" he cried, gripping her shoulders and shaking her slightly. Old fears too recently buried resurfaced and she drew back from him, her eyes wide with terror, her breathing shaky as she waited for him to go on.

"What do you want of me?" she cried.

Temple's strong fingers still gripped her soft shoulders, biting into the tender flesh. "Do you carry Cort's child?" he demanded.

Brynna gasped and drew back further. "Are you mad?" she asked.

"Don't evade the question."

Brynna stared into his dark eyes, anger growing from a deep well of pain. "How dare you come to me in the middle of the night to make this accusation," she whispered scathingly. "I am your wife. I've made my vows before God. I have not dishonored them." She jerked free of him.

"Neither have I," he answered, puzzling by her accusing tone.

Brynna sat with her knees drawn up, nursing her bruised shoulder. Her golden hair tangled around her in disarray. Her gaze was drawn to Temple's eyes, wide and dark and filled with all the same pain and doubts with which she'd struggled these past weeks.

"Why did you ask me this horrible question?" she demanded. Sighing, Temple slumped onto the bed, then raised his gaze to hers.

"I didn't doubt your faithfulness to our marriage," he said finally. His voice dragged with fatigue and something more. "I only wondered about your association with Cort."

"He's your friend, Temple," she said with more gentleness than she'd felt some moments before. "He would not dishonor you in any way. Nor would I."

"He's in love with you and he has a way with women, even proper young ladies."

"He was always a gentleman with me. Besides, have you no trust in my feelings? I don't love Cort. You judge me too harshly. I wonder that you even married me since you carry such a low opinion of me." She rose from the bed and stalked across the room. The lamplight shone through the thin cotton of her gown, outlining her slender limbs and lush body. Temple felt desire grow. Too many nights had passed since he'd made love to his wife. He realized he'd angered her with his accusations, and there was little chance of wooing her now.

"I'm sorry," he said. "You've seemed so aloof of late and you're often tired and I thought—"

"I'm perfectly aware of what you thought," she snapped. "Am I always to remain cheerful and energetic for fear my husband will think me a wanton?"

"No, of course not," Temple said, finding himself ensnared in that timeless role of the offending male who must now placate. "It's just that if you had been indiscreet, I wanted you to know that—that I wouldn't divorce

288

you. I would have taken the child and raised it as my own."

"Surely you don't expect me to feel grateful for this magnificent gesture, when it offers me the greatest insult a woman could receive from her husband."

"I didn't mean it that way," Temple said. "I only want to tell you that whatever happened before our marriage is behind us. I wouldn't hold it against you, just as I would hope you wouldn't hold my past peccadillos against me."

He'd hit so unerringly close to the real truth for her unhappiness that Brynna could only stare at him dumbfounded. He was apologizing for whatever he'd done before their marriage. Did not his very words condemn him, did they not add credence to Cyra's accusations? Heartsick, she sat looking at him.

"Let me see if I have this correct," she said, chin high, eyes snapping. "I'm to forgive and forget your past romantic liaisons and in exchange you will do the same for me."

"Yes, I think that's fair, don't you?" Temple said, smiling. Perhaps they would make up yet this night and he could make love to her after all.

"More than fair," she said sweetly. "Need I tell you about my . . . indiscretions?"

Her question drove the breath from him. He eyed her warily. "No, you don't need to c-confess particulars."

"Good," Brynna said, feigning a yawn. "I'm much too tired to discuss all of them tonight."

"All of them?" Temple said, moving to one side as she scrambled back into bed and pulled the covers up to her chin. "How many were there?" he demanded.

"You said I needn't confess them, and I really think that's wise," Brynna said. "And I shan't ask you who and what."

Dumbly, Temple undressed for bed and slid in beside her. Thoughts were tumbling through his head. She'd been a virgin when he married her. He'd felt the stiffness of her maidenhead and seen the smear of blood on the bridal sheets. Such things could be faked, he reminded himself. But Brynna wasn't a devious woman. She was too young and innocent. But no woman was totally innocent of wiles. Brynna loved him. He loved her. He'd said he would forgive her any indiscretions, believing she had none. Now he tossed on his marriage bed, going back over their conversation. He'd come to accuse her with some basic part of himself, knowing the accusations would prove false, yet new doubts were born.

Brynna stirred beside him, wrapping her legs over his in a movement that would have ended in prolonged love-making, but Temple made no move to touch her. He lay rigid and preoccupied. Brynna sighed and settled against his side. For the first time, the unhappiness she'd felt receded. He'd asked her to forgive his past, which meant he would not repeat his past transgressions. Although she disapproved of his behavior, she must forgive him as he had asked. She must take heart that he so obviously loved her. She thought of his accusations. Clumsy as they'd been, they'd been a declaration of love from a man who was not usually clumsy about such things. She'd sensed the depths of his despair and been angered that he could think her capable of having other lovers before him. She nearly chuckled out loud as she thought of his face when she accepted his forgiveness. Right now, he must surely be worrying over what she'd needed forgiveness for. She'd let him worry a while.

The silken cords that bound her seemed less confining now, for she recognized that if she were indeed trapped in her marriage, it was more by love than anything else and that Temple was as much a captive as she. She longed for him to make love to her, but he turned away, presenting his broad back to her. Brynna snuggled against his warmth and slept the first sound sleep she'd enjoyed for weeks.

Temple heard the deep, even breathing that signaled his wife was asleep. How could she slumber so innocently? he wondered. What manner of woman had he married? By God, if he ever heard of one man who'd touched her, he would call him out in a duel. Temple slept fitfully only to rise in a foul mood. In the days that followed, Jessica observed that now it was Temple sunk in the dark moods of depression which had once claimed Brynna, while Brynna was once again her sunny, cheerful self. Jessica wasn't sure what had brought about the changes, but this time, wisely, she did not interfere.

Chapter Fifteen

October melted into November. Temple was seldom home in the evenings, working till dark before releasing the slaves from the fields. When he was home, he was stiff and aloof. At first Brynna had tried to cajole him from his foul moods, then she tried to explain the prank she'd played upon him, but he refused to listen. Finally, in anger, she elaborated upon her imaginary indiscretions, dropping a name here and there, leaving a half-written letter on her desk.

"I remember . . ." she would begin, then pause and shake her head, her lips curved in a fond smile. Temple's mouth would tighten in a straight line and he would stalk outside to the gallery to smoke a cheroot.

"Do you ever intend to tell him the truth?" Jessica asked one evening when Temple had fled in tight-lipped fury.

Brynna's mischievous smile dimpled her cheeks. "Whatever do you mean, Aunt Jessica?" she asked sweetly.

"At first, I didn't understand what was happening," Jessica said, laying aside her needlepoint and folding her hands in her woven-silk lap. "I promised myself I wouldn't interfere and, in fact, I've found some humor in what is occurring between you and Temple, but, my dear, you must have a care not to carry things too far."

"I've tried to tell him the truth, Aunt Jessica," Brynna said. "Do you realize he had the audacity to ask if I . . . if I . . ., well, it doesn't matter."

"I'd guessed as much," Jessica said, nodding her head, "and I quite agree he deserves some of what he's gotten, but he loves you terribly and he's suffering."

Brynna's face flushed contritely. Her gaze darted to the French doors. Beyond, Temple could be seen passing the gardens. "I don't want to hurt him," she cried. "I love him."

"Then perhaps you should remind him of that," Jessica said gently.

Brynna was already on her feet and hurrying from the parlor. Jessica reprimanded herself for having once again meddled, but as she watched the young figures bend their heads close, she thought she might be forgiven this once. Folding her needlework, she rose and went up to bed.

"There never have been any other men," Brynna whispered. "You made me so angry with your accusations and assumptions, I just wanted to hurt you back."

"I never meant to hurt you," Temple cried, sweeping her into his arms. "I don't know why those thoughts were ever in my head. I know you're honest and true. Forgive me." He pulled her into his arms and showered her face with kisses.

"I'll always forgive you anything, Temple," she whispered. "As long as I know you love me."

She meant the words she uttered. Whatever he'd done, it was past. He had been as much a victim of their way of life as she. But that would change. *They* would change.

293

They'd grow stronger and learn from mistakes. Temple's kisses awakened hungers in her that had been held in abeyance for too long. Temple swept her up in his arms and carried her from the moonlight gardens up the sweeping stairs to their room where he made love to her with a passion that caused her to cry out.

In her room, Jessica heard the cry and smiled. The years had not dimmed her own memories of Temple's father and the passion they'd shared. Soon, she thought, Langtry would have children filling its rooms and there would be no doubt in anyone's mind as to who their father was.

Autumn slid into winter. The rains came, cold and damp, but the days were filled with such happiness, it seemed the sun shone every minute. She had never told Temple or Jessica what she'd seen in the woods that summer night and she seldom thought of Cyra.

The social season was upon them. Invitations filled the silver tray on the hall table. Brynna's days were filled with trips to New Orleans and Madame René's for new gowns and accompanying Jessica to teas at the house of the other planters' wives. They'd long since put aside their snobbishness of the summer and begun to accept her as one of their own. In the evening, the three of them attended balls and formal dinners in the other great mansions. Brynna often ran into the irreverent Francine or Alicia and Cort. Though she much preferred Cort's company over that of his sister, she took extra care not to seek him out.

Christmas loomed and, with it, a hundred extra tasks as Jessica and Brynna prepared gifts for their slaves. Each man, woman, and child would be given new clothes and new shoes as well as a gold coin. The girls would receive new rag dolls and the boys, carved horses. A pig would be killed and roasted over an outdoor pit, and cups of new rum handed out to all. As the holiday approached, slaves dragged cane stalks to the riverbank and made a huge pile.

"Whatever are they doing?" Brynna asked, watching them from the gallery. The sun was shining brightly and she'd come out to enjoy the fresh air.

"There's to be a Christmas bonfire to welcome Papa Noel," Jessica explained. "It's become a tradition all along the river. The slaves would be disappointed without it."

Brynna stood remembering past Christmases. Beaumont Hall had never enjoyed the generous festivities of the holiday the way Langtry did. She'd never get used to the joy of being here.

"Hello," Temple called, riding by on Chandra. "What do you think, Jessica. Will the bonfire be big enough this year?"

"I don't see why not. You make it bigger every year."

"We have to make a good showing this year. Brynna's never seen this custom," he said, eyes twinkling. He was like a little boy, Brynna thought.

"Are you coming to kiss me?" he demanded, and she ran forward to the side of his horse. Temple leaned sideways in his saddle to swoop her up.

"Put me down," she cried, laughing gaily.

"Not until you pay the price I demand," Temple cried, setting a spur to Chandra's sides so he leaped ahead.

"Temple!" Brynna called in alarm, although he had her tightly clasped to his side. The ground flashed by below the stirrup in a dizzying speed. The slaves watched the master and mistress with smiling faces. Brynna knew Temple was putting on this display for their benefit. Whooping and howling, he galloped down the drive and back, then claimed his kiss in front of all before setting her on her feet again.

Brynna swayed and clutched at his leg to keep from falling. Her stomach felt strange, her face hot.

"Are you all right?" Temple asked anxiously, his rowdy mood dampened by concern for her. Brynna steadied herself and stepped back from his horse.

"You take my breath away, sir," she answered laughingly. When he was certain she was all right, he gave another whoop and galloped away. After he'd gone, Brynna placed her hand against her flat stomach, willing the nausea away. She thought of Aunt Jessica's bout of fever the summer before and hoped she wasn't coming down with something similar. The season for fevers was past. After a moment or two the nausea left her and she turned toward the gallery where Jessica stood watching her. Beyond Jessica, at the corner of the house, stood Cyra, her dark eyes fixed on Brynna. For a moment the two girls stared at each other, then Cyra turned and disappeared.

Strangely bothered, Brynna hurried to join Jessica, but as they supervised the baking of cinnamon cookies and pralines, she found her holiday mood had fled. Later, when she made her way to her room to rest a while, she found a carved doll lying against her pillow. Curious, she picked it up. It bore a chestnut ringlet of her hair and a scrap of silk from a cast-off gown. Obviously, it was meant to represent Brynna. In the heart of the doll, a nail had been driven. As the portent of this crudely made figure became clear, Brynna let out a cry and threw it from her. Who would have left such a thing here on her pillow? The memory came of Cyra standing at the corner of the house. She'd felt the intensity of Cyra's hatred even then.

296

This was only another symbol of it. Kneeling, Brynna picked up the menacing doll and stared at it.

"Oh, Cyra," she said in despair.

She never showed the doll to anyone. She stuffed it deep into a drawer and tried to forget about it, but the image of it haunted her. She tried her best not to let what had happened throw a cloud over the Christmas preparation. Temple was so immersed in the gaiety, she didn't want to dim his happiness. He'd labored hard in the fall; he deserved this rest.

His labors had been rewarded. In spite of the fields lost to the storm, his new methods had yielded more sugar from his remaining crops. Temple was jubilant and advocating changes to any planter who showed an interest in his methods. Life seemed incredibly blessed.

Christmas Day dawned clear and sunny. The field hands gathered on the front lawn. Temple made a ceremony of handing out the gifts and praise for the months of hard work. Brynna and Jessica passed out toys and candy to the children. There was much laughter, and when Temple was finished, the slaves broke into Christmas carols, sung with a cadence and rhythm Brynna had never heard before. The adults clapped their hands and the children aped their parents, their eyes bright with excitement. The good cheer lasted long after the slaves had returned to their quarters. Singing and sounds of merriment could be heard clear up at the big house throughout dinner.

"It's time to give my beautiful wife a gift," Temple said after dinner, dropping a kiss on Brynna's exposed nape. She'd drawn her hair high on her head with a cluster of curls dancing fetchingly behind each ear. In honor of the day, she'd donned one of her new gowns, an emerald-green velvet that made her feel elegant and grown-up.

297

She'd required May to lace her corsets tighter than usual, for it seemed the infallible Madame René had erred in her measurements and the waist was snug. As Brynna settled on the sofa before the tree, she had to struggle to draw a deep breath. Temple's dark eyes were bright with admiration and love as he handed her a ribbon-bedecked box.

"I'm sorry it's not another puppy," he laughed, bending to ruffle Beauregard's ears, "or another pony."

"Perhaps it's just as well," Brynna said lightly. "I wouldn't want either of them to be jealous."

"Neither would I," Temple said. "As for me, I shall always be a little bit jealous of anyone who captures the affections of my adorable wife."

"There's no need for you to be," Brynna answered, forgetting the present he'd given her. His eyes held all she needed or wanted. "I shall never love anyone as I do you."

Temple bent to kiss her deeply, then drew away and took a place near the fire. "Open your present," he ordered.

Brynna did as he bid and found within the velvet box a necklace of diamonds that took her breath away. Even if she had no craving for jewelry of this magnitude, she could clearly see the extravagance of his gift.

"These must have cost a king's ransom," she exclaimed.

"As well they should for a queen," he answered. "Do you really like them?"

Dimples flashed in Brynna's cheeks. "Not as well as Malka or Beauregard," she answered, "but they are beautiful and I shall cherish them."

Temple's laughter rang out. "Now a gift for Jessica," he said, handing her a package. He'd given her a necklace of jet, which Jessica put on immediately. There was more—

chocolates from New Orleans, a length of Chinese silk, a music box. Brynna timidly offered him the silk scarf she'd made, the new pipe and English tobacco, a rare coin, and a gold-tipped cane, which he brandished dramatically as he paced the room. There was a new reticule for Jessica and a lace fan to match one of her new gowns.

"It's perfect," Jessica said, opening the fan to study it from different angles. Sighing, she leaned back against the sofa. "This has been the best Christmas we've had in years."

"It's the best Christmas I've had in my whole life," Brynna said with such feeling, Temple and Jessica exchanged glances. Brynna had become so much a part of their lives, they sometimes forgot she'd ever lived elsewhere. Now they sat speculating about her earlier Christmases. She seldom spoke of her life before she came to Langtry.

" 'Scuse me, suh," Absalom said from the door. "The slaves are gathering down by the river, whenever yo' ready to go down."

"Is it time for the bonfire?" Brynna exclaimed with such excitement that Temple and Jessica laughed at her.

"It's time," Temple said. "Fetch your shawls and we'll walk down."

Bundled against the river dampness, they walked under the branches of the live oaks down to the river where the blacks had indeed gathered to sing hymns and visit. Voices rang out excitedly on the night air, then fell silent as Temple stepped forward to say a few words to his people before setting a torch to the pile of dry stalks.

"This has been a good year at Langtry," he said, looking around the circle of eager dark faces. "We have a new mistress. She will love you and care for you the same as Miz Jessica. I think she has also brought us good luck. The hurricane did much damage to the crops, but no lives were lost. Yellow fever never found its way to us from New Orleans. Our yield from our crops, in spite of the damage from storm and drought, was sufficient. Our people remained healthy. We have many reasons to give praise tonight. We pray the New Year will bring us future blessings and future heirs." Temple looked at Brynna, his eyes glittering with love and pride. Her heart was overflowing. She, too, hoped for a baby in the New Year.

The slaves sent up a cheer as Temple touched the torch to the dry stalks. They blazed to life. A river breeze fed the bright flames so they leaped higher, towering over the gathered throng. As the fire grew hotter, Brynna drew back from the crackling, spitting flames. The red-orange light shone like a beacon on the broad faces of the slaves. Temple came to stand beside her and place an arm around her shoulder. In that moment, it seemed they truly owned the world, so invincible did their happiness make them.

They stood watching until the intensity of flames had died down a little. As the fire ebbed so did the excitement of the watchers. By the time the bonfire was only a pile of coals on the riverbank, people had already begun to drift back toward their cabins.

"Fire! Mistah Temple. Theah's a fire."

At first Brynna looked back at the river, thinking the coals had flared up again and caught the dried grasses on fire, but the riverbank was dark. All around her slaves had begun to run and point excitedly.

"Mistah Temple. It's da mills and warehouse," someone cried, and Brynna turned to gaze at the orange glow rising over the treetops.

"Oh, no," she gasped, knowing much of Langtry's

300

sugar yield was still in the warehouse awaiting shipment down to New Orleans.

"Brynna, take Jessica to the house and stay there," Temple ordered, and ran off through the trees in the direction of the mill.

"Come on, Jessica," Brynna said, walking her aunt toward the house, although she longed to run after her husband. She spied some of the house servants. "May!" she cried. "See Aunt Jessica gets back to the house safely."

"Where are you going, Brynna?" Jessica asked worriedly.

"I've got to go down to the mill. Temple may need me," she answered, gathering her full skirts in her hands preparing to go.

"Be careful, child," Jessica said, knowing she couldn't keep her niece away. She watched silently as Brynna sped across the yard after the firefighters.

Dusk had turned to dark, so she couldn't see the limbs that lashed out at her. She took no time to avoid them, taking their stinging slaps and scratches without pausing. She was gasping for air by the time she reached the mill and paused to take in the scene before her. It seemed like something from hell itself.

The new mill, with its steam engine and steel rollers, was blazing furiously. Counting it lost, Temple directed the efforts of his slaves toward saving the barns where the sugar was stored. A stream of buckets were filled at the river and handed along a row of slaves to men who threw the pitifully inadequate contents against the burning wood.

Temple had taken off his jacket and beat at the flames with it. Other men rushed to join him. Brynna saw a gap in the brigade and ran to take her place there. The buckets were heavier than she'd expected and she almost

301

dropped the first one handed to her. She steadied herself and passed it on, grabbing the next and the next until it seemed she had ceased to be a human and was a mere cog in a machine all too inadequate against the roar of the flames. One slave got too close and ran past them screaming, his clothes afire. Hands grabbed him and threw him in the cold river water. Sputtering, he climbed out and ran back to the burning building to beat ineffectually at the flames.

"Let it go," Temple cried finally. His face was blackened with soot, his eyes red-rimmed. "We can't stop it," he called.

"No," Brynna cried, feeling his pain. "We can put it out. We can!" She ran forward to throw the bucket of water at the flames. She tossed the bucket aside and, picking up a discarded blanket, she beat at the flames.

"Brynna!" Temple called. "Get back." She didn't hear him above the fire's roar. "Brynna!"

She heard him then, and some of the panic in his voice warned her. She looked up and saw a wall of fire plunging down toward her. She screamed, throwing up her hands to shield her face. Strong hands jerked her away and she felt herself thrown clear, felt pain shoot through her temple, and the flaming holocaust was lost to her, shut away by the velvet darkness that claimed her.

She came to on the parlor sofa at Langtry. Jessica knelt close by applying cooling wet clothes to her brow. "Poor thing, she's coming to," she said when she saw Brynna's eyelids futter.

"Brynna!" She heard the urgency in his voice and wanted to tell him she was all right, but her eyes wouldn't focus and her throat was clogged with smoke.

"Here, drink this," Temple said, lifting her and holding a glass to her lips. Brynna drank and felt the fiery whiskey burn a path down her throat. She gasped and coughed. Temple laid her back against the sofa arm.

"Thank God," he said, and turned away, but she'd seen the sheen in his eyes and was warmed by it.

"D-did you lose the warehouse?" she asked.

"Yes, you little fool," Temple said, rounding on her. "But that's nothing compared to the fear of losing you. Why didn't you do as I said and stay here with Jessica?"

"I wanted to help," Brynna said. "I'm sorry I worried you." Sighing in resignation, he crossed the room to draw her into his arms.

"You worried me mightily," he said, rocking her gently. Brynna lay against him, grateful he was all right. He smelled of smoke.

"Does anyone know how it started?" she asked. Temple drew away and paced the room, raking his hand through his dark hair impatiently.

"No one saw anything," he answered. "They were all down by the bonfire, but I found this when I first arrived." He reached inside his pocket and pulled out a pouch decorated with colored pebbles and chicken feathers. No one said a word. They all knew the significance of the pouch. Brynna thought of the carved doll upstairs in her drawer and was unable to meet Temple's eyes. Surely Cyra wouldn't have had anything to do with the burning of Langtry's crop.

"We'd better get some rest," Temple said finally, tossing the pouch on a table. "Let's hope the New Year begins better than this one has ended."

"Amen," Jessica said, and got to her feet. "Do you need some help, dear?"

"I'll carry her up, Jessica," Temple said, coming to gather Brynna in his arms.

"You're tired. Let me walk up with you," she said, and

303

Temple released her. Brynna guessed he must be even more tired than he looked. As they made their way up the stairs, she looped his arm over her shoulders and placed her arms around his waist. "Lean on me a little," she urged, ignoring the strange fluttering in her stomach.

Her words brought a smile to his face. "No matter how bad things seem," he said, "you make me see how lucky I really am." He leaned on her then, letting her feel his weight slightly, letting her know in ways words could never have conveyed how much he needed her. Together they reached their room and helped each other undress. The beautiful new gown was ruined. Brynna poured water into the china bowl and brought it to the bed where she bathed Temple's face and then her own. Finally, she crawled into bed beside him and cradled his head against her breast. Whatever the New Year held, it could never give her as much as the old one had.

She thought of the pouch lying on the table below. She'd ignored too much for Cyra, trying to protect her. In doing so, she'd caused the man she loved more than anything in the world to be hurt. She would not defer to Cyra again. Tomorrow she would speak to Cyra and this time, there would be no doubts that she was mistress of Langtry and Cyra her slave.

Temple awoke with Brynna snuggled in his arms. He peered down at her soot-smudged face and thought he could never love her more than now. He thought of her standing in the brigade passing buckets and beating at the flames. She'd come to Langtry a child, she'd become a woman any man would feel pride in claiming. Love welling, he bent to kiss her eyelids, cheeks, and nose. By the time he'd reached her mouth, she was waking, stirring against him all warm and soft and pliant. Then she remembered the fire, and with a cry sat up.

"I was hoping I was dreaming," she moaned with regret.

"I wish it had been a dream." Temple threw aside the covers and reached for his trousers and boots.

"Where are you going?"

"I want to assess the losses."

"Do you think any of the sugar escaped the fire?" Her eyes were deep with worry.

"No," he answered honestly. "The fire was too hot."

"Could the fire have been an accident?" Brynna held her breath, waiting for the answer.

"Someone set it." He pulled on his boots and straightened. She saw the anger in his dark eyes and the set of his mouth. He dropped a quick kiss on her lips and hurried off, his mind already on the burnt mill and warehouses.

Brynna got out of bed and felt a wave of dizziness claim her. She'd risen too quickly, she chided herself, waiting for the room to right itself. Catching sight of her soot-smudged face in the mirror, she immediately ordered a bath. The warm water soothed her aching muscles and dulled the pain that had started low in her middle. She must learn to worry less, she told herself, and thought of Cyra. Her resolve was stronger than ever. She dressed quickly and set out for the slave quarters at a determined pace.

Cyra was sitting on the littered porch of her cabin. She smiled when she saw Brynna coming.

"Did you set fire to the mills last night?" Brynna demanded without preamble.

"Good mahnin', Mistress Brynna," Cyra said mockingly.

"I asked you a question. Did you set fire to the mills and warehouse last night?"

"Why, Miz Brynna, why would Ah do a thing like that."

"I don't know why, Cyra." Brynna answered. "I'd like to think you didn't do it, but someone did, and whoever it was, left this behind." She tossed the voodoo pouch on the porch beside Cyra.

Thoughtfully, Cyra picked it up, kneading it between her slim brown fingers. Finally, she raised her dark eyes to Brynna and they held a world of secrets that Brynna realized she would never know. "Nearly ever'body's got a bag of gris-gris," Cyra said.

"I know what gris-gris is, Cyra. I know about the special powers it's supposed to possess, and I know how people like you prey on the fears of the ignorant slaves."

"I ain't doin' nothin' wrong," Cyra snapped.

"You aren't doing anything right," Brynna answered. "I've warned you before and now I'm telling you. If there's any more evidence of voodoo being practiced here on Langtry I'll—"

"Tell on me. That's what yo' said befo'," Cyra finished for her. "Why ain't yo' don' that, Miz Brynna?" Her lips curled with contempt.

Cat-quick, Brynna stepped closer and slapped Cyra across the cheek. Cyra's smiled faded. Hatred shone in her eyes.

"I don't have to tell on you to anybody," Brynna said. "I am the mistress of Langtry and you are my slave. If you cause any more trouble, I will sell you away to the first buyer."

"No you won't!" Cyra cried defiantly.

"Yes I will!" Brynna's gaze was unflinching. Cyra rubbed her cheek and studied the white girl.

"Yo' got yo' daddy's look right now," she said.

"If I need to, I can be my father's daughter, Cyra. This is my last warning to you. Do you understand?"

"Yes, ma'am," Cyra said, uncowed and hostile. "Ah's be good, Miz Brynna. Ah's be good!"

Defeat was bitter in Brynna's mouth, but she would not leave the confrontation bested by this bitter woman. "You've thrown away any chance for love and understanding between us. Have a care, Cyra."

Turning, Brynna stalked away. She could feel the hatred of Cyra's gaze on her back. She wanted to weep for the shiny-eyed girl she'd once known and loved, but those days were forever behind them. Each of them moved on opposing roads toward their own destinies. Brynna felt a load slide away from her and recognized it as guilt, the guilt she'd carried for Cyra and the wickedness of her father. In letting go of the past, she stepped forward toward the future with greater confidence. She was no longer Brynna Stanton, frightened and ashamed. She was Brynna Sinclair, the wife of Temple Sinclair and mistress of Langtry. With a start she realized she no longer counted her love of Langtry ahead of her love for Temple. Without the man, the land meant nothing. With renewed buoyancy she followed the path toward Langtry.

"Good morning, Brynna," Betty Hewitt said from the gatepost. "That was some bonfire last night. Ah believe the biggest we've evah seen round about these parts."

"You know, of course, it was no bonfire, but the mills and warehouse."

"Yes, ma'am, I surely do," Betty said. "It's a shame. Looks like Temple won't have the extra money to buy you fancy doodads for a while."

Brynna had been about to proceed down the path, but now she paused and turned to confront the impudent girl.

This was her day to take care of many loose ends, she decided, and smiled benevolently.

"Betty, dear," she said with some condescension and great firmness. "Beginning with the New Year, I'll expect you to take over the supervision of the weaving and sewing sheds."

The vapid smile disappeared from the pretty face replaced by outrage. "Ah am not one of Langtry's niggahs," she declared hotly.

"Indeed you are not," Brynna said. "You are the overseer's daughter and as such you hold a certain position on this plantation. Therefore you will perform your duties, as Aunt Jessica and I must do. I will expect you to join us first thing tomorrow morning." Without giving the girl time for rebuttal, Brynna continued down the path. When she reached the kitchen, she had to pause for a moment to knead the pain in her middle. When the spasm had passed, she entered the kitchen.

"Lala, I need to talk to you," she said, and no longer did she sound like the mistress of Langtry.

"W'at yo' need, Miz Brynna?" Lala asked, pausing at her task of kneading bread dough. Her great brown arms gleamed, her hands were white with flour.

"You must tell me everything you know about voodoo and how I can get rid of it from Langtry."

Lala's expression reflected fear. "Ah cain't tell yo' nothing 'bout dat, Miz Brynna. Don't ask me dat," Lala said.

"I have to ask you and you have to tell me. Something bad is going on here at Langtry and I want to stop it."

"Lawd, don't say dat, Miz Brynna. Yo' cain't stop it," Lala whispered. "Evil spirits been called up f'om de grave and dey ain't never going back."

"Lala, listen to me." Brynna leaned forward to grip her arms. "We have to try. Langtry may be destroyed if we

308

don't." Lala stood for a long time, considering, and Brynna saw the struggle in the big woman's eyes. At last Lala nodded her head.

"W'at yo' want t' know, Miz Brynna?" she asked resignedly.

"How many of the Langtry slaves are involved with voodoo?"

"Ah don't know that fo' sure," Lala said. "Dat new man Mistah Temple bought last' summer, he force some of de slaves into it. Dey don't want to, dey scared of de spirits, but he say, dey got to follow him and do what he say. Mah son, Jacob, he got t' do lak' Thomas say an' he don' wan' to."

"He won't have to anymore," Brynna reassured the frightened cook. "I'll speak to Mister Temple and this will be ended."

"Yo' cain't never end it wit' de spirits, less'n dey want yo' to."

"We'll find a way. Tell Jacob. Tell all the slaves. They must stay away from the woods where the rituals are held."

"Ah tells 'em, Miz Brynna. Ah'm not sure dey believe me."

Brynna left the kitchen and made her way back to the big house. She was tired and needed some time alone to think. Although Jessica sat in the parlor sewing, Brynna took the back stairs and went straight to her room. She must find some way to end this voodoo spell Cyra and Thomas seemed to have cast over the slaves. She'd tell Temple about everything as soon as he returned. At the top of the stairs, she paused and gripped the banister to keep from falling. Pain gripped her stomach, doubling her nearly in half. She breathed deeply until the pain and nausea passed, then slowly made her way down the hall.

She'd skipped breakfast and run up the stairs too quickly, she chided herself. She'd lie down and rest until this malaise passed. Sweat beaded her brow by the time she reached her room. Gratefully, she closed the door and leaned against it, drawing strength to make her way to the bed. Through a haze she saw the ugly thing on her pillow, the twisted, broken doll with the red-gold curl and the nail driven into its middle. The pain in her stomach was greater now, building until she feared it might consume her. Staggering to the bed, she gripped the post in an effort to stay on her feet. She was going to faint, she realized dimly. Still, her gaze was fixed on the voodoo doll. It wavered as if it possessed a life of its own. Brynna felt the darkness rush at her and heard her own anguished scream.

Chapter Sixteen

"Brynna, darling," Temple whispered against her pale brow.

Brynna felt him near her and her arms reached out to clutch him.

"Make it go away," she whimpered.

"What, my precious girl?" Temple muttered, soothing her.

"The doll!" Brynna cried out, opening her eyes at last to look at him.

Seeing the terror in her gaze, he drew back. "What doll?" he asked worriedly.

"The voodoo doll. It was alive. It was coming at me." She struggled to sit up.

"Brynna, lay back. You've been sick."

She lay quietly, her golden eyes pinned on him trustingly. Temple's hands smoothed the chestnut strands from her damp brow.

"I've been sick?" she repeated. "Did I have a fever like Aunt Jessica?"

"No, dearest." Temple looked away then and she saw his shoulders shake briefly before he controlled himself.

Jessica crept forward from the foot of the bed to take her hand and grip it tightly. "Oh, Brynna, I'm so sorry," she whispered. "You must be brave, my child."

"What is it? What's wrong with me?" Her gaze settled on Temple demanding an answer.

He raised his tear-stained face to her and brought her hand to his lips. "You were carrying our child, Brynna," he said, "and it's lost."

"It wasn't your fault, child," Jessica said quickly. "It was the shock of the fire and everything."

"No!" Brynna said disbelievingly, looking from Temple to Jessica and back again. Then the extent of what had happened closed in on her. She hadn't acknowledged yet that she was pregnant, but the suspicion had been growing. The tight Christmas dress, the unexpected nausea, had been clues she'd hugged to herself, waiting for just one more thing to tell her it was really true. Now before she'd even had the chance to revel in the joy of carrying a child, she'd lost it. Grief welled from some deep pool within her.

"No!" Her denial was a loud cry that echoed through the house and into the yard where Lala and the other house slaves waited.

Lala crossed herself. "I tol' her," she muttered. "I don' tol' her, you cain't make the spirits mad at yo'."

Temple held his sobbing wife, feeling her slender body tremble against him.

"Not our baby," she sobbed. "Not our baby!"

Jessica sat nearby weeping silently. Tears ran unchecked down Temple's cheeks. He'd lost so much these past few days, but this was the greatest loss of all. He'd vowed to protect her from grief and unhappiness, but how could he have protected her from this? He wept with her until her grief had drained her of every ounce of strength.

He placed her gently against her pillows and held a glass to her lips.

"Drink this, darling," he urged. "It will make you sleep." Obediently, Brynna swallowed the milky liquid, welcoming any respite from this pain she felt, a pain greater than any suffering she'd ever known. Thankfully she sank into a dreaming half-world where pain and joy were not known and therefore not felt.

"Let her sleep," Jessica said, coming to place a comforting hand on Temple's shoulder. "When she wakes, she'll feel a little better."

"I shouldn't have let this happen," Temple said, gripping Brynna's limp hand. "I saw her at the fire, lifting those pails of water and I didn't want to stop fighting the fire and send her home."

"It's not your fault, Temple. You can't blame yourself," Jessica said. Her eyes dimmed with tears as she watched her stepson's grief. "Brynna went there because she wanted to help you. She would have hated it if you'd sent her home like a child. There will be more children. She's young and healthy and you love each other. Think of that."

Temple nodded in agreement, but she knew it was too early for him to find comfort. Time would heal this loss, but now was a time of grieving.

"I'll leave you alone. If you need me, I'll be close at hand." Jessica left him then, knowing there was nothing more she could do. She closed the door behind her, carrying with her the glimpse of Temple on his knees beside Brynna's bed, his dark head resting against her breast. She carried with her the memory of Brynna's words. A voodoo doll, she'd cried out. Thoughtfully Jessica returned to her own room. There were undercurrents here at Langtry for which she had no liking.

* * *

All pleasure and joy in living was gone, it seemed. Brynna's body recovered, but her heart and spirit did not. Temple and Jessica did their best to maintain a cheery atmosphere around her, but to little avail. Sometimes, defeated by the sadness of his wife's eyes and his own regrets for things never to be, Temple would saddle Chandra and ride out over the fields of Langtry. But they gave him no joy. As he viewed his scorched fields and the ruin of his mills and warehouse, he felt no urge to rebuild and he wondered at the impasse they'd all been brought to. Sitting on Chandra's back, he wondered about the child they'd lost, the son who might have ridden beside him or the daughter with great golden eyes like her mother's and he hung his head and wept, great gulping sobs that only a man can weep when his soul has been wounded.

But spring was coming, and from the scorched fields sprang the first green shoots of a new cane crop. Temple lifted his grief-stricken eyes and began to hope again. And he carried that hope back to Langtry to his wife.

Brynna didn't want to see the spring, the renewing of life. The precious life within her had died. There would be no quickening of a tiny heartbeat beneath her own, no wonder of movement, no crying grasp for life. It was gone and she couldn't understand why it should be so. Slowly she resumed the running of Langtry, portioning supplies, supervising the house servants and skilled workers in the planting of new gardens.

The weather warmed, so Jessica and Brynna could sit on the front gallery and work at their stitchery. But the chill of the evening drove them indoors to the warmth of the fires. It was not yet March and the gulf air sometimes blew cold and damp.

Occasionally when Brynna went to the slave quarters, she saw Cyra. The slave woman would pause and stare at her unblinkingly. Brynna never acknowledged her presence, turning away as if she hadn't seen her. Nor did Brynna ever speak to Lala again about the voodoo practices of the Langtry slaves.

Sometimes at night she woke from a nightmare, sweating and crying out against the demons that taunted her, against the voodoo doll that had never been found and still haunted her. Temple would soothe her fears and hold her while she poured out a jumble of grief, old fears and unhappiness from her childhood, the horrible death of her mother, the brutality of Wes Stanton toward Cyra and his other slave women. Temple held her and soothed away the hurt and cursed the cruel man who'd sired this beautiful girl and then terrorized her so.

Sometimes he tried to make love to her, certain that if she became pregnant again, her grief would dissipate, but Brynna pushed him away, turning to her side of the bed. He didn't know how to reach her this time. He'd promised to protect her. He'd failed.

They'd ceased entertaining. The flux of invitations turned to sympathy cards, then dwindled away. They seemed locked in their gray, unhappy world at Langtry, and so they missed the first rumblings of trouble.

One warm day as Jessica and Brynna supervised the planting of early potatoes, a group of riders cantered up the oak-lined drive.

"Looks like trouble," Jessica said, peering from beneath the broad straw brim of her bonnet. "Benjamin, run down to the fields and get Master Temple." The boy took off at a run, grateful to be free of his duties in the garden.

315

"That looks like Cort de Jarreau and his father," Brynna said.

"Yes, it does," Jessica said. "Let's go to the house and greet them." Brynna followed her to the front gallery.

"Bonjour, Madame Sinclair," Sidney de Jarreau called as the men reached the front of the house.

"Good day to you, Monsieur de Jarreau," Jessica greeted. "Won't you come inside for some coffee?"

"We've come to see Temple," Jarreau said, dismounting. The others followed suit.

"I've sent for him. Please, gentlemen, won't you come in." They all trooped into the parlor.

"I heard about your loss, Brynna," Cort said. "I'm truly sorry."

Brynna couldn't bear to acknowledge his words of sympathy. Gripping her hands tightly in her lap, she forced a smile to her lips. "Tell me, Cort. How many pretty heads have you turned this season."

His dark eyes studied her a moment, taking in the pale face, the delicate facade of gaiety she forced upon herself, and he played the game she expected of him, although it was a game he'd long since abandoned.

"None worth the counting," he said, "since the one I value most is not to be turned."

A pot of hot black coffee was brought, and Brynna quickly positioned herself to pour.

"Gentlemen, what is the reason for this honor?" Temple asked from the door. He strode into the room and greeted each man. "Would you like whiskey for your coffee?" he asked, and personally served each man.

"Temple, we know how stable Langtry's people have always been. Except for those rumors last fall, we've never heard a hard word against your slaves. But trouble with

316

other plantations has increased and we're looking into everything to see what's got the slaves riled."

"I'll be happy to cooperate in any way I can. Ever since the fire that was set at Christmas time, things have been quiet around here."

"Have you seen any more signs of voodoo?" Cort asked.

"Only the pouch. What other signs should we look for?" Temple asked.

"Pouches, feathers, rough drawings, or carved dolls." The cup slid from Brynna's hands with a clatter and fell to the Persian carpet. The men turned and stared at her. Face white, mouth gaping, Brynna stared back.

Temple crossed the room to stand beside her and grip her shoulder reassuringly. "You'll have to excuse my wife, gentlemen. She's been not been well these past weeks."

"So we've heard. My apologies to you, Mrs. Sinclair, for bringing this unpleasant subject to your parlor."

"Jessica, perhaps you would take Brynna to her room," Temple suggested.

"No! I want to stay," Brynna said sharply.

Jessica sank back in her chair.

"Well, we've finished, really," Jarreau said. "If you see anything out of the ordinary, please let the rest of us know, and in the meantime, be careful. Keep your womenfolk close to the house."

"My goodness, surely there's no danger," Jessica exclaimed. "Our people have been with us for years."

"Mais oui," Jarreau said, shrugging his shoulders. "We may be worrying for no reason. But Alaric Tyson's wife was found drowned in a pool on their land and a plantation house down near Houmas caught fire mysteriously. The Houmas man had whipped one of his field hands for

stealing and Madame Tyson was known for her heavy hand with her slaves."

The room was silent. The planters looked at each other uneasily. They'd heard this before, but each time it was repeated, it seemed to gather credence.

"But why would anyone want to do us harm?" Jessica asked in dismay. "Why would our people want to burn the mills and warehouse, Temple? You've never treated them badly."

"No, but Kyle Hewitt does," Temple said. "I've caught him at it and given him warnings."

"And there are the mulatto babies born the last few months," Jessica said thoughtfully. "At first I didn't notice them after my bout with the fever. Their mothers don't want to talk about them for fear they'll be punished."

"Hewitt!" Temple said, driving a fist into the palm of his hand. "I'll dismiss him at once."

"This trouble may not be caused by your people," Harcourt explained. "We know slaves are moving from one plantation to another. Keep tight rein on your people and pay attention if you have a strange Negro show up."

"Yes, I will," Temple said.

"Send for help if you have any problems and arm your women."

"Isn't that getting a little drastic?"

"Perhaps," Jarreau said. "But if what we suspect is really happening, no precaution is too drastic. Why take a chance with our women?"

Brynna felt a chill run through her and she crept closer to Jessica as Temple showed their guests to the door. His face was somber when he returned.

"You heard what they said. We must be cautious. Don't go far from the house without each other." He strode to a cabinet and took out a key, and opened it.

318

Pulling out a small pistol, he loaded it and turned to Brynna. "Jessica already knows how to use this. Come here and let me show you."

"I couldn't," she whispered, recoiling.

"Could you use it to save Jessica or me? Come here." His tone was brusque, his face bleak. She knew he would brook no argument on this. Timidly, she took hold of the pistol, her hand dipping slightly as she felt the weight of it. Temple showed her how to cock it and where the trigger was. When she was able to handle it with some familiarity, he took her into the backyard and set up targets for her, making her shoot at them time and again until she hit them more often than she missed.

"That's enough," he said finally. "You or Jessica keep this gun with you at all times, especially when I'm not here."

"Temple, you're frightening me," Brynna whispered.

His long arms pulled her against him. "I don't mean to do that," he murmured against her temple. "God knows we've been through enough these past weeks. But you mustn't ignore the danger." The image of the voodoo doll came to her and she hid her face against his chest.

"Hold me," she whimpered, and he held her close, feeling her softness, breathing the fresh scent of her hair and body. Desire pulsed through him. It had been weeks, and his body hungered for her, but he knew this moment was not the time. She was frightened and he must practice patience.

Why hadn't she told him about Cyra and Thomas? she wondered. Why hadn't she warned him? She owed the slave woman nothing. Yet the memory of the voodoo doll and the loss of her child were somehow entangled in her

319

mind with her threats to expose Cyra. What would happen if she told about the things she'd seen? Would Temple be killed? She couldn't bear the thought.

Now began a season of fear. Each morning as Temple mounted his horse and rode out to his fields, Brynna stood on the gallery wondering is she'd see him alive again. She carried the small pistol in a concealed pocket of skirts at all times, although she was still certain she would never be able to use it. The slaves were frightened as well. Nothing was ever said or done without their knowledge. They'd heard of the Houmas fire and the Tyson woman's death and more. They were quiet as they went about their tasks, their eyes filled with fear and uneasiness. Jessica and Brynna spent as much time reassuring the house servants as they did themselves.

The days passed without further incident. Brynna grew used to the weight of the gun tugging at her skirts. Seeing Jessica and Brynna go about their business, the house servants began to relax. To keep them too busy to speculate, Brynna and Jessica began spring cleaning early, ordering the chandeliers lowered and polished, the draperies and thick woolen rugs beaten and aired, the wood floors waxed, the silver polished. Every closet and drawer was turned out and put back again.

"I think it's done," Jessica said, looking around. "I can't think of one corner we might have missed."

Brynna laughed. The sound was unfamiliar to her. "It's wonderful to see Langtry like this, all shiny and bright, like a grand dame in her best jewels." Jessica said nothing, but her steadfast smile was enough. Brynna turned to her. "It's good to laugh again," she said. "I'm sorry I lost the baby."

"Don't ever say those words again," Jessica scolded gently. "It couldn't be helped."

"Maybe not. Only God knows that."

"There's something I've wanted to ask you ever since that day," Jessica said, "but I haven't wanted to bring it up and cause you pain."

"What is it?"

"The voodoo doll you saw. Tell me about it."

"It was there, Jessica, on my pillow when I walked into the room. But that wasn't the first time. Before Christmas, I found a voodoo doll on my pillow."

"What did you do with it?"

"I pushed it back in my drawer. I—I thought it was a prank."

"You thought Cyra was playing a prank on you."

"Yes. She used to do that when we were girls and she tried to make me do what she wanted. That's why I never said anything to you or Temple. I knew you'd be angry with her, but she . . . she can't help the way she is."

"Do you still have the first doll? The second one was never found."

"I think so. It's still in my drawer."

"Go get it, Brynna. We must tell Temple about this tonight."

"Yes, of course, you're right." Brynna hurried to her room, but when she searched through her drawer, the doll was missing.

"It's gone," she said, feeling alarmed.

"Are you certain? Let's take everything out." Jessica helped her turn the drawer out, but the doll was gone.

"But how did it disappear?" Brynna asked faintly.

Jessica saw the fear in her eyes and shook the girl. "Don't begin to believe all this nonsense, Brynna. Obviously whoever put it there came back and got it."

"I didn't used to believe in voodoo," Brynna said slowly, "until I lost the baby. Then I thought—"

321

"You were sick with grief then," Jessica said, looking into her eyes. "You aren't now, Brynna. We must fight this together, and the first thing we must do is tell Temple everything."

"Yes, oh yes, Jessica. I'm sorry I haven't done so already. I meant to, and the baby— But I will now, tonight!"

Anxiously, the women awaited Temple's return. Dusk fell and deepened into night and still he didn't come. Brynna paced the parlor. Jessica steeled herself to stitch neatly when all the while her heart pounded painfully in her chest. Finally, when the tall corner clock struck ten times, Brynna could stand the suspense no longer.

"I'm going to look for him," she cried. "I know something has happened."

"Brynna, no. You can't."

"I can't sit here waiting, when Temple might need me."

"Do you have the pistol?"

"Yes." Brynna gripped the reassuring weight, longing to hear Temple's horse in the drive, but the night was silent. "May!" Brynna called, and when the young black girl appeared, Brynna took up a lantern. "Master Temple is not home yet," she said. "We're going to look for him."

May's face gleamed with fear. "Yes, Miz Brynna," she said faintly. Brynna held out her hand and took the girl's hand. "Remember the hurricane last summer, May?" she asked lightly. "We were very brave and nothing happened to us then. Nothing will happen now."

"No, ma'am," May said, and followed her out of the house.

"Be careful," Jessica called after them.

"Tell Lala to have supper ready for us when we all get back," Brynna called gaily, to give herself as much as

May, courage. They made their way down the dark path to the barn where Brynna ordered Jarib saddled. Chandra snorted and stamped in his stall as if he knew she was going to find Temple.

"Has the horse Master Temple rode today returned to the barn?"

"No, ma'am, Ah ain't seen him," the stable boy answered.

Chandra whinnied.

"Saddle Chandra as well," Brynna ordered. "May can ride him."

"No, ma'am, Miz Brynna. Ah ain't never rid no horse." May rolled her eyes in fear.

"I can't go alone," Brynna said, trying to think of what to do. No moon shone to light the way, and the vast blackness beyond the glow of the barn lanterns was daunting. "May, run to the overseer's house and see if Hewitt has returned."

"Yes, ma'am." May grabbed up a lantern and set off at a run. Impatiently, Brynna helped the boy saddle up the two Thoroughbreds. Leading Jarib to the mounting block, she settled herself astride the nervous horse and took the reins the stable boy held out to her. Wheeling about, she made her way first toward the overseer's house. She could see the weave of May's lantern as she ran to meet her.

"Miss Betty say she ain't seen her daddy all evenin'," May gasped.

Fear clogged Brynna's throat. "Get Betty and go up to the big house. Tell Aunt Jessica to send Absalom to the Jarreau plantation for help."

"Maybe yo' should wait, Miz Brynna, 'till Mr. Jarreau come."

"I can't wait," Brynna cried over the stamping of

323

Jarib's hooves. "Temple is hurt. I must find him. Give me your lantern."

May handed it up, and Brynna spurred Jarib forward. The spirited animal broke into a hard gallop. Chandra followed behind them. Brynna gave the horses their heads, trusting in their instincts. They knew the pathways of Langtry better than she. Through the black night they galloped, the wind whipping her hair free from its pins. She might have despaired of finding Temple if not for Chandra. Abruptly, he broke free, and with his reins trailing veered down a side path. A sturdy roan stood in beneath an oak tree, its head down, its saddle empty. Instinctively, Brynna knew this was the horse Temple had ridden out on. She raised the lantern high, peering into the dark shadows beneath the tree.

"Temple?" she called, and her voice sounded loud and frightened in the still night. There was no answer. Even the frogs along the riverbank seemed to have stilled their song.

"Temple!" she cried again, her voice edged with fear. Chandra had trotted ahead and Brynna nudged Jarib to follow. Down the narrow path they traveled with branches tearing at her hair and skirts. The fields on either side were overgrown and the ground beneath swampy and untillable. Surely, Temple would not have been here. A sound made her pause. A moan! Chandra whickered. The moan came again.

"Temple!" Brynna screamed and kicked at Jarib's sides to urge him forward.

He lay at the side of the path, half submerged in a shallow, muddy pool. Crying his name, Brynna slid from the saddle and ran to him. Placing the lantern on a dry piece of ground, she knelt beside Temple. He was bleeding badly from a deep gash across his shoulder. His face

324

and body were battered, as if he'd sustained a horrible beating. Frantically, Brynna tore away a piece of her petticoat and, dipping it in the muddy water, dabbed at his bloodied face. Then she attempted to bind his gaping wound.

"Temple," she crooned over and over. "Please be all right. Please." Desperately, she looked around. She had to get help for him. No one would find them here and she couldn't leave him alone. What if in his pain he rolled face down into the pool of water? He would drown. She had to get him onto the horse. Temple groaned again, and she took heart.

"Temple," she said, patting his face lightly. "Wake up, Temple. You have to wake up and help me, do you hear? There's no one else, just you and me, and I can't get you on the horse. Do you hear me, Temple? You have to help me."

With a loud groan he rolled his head and opened his eyes. They were glazed with pain and she wasn't sure he recognized her, but she'd gotten some response and she had to insist on more.

"Get up, Temple," she said, tugging at his arm. "You have to get up on your feet. Come on, Temple. No one else can do it but you. That's good." He was trying to rise. Brynna knelt and placed a shoulder beneath his arm, then cajoling and commanding him, she managed to get him to his feet. His large body sagged against her slender one, nearly knocking her to her knees. But she had too much to lose if she let him slide back down to the muddy swamp.

"Chandra!" she called, her voice breaking with strain. As if he understood her urgency, the Arabian came to her. With just a couple of steps, they were beside the Thoroughbred, clinging to his saddle. For a moment, Brynna stood sobbing, wondering how she'd get Temple into the saddle, but do it she must.

Taking his hand, she placed it on the stirrup. "Temple, put your foot in the stirrup," she ordered. His hand flopped away and his knees sagged.

"No!" she cried, making her tone unyielding. "Climb into the saddle, Temple. You must." For a long while he stood breathing heavily, his head leaned against his stallion, then slowly, laboriously, he pulled himself up into the saddle. Brynna pushed from behind, guiding his foot to the stirrup, lending her weight, and when at last he lay against Chandra's neck, she took off her petticoats and tore them to shreds, to tie his feet in the saddle and his hands around Chandra's neck. Then, trembling with her efforts, she climbed onto Jarib's back and slowly walked the horses back toward Langtry. She had no idea how much time had passed. She was surprised to see men gathered in front of the big house, lanterns in their hands. When they heard her coming, they rode out to meet her.

"My God, Brynna," Cort exclaimed. His voice held dread. "Where's Temple?"

Wearily, she nodded toward Chandra.

"Temple!" Cort swore softly and, dismounting, untied Temple. "Let's get him inside." Men rushed to carry him into the house. Jessica had already fetched her medicines and a pan of water. They placed Temple on the satin sofa and Brynna knelt to help Jessica wash him.

"Where's my daddy?" Betty Hewitt cried, her pretty face twisted with fear.

"I don't know," Brynna said without looking up. "I didn't see him." Betty began to weep noisily. Brynna turned away. Cort studied the pale face before him. There was no sign of weeping, only a grim determination to help her husband and an overwhelming fatigue.

326

"What happened?" he asked softly. "When Temple didn't come home by dark, we knew something was wrong. I went out looking for him."

"By yourself?" The other men stood around the parlor. Brynna recognized many of them from their last visit here to warn of dangers.

"There was no one else," she said, looking around the circle of grim-faced men. "Do you think Kyle Hewitt is still out there?"

"We'll look for him," Harcourt said.

The other men nodded in agreement.

"Where did you find Temple? Maybe Hewitt was nearby."

"I never thought to look," Brynna confessed. "Follow the wagon road down to the bend. Take the side road as far back as you can go. Those fields haven't been drained yet. It starts to get pretty swampy."

The men filed out. Brynna turned back to Temple. He looked a little better with the blood and mud washed away, but a dark bruise above one eye testified he had been struck with something. The gash across his shoulder gaped open.

"Oh, no," Brynna cried upon seeing it. "What could have caused such a monstrous wound?"

"Machete," Jessica said and, taking out a needle, calmly threaded it. "Now, Brynna," she said. "You must be very brave. You must take that bottle of whiskey and pour some of it over my hands and needle and then in the wound."

"Oh, no!"

"You must, else this will become infected and we'll lose him."

"I'll do it, Jessica," Brynna whispered. Tears filled her eyes and rolled down her cheek, but she took no time to brush them away. With a steady hand, she did as Jessica had instructed. When the alcohol was poured into the wound, Temple twisted on the sofa and shouted with pain. Brynna hesitated only for a moment before continuing until all of the gash had been washed with alcohol.

"Try to get some down him," Jessica said, and Brynna held the bottle to Temple's lips, letting the fiery contents dribble into his mouth. Jessica set the needle to the jagged edge of the wound and drew it through the bruised flesh. Brynna clamped her teeth over her lips to keep from crying out. Steadily, Jessica worked, and when the wound was closed, she cut the thread and sat back on her heels. The hands that had been steady while she stitched her stepson's wound were shaking so badly, she could scarcely place the scissors back in her sewing basket.

"Oh, darling Jessica," Brynna cried, hugging the older woman. "You were splendid."

"No, Brynna, *you* were the splendid one, going out into the dark night to search for him and miraculously finding him."

"I didn't find him. Chandra did," Brynna said, and looked at her sleeping husband. "We all love him so. Do you suppose it will be enough to save his life?"

"I think it will, child," Jessica said. "Let's call someone to help get him upstairs. I've sent Absalom for a doctor, but he likely won't come now before morning."

With the help of the house servants, they carried Temple up to his room and settled him in bed. He stirred now and then, moaning with pain. When she was sure he was resting well, Brynna sank into a chair by his bedside. The skirts of her gown were muddy and damp, but she had no energy left to change.

"Why don't you try to sleep, child, and I'll sit with him."

"I can't, Jessica," Brynna said. "I just want to sit here and look at him. I was so frightened that I would never see him again."

"I know, I know," Jessica said.

Despite her disclaimer, Brynna did sleep, sitting in her straight-back chair with her head resting against Temple's bed. A sound brought her upright and she realized voices were coming from below. She hurried to the landing and looked down. The men had returned. They gathered in the great hall, looking worried and uneasy.

"We found Hewitt, Jessica," Jarreau said. "He was on down a ways from the place Brynna said she found Temple."

"Is Mr. Hewitt all right?" Jessica asked.

"He's dead, Miz Sinclair," Beynaud said. "He was cut up pretty badly with a machete."

"That poor man," Jessica whispered.

"We'll have to wait till morning before we start looking for the culprits. Do you have any idea who could have attacked them?"

"None," Jessica said.

"I know who did it," Brynna said and walked down the stairs, her eyes dark with anger, her head high with purpose. Halfway down, she paused and looked at the men. "The murderers are a field hand named Thomas and a mulatto woman named Cyra."

Chapter Seventeen

"Brynna, are you sure?" Jessica cried, staring up at her.

"Cyra killed my father and set fire to Beaumont Hall."

"But why, *chérie?*"

Brynna didn't hesitate, although the eyes of the planters were fixed on her. Once she'd kept her secrets and it had nearly cost her everything she held dear. Now she squared her shoulders and spoke without fear.

"My father mistreated his slaves. They feared and hated him. I've known for some time Cyra was involved with voodoo," Brynna said dully. "She and Thomas have performed rituals here on Langtry and they forced some of the other slaves to participate. Time and again I warned her, but she refused to believe she would be punished. When I lost the baby—I didn't think about Cyra and what she was doing. My failure to do anything about her cost Hewitt his life and nearly brought about the death of my husband." Brynna began to weep, making no effort to cover her face.

"With your permission, Miz Sinclair, we'll go down to the slave quarters now and apprehend them."

"Yes, of course," Jessica replied.

Cort ran up the stairs to Brynna. She crumbled in his arms. Jessica hurried up to help, and between them, they carried her down the hall to the bedroom Brynna had once used.

"Go ahead with the others," Jessica said.

"You have your hands full, Aunt Jess. Do you need me to help?"

Jessica shook her head. "Just send up May when she has the Hewitt girl calmed down."

Cort walked to the door and looked back at Brynna. "They've had their share of misfortune," he said softly.

"Yes, they have," Jessica replied. "But they're strong and they have each other. They'll survive."

"Yes. They have each other." Cort closed the door softly behind himself.

Brynna slept as if dead and woke with a start, her first thought of Temple. Throwing a cover over her nightdress, she hurried down the hall and burst into his room. Temple sat up in bed, looking pale and tired, but awake. A large bandage covered his shoulder and crisscrossed his chest. The bruises on his face and torso were ugly and painful-looking. With a cry, Brynna tore across the room and flung herself on the bed, her arms wrapping tightly around him. Temple winced, then gathered her close. Tears dripped from her chin onto his bare chest and he tightened his grip, aware of how close he'd come to death and how much he loved this woman who clung to him.

"Come now, Brynna," he admonished softly. "You saved my life. Is that a cause for tears?"

"I came so close to losing you," she whispered. "I couldn't have lived without you." Her strong young arms tightened around him convulsively. He endured the added pain because it was Brynna who held him and he wanted her there in his arms.

Cort and Jessica stood at the foot of the bed. They'd been conversing with a short, balding man wearing spectacles. Now all fell silent and watched the two people on the bed. Brynna's chestnut strands fanned behind her, her slim, young body was outlined in the cotton nightdress, the rich coverlet contrasting sharply. They were handsome together, and the mutual depth of their feelings heartwarmingly clear.

Cort saw the beauty of the woman and felt regret deep in his soul that he'd hadn't won her love, but then, he acknowledged, he'd never really had a chance. Brynna and Temple had belonged to each other from the beginning. He could only hope that one day he might find someone like Brynna, someone who'd look at him with that same depth of love.

Dr. Saunders cleared his throat and Brynna raised her head and looked at him. "Is he going to be all right?" she whispered pleadingly.

"Thanks to you and Jessica, he will most certainly live," Dr. Saunders answered. "As to whether he'll be all right, I'm not sure he ever was." The doctor grew serious. "If you hadn't found him when you did and hadn't gotten him back to the house where he could be treated, Langtry would be having two funerals instead of one. Jessica, your skill with the needle is unsurpassed. If ever you think of practicing nursing, I could use some help in my office."

"Thank you, doctor, but I have my hands full here," Jessica answered. Her smile was bright, but her face and the slump of her soldiers showed the strain she'd endured.

"What about Cyra?" Brynna asked, sitting up. Her eyes were wide with dread.

"Cyra and Thomas and a handful of other Negroes couldn't be found last night," Cort said. "We think they fled into the swamps. We've got men and dogs coming today to track them down."

Brynna leaned back, her face bleak. An image of Cyra fleeing with a pack of hounds and men after her was distressing. Then Temple moved beside her, trying to ease the pain of his wounds, and her heart hardened again.

In the days that followed, many men came to Langtry, their faces grim with purpose, their waists girded with gun belts, their horses bearing rifles and whips. Their hounds yipped in the front yard, snarling and fighting with each other over the slightest provocation. Watching them from the parlor windows, Brynna imagined those teeth ripping into human flesh and, shuddering, turned away.

Kyle Hewitt was buried in the family cemetery with all the slaves of Langtry in attendance. Jessica stood with her arm around a sobbing Betty Hewitt. Brynna stood beside Temple, who'd insisted on rising and attending the funeral. He was white-faced from the effort by the time it was over. Brynna helped him back to his bed and sat beside him the rest of the day. The afternoon of the funeral, Betty Hewitt made her way upstairs and hesitated in the doorway.

"Is he sleepin'?" she asked timidly.

Brynna glanced up from her needlework.

"I'm awake, Betty," Temple said. "Come in."

Betty advanced to the side of his bed, her eyes fixed on his face. When she saw his bandages, she broke into tears. "Oh, Temple," she wept wildly, and for a moment, Brynna thought she meant to throw herself at him. She remained where she was, weaving on her feet until Brynna rose and brought her a chair. Perching on the edge, she raised round blue eyes to Temple.

"I'm sorry," she said. "I didn't mean to add to your troubles by bringing you mine."

"You've been through a great loss," Temple said. "We understand your tears."

"It's just that Ah was partial to my daddy," she said, twisting a handkerchief in her hands. "He always took care of me and now I don't know what I'm to do. I'm all alone." The final words were nearly lost in a fresh flood of tears.

"You're not alone, Betty. You have us—Brynna, Jessica, and myself."

Betty raised her head and stared at him. "But I ain't . . . I'm not like real family to you."

"Have you family anywhere else?" Brynna said. "If so, we'll see you get to them."

Betty cast her a baleful glance. "I have no other family, no one to take me in. I suppose I could go into New Orleans and find me a job as a shop assistant. Perhaps at Madame René's."

Brynna thought of Betty's pathetic attempt at needlework.

"You needn't worry about that now," Temple was saying. "You've just buried your father today. You're welcome to stay at Langtry as long as you wish, isn't she, Brynna?"

"Yes, of course," Brynna said faintly. Betty's expression turned triumphant as she glanced at Brynna. Quickly she hid it and assumed a subdued air. Her eyes, however, were joyous as she faced Temple.

"Thank you, Temple," she said softly. "That eases my mind some to know Ah don't have to leave the only people Ah know in this world. You are kind and generous, sir."

334

"No need for thanks," Temple answered, and his voice was ragged with fatigue.

"He's very tired," Brynna said. "We'd better let him rest a bit." Betty seemed to hesitate, so Brynna preceded her from the room. Betty had no choice but to follow.

In the hall she paused and looked around with a proprietary air. "Which room am Ah to have?" she asked abruptly.

Brynna's brow wrinkled in puzzlement. "Why, I thought you were comfortable enough in the downstairs guest room."

Betty shivered delicately. "Not at night," she stated. "Ah'm frightened down there all by myself. Why, Ah imagine if them niggers come to the house, I'd be the first one they'd find down there. Ah want to be near people even when Ah'm sleeping."

Vexed, Brynna drew a breath and let it out slowly. "Perhaps you'd better see Jessica," she said. "I believe she's in the parlor."

"All right," Betty said, and sashayed toward the stairs. Watching her, Brynna thought she'd never seen anyone less touched by grief. Pushing Betty from her mind, she returned to Temple, and seeing he already slept, she lay down beside him and wrapped her arms around him. After a while she, too, slept and dreamed of a happier time at Langtry.

Cyra and the other slaves were not found. "They've gone too deep into the swamps," Cort said. "They'll have to come out eventually."

"Aren't the swamps dangerous?" Brynna asked.

"There are deadly snakes and the like," Temple replied. He'd come out on the gallery to sit in the sunshine. "Anyone who knows the swamps could live in there for

335

some time. They can fish and trap alligators for food. It's rough living, but the Cajuns do it."

"If only they don't come out to kill again," Brynna said.

"Amen to that," Cort answered, and, spying Betty in the door bearing a tray, he quickly rose. "Good morning, Miss Betty," he said, bowing slightly.

Betty Hewitt dimpled prettily, and with mincing steps brought the tray to the wicker table. "I thought we might all like a glass of lemonade," she said grandly, and proceeded to pour and hand the glasses around. "Would you like a tea cake with your lemonade, Brynna? These are Lala's special recipe."

"No, thank you," Brynna answered, biting off her words. Little chance Betty would know if this was Lala's favorite recipe or not since she never set foot in the kitchen. In fact, since the funeral, Betty hadn't turned her hand at any of the chores and indeed added to them by sending the house slaves running on errands for her. Now she settled herself in the remaining chair and glanced around, her gaze settling hungrily on Cort.

"My gracious, Cort, you certainly look handsome this mahnin'," she said coquettishly.

"Why, thank you, Betty. You're looking rather fetching yourself."

"In this old thing?" she said. "Ah've been meanin' to get down to New Orleans and have some new gowns made, but with all that's happened, Ah just haven't had the inclination. You're awfully kind to say Ah look nice, though. It lifts a woman's spirits."

Temple glanced at Brynna, barely concealing a smile.

"Have you seen the garden, Cort?" Betty asked. "New shoots are just comin' up everywhere. It makes a body feel renewed to know life is like that." In her enthusiasm she jumped to her feet. "Why don't you come with me now.

Ah'll show you the peas and beans and those funny little herbs Jessica's so fond of." She tugged at Cort's hand and, laughing, he rose.

"Ya'll excuse me," he called over his shoulder.

"How can he endure that woman?" Brynna scoffed in exasperation once they were gone.

Temple studied her face. "You aren't jealous, are you?"

Her head jerked up. "How can you say that to me. You must know how much I love you."

Temple had the grace to look embarrassed. "That was a fool thing for me to say."

"Yes, it was," Brynna answered. "And for that you must return to your bed."

Temple grinned engagingly. "Only if you come with me." The dark lights in his eyes made his meaning all too clear.

"You're ill," Brynna cried in dismay.

"I'm better, much better." She could feel the heat of his dark gaze and an answering flare within herself. They hadn't made love since Christmas morning, before the fire, before the loss of their baby, before the trouble with the slaves. Now that all seemed behind them and her body raged with desire. Temple saw the flickering passion in her eyes and, getting to his feet, took her hand to pull her to their room.

"Cort and Betty will be back soon. What will they think?" she protested faintly.

"They'll probably not make the gardens," Temple replied. "Betty had something else in mind. No doubt they're even now in her room."

"That's disgusting," Brynna said. "How could Cort?"

"She's pretty enough, and accommodating," Temple said, beginning to unfasten her gown. "But let's not talk

337

about Cort and Betty." He lowered his head and nuzzled the soft white throat he'd exposed. Brynna shivered with delight, then buried her hands in his dark locks and tugged his head up so she could look deep into his eyes.

"Do you think Betty is pretty?" she asked.

"Not as pretty as you."

"Did you ever go to Betty's room?"

Temple's nibbling kisses stopped and he drew back. "Betty and her father worked for Langtry. I couldn't have taken advantage of that."

"But what about the slave wom—" She'd blurted it out before she could stop herself.

Once again, Temple drew away and studied her face. His eyes were dark and serious. "Some men use their female slaves," he said softly, "but my father and I have never done so. We consider it an indecent act against people who are dependent on us. My son will be taught to feel the same way."

Brynna's heart swelled with love. "I should have known you could never be like that," she said, throwing her arms around him. "You're good and noble."

"And much in need, Brynna. Can we stop talking now?"

"Only words of love," she answered. "I love you, Temple." She laughed as he swooped her up in his arms and laid her on their bed. She saw the dark shadows in his eyes and knew the gesture had cost him pain, but he bent over her, stroking and petting until she was limp with need. They'd wanted to take their time, but denial had taken away restraint. They tore away some of their clothes and left those that didn't interfere. Their coming together was intense, hot, and tumultuous, leaving them gasping and sweating as they descended the heights of fulfillment and fell into a dreamless, painless sleep.

* * *

Temple improved steadily and soon, over Brynna's protests, mounted his horse and took short rides into his fields. The de Jarreaus had sent over their overseer to help out until Temple could hire another. Cort had come every day to help, and Brynna was impressed at his skill as a planter. She'd thought him a philanderer and little else. Yet every day he disappeared for long periods and Brynna guessed he was with Betty. Betty had informed Jessica she preferred to keep her room on the ground floor. Brynna thought of revealing to Jessica Betty's liaison with Cort, then decided against it. Very little escaped Jessica; and Cort was like a favored nephew to her.

The crops were planted and the heat of an early summer was making itself felt. The planters began to relax and loll on their balconies, mint juleps close at hand. Their tranquility was rent by the shocking news that another plantation south of the river had been fired and its owners killed. Suddenly, Temple and Cort were packing their saddlebags with a fresh change of clothes and extra ammunition.

"Must you go?" Brynna cried. "What if something happens? What if you're injured again?"

"I won't be," Temple said. "I'll be riding with a group of men and I'll be expecting trouble this time. I have to help, Brynna. These men came to help me when I needed it."

Silently she stood back, but once he'd gone, she threw herself into Jessica's arms and wept bitterly.

"It's my fault," she sobbed. "I brought Cyra here."

"Cyra didn't start this, Brynna," Jessica explained. "She only joined in a movement that was already at hand.

339

There would have been an uprising of the slaves without her."

"How can you be sure?"

"Because it happens anytime people are oppressed," Jessica said, staring off into the distance. "One day our way of life will end for this reason."

"Jessica, you sound as if you disapprove of slavery."

"I suppose I do, a little bit," Jessica said. "Injustice wasn't born in the slave system. It's existed among men since the beginning of time. There are always unscrupulous men who take advantage of society's laws and our complacency toward others, suffering to satisfy their own desires. Life truly is a survival of the fittest even in an advanced civilization such as ours. We've tried—Temple, Etienne and I—to do something toward righting those wrongs. That's why our people are treated well, Brynna. We've freed many of them, those we knew could care for themselves, but some will always be dependent on us for their livelihood."

"You make me see things in a different light," Brynna said.

"No, child. You've known from the beginning. I've seen it in the way you've treated our slaves and the way you were with Cyra."

"Sometimes I've felt so ashamed for—"

"You're making a difference, Brynna. One day you may be called upon to do more. Learn and prepare yourself."

Brynna hugged the older woman. "I wish I could have helped Cyra," she whispered.

"Cyra has chosen her own path."

Brynna drew comfort from the things Jessica had said and she pondered her future role in this closed, carefully guarded society of wealthy planters and palatial homes.

No one believed such a brilliant world would ever change, yet Jessica had said it would one day. Would Langtry survive such a change? Perhaps that was her role, to preserve the strength and beauty of Langtry. She went about her tasks with a new regard.

The men didn't find the renegade slaves. Once more they'd fled into the swamps and bayous. Angry voices were raised among the planters, demanding the authorities do something. A vigilante group was formed, and Temple returned white-lipped from their first meeting.

"I won't join such an organization," he declared, pacing the parlor like a caged animal. "Many of those men aren't even land owners. They have nothing at stake. They're little more than bounty hunters. I won't contenance the cruelty they represent."

Summer progressed with unrelenting vengeance, the heat as oppressive as the fear that haunted the river country. Rumors of more runaway slaves joining the renegades dominated every social gathering. A plantation farther west toward Lafayette was burned, but its owners managed to escape. The mutilated bodies of black slaves began to turn up. Freed Negros claimed it was the work of the new vigilante group; planters claimed it was the work of Thomas and his renegades, intent on revenge toward any Negro who gave information to the whites.

The new furor caused terror among the plantation slaves. No longer were Jessica and Brynna greeted with smiles when they entered the kitchen or worksheds. Dark eyes, filled with mistrust, watched them warily. Though they were outnumbered, the whites had the power to wreak horrible deaths upon the blacks. Everyone knew even the finest lady visited the New Orleans premises of

341

Marie Laveau for the express purpose of a love potion or charm. How did they know those same genteel ladies did not purchase the powerful gris-gris that brought death and mayhem?

"Lala," Brynna said, standing beside the brick fireplace. "You know we would never hurt you. We love our people."

"Ah know, Miz Brynna," Lala said without looking up. Gone were her smiles and advice on a hundred different things. Perhaps that was the thing most unnerving, the silence of Langtry. Children no longer played in the dusty street before their cabins, calling to one another in childish games. No voices were raised in hymns, no banjos played in the warm summer nights. A silence of fear lay over the land.

"How will this all end?" Brynna wondered aloud.

"We must be patient and steadfast," Temple said, patting her back. "Once these renegades are caught and punished, the black people will stop being afraid and start trusting again."

"Surely, they know you aren't a part of the vigilantes," Brynna insisted. "They have no reason to fear us."

Reason seemed to play no role in the mood of the slaves. Though Brynna thought of Cyra and Thomas often, they seemed like strangers to her. The Cyra who hid in the swamps and came out to kill and plunder was not the same Cyra with whom Brynna had shared her childhood. That time was gone forever. Brynna concentrated on the care of Langtry and its people.

One day as she walked the path from the slave quarters back to the big house, she saw a figure lurking around the overseer's house. With the unrest among the slaves, Temple had not yet found a new overseer, so his house sat empty, the yard overgrown with weeds. At first, Brynna

342

thought the figure was one of Langtry's slaves, and she opened her mouth to call out. The figure stepped out of the shade of the building into the sunlight and the sound died in her throat.

"Cyra!" she gasped. The black woman remained still, her dark eyes staring at Brynna with a dark, unfathomable look. Her cheekbones stood out in bold relief, her body was thin and dressed in a ragged gown. At first Brynna felt a rush of relief, then fear crept over her. Brynna's eyes rounded with terror and she thought of the pistol she'd left on the dresser in her room. Where were Thomas and the other runaway slaves? Were they even now at the big house massacring Jessica and the others?

"No!" she screamed. The supplies she carried slipped from her nerveless hands. Grabbing her skirts high above her knees, she ran pell-mell toward the house. "Jessica!" she screamed. Lala and her assistants came out of the kitchen and watched in openmouthed astonishment. At least they were safe, Brynna thought.

"Get inside," she yelled, waving her arms. "Lock the door." Lala waddled back inside the kitchen, her assistants scrambling after her. Brynna heard the bolt slide home as she ran past. She gained the gallery. Everything looked quiet, too quiet. Sobbing now with terror for what she might find, she dashed inside the house.

"Jessica!" she screamed, running down the hall.

"Brynna?" Jessica answered from the parlor. Brynna skidded to a halt and slowly, disbelievingly, walked to the parlor door. Everything within was normal. Betty sat at one end of the sofa, her mouth crammed with a bonbon, her eyes wide and startled. Jessica stood beside her chair, her stitching on the floor where she'd dropped it.

"What is it?" Jessica cried, rushing forward. "Are you hurt?"

Brynna gazed at her in dismay, taking in every detail of Jessica's face and clothes. "You're alive!"

"Of course I am, child. What's got in to you?" Jessica paused. Her face blanched as she understood what had propelled Brynna into the house in such a panic.

"Have they come to Langtry?" she asked quietly.

"Yes. I saw Cyra down by the overseer's house."

Betty immediately began to scream, sugary streams of chocolate running down her chin. "Stop it," Brynna ordered. "Stop that screaming or I shall slap you."

Betty stopped her wailing and gulped down the rest of the bonbon. Her pale-blue eyes brimmed with tears.

"We must send for help," Brynna said. "Absalom!"

"Yes, ma'am, Miz Brynna." The black man came forward, sweat gleaming on his bald scalp.

"Go for Temple. Keep to the trees and cover as much as you can."

"Yes, ma'am." The old black man shuffled out to the gallery dodging behind the pillars to peer around before proceeding.

"Betty, collect all the slaves in the house and take them upstairs. Come on, Jessica. We'll be safer upstairs." The frightened women fled to the upstairs bedrooms, where they crouched in corners and waited. Brynna peered out the curtained French doors for a glimpse of Temple. She could see no sign of Cyra or Thomas or any strange Negro. The plantation lay still in the afternoon heat.

After an interminable time, Temple came galloping along the path. Brynna grabbed up the pistol and went out on the gallery. Her pistol would be ineffectual against a horde of rebelling slaves, but she might protect anyone who tried to attack Temple until he reached the safety of the house.

"Brynna," he shouted when he saw her. "Get back

344

inside." He leaped off his horse before it had come to a complete stop and ran for the door. Brynna flew back along the gallery and to the stairs to throw herself into his arms.

"What happened?" he demanded.

"I saw Cyra down by the overseer's house."

"Was she alone?"

"As far as I could see."

"Go back with Jessica and stay inside," he ordered. "I've sent Absalom for reinforcements. They should begin arriving shortly."

"What are you going to do?"

"Get guns and ammunition ready," Temple called over his shoulder. She could hear the anger in his voice and knew it was directed at himself. Save for the holstered pistol strapped at his waist, he'd stopped carrying firearms. Now she stood at the top of the stairs hearing him at the cabinet in his study. Soon he was back carrying extra shotguns.

"Give one of these to Jessica. Tell her to shoot if she has to." He headed toward the gallery.

"Let me come with you," Brynna pleaded.

Temple's fingers were biting on her arms. "I'm just going to patrol the gallery. I can see better from there if they try to rush us. You go back with Jessica."

"All right!" She made no further demur.

"It will be all right," he reassured her, and dropped a quick kiss on her lips. Brynna went back to Jessica's room and waited.

It seemed they'd waited an eternity before the first horse pounded down the drive.

"Tem," Cort called, and Brynna cried out in relief. Cort and his father and the White Hall overseer climbed the stairs and joined Temple on the gallery. Now each man patrolled a side and soon more men joined them.

With the advent of more men present, the women crept out on the gallery and peered down at the posse.

"Have you changed your way of thinking, Sinclair?" Harcourt declared when he'd alighted from his horse.

Temple's lips remained tightly clamped and he made no answer.

"Now is not the time for a debate, monsieur," Jarreau said. "We have gathered to hunt down this mob and bring them to justice."

"Ah aim to do that, suh," Harcourt declared, offended at the reprimand.

"Be forewarned," Temple said. "I want none of my people injured. Be very sure who you're shooting at." He glared at the circle of faces. Silently, the men moved out amid a clatter of hooves and the baying of hounds. A guard had been left behind, but still the women didn't feel safe. Betty smiled at Shepherd and, citing fear, managed to stay close at his side. For once, Brynna was willing to concede the girl might not be pretending.

For the rest of the day, they waited in tense silence. Jessica and Brynna went down to the kitchen and persuaded Lala to unlock the door and prepare some food and large pots of black coffee. The men would be hungry when they returned. They discovered the spring house and storage sheds had been raided, although not as much food had been taken as one might have thought.

"You must have scared them off when you saw Cyra," Jessica said. "It's a wonder they didn't kill you to silence you."

Brynna shivered.

When they hadn't returned by dark, Brynna ordered supper to be served, for no other reason than that it ended the desperate watching and waiting to hear something. The women picked at their food, shoving it around their plates. Shepherd ate heartily, belching afterward and picking his teeth.

The men returned sometime before midnight, their faces tired and scratched, their boots muddy. Jessica ordered the food and coffee brought for them. Brynna moved among them, filling their cups with the black liquid.

"Did you find any trace of them?"

Temple shook his head. "They were out there, though. And they're getting desperately low on food."

"What move do you think they'll make now?" someone asked. The other men looked away without answering. They were afraid of what that answer might be. Tired and discouraged, they broke up, some who lived close by returning to their plantations, others bedding down where they could find the space. They would hunt again in the morning. Some made pallets on the upstairs gallery. They'd stand watch during the night just in case.

"We'll be back in the morning," Cort said. "I wouldn't worry, Aunt Jess. Wherever they are, they won't bother you here tonight."

"Good night, Cort. Thank you and your father for coming to help."

Cort paused beside Temple, his dark eyes on Brynna. "Maybe you should consider sending the women down to New Orleans until this is settled. Alicia's already gone down."

"I've thought of that," Temple said.

"I won't go without you," Brynna said, meeting her husband's gaze unwaveringly.

Wearily, he put his hands on her shoulder and drew her near. He rubbed his forehead against hers. "For once you may have to follow your husband's orders," he said lightly.

"Not without you," she repeated, wrapping her arms around his waist. They stood thusly entwined, drawing strength from each other.

The next morning, against her protests, Brynna, Jessica, and Betty, along with several of the house slaves, were bundled into carriages, and with men riding guard, were taken to safety in New Orleans.

Brynna railed at the separation, refusing to indulge herself in the shops and tea houses, refusing even to call on anyone.

At Langtry, Temple tried to carry on by himself, but the big house had never seemed so empty. At any moment he expected to hear Brynna's voice or her running footsteps on the stairs. In the evening he sat in the empty parlor and smoked his pipe, and contemplated how life would have been if she'd never come to Langtry. It was impossible to imagine. Two weeks had passed and they seemed like an eternity. As he sat lonely and disconsolate, he heard a carriage on the drive. A door opened and familiar footsteps ran along the hall. Sure he was only imagining that which he desired so much, Temple sat where he was until a flash of color appeared in the parlor door.

"Brynna!" he exclaimed, sitting upright. "What are you doing here?"

"I came back to Langtry where I belong," she said. "You can't make me go back."

"It's safer there."

"It's safer here. There's yellow fever in New Orleans."

There were no arguments left. Temple opened his arms and Brynna flew into them. "Don't ever send me away again," she whispered. "Promise."

348

"I promise," Temple vowed, and even as he said it, wondered if he could keep such a pledge. They had not yet found Thomas and Cyra, and his fear for the destruction they could bring was greater than ever.

Chapter Eighteen

Cyra and the runaway slaves looted plantations up and down the river, carrying off supplies of food and blankets and clothes before disappearing back into the swamps. Even Acadian villages along the bayous weren't safe from the marauders. A Cajun man was found, brutally hacked by machetes and his pirogue missing. The planters and their slaves stayed on a fine edge of preparedness.

Jessica returned to Langtry, declaring she'd rather risk the dangers of a slave uprising than the heat and noise of New Orleans. Betty Hewitt seemed to prefer the gaiety of city life to the dullness of the country.

"She's got a job sewing ribbons on hats," Jessica said, "and good riddance. I gave her a voucher for one hundred dollars as Temple instructed me. If she handles it wisely, she can live comfortably until she finds a man to marry her."

"Do you think she will?" Brynna asked. It was good to have Jessica back and hear the latest gossip from the city.

"Indubitably," Jessica declared. "Betty's not a bad girl. She just needs to find a man who'll take care of her and pay her a little attention."

"Look to you, Jessica, to find some good in everyone," Brynna said, gripping her hand tightly. "I've missed you."

"Well, tell me about Langtry. Are my gardens yielding yet? Have you started the canning? Did Lala make that gooseberry jam like I told her?"

"It's all done, Jessica," Brynna assured her. "Come and see."

The days passed, blending one into another, and Brynna forgot the terror around them, lost in the peace and contentment of the plantation. Cyra had come to the plantation for food and supplies. She'd come back because she was hungry and this was the place that had once been her home. She and Thomas had done nothing to the inhabitants of Langtry, and Brynna began to believe they never would. Cyra still held some loyalty for her.

Death came creeping in the night, silent and insidious as the swamp mists. Death came sweeping on a blood-curdling cry of vengeance and terror and was purified in the cleansing flames of fire that swept through a plantation home, destroying all semblance of elegance and beauty. Death came to White Hall and to Monsieur Sidney de Jarreau.

"No," Jessica cried when the messenger brought the news. "No!" She sat down abruptly and placed her hand against her heart. Her gardening gloves and hat lay nearby on the black soil, everyday things forgotten in this new atrocity. Brynna sent for Temple and helped Jessica to the house where she urged a glass of brandy upon her. Jessica's color came back, but she still bore the glassy-eyed glaze of shock.

Once again Temple gathered his weapons and supplies and rode out to join the vigilantes who were searching every bayou and field. Once again, Brynna and Jessica huddled in the main house waiting for news. Late in the afternoon a lone carriage rolled down the drive and came to a halt. Before they could go to the door, it was flung open and Alicia de Jarreau entered. Her face was ravaged by tears, her coiffure wind-blown and straggly.

"Temple!" she cried. "I must see Temple."

"He's not here," Jessica said, going to take the distraught woman's arm. "He's gone to join the men."

"They've killed my father," Alicia cried, and Brynna was moved by her anguish.

"We know, Alicia," Jessica said gently.

"We're so sorry," Brynna added, coming to offer her condolences.

Alicia drew herself away from Jessica's consoling touch and glared at Brynna. "You!" she cried, shaking with rage. "It's all your fault. You brought that . . . that murdering Nigrah down here."

"Shh," Jessica chided her. "It's not anyone's fault. It just *is*, that's all, and we've got to get through it the best way we can until our men find them and stop this killing spree."

"Until I die, I'll hate you, Brynna Stanton," Alicia cried, refusing even now to acknowledge her marriage to Temple. Her eyes spat fury and hatred. "I'll pay you back for this, I swear."

"Enough!" Jessica said sharply. "Now, Alicia, you're a guest in this house and you're welcome to stay here, but I won't have you blaming Brynna. No one person is the cause for what another person does. You should know that. Now come to the parlor, child, and let me pour you a glass of sherry. You've had enough shock for one day."

Obediently, Alicia followed Jessica, but her words echoed in the elegant entrance hall. Quietly, Brynna crept upstairs and threw herself across her bed to weep in misery.

For days the men searched the swamps and fields, without success. Work on all the plantations had come to a halt as more planters joined the hunt. Temple and Cort stopped only briefly to bathe and have a hot meal. They both looked tired. Three days after the attack on White Hall, Sidney de Jarreau was buried. Temple and Cort accompanied the three women to the cemetery on White Hall land. Brynna was shocked when she saw the beautiful manor house. It had been nearly destroyed by the flames. Alicia refused to look at it, her face buried in a lacy handkerchief.

Cort stood stiff and unblinking at his father's grave. A muscle twitched in one cheek. He was using tremendous control not to break down.

The White Hall slaves stood respectfully silent. Some of them wept copiously. One raised his voice in a sorrowful hymn. The preacher read the service and three strong field hands threw the dirt down on the rich oak coffin. Another man had been buried.

"I'm so sorry, Cort," Brynna said, laying a small hand on his sleeve. "What will you do now with White Hall?"

"Rebuild it," he said brusquely.

"I'm glad. I think your father would be very pleased with that." Cort looked at her then, his brown eyes were bright with tears. Temple patted his shoulder, and the two men embraced.

"Langtry is your home until you've rebuilt," Temple said.

They all got back in their carriages and drove back to Langtry. In the days that followed, Brynna seldom saw Temple or Cort. They divided their time, as did all the planters, in trying to supervise their slaves and track down any new rumors about the runaway slaves. Cort had gained a somber maturity in recent weeks. Gone was the flippant roué and in his place was a man determined to rebuild his family home. He'd already set his slaves to clearing away the debris of the once-stately mansion. At night he slept there eating with his slaves, bathing in the pond. When he could spare a moment, Temple rode over to help Cort.

Alicia was bitter and aloof following her father's funeral. Brynna tried to stay out of her way, knowing she was grief-stricken and knowing she still held Brynna responsible because of Cyra. Going about her business, she sometimes paused and fell to thinking about all that had occurred. There'd been so much sorrow. The season of laughter seemed very far away, yet looking at the gleam of sun on the grass and treetops, she knew it was a season that would return. Soon, she prayed. Soon!

Temple and Cort had come home unexpectedly for supper. Brynna had ordered Lala to prepare her best, and in spite of the short notice, a meal of sweet pink ham, shrimp Creole, and fresh garden vegetables was put out. Looking strained, the two men sat down and simply looked at the gleaming place settings and delectable food. They'd been eating food from their hands or from a tin plate. This all seemed too elegant now.

Heart filling with joy at just having Temple near again, Brynna took nothing on her own plate, but simply sat and watched him eat. They'd just finished dessert when the sound of hoofbeats, coming at a hard gallop, interrupted them.

Casting an alarmed glance at each other, they rose and hurried to the front gallery. A lone rider came to a sliding halt before them.

"What is it?" Temple asked, running to greet the boy.

Gasping for breath, the young messenger looked around the circle of anxious faces.

"Mr. Harcourt sent me. They've got 'em, sir. They've got 'em cornered down at Bayou Teche. They want as many men to come as they can round up."

"We're leaving now," Temple said, racing inside to get his gun and ammunition. Cramming extra bullets into his pockets and belt, he ran past, pausing only long enough to drop a quick kiss on Brynna's mouth.

"Temple!" she cried, and when he turned, she clamped her hands together. How she longed to utter a plea on behalf of Cyra, but it would not be welcomed. "Be careful," she whispered instead. All night they waited, knowing they would hear nothing, yet unable to go to bed. Finally, toward dawn, Brynna lay down on the sofa and slept.

At midmorning the same young messenger made his way up the drive.

"Miz Brynna Sinclair?" he asked, looking at the three women.

"I am she," Brynna said, taking a step forward and peering at him anxiously. "Wh-why are you here?" Her heart seemed to have stopped beating, her breathing was suspended. She stood in a void, waiting for him to utter the words that would plunge her into torment.

"Mr. Sinclair sent me to tell you he and Mr. Jarreau are all right. They got the leaders and they're bringing them back to the Jarreau plantation this morning."

"Are they there now?" Alicia asked.

"They left after I did, ma'am. They should be getting there soon."

"I'm going over. Absalom, order the carriage immediately," Brynna cried.

"I'm going with you," Alicia said. Her eyes were hard. "I want to see the murderers of my father."

Brynna knew it would do little good to try to dissuade

her. Taking down the wide straw bonnet she wore in the garden, Brynna filled a basket with bottles of whiskey, bread, and ham. By the time the carriage arrived, she was ready. Alicia climbed into the carriage beside her. The Creole girl's manner was defiant and bitter. Brynna made no effort to convince her to stay behind.

Taking the whip in hand, Brynna drove the carriage herself, urging the horses to a faster pace until they were in danger of overturning on the winding road. She had to get to White Hall before the vigilantes did. She had to see Cyra again.

She arrived at the Jarreau gate just moments ahead of the posse. Her eyes sought out Temple first, and when she was certain he was unharmed, she looked for Cyra.

She sat among the other captives on the bed of a farm wagon, her head held regally high, her pitifully thin shoulders straight. Thomas stared straight ahead, acknowledging the presence of no one else. Cyra was at his side, and now and then she glanced at him, her look at once proud and protective. That single look was more wrenching than anything else she could have done. There was love in Cyra's eyes, and if they shared no other common ground now, Brynna knew they shared at least this much. Each of them loved a man with all her heart and soul. Each had followed her own destiny.

"Killers! Murderers!" Alicia shouted, startling Brynna back to the grim horrors Cyra and Thomas had perpetrated on them all. As the wagon drew near, Alicia stood up in the carriage and spat at the prisoners. They sat perfectly still, unmoved by her tirade. The eyes of some reflected their dazed, hopeless state of mind, but Thomas and Cyra's eyes were hard and defiant.

Alicia began to weep, her body shaking. Brynna feared

she might fall. When the wagon drew level with them she dug into her bag and brought out a small pistol.

"Alicia, no," Brynna cried as she took aim and fired. One of the slaves seated near Cyra screamed and fell forward. The other slaves struggled to get out of the wagon, but they were chained hands and feet. Alicia took aim again. For one brief second, Brynna saw beyond the shiny barrel of the pistol to Cyra's face. She saw the fear and shock reflected in her brown eyes, saw the instinctive, protective shield her thin arms made over her rounded belly.

"She's pregnant, Alicia. You don't want to kill her," Brynna cried out, but the Creole girl cocked the pistol with deadly intent. Desperately, Brynna looked around for help. The weary men had turned at the first shot, their pistols drawn. When they saw Alicia had fired, they reholstered their weapons. She could expect no help from that quarter, Brynna thought, and picking up the buggy whip, she flicked it over the heads of the horses. They jumped ahead. The carriage rocked crazily. The gun went off as Alicia fell back in her seat.

Brynna brought the confused horses to hand and turned on Alicia, but the hatred reflected on the Creole's tear-ravished face made her pause. Alicia had a right to her grief. Wearily, Brynna took the pistol from her nerveless hands and guided the carriage down the road and into the yard of the once-elegant plantation. Temple was already there astride Chandra. He came to them at once.

"Are you all right? I heard a shot."

"We're fine." Brynna said.

Temple eyed the weeping Alicia. "You shouldn't have come."

"You know I couldn't have stayed away and I couldn't

make Alicia stay behind. We've brought some food for the men and prisoners."

The wagon rumbled into the yard, surrounded by men on horseback.

"What will they do with them?"

Temple's lips tightened as he watched the men usher the prisoners from the wagon. One moved too slowly, and Shepherd yanked him forward by his chains. The man fell and the slave trader was upon him instantly, pounding him with the butt of his rifle.

"Shepherd," Temple shouted, and wheeled his horse. The burly man had raised his rifle yet again to smash down on the helpless prisoner, but Temple rode at him. Chandra's deep chest brushed against the slave trader and sent him rolling across the ground. Temple sprang off his horse ready to fight if he had to. Shepherd got to his feet. His face was ugly as he drew his gun and aimed it at Temple.

"No," Brynna cried frantically.

"I've had about enough of you, Sinclair," Shepherd said. "You been ordering me around ever since we captured these here Niggahs."

"I told you at the beginning, Shepherd. I won't have them brutalized no matter what they've done."

"Ain't that nice?"

"Shepherd," another voice called out. "Put the gun away."

Brynna looked at Cort gratefully. His clothes were dirty, his chin covered with stubble, his thin, handsome face weary. In his hand he held a pistol directed right at Shepherd's middle.

"I'm aiming to kill this gentleman," Shepherd sneered without taking his eyes off Temple. "We'll call it one of them duels gentlemen are always fighting."

"If you pull that trigger, it will be cold-blooded murder and you won't live to reholster your gun."

Shepherd looked at Cort then, and his eyes grew wide as he took in the cocked pistol.

"It's your choice, Shepherd," Cort said softly.

The other men stood silently watching. Shepherd shifted from one foot to the other. "Aw well, Ah weren't going to do it. Ah was just mad," Shepherd said, speaking to the circle of men at large. "You know me. Ah got a temper and Mr. Sinclair there's been mighty bossy to me. When he knocked me down here in the dirt in front of them niggahs, Ah just lost my temper."

"I've said it to you more than once and I'll say it again. You are not to mistreat the prisoners."

"All right, Mr. Sinclair, if you say so," Shepherd shrugged and put his gun back in its holster. "Ain't goin' t' matter in a little bit anyway. They'll all be dead."

Temple glanced around the ring of men. "What's he talking about?"

"We're going to hang them, Tem," Cort said. "That's why we brought them back here." His dark gaze was unwavering.

"You're going to kill them without a trial?" Temple demanded.

"They've had their trial," Harcourt said. "We brought them here for their execution."

"What if some of them are innocent."

"None of them are!" Cort flared. "You know that, Tem."

"Will you side with a vigilante, Cort? Is this the way your father would have wanted it done?"

"An eye for an eye, a tooth for a tooth," Harcourt intoned.

"You can't hang them without a trial," Brynna appealed to Cort. "You don't want to hang them here on White Hall land. Think of Alicia!"

Alicia stood up in the wagon, and her beautiful mouth twisted into a vengeful grin. "Hang them," she said hoarsely. "Hang them from that oak tree yonder, and every day of my life I will rejoice when I look at it, knowing my father's death was revenged."

"This is not about revenge," Temple said. "What about justice, law, and order?"

"This *is* justice," Cort said. "Vigilante justice, vigilante law."

"This is not like you, Cort," Temple said. Cort sensed his disappointment in him, but he didn't back down.

"I've lost my father. White Hall was burned. I've seen the terror and mayhem these people have wreaked on the countryside. They have no rights."

"If you have no stomach for this, Sinclair, go home," Harcourt ordered, and the other men nodded in agreement.

"Come on get those niggahs out of that wagon," someone called.

Defeated, Temple led Chandra back to the carriage. "Go home, Brynna," he said. "This is no place for you and Alicia."

"I'm staying," Alicia cried, her eyes shiny and hard with unshed tears.

"I must stay," Brynna said. "I must find some way to stop them. They can't hang Cyra." Her voice broke and she shut her eyes tightly against the pain.

Temple touched her arm. "You know the crimes she's committed," he said gently. "Nothing can save her."

Brynna opened her eyes and stared at him pleadingly. "We have to find some way, Temple. She's my sister."

"My God," Temple whispered. Even Alicia was silent.

Brynna folded her hands in her lap and turned her head away from him. "I grew up with that knowledge," she whispered. "My father . . . is her father. Her mother lived in the big house with us until one day she just disappeared. But my father kept Cyra to be my playmate and later my maid. He used to taunt my mother with Cyra's presence, thinking he could make her hate Cyra as much as he did, but Hope loved her and was always kind to her." Brynna raised her head and looked at him. He thought he'd never seen so much anguish in one person's eyes. "I loved her, too," she said through her tears. "She's my sister." Her small frame shook slightly, her slim shoulders hunched in misery. Temple pulled her down in his arms, cradling her against him. Brynna put her arms around his neck and wept.

"We'll find a way to save her," he said gently.

"Niggah lover," Alicia spat, and got out of the carriage. Without a backward glance, she sped across the overgrown lawn to the knot of men.

"She's telling them about Cyra," Temple said against Brynna's cheek. She drew back and looked into his face.

"I don't care. I'm not ashamed anymore," she said tiredly. "Will you be?"

Temple touched her small chin. "No," he said. "There are too many mulattoes in the South for anyone to point a finger of accusation. Besides, the shame wouldn't be yours, Brynna."

The crowd of men approached the carriage, Cort at their head. "Is what Alicia says about Cyra true?" he asked.

Mutely, Brynna nodded. She saw the inner struggle reflected in his eyes.

"We can't let her go free," he said finally. "But we can spare her from the hanging."

The men muttered in disagreement among themselves. "No," Alicia cried. "Hang them all. She's just as guilty as the rest."

"Alicia, be still!" Cort commanded and, dazed that he should use such a tone to her, she obeyed.

The other men exchanged angry glances and Brynna guessed they hadn't all agreed with Cort's gesture. Finally Harcourt shrugged.

"I've not had any member of my family or my slaves hurt by these animals," he said. "Otherwise, I couldn't go along with what you're proposing. You lost your daddy, so if you can let the woman off the hanging, I'm with you." Slowly, the majority of the men came around. Disgruntled at the way things had gone, Shepherd cursed and walked away. He'd been a major opposer.

"Thank you, thank you all," Brynna said.

"We're not letting her go free, Miz Sinclair," Harcourt explained. "She has to go to New Orleans. She may have to face the hangman's noose yet."

"Thank you for giving her a chance . . ." Brynna paused and looked around. "You've risked your lives to protect us all, and we're beholden. I've brought some whiskey and food for you. It's in the basket."

The men took down the basket gratefully and passed around the bottles of whiskey. Chunks of bread were divided, along with slices of ham. The way the men wolfed them down, Brynna knew they hadn't eaten for some time.

"May I give some food to the prisoners?" she asked, and the men paused and stared at her.

"You've got a kind heart, Mrs. Sinclair, to think of those murdering devils after what they've done," Alec Frontier said. "But we won't be giving them any food today. They'll be dead within an hour."

362

"May I give Cyra something? It's a long ride to New Orleans."

"Yes, ma'am, I believe that would be all right. I'll have someone cut her out of the others. You can feed her then."

"Thank you." Brynna's eyes stung with tears, but she blinked them back.

The slaves had been made to sit on the ground and now the men moved forward. Cyra's chains were loosened from the rest and Harcourt pulled her away from the mob of Negroes. When the slave woman saw she was to be separated from the rest, she screamed, crying out in wordless sounds for Thomas to help her. The black man leaped to his feet, struggling against his chains. Two men ran forward to subdue him. A rifle butt landed behind his ear and he went down.

"No!" Cyra shrieked, fighting the man who propelled her forward. When she saw it did little good, she went limp, refusing to take one step away from the man she loved.

Brynna saw her struggle through tear-filled eyes. "Cyra!" she whispered, and felt the other woman's pain. The man dragged her limp body through dust and weeds to the corner of the burned-out shell of the plantation house. Cyra lay in the grass sobbing, then slowly sat up, leaning back against the wall. Her mouth was a defiant slash in her face, her eyes filled with hatred as she glared at the man assigned to guard her.

Taking a piece of bread and ham, Brynna made her way to Cyra, kneeling beside her. Cyra's head jerked around and she stared at Brynna.

"Are you hungry?"

"I don't want your food," Cyra snapped.

"Try to eat something. You'll need your strength."

Brynna held the food out to her. With a snort of contempt, Cyra knocked it from her hands. A commotion at the oak drew her attention, and she stiffened as ropes were thrown over the branches.

"Don't be afraid," Brynna said. "They've promised to take you back to New Orleans for trial. You're safe for now."

"Ah don't want to be safe," Cyra cried. "Ah want to be with Thomas." She began to fight against her chains, twisting and flailing out until the steel cuffs cut deep into her flesh. The chains were soon coated bright red with her blood; still, she struggled.

"Stop that," the man guarding her ordered.

"Cyra, please, you must stop this," Brynna cried, throwing her arms around Cyra's shoulders. Cyra kicked her away. Brynna fell backward.

"Brynna," Temple ran forward and helped her up. His angry gaze took in the crazed woman. "You've done all you can. I want you to leave. Now, Brynna."

She was weeping as she looked at him. "I can't. Cyra needs me," she said. "I can't let her go through this alone."

White-lipped, Temple turned to the guard. "Take the woman to the other side of the house," he ordered.

"I don't believe I can, Mr. Temple. She's fighting me too hard."

"I'll get help," Temple said, and turned away. A scream, like that of a wounded animal, brought them up short. Brynna turned to Cyra, who sat staring at the oak tree. The cords in her throat stood out, her mouth was opened in a scream that had gone silent but was no less agonized. Brynna looked at the oak tree. A line of black men danced at the ends of a dozen ropes, their bodies jerking in the final throes of death. Thomas was one of them.

"Oh, no!" Brynna whimpered, and covered her eyes. Temple grabbed her, burying her face against his chest so the horrible scene was blocked from her view. But it was etched in her mind, the men on the ground cheering, the slaves hanging by their necks, and Alicia standing to one side, her face bright with glee, her laughter shrill with madness.

Slowly, Brynna pushed away from Temple and looked at Cyra. The black woman sat as if dead, her dark eyes blank.

"Cyra?" Brynna whispered, kneeling to put her arms around her. Cyra made no response. She seemed lost in some world of her own. At the tree, men passed the whiskey bottles. Finally, looking grim-faced, they traipsed back to their horses. The deed was done, the slaves had paid for their crimes. Their bodies would hang here for days as a warning to any other black slave who thought to defy white authority. The men wanted only to put all the terror and ugliness behind them and resume their comfortable lives. Watching them go, Brynna wondered if any one of them gave thought that they might have been part of the problem themselves.

Cort put his coat around his sister and led her back to the carriage.

Harcourt and Shepherd walked to where Cyra was held. "We'll take the woman now," Harcourt said.

Brynna eyed Shepherd distrustingly. "Will you see that she arrives in New Orleans without injury," she said.

Shepherd's lips tightened. Harcourt nodded. "I'll be riding along," he said. Bending, he caught Cyra under one arm. Shepherd took the other. "Come on, Cyra. Time to take a ride."

Obediently she walked between them and climbed into the wagon. Brynna followed, and when Cyra was settled, she placed the bread and ham on the wagon bed beside her. "You may want it later," she said.

"Do you think your scraps of food will make everything right?" Cyra sneered. "Do you think it will ease the pain of losing yore man? Ah'll remember this day. Ah'll remember for my son." Her arms wrapped around her stomach. Her eyes were bright and bitter.

"Cyra, do you feel no remorse for what you've done?" Brynna asked.

Cyra's laugh was filled with contempt. "Ah'm sorry for what Ah didn't do," she hissed. "Sorry Ah didn't kill you that afternoon we came to Langtry to steal food." Brynna's eyes registered shock. "Yo' would have killed me," Cyra went on. "Ah saw it in your face. Ah thought yo' had a gun in yore pocket the way yo' went for it. But, Ah ain't evah goin' t' kill you. Ah'm goin' t' kill yore man, so yo' hurt as much as Ah do." She grinned then, an evil, vengeful twist of her mouth.

The wagon rolled away then, leaving Brynna standing in shock with Cyra's final words ringing in her ears. Temple saw the slump of her shoulders and came to put an arm around her and lead her back to the carriage. Alicia was silent and limp now, as if all feeling had been drained from her.

"Tie Chandra to the back of the carriage," he told Cort. "I'll drive." He climbed into the seat and took up the reins. Cort stood back.

"Aren't you coming?" Temple asked stiffly.

Cort shook his head. "I won't be coming back to Langtry for a while," he said. "I believe it's best."

"Perhaps you're right," Temple said, and Brynna knew

366

the events of this day had caused a chasm between the two men that could not be ignored.

"I'd appreciate it if you would watch out for Alicia for a few days until I can make arrangements for her to return to New Orleans. I'm afraid she's going to need some extra care."

"Of course we will," Brynna said.

Temple whipped up the horses and they turned down the lane away from the plantation, away from the men dangling at the end of their ropes, the horrible legacy that had become White Hall's.

"I have to go to New Orleans," Brynna said when they'd gained the road toward Langtry.

"I know," Temple said.

"I have to stand by Cyra through this."

"I know." They said no more on the drive home. Once there, they concentrated on getting Alicia inside. Jessica saw their faces and knew they'd witnessed terrible things this day. Wisely, she did not ask. They put Alicia to bed, and Brynna went to her room to change her clothes and pack for New Orleans. She wanted to leave immediately. She would have to engage a lawyer and see that Cyra was housed and fed properly in prison. If she could do nothing to stave off the inevitable end Cyra must face, at least she could ensure Cyra's last days on earth were comfortable.

When she was packed, she carried her small portmanteau downstairs. She crossed to Temple's study, then hesitated at the sound of voices within. Temple stood at the fireplace, a glass of whiskey near at hand on the mantel. Alicia, clad in a sheer nightdress and robe, stood before him. Her voice was wheedling.

"Send Brynna away, Temple," she pleaded. "She can never be a proper wife to you. She'll only bring shame to the Sinclair name."

367

"You're distraught, Alicia. Go back to your room," Temple ordered sharply.

"I love you, Temple. I always have," Alicia continued as if she'd not heard his reprimand. Her hands clutched at him. "I should have been your wife, not her. You can change that. Send her back North, where she belongs. You can get a divorce. Everyone knows she's a woman of loose morals. I've told them so from the beginning. No one would fault you."

"You've spread filth about my wife?" Temple asked in disgust.

"I had to," Alicia whimpered. "I had to drive her away so you'd be free again to marry me. I love you, Temple, and you love me. I know you do."

"Listen to me," Temple said, grabbing her shoulders and shaking her none too gently. "I've never loved you. We would never have been man and wife even if Brynna had never come here. But she did come, and I love her. There can never be any other woman for me."

Alicia blinked as if waking from a long sleep, then, tearing herself away from him, she backed toward the door. When she saw Brynna, her black eyes widened.

"Hello, Alicia. I hope you're feeling better," Brynna said gently, then turned to Temple. "I'm ready to go now."

Alicia fled up the stairs, her dark hair flowing behind her. Temple and Brynna looked at each other until they heard the door of her room slam, then they went into each other's arms.

"She's been spreading rumors about you," Temple said.

"I heard. It doesn't matter, nothing matters as long as I have you and Jessica."

"And Langtry," Temple added.

Brynna drew back and looked at him. "I love Langtry, but it means nothing to me without you." Temple hugged her close again, rocking her like a child, yet feeling her sweet, womanly body. They didn't hear the approaching horse, until Jessica cried out from the hall. Swiftly, Temple and Brynna made their way to her.

"What is it? What's wrong?" Temple demanded. The same young boy who'd come before as messenger stood in the doorway, crumpling the brim of his hat nervously.

"Timothy!" Brynna cried.

"The woman got away, Miz Sinclair. Mr. Harcourt sent me to warn you, 'cause he said he heard the woman threaten you. He'd have come hisself, but he's been injured pretty bad. Shepherd was killed."

"When will it end?" Jessica said.

"Thank you for coming," Temple said. "Go around to the kitchen and tell Lala to give you some food."

"Thank you, sir." The boy hurried out.

Brynna was silent. Temple took her arm. "You can't do anything more for her."

Brynna raised her great golden eyes to him. "It isn't Cyra I'm worried about now," she said. She threw her arms around him and held him tightly. Cyra's last words rang in her ears. Cyra wouldn't kill Brynna. She meant to kill Temple.

Chapter Nineteen

She was a prisoner in a smoke-filled place. She couldn't breathe, the smoke burned her lungs so. She couldn't see for the billowing black cloud that encompassed her. A river wind blew the smoke away, and in the distance she could see men jerking at the end of the rope. One of them was Temple and she screamed reaching for him. She woke drenched in sweat, her arms flung across Temple's pillow. It took her a moment to realize he wasn't there, a moment more to realize something was wrong, terribly wrong. She tried to draw a breath and tasted the acrid blackness of smoke. She hadn't been dreaming, she thought, alarms clanging.

From the open window came the cries of people. The warehouse and mills were on fire, she thought in a haze, then realized they'd already burned. Barns then or sheds or . . . Terror burned away the lethargic haze that claimed her. She bounded out of bed and staggered, gripping the bedpost to steady herself.

"Temple," she screamed, knowing he wasn't there. Billows of smoke poured from under the door. Brynna shoved away from the bedpost and staggered to the door, throwing it open. Flames crackled along the hallway, feeding hungrily on the thick wool rug. Gasping, Brynna slammed the door closed and looked around in desperation. Where was Temple? Where was Jessica? Fear for their safety propelled her toward the French doors and the gallery beyond. She staggered against the railing coughing and drawing in huge gulps of fresh air. When the spasm had passed, she pulled herself along the gallery toward Jessica's room.

The doors were closed.

"Jessica," Brynna screamed, pounding on the wooden frame. No answer came from within. Peering through a pane, Brynna could see the room was smoke-filled. Jessica lay on the bed, asleep or unconscious. She had to do something. Wildly she looked around for something to break the glass. The wicker chairs were too heavy to lift. Wrapping her fist in a corner of her gown, Brynna punched the doorpane. It shattered and fell inward. Ignoring the jagged shards of glass that slashed at her hands, Brynna reached inside and unfastened the lock.

"Jessica," she cried, hurrying to the bed. The old woman made no response. The smoke filled Brynna's lungs, so she feared she might faint. Hooking her arms beneath Jessica's shoulders, Brynna tugged her off the bed and onto the floor. Kneeling beside her, Brynna fought for breath. She could do this, she told herself. Hadn't she gotten Temple on his horse, and he was much bigger than Jessica. But the smoke stole her breath and her strength and burned her eyes. She wasn't sure she was even moving toward the French doors or deeper into the smoke-filled room. Inch by inch she pulled Jessica and herself across the floor, and when she reached the sill, she gave a mighty tug that carried them both out onto the gallery.

"Here, Jessica, breathe," she said, propping Jessica

371

against the railing. Frantically, she patted Jessica's cheeks and the back of her hands, trying to arouse her. A sense of urgency made her peer over her shoulders at the fire. Where was Temple? her mind screamed.

The slaves had reached the house now. May came running around the corner of the gallery.

"Are yo' all right, Miz Brynna? We got Miss 'Licia out. She's down in the yard. Oh, Lawd, Miz Jessica." May fell to her knees beside the old woman.

"Get someone to help carry her down to the yard," Brynna ordered.

"Where yo' goin', Miss Brynna?"

"I have to look for Temple."

"Yo' cain't go back in theah," May cried. "Not even yo' can get out a' theah, Miz Brynna."

"I have to," Brynna cried over her shoulder. She ran around the gallery and entered the hall from the opposite side. The fire was less intense here, and she was able to take the back stairs. There was an eerie kind of reality to the untouched lower floor. The fire was on the floor above and hadn't descended yet. Brynna walked along the hall. Something warned her not to call out Temple's name. She rounded the sloping curve of the main staircase and paused. The darkness seemed to breathe with a life of its own. Something waited for her there in the shadows.

Swallowing against her fear, Brynna moved toward Temple's study door. It gaped menacingly. Without opening it further, she slipped inside and pressed against the panel wall.

"Ah've been waitin' for yo'," a soft voice said.

"Hello, Cyra," Brynna said, blinking her eyes to help them adjust to the darkness. What she saw almost made her cry out. A square of moonlight lay across the floor. Temple lay sprawled in the pale golden light, a dark pool growing beneath his head. Brynna bit her lips to remain silent. She must not show weakness in front of Cyra now.

"Is he dead?" she asked quietly.

"Not yet," Cyra answered. "I waited so you'd be here to see it."

"Cyra, you can't want to do this," Brynna said, desperately stalling for time. She slid along the wall and felt a bookshelf behind her. Hope rocketed through her as she remembered the gun Temple had once shown her he kept hidden there.

"There's enough bloodshed, enough terror to last us all a lifetime." Which shelf had it been? she thought. Her fingers were slick with sweat and she pushed against the books, feeling them slide deeper into the shelves.

"What about your son? Can't you forget all that's happened and think of his future?" She pushed against a thick book and felt it resist. She pushed again. The gun was behind this book. It had to be.

"My son ain't got a future," Cyra was saying, "'cept to be a slave, to be beaten and worked to death and to be hanged like his daddy."

"You could go north, Cyra. There's money there in the desk that would buy you passage. You could raise your son to be free." Her fingers tugged at the thick tome. It was wedged too tightly and she feared she couldn't dislodge it without revealing her actions to Cyra.

"It's too late for that," Cyra was saying. "Maybe if Thomas was alive."

"You have to go on living, Cyra. For Thomas's son." The book was free. It clattered to the floor.

"What was that?" Cyra cried, leaping into the patch of moonlight. Her eyes were wide and wild-looking. In one hand she held a knife. Now she crouched, placing it against Temple's throat.

"No," Brynna cried. "I only knocked a book off a table."

"Stand in the light, so I can see you," Cyra ordered.

Brynna hesitated. "What are you going to do?" she stalled while her cold fingers closed around the pistol.

"Ah want to see what yo're doin'," Cyra said. "Do like I said now, or else." She raised the knife, preparing to strike.

"I'm here," Brynna said, moving forward into the square of moonlight. The gun was hidden in the folds of her gown. Her shaking fingers sought and found the hammer. The roar of the fire and the crackle of flames eating through the ceiling covered the sound as she cocked the pistol.

Cyra laughed quietly. "'Member that Latin class yo' took, where yo' read 'bout that king who played his fiddle while Rome burned."

"I remember," Brynna said.

Cyra's laughter died, and she turned her gaze on Brynna. "Yo'll have lots of memories, just like me," she said sadly. "Yo'll 'member how it was to see your man die, and yo'll always 'member it was me that done it." She raised the knife high over Temple's still form. Brynna could see the moon glinting on the blade as it began its downward plunge. Her hand was steady as she fired at Cyra.

Cyra cried out. The knife spun away. Cyra stood at the edge of shadows. Brynna could see only her bare toes. She'd missed, but she'd stopped Cyra from murdering Temple. Then, softly as a petal drifting to the ground, a droplet of blood fell on the edge of moonlight.

"Cyra," Brynna whispered, watching as the droplets increased. Then they stopped. "Cyra!" There was no

374

answer. A shadow blocked the stream of moonlight, then was gone. "Cyra!" Brynna called, then, certain she was alone, she threw the gun aside and rushed to Temple's side. He groaned and tried to sit up.

"Brynna," he grunted.

"I'm here," she said.

"Cyra!"

"I know, darling. She's gone now. We have to go outside, Temple. Can you walk?"

"Can walk," he said, and stumbled to his feet. Together they made their way to the French door leading out to the gallery. A brigade line had formed and the flames that ate at Langtry were already being diminished. Somewhere in the weaving shadows, a wounded black woman used the confusion to effect her escape. Brynna prayed Cyra would make it, prayed that one day she would find some peace for her troubled soul.

With tears pouring down her cheeks, Brynna watched the slaves fighting to save the stately mansion.

"Look, Temple," she said, gripping him tightly. "Our people are fighting to save Langtry. They won't let her die!"

Temple raised his head and gazed at his home, seeming to take strength from the noble columns and graceful lines. "Our people," he said, looking into the glowing golden eyes he loved so much.

"Our legacy to our children," he said, and Brynna knew it was true. The people made Langtry what she was. Brynna had come to Louisiana seeking asylum from a brutish father and found everything that mattered in life. Her arms tightened around Temple. Nothing could ever defeat her again. She was well and whole.

Jessica had recovered from the smoke. She came and

put her arms around them both. Together they stood watching the first glimmer of sunlight rise over the distant horizon. It gilded the live oaks and the river beyond and reflected on the gentle beauty of Langtry.

Epilogue

"Mama!" The squeal of children echoed down the hall. A small body hurdled into Brynna's room and threw itself against her.

"What is it now, Stephen?" she asked, putting down her brush and turning to her child.

The four-year-old boy rubbed his dark eyes with a pudgy, dirty hand and stared up at her rebelliously. "May says Ah have t' take a bath."

"That's right, you do," Brynna said, fondly ruffling his dark curls. "We're having a party and our guests will soon be here."

"Don't want no party if Ah have t' take a bath," the boy said stubbornly.

"You always run to Mama," a high, piping voice reprimanded him from the doorway. Brynna turned and smiled at her daughter. Two years older than her brother and already displaying a sister's disdain for boys in general, Aimee was tall for her six years, with a quick, slim body that was seldom still. Stephen was in awe of her.

Prissily, Aimee fluffed the ruffles of her pale-blue gown and seated herself on the edge of a boudoir chair next to her mother's dressing table. Beneath the short hem of her high-waisted gown peeked white, lace-trimmed pantaloons. Her slender feet were covered by black satin slippers; trim, stocking-clad ankles were primly crossed. Chestnut curls tumbled to her waist, caught back from her delicate features by a blue satin ribbon. Unlike most children, Aimee didn't fidget. When she grew bored or restless, she simply got up and moved to something else.

"How pretty you look, Aimee," Brynna complimented her daughter, knowing it would please her. "Did Meme tie your sash? It's so nicely done."

"*Oui,* Grandmère tied it," Aimee replied, disdaining the childish nickname they'd used for Jessica. "Is Cort coming to our party?"

"Umm! *Uncle* Cort, Aimee. You mustn't be disrespectful."

"He isn't really my uncle, is he?" Aimee insisted, her golden eyes speculative.

"No, but what difference does that make?" Brynna asked absently.

"One day I'm going to marry Cort," Aimee stated serenely. Startled, Brynna glanced up at her precocious daughter. The memory of a young Francine d'Abbadie came to her and she laughed despite herself.

Aimee frowned at her mother. Grown-ups always laughed at children when they didn't know how to answer them. Pert, freckled, nose high, she regarded her brother. "We must do something about this odious child. He'll spoil our party."

Brynna bit back a sharp reprimand. She'd raised her children with much love and sometimes when she confronted her feisty daughter, she wondered if she'd spared the rod too much.

"*Mon Dieu,*" Temple exclaimed from the doorway.

"Where has my family gone and who are these beautiful princesses?" With long strides he crossed to Brynna and dropped a light kiss on her soft lips. "As always, my sweet wife, you are stunningly beautiful."

"Thank you, monsieur. How kind of you to notice."

"If only my ugly daughter had taken after her beautiful mother," Temple teased.

"Oh, Daddy," Aimee squealed, dancing to her father and throwing herself into his arms. He lifted her and spun around. Her laughter spilled into the room like the tinkling bell sound of the swamp frogs Temple had shown Brynna when she first came to Langtry. Watching her husband with their daughter, Brynna smiled with happiness. Just that quickly, Aimee had changed from a prim adult into a giggling little girl. Stephen left his place at her side and ran to wrap his arms around his father's leg.

"Give me a ride, Daddy," he demanded, stepping on to his father's boot. Temple set Aimee on her feet and stalked around the room, his squealing son clinging to his leg. Aimee jumped up and down, clapping her hands.

"Goodness, what's all the commotion?" Jessica asked, coming into the room. She wore a soft gown of gray silk. Though her shoulders slumped a little, and she now wore spectacles all the time, she'd aged very little over the years. Now she pushed her glasses higher on her nose and smiled at Brynna.

"You look lovely, *chérie*. You outshine even Langtry."

"Thank you, Jess," Brynna said, lightly getting to her feet and smoothing the full skirts of her cream-colored silk gown. She'd chosen it because it reminded her of her wedding gown. Like Aimee, she fluffed the lace trim and tugged at the low-cut neckline. She would never grow used to such daring décolletage, although her gown was modest by most standards. The neckline revealed her creamy shoulders. Her glorious hair was caught high on her head with small curls bobbing behind each ear. Certain she did indeed look her best, Brynna turned away from her mirror and regarded her family. Her heart was overflowing with love as she watched them all, from dear Jessica to her rapscallion son.

May entered the room and Brynna signaled her forward to take Stephen to his bath.

"No," he cried, refusing to let go of his father's leg. "I don't want a bath."

"What? A man who doesn't want a bath? I've had mine, son." Stephen got to his feet and looked up at his father, his head tilted far back. Temple stroked the soft, rounded cheek of his son. "You'll have to start shaving one of these days," he said solemnly.

Stephen felt his chin, his brown wrinkling with consternation. "Do you think so, Daddy?"

"Tell you what, let's go wash that dirt off and take a close look." Temple winked over his son's head, then hoisted him on to his arm. Shaking her head with laughter, May followed them down the hall.

"I swear, Brynna. Langtry has never looked so magnificent. You can't tell there ever was a fire here."

"We know, though, don't we, Jessica?"

"Yes, we'll always remember. You've never heard anything more about Cyra?"

Brynna shook her head. "Temple thinks she got away down the river in a rowboat. That's where the blood trail ended. Her body was never found and someone thought they spotted her in Memphis."

"She brought a lot of grief to this country," Jessica sighed, "but I hope she got away."

"I think she did. Somewhere, right now, Cyra is watching her child at play and maybe she's stopped hating us a little bit."

"Who's Cyra?" Aimee demanded curiously. Brynna smiled and hugged her daughter and turned toward the door.

"She was someone I knew once . . . I hear the first carriages arriving. Come help Jessica and me greet our guests."

Together they walked down the hall to the great, curving stairs. Coming from the room where his son had finally submitted to a bath, Temple paused and watched the three women. They represented the very best of all that was the South.

He would remember until he died the day Jessica came to Langtry. She'd healed the heart of a grief-stricken father and given love and guidance to a troubled, rebellious boy. As for his daughter, great beauty and intelligence were already evident in her delicate face, but, like her mother, Aimee had a mind of her own.

Temple studied his wife, the source of his happiness. Her beauty was legendary among the Louisiana planters, her gracious hospitality eagerly sought. He'd seen men of great worldly experience fall under her spell in a matter of minutes. He was still as susceptible to that beauty as the first day she came to Langtry. He longed to take her back to their room and strip away the finery and spend the long hot afternoon making love to her, but this was a special day for them all, a day of celebration. A day to commemorate their years together here at Langtry, years that had passed with surprising swiftness and contentment.

Pausing at the top of the stairs, Brynna seemed to read his thoughts. Her smile held all the love in the world.

Slowly she held out a slender hand and grasped his. Arm in arm they followed Jessica and Aimee down the stairs and out to the shaded gallery to welcome their guests to Langtry.

Author's Note

Above New Orleans along the banks of the Mississippi River, Oak Alley sits in classic southern beauty at the end of a quarter-mile-long alley of centuries-old live oaks. The trees, twenty-eight of them placed in two rows of fourteen trees apiece, were planted sometime around 1718. The present plantation house has been designed with twenty-eight columns, measuring eight feet in circumference with deep-shaded galleries above and below to offset the fierce Louisiana summer heat. Originally called Bon Sejour, or Pleasant Sojourn, the plantation has always been known as Oak Alley because of its beautiful trees. Though more than two hundred and fifty years old, all of the original trees are still standing. A similar alley was planted at the back of the house at a later date.

Having traveled to Oak Alley and walked beneath those trees and rested on those hospitable verandahs drinking mint juleps, I envisioned the men and women who must once have lived and worked there, and thus the Sinclairs and Langtry were born.